2ND ITERATION

ADVENT

A.P. BLANCHARD

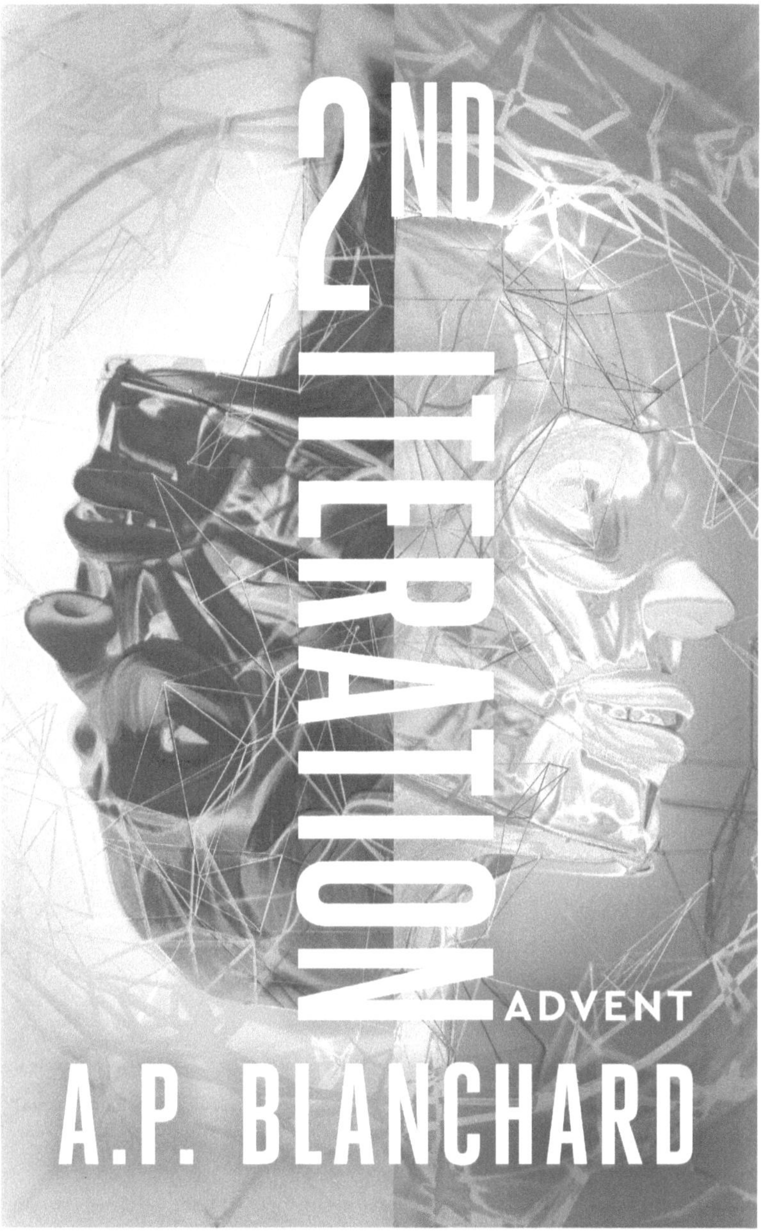

Blanchard Educational Services

PROLOGUE

A FLICKER AT THE edge of Jaxon Beck's vision—there, then gone. He blinked hard. It returned, a silvery ripple, like heat rising from summer asphalt. His stomach knotted as the ripple expanded, fracturing into jagged prisms of color that pierced his view. The familiar starburst pattern bloomed outward, its edges pulsing with electric blues and violent purples. His fingers tightened on the handlebars.

Jax's throat seized around a guttural sound that was half-curse, half-prayer, "Oh damn—not now!"

Moments earlier, he had been blissfully gliding through the city streets on his mountain bike. Late spring offered a brief interlude between cold and heat, though the air still carried a touch of winter. Ahead, snow-capped mountains blushed under the morning sun, crowned by a deep azure sky. Jax had inclined his head and inhaled the beauty around him.

Hoping to avoid the crush of morning commuters, he'd chosen the longer, more precarious route. The narrowing road could be intimidating—the tightly parked cars on either side reminiscent of a slaughter chute for cattle preparing for sacrifice. His breathing deepened as the road beckoned and aroused him. Succumbing to the taunt, he pushed his muscles beyond their accustomed limits.

Rising onto the bike's steel pedals, he had demanded more of himself, accelerating until he matched the rhythmic flow of traffic. Bike lanes nonexistent, he smoothly merged onto the crowded roadway, joining the tidal surge of cars and trucks.

But then the shimmer had arrived, and elation gave way to alarm. His expression screwed into a mask of fear as he grasped the danger he faced. The euphoria of the morning and the rush of speed had dulled his wits. A single bead of sweat slowly slid from beneath his helmet and dropped to his bearded cheek.

The starburst before him spun wildly, swelling and shrinking in a maddening rhythm before giving way to a darkening fog at the edges of his sight. Tunnel vision was creeping in. Cresting the steep hill, his momentum increased. The torrent of vehicles distorted into mere streaks of color.

His vision continued to collapse, dragging his focus down with it. Through the murky haze, a red pickup appeared, blocking his path—then vanished—a hallucination.

The sharp descent worsened his dread. It was futile to believe he had enough time to reach safety. The cursed thing within him had awakened—demanding its due.

Then, through his failing sight, he glimpsed a white SUV pulling out from the opposite curb. An icy jolt hit his gut as he made the choice—his only choice.

As the SUV cleared, Jax yanked his handlebars hard to the left, cutting across traffic and narrowly missing an oncoming sedan. Horns blared angrily, but he didn't care. He'd made it through the gap and yet...he hadn't slowed down!

Intuitively, he pulled up on the handlebars, willing the bike to jump the curb. For a few heartbeats, time stood still. He was weightless. Then he felt the jarring thump of tires as he landed on the narrow sidewalk. Clutching the brakes, the wheels shrieked in protest as the bike skidded to a halt. He exhaled forcefully as all momentum ceased.

Then a dark awareness slithered into his thoughts—*that shriek wasn't metal*. Through his last sliver of sight, he saw and understood...he'd come within inches of crashing down onto an elderly woman. It was her panicked scream, not the bike's wheels, he'd heard objecting.

He dismounted, doubled over, and gasped for breath. Eyes squeezed shut, his trembling fingers managed to rummage a small tablet from his pocket and place it on his tongue. Yanking off his sweat-soaked helmet, he tried to breathe and waited for the medicine to ease the pounding in his skull.

Eyes still closed, Jax sensed the woman scurry past. He raised his hand in a weak apology, but she slapped it away and cursed him loudly in an unrecognizable language.

All he could do was sink to his knees and nod in silent agreement...*fool!*

1

Classroom

By the time Dr. Beck finally arrived at the stone-faced building on the university campus, his vision had almost returned to normal, and the pain in his head had retreated to a manageable dull ache. Standing just shy of six feet tall, Jax was lean and generally in good health. He hoisted the bike up onto his shoulder and easily carried it up the short flight of concrete stairs.

Once inside the entranceway of the building, he released his grip and set the tires gingerly on the worn green tiles. He made his way down the hallway, where he noisily pushed through a metal door.

Entering the theater-styled classroom, Jax raised one hand to the assembled students while using his other hand to lean his bike against the entrance doorframe. As he started to move away, the bicycle lost its fight with gravity and collapsed to the floor, the loud clatter reverberating through his aching skull. He returned to his fallen machine, used both hands to pick it up, and, this time, ensured it was securely balanced against the wall before stepping away. He attempted a good-natured smile while silently cursing his clumsiness and the residual pain it had caused.

"Sorry. I'm sorry I'm late, everyone. Give me just a minute, and I'll be right with you."

Removing the pant clips from the cuffs of his tan slacks, he placed them into his inverted helmet. He unsteadily strode over to his teaching assistant, who was standing behind the wooden lectern.

"Morning, Amy," Jax said, nodding to the younger woman.

Sliding his backpack onto one arm and handing it to her along with his bike helmet, he touched a finger to his head and muttered, "Another one for the logbooks."

Serving as his senior lab assistant and classroom aide, she understood immediately what the gesture meant.

"Sorry, Jax," Amy whispered. "I just got through handing out the students' graded papers from last week and was going to start a review of the highlights you've covered this semester."

Brushing off the sleeves of his faded sports coat, Jax ran his fingers back through his longish brown hair, then extracted his glasses from the coat pocket. Glancing around the room, his hazel eyes could only make out a blur of faces that filled the crowded auditorium. Exhaling loudly, he absently rubbed his temples before picking up a small remote from the podium. Taking a couple of careful steps backward, he pointed up at the large screen.

Jax's thumb found the familiar rubber button on the remote. A soft click, then a mechanical whir as the projector warmed to life behind him. The screen blazed blue-white against the dim lecture hall, making several students squint. Bold black letters materialized against the harsh glow, *Introduction to Neuroscience.*

"So, you will recall that in addition to teaching this class, I am also one of three lead researchers for the Rocky Mountain Neurosciences Center here at the Colorado Health Medical Campus.

"In this class, we've presented an overview of the brain, or what we know of it so far. You have read how different segments are known to control certain activities, such as the movement of our limbs, breathing, forming thoughts and emotions, and storing memories."

Jax made fists with each hand, then squeezed them together and held them straight out to the class.

"This powerful mass of cells is roughly the size of your fists when you put them together like this. Of course, this is just an approximation to provide you with a visual representation.

"The brain is an organ that serves as the center of the nervous system and consists of billions of nerve cells called neurons. These neurons communicate with one another throughout your body in a remarkably intricate network. It is the study of these cells and their systems that we call neuroscience.

"As I mentioned a moment ago, the Rocky Mountain Neurosciences Center is tasked with examining causes of some of the most prevalent ailments and diseases that affect the brain.

"The brain is comprised of three main sections, the cerebrum, the cerebellum, and the brainstem. The cerebrum occupies the upper part of the cranial cavity and is the largest part of the human brain. Its primary role is that of higher brain functions, including thoughts, actions, emotions, and the interpretation of sensory data from throughout the body.

"The cerebellum is located at the back of the brain and coordinates voluntary movements such as posture, balance, coordination, and speech. Then we have the brainstem, which connects to the spinal cord and also to the midbrain.

Jax stretched out his fingers so the thumb and forefinger of each hand touched, forming a crude web. He held his hands up over his head, then lowered them to chest height.

"One of the fascinating things about the brain is the cerebral cortex, which covers the cerebrum and serves much like a helmet. If you were to flatten out all the wrinkly parts, the cortex would only cover an area about the size of my hands right now. And the thickness of this area would be as thin as that credit card in your wallet or purse.

Jax lifted his arms over his head, clasping his fists. He stretched his back, then rolled his shoulders forward until he felt a little pop.

Pausing, he looked over each row of eighty or so students from front to back, confirming to himself that he had their attention.

"The thing about neuroscience is that it encompasses so many interdisciplinary areas of study. In addition to neurobiology, which we just briefly touched on here, it also includes chemistry, health sciences, and, of course, psychology. What most people don't realize is that it also includes aspects of engineering and physics.

"The Center is dedicated to helping patients with a wide variety of neurological conditions, including stroke, Parkinson's, and Alzheimer's, but my area of concentration deals specifically with chronic headaches and migraines. We examine the potential causes and current treatments.

"Research tells us that, although women are more likely to experience migraines, children, teenagers, and adult males can also experience them. How do I know this is true? Because not only do I conduct research surrounding this phenomenon, but I am a victim of migraines as well.

"A migraine typically progresses through four stages. These are prodrome, aura, attack, and postdrome. Not everyone who has a migraine goes through each stage. For example, I often skip the cues of the prodrome stage and jump right to an aura."

A woman seated near the front asked, "So, Dr. Beck, do you experience the same nausea and sensitivity to light and sound that some others do?"

Jax turned to confront the young woman. He wondered if her question had made him angry because his head still hurt from the migraine, or because she had interrupted his train of thought. He paused to compose himself before answering the question.

"Yes, Pam, sometimes it does get to that level, but not always—I mean not often."

Gently shaking his head, Jax tried to clear his muddled thoughts and get back on track.

"These visual disturbances, or auras, can manifest as flashes of light, zigzag patterns, or blind spots in one's field of vision, and may include visual or auditory hallucinations.

"After the aura is the attack stage. Forming words and understanding the speech of others can be difficult. This is sometimes misdiagnosed as a form of stroke. We believe that the electrical impulses throughout the brain will, for lack of a better term, misfire."

He turned his back to his students and rubbed his neck. He tried desperately to remember the point he had been trying to make, but his thoughts faltered. He clasped his hands together, both in supplication and frustration. He stared at the screen—then glanced up at the shadowed audience—then back to the screen. He willed his mouth to form the words he'd spoken a hundred times before.

"From...from here, the patient will typically progress to experiencing a throbbing or pulsating pain in the head, neck, maybe even in the shoulders and back. This pain will usually manifest on one side of the head, but it isn't—it isn't consistent..."

A young man from the middle row called out, "How long does it take someone to get through this—well, these events?"

Jax gently rubbed his eyes and clenched his teeth, then jabbed his index finger at the screen. He acknowledged the unavoidable reality... His lecture had become a muddled question-and-answer session.

"Well, Kevin," he said testily, "the reading assignment should have mentioned this point. From onset to the postdrome stage can take a few hours or last up to a few days."

Jax's throat began to tighten, and the back of his neck was cramping. He forced the semblance of a smile on his face and took a deep breath. The remote was sweaty in his shaking hand as he stared out at the class. Not focusing on anyone or anything.

Another student lifted her hand to ask a question. Sensing movement, Jax glanced in her direction with a blank expression, and her arm gradually lowered back to her side.

"You know what?" Jax pronounced in a monotone. "Why don't we stop here for the day? That way, everyone can catch up on the reading assignments and participate in the discussion. And—and, oh, yes, your research papers. Don't forget. Your papers are due in two weeks."

He scanned the room searching for Amy, but his vision was still blurry. He knew he was reaching a point where he might say something inappropriate. He needed her help, or he might make another scene. He needed her to intervene...now.

From the side of the stage, Amy could see the change in Jax's posture and speech. She quickly stepped out of the shadows and stood at the front of the room.

"Yes, people," Amy said, "so please don't make me chase you down to get those papers submitted. Just a reminder to you. If you send them to me early via email and ask nicely, I will make edits and allow you to make corrections. But don't wait until the week before they're due to submit them and expect this consideration—it won't happen."

Having recovered a bit, Jax added, "Also, we only have a few weeks until finals. I don't care if you think it's extremely old-school, but I will require your physical presence for a paper-and-pencil test. That's it for today. See you next week."

From the departing crowd, Jax was certain he heard someone utter, "What a dick!"

2

REFLECTIONS

THE LAST STUDENT FINALLY backed away, notebook clutched to her chest. Jax's temples throbbed as he glanced at Amy, who gave him a slight nod. "I'll grab sandwiches from that food truck," she said, already shouldering her bag. "Meet you at the lab."

Outside, Jax gripped his handlebars with white knuckles, the rubber warm from sitting in the sun. Each step sent a jolt through his skull as he pushed his bike along the cracked sidewalk.

The Neurosciences Center mirrored the six other university buildings surrounding it, each with its own group of scientists specializing in various health abnormalities. These buildings were the original classrooms when the university was first built, but were later converted to various science labs when a multi-million-dollar addition was added.

What Jax really wanted was to spend more time on his research and not be forced to teach these...children. The one shining light in this arrangement had been Amy.

Amy Taylor was just an undergraduate student when they first met, and she was also the first person Jax asked to join his research team. He'd recognized her intelligence immediately, and now she was close to earning her doctoral degree in neurochemistry. Damn, where had the years gone?

Jeez, he was full of himself during that time. A newly minted MD with a PhD tagged on to that. He'd just been offered his own research laboratory and was just starting to set up the equipment. The rising star on campus who had it all—

Smacking the seat of the bike with the flat of his hand, Jax jolted himself back into the present moment, chiding himself for pining for a fantasy. Glancing around, he was confident that no one had noticed his mental malfunction.

Of course, that fantasy vanished when the COVID crisis struck, and he was pulled into helping run the clinic here at the hospital. He hadn't even gotten all of his equipment uncrated before that shit storm hit. The twelve-hour shifts blurred into 14 and 16-hour marathons. Him not even making it home to his shitty little apartment, but instead crashing in his empty new lab most days. He'd lived off cafeteria food and the nearby patio bar. The campus was closed down, so the hospital staff were basically the only customers.

Worst of all were the deaths. The sheer number of deaths he had overseen before he was released from those two years of indentured servitude. Thank God for Tessa.

As he continued walking, he noticed groups of students huddled under budding aspen trees, talking animatedly. Still others were rushing to their next class or texting on their phones. All of them were simply oblivious to what had transpired here just a few short years ago. He found it all...haunting.

When his path was abruptly blocked by a set of concrete steps, he stood motionless and gazed up at the Center's entrance. He had no recollection of how he got there. The stone facade seemed to be studying him—accusing him. He mumbled to himself, "So fucking predictable."

Shaking his head, he guided his bike up the short steps. The building was neatly divided into two main wings, each with offices on either side of the aisles. Veering to the right, he strode down the aisle until he came to a door with his name stenciled on the glass. Inserting the key he kept hanging around his neck, he worked the rusting metal latch until he heard the slight pop of the simple lock. Pushing his bike through the door, he found its designated spot against the office bookcase.

He slid off his backpack and laid it on his weathered desk. Unencumbered by bike and bag, he allowed himself to uncoil into the cool leather of the chair. He allowed the coolness of the chair's headrest to seep into his neck, easing some of the tension that remained. Aside from his computer, the chair was the only modern addition to the archaic room. The small space had smelled like a tomb when he had first occupied it, and it retained the same musty odor years later, regardless of what remedies he tried

A beam of sunlight sliced through the window, catching the edge of a silver frame on his bookcase. Tessa gazed back at him from behind the glass—wind-tousled blonde hair, that knowing half-smile that still made his pulse quicken after all these years. Damn. He'd meant to call her hours ago, before the morning went to shit. His fingers found the cord for the blinds, twisting until the harsh light retreated. In the new dimness, he pressed his palms against his closed eyelids, seeking relief.

The silence of the office wrapped around him like a cool compress. Another neck stretch, another vertebral click. His mind finally settling, he fished out his phone and dialed Tessa's number. Voicemail. Right—Tuesday's clinic hours. No interruptions. He slipped the phone away, eyes drifting back to her photograph. More than five years had passed since they'd met in that same hospital where she now treated patients. She had captivated him with that same smile, but it was her sharp wit and brilliance that led him to propose.

Turning to log onto his computer, a hint of yellow caught his attention. A small note was attached to his monitor. He hated notes and all they suggested. He plucked it from its sticky perch and saw it was from the Center director—a request for Jax to come by his office. Such a summons was not uncommon from his boss. He crumpled the paper. Tossed it at the corner barrel. Missed.

Taking one last deep breath, he stood and gathered his things. Closing the door, he turned and strolled down the hallway, unaware his instinct had been prescient.

After exiting class with Jax, Amy walked to the procession of food trucks lining the street. She had always been the first person to volunteer for such tasks. She was also the first to capture the attention of most men… and many women. Careful not to encourage the wrong type of attention, she tried her best to downplay her attractiveness. She'd lost all patience with dating during her freshman year, choosing to focus on her studies instead of dating and sex.

After placing her order, she turned and found a small group of athletic male students trying to flirt with her. Ignoring their vulgar observations about her figure and requests for her phone number, she merely turned and gazed at the ground. Here she was, a couple of months away from her doctoral degree. Yet without resorting to wearing a burka or rags, it always came down to her figure. The thing that society always reminded her was the thing it valued most.

By the time her food request was completed, she could feel the frustration congealing—at Jax, the director, but mostly herself. She vowed not to wait for respect to be given. If this was the way things were going to be played, then so be it. Respect came from two things, admiration and fear. If not the first, she would settle on the latter. She held her head high as she walked purposefully through the group of boys who had made those lewd suggestions—both of her hands grasping the bags—knuckles white.

3

Bad News

For Jax, Dr. Steven Mason was the catalyst for his decision to remain at the Center. When he first graduated with his MD and PhD, Jax was approached by many of the top universities and their research centers.

There was no doubt in his mind that he would stay in Colorado when Dr. Mason showed up one day and promised him carte blanche if he would consider staying at the Center. That was six years ago, and Jax hadn't regretted his choice, even enduring the two years he had been conscripted to the hospital's Covid Clinic before finally returning to his lab. In fact, it was that very clinic that led him to meet Tessa.

Ensuring his glasses were secure in his coat pocket, he walked the short distance down to the director's office positioned near the center of the building. The meds Jax had taken a couple of hours ago had helped with the roughest pain. Still, the back of his head was tender, and his neck cramped, so he would need more ibuprofen later.

Jax stuck his head into the open office doorway and looked around for his mentor. Partially hidden behind the large computer monitor sat a man of indeterminate age with rich black skin and a shiny bald scalp reflecting the light overhead. Tapping the door frame, Jax leaned in and asked, “Hey, Steve, you wanted to see me?”

Startled, the man looked up from his computer screen. “Jax, my boy!” Dr. Mason said, “Come in, come in. Please, sit.”

Raising one hand, Jax motioned in a way to stop the man, “Actually, Steve, I have my crew waiting. I just wanted to check in before heading down to the lab.”

“Please, Jax. Come in and close the door. We need to talk.”

“Sure, Steve. But that look on your face does not instill a lot of joy in me.”

He entered the large office and closed the door behind him as requested. Dr. Mason had two stiff wooden chairs in front of the large, overcrowded desk. Jax took the first chair, settling onto the edge of its thinly padded seat.

“Yes, yes, I get that. Unfortunately, I do have some...well, something that we need to discuss about the Center that I haven’t even shared with the other lead scientists just yet. I wanted the chance to talk with you first about this matter.”

“Sure. I mean, thanks...I guess.”

Dr. Mason rubbed a hand over his smooth pate, then gently pushed the computer monitor to the side of his desk so he could look at his visitor unobstructed.

“I’m not going to beat around the bush with you, Jax. I hate to convey bad news, but we’re going to lose some funding, and it’s going to happen rather soon, I’m afraid.”

“But I—wait, I have grant money. It’s been earmarked for at least twelve months!”

“Jax, you’ve seen the political shit storm this nation is facing. They’re cutting everything, everywhere. It was simply inevitable that the university would feel the pinch sooner or later. As it turns out, it’s going to be sooner.”

“Sure, I could see the writing on the wall like the next guy, but why are you telling me specifically about this? Won’t our cuts be evenly split among our three research labs, and what each of us is trying to do?”

“It simply is not that clean, I’m afraid. Most of the funding the other two labs are getting has to do with patients suffering from specific neurological disorders. Every one of those conditions has charities and benefactors who fund research to find treatments, or even a cure, for those diseases. Yours, I’m afraid, does not.”

Jax rubbed his neck and took a deep breath before asking, “What kind of timeline are you talking about here, Steve? My team deserves to know. Shit, I deserve to know.”

The older man took a second to gaze out his window, then turned back to face Jax.

"Jax, you know I believe in you and your team. But the fact is you haven't really produced anything that our outside sponsors can use..."

"That's bullshit, and you know it! We have ongoing collaborations with the top ten teaching hospitals in the country on several promising treatments. Damn it, we've had nearly a dozen articles published in the last three years alone!"

"I agree with you! But you know damn well that a lot of the funding that comes your way, aside from what used to be government grants, is from the private sector."

"You mean Big Pharma, don't you?"

"If I'm putting all my cards on the table, here is what I'm talking about. Epilepsy is identifiable. Parkinson's, Alzheimer's, and Huntington's are all identifiable diseases. Then you have ADHD, autism, or Cerebral Palsy. Each of these is known to the general public and is either life-altering or fatal."

"And migraines are just bad headaches and a simple inconvenience that millions endure for a short period. Shit, I've heard all that crap before—too often!"

"Also, Jax, can you name any significant breakthrough your team has produced in the last year—one that the public can use? You should know as well as anyone that in science, excellent work does not translate into real-world applications."

"You want me to apologize for not having a neurological disorder that has a million-dollar charity to promote funding for research? That we haven't whipped together a sexy enough product for doctors to push on their patients?"

"That's unfair, Dr. Beck, and you know it. How many times have I gone to bat for you? Well, let me tell you, it's been several times. Actually, I've put my ass on the line for you, your research, and your lab more often than I care to admit."

"So, how much time am I really looking at before I have to shut the doors here?"

Dr. Mason rotated his chair to the printer behind him and pulled out a sheet of paper from its plastic tray. He turned back and placed the paper down on the opposite side of the desk and tapped it once with his finger.

"I was just reviewing that very issue. Assuming I can shift some things around here and there, I believe I can give you until the fall before we must let your team go."

Looking at the spreadsheet laid out before him, Jax could make out some of the larger words. For the most part, the page was an unfocused jumble of letters and numbers. He rubbed his temples to fight back the rising pain he had just been able to tamp down earlier and slid the paper back across the desk.

"Goddamn it, Steve. So, that's it. I get just a few more months, and then... what? The team is done, over, gone?"

The Director looked at the dejected face of the man who had been his student, then his employee, and eventually his colleague. All he could manage was a simple, "Yes."

4

Review of Work

The three Center labs stood in stark contrast to the surrounding offices. Instead of aged wood paneling, they featured stainless steel walls and sinks, state-of-the-art lab equipment, and sleek office décor. Fluorescent panels cast an even, shadowless light across every surface. In the center of the main room sat a single patient station, its adjustable partitions hung on ceiling tracks, their frosted panels waiting to slide into position. Along the periphery were open workspaces, a small conference room, and a control booth for recording patient readings.

Jax's lab was isolated at the far eastern end of the building, while the other two labs occupied the entire west wing. Although he had his personal office just down the hall, he often worked from an empty cubicle at the farthest point in the room. He liked to stay close to his team and the work being done.

Jax slipped into the lab during the lunch hour, raising his hand in a perfunctory greeting before making straight for the half-empty coffee pot. Mug filled to the brim, he retreated to the far cubicle and powered up his workstation.

Through the glass partition, he could see his team gathered in the conference room, already halfway through their meal. They'd long ago stopped waiting for him to join them. Amy Taylor ran point as Senior Lab Assistant, while Gabriel Torrez handled the junior position, tracking emerging technologies and trial results from competing research centers. At the end of the table sat Sita Singh, their technical specialist, whose expertise kept their complex array of scanners, analyzers, and software systems functioning at peak efficiency.

Jax sipped his coffee, the weight of dread pressing down on him. The meeting with the Director had left him drained, going through the motions without much thought. It didn't feel like the right time to tell the team what he'd learned—he needed to mull it over before dropping something that could blow up.

Looking up from his monitor, Jax saw the team finishing lunch and wandering back into the main lab. He wanted to approach the funding problem coolly—scientifically. First, examine the known facts, identify what was missing, and maybe—just maybe—find a new way forward.

Without further thought, he called out, "Hey, guys, before you dive back into work, would you mind if we carve out a few minutes for a quick review?"

Although hesitant, they all nodded their agreement. Jax pointed back towards the conference room they'd just left. Retrieving their laptops, the three followed Jax into the room and reclaimed their seats. Jax stood before the whiteboard and wrote across the top, *'Summary of Work'*.

"Amy, could you start us off with a pharmacological overview?"

"Certainly." She stood and uncapped a marker, ready to write out her thoughts. "We've seen promising results with CGRP antagonists—calcitonin gene-related peptide inhibitors. These block the peptide that transmits migraine pain. Drugs like—"

Jax lifted his palm in a halting gesture. "Let's take a step back from the technical details. Can you walk us through the basic mechanism? I'm looking for the big picture of what triggers these migraines and how these compounds actually interrupt the pain cycle."

Amy's eyebrows lifted slightly. "Well, sure, if I need to go back to high school-level explanations." She capped the marker with a sharp click. Then stepped forward and gestured to the side of her head, spreading her hand wide.

Amy sighed. "Think of it like this. Your brain has a major alarm system—the trigeminal nerve. When that alarm gets tripped, it floods your brain with chemical messengers that basically scream 'pain!' These messengers inflame the protective covering around your brain, and that's what you feel as a migraine. What our drugs do is intercept those messengers before they can complete their mission. It's like having security guards that catch the alarm signals before they reach the control center."

She started to list off drugs using the closed marker against her other hand. "Drugs like Lasmiditan can be used for acute pain or prevention. Other drugs work similarly but are stronger and still undergoing clinical trials—"

"What about GABA?" Jax interrupted. "Like with epilepsy?"

Amy crossed her arms and held a slight edge to her voice. "GABA, or Gamma-Aminobutyric Acid, is the brain's primary inhibitory neurotransmitter. It calms neural signals. Aside from epilepsy patients, some supplements do exist, but dosages aren't standardized, and it's unclear if they cross the blood-brain barrier—"

"Okay, thanks, Amy. Gabe, you've been tracking non-pharmacological approaches. Can you give us a quick overview?"

"Sure," Gabe said, stepping to the board as Amy sat down. Jax took a second to study the thin, wiry man. Gabe was always cheerful, something that had been lacking in himself lately.

Gabe's eyes lit up. "Neuromodulation is where the real excitement is happening. Our TMS—that's the Transcranial Magnetic Stimulation machine—is showing promise, and those Vagus nerve stimulators are creating quite a buzz in the field." He traced a line from behind his ear down his neck. "The Vagus nerve runs from here all the way down to your vital organs. The best part? These are all external methods using magnetic or electrical pulses—no surgery required!"

He grinned at the group. "Fun fact: you can actually buy over a dozen different Vagus nerve stimulators online right now. Results vary from person to person, of course, and the lack of standards means we don't have rock-solid studies yet—but the potential is definitely there."

"Thanks, Gabe. Let's move to our own work with the TMS. Sita, any measurable trends in the data?"

Jax recalled that the young woman was one of Amy's first hires for this team. Standing just under five feet tall, her blend of punk and goth styles gave her an air of authority that belied her petite stature and Hindu upbringing. Although she was required to remove her metal studs for this job, she still displayed a flamboyant collection of tattoos that covered both arms to the wrist.

Sita cleared her throat as she replaced Gabe at the board, tucking a strand of hair behind her ear. "Exit surveys show a small but statistically significant decrease in attack frequency," she said, her voice steady despite her slightly quickened speech.

She glanced at Jax, then back at her notes. "Let me back up." She raised one finger, her silver rings catching the fluorescent light. "The machine sends repetitive magnetic pulses through the skull, stimulating nerve cells and inducing electrical currents that alter neural activity." Her confidence grew as she delved into the technical details. “Some call it rebooting the brain, which is not too far off.”

“It’s also used for OCD, depression, even smoking cessation,” Jax added. “Like with the vagus nerve stimulators, there’s a placebo effect going on there. But I’ve also heard about some complaints from volunteers. Are those concerns valid?”

“Not really. Our trials go back just over a year,” Sita said. “Aside from grumblings about mild side effects, there’s nothing significant—Amy’s even written a paper on this. Really, we’ve basically just verified the results from existing studies. Nothing new there.”

Amy crossed her arms and leaned forward slightly. “But don't forget,” she added, her voice sharper, “we've seen reduced reliance on rescue meds. Not dramatic, but it's there in the data. The placebo effect is a confounding factor, sure, but that doesn't invalidate our findings. We'd need a much larger sample size to draw firm conclusions—which, if you'd read my paper, you'd know I already recommended.”

As Sita returned to her seat, Jax stood and reviewed his notes before looking at the assembled group.

“No. TMS isn’t portable, so it’s impractical during a patient's episode. We also can’t prove the relief comes from the intervention itself. The same goes for Vagus stimulation. Let’s wrap those up. We can’t afford to keep chasing something we can’t prove.”

"We've already ruled out supplements and lifestyle changes," Sita said. "Too much variability."

"True," Gabe added. "The gut-brain link is being explored, but it's speculative. A few small trials on probiotics showed minimal benefit. As Amy said, we need larger studies, but at the moment, there are too many confounding variables."

Amy leaned forward, tapping her pen rapidly against her notepad. "What about psychedelics?" Her voice rose slightly. "Microdosing psilocybin or LSD for cluster headaches is an established therapy—so why shouldn't there be crossover potential? We're ignoring an entire avenue of treatment here."

"I admit it's an expanding area. Most studies focus on cluster headaches, but there are anecdotal reports and pilot studies suggesting benefits for migraines, especially chronic, treatment-resistant cases. Realistically, given our current politics and regulatory hurdles, the university has balked at the idea of us studying that here. But let's not eliminate it just yet. Maybe there's a way around the politics I haven't thought of yet."

"Anything new in behavioral techniques?" Sita asked.

"Yes," Jax said. "Tessa's mentioned they're tracking trends in psychology. Using biofeedback apps and smartwatches for early warning and self-regulation, then combining that with guided relaxation or cognitive therapy."

Amy's pen stopped mid-tap. "So, we're just—what—abandoning neuroscience to chase psychological factors now?" Her voice rising with the last three words.

"Maybe. Think about it. If TMS and Vagus nerve stimulation have shown placebo effects, then all these other devices may lead to some form of behavior modification. You know, a train-your-brain type of process."

"Damn it, Jax," Amy said, "we are currently knee deep in examining the effects of neurochemistry and mapping electrical and vascular changes in the brain. But you want us to—do what? Dump all the work and data we've gathered and go looking for behavioral changes instead?"

"Amy, I'm not trying to throw your work away, but we—"

"What, Jax? What the hell is this all about? We had a plan. This team has been working with defined goals. Now that's not good enough? And what is the actual reason you're putting us through this exercise today?"

Jax stood looking at her, not having a good answer. He had wanted to get them motivated—to think differently—anything to keep from talking about budgets.

"I believe it's prudent that we look at trends as well as treatments that haven't been fully investigated, that's all. Damn it, Amy, our work with neurochemicals has been going on for two years! Honestly, what exactly do we have to show for it?!"

Wordlessly, Amy stood and glared at Jax for several seconds. Then, she gathered her things and left the room. A moment later, the loud bang of steel doors slamming closed reverberated through the lab. Jax glanced at the whiteboard, then turned to his two remaining team members, who kept their eyes riveted to their laptops. He tried to write something on the whiteboard, but he was too rattled.

His phone indicated an incoming text. Removing it from his pocket, he saw it was from Amy. After silently reading the curt message, he just shook his head slowly.

"Look, we've been pushing hard this whole semester. What say we call it early, and let's all take a long weekend. I know I could use the break, and I believe Amy already beat us to it. So please, Gabe, Sita, go relax, and we'll pick this up on Monday."

Tessa had looked at her phone when she felt it vibrate and saw the call was from Jax. She knew he would understand her not answering, as it was a part of the job to put work before personal considerations. They both shared this same outlook, and he would have acted the same if she had called him.

This particular moment was an especially bad time for her. She was conferring with Terry Adler, one of the psychologists she worked with at the hospital. Terry was in the middle of conducting an EMDR session with a 29-year-old man named John, who had suffered a trauma while serving in the US Army a few years ago. The room where the therapy was being conducted had muted lighting. The observation room where she sat was completely dark.

Through the window, Tessa watched Terry's fingers move rhythmically from left to right in front of John's face, his eyes tracking the movement while his jaw muscles clenched and unclenched. Terry's voice filtered through the speaker as a low murmur, punctuated by longer silences where John's responses were too quiet to catch.

She'd skimmed Terry's case files for years, signing off on treatment plans with clinical detachment, but lately found herself lingering behind the glass. The stack of research papers on her desk had grown—dog-eared journals detailing cross-over applications for this treatment. When the second EMDR therapist was hired last quarter, Tessa had personally conducted the interviews, peppering candidates with questions about adaptations for non-combat trauma that left HR raising eyebrows. The multiple military bases scattered throughout the state kept both therapists' schedules full.

Pulling her long blonde hair up into a ponytail, she reviewed John's history to better grasp the trauma he was dealing with. As one of the last of the troops to be pulled out of Afghanistan, John had stood at the airport gate, his commanding officer screaming in his ear to move while his Afghan interpreter, Farid, pleaded from the other side of the barrier. John's hand had hovered over the gate release and was about to act until another soldier yanked him backward. His final image of Farid was a split-second tableau—recognition, betrayal, then nothing as Taliban gunfire erased his face.

John had managed two years of civilian life after Afghanistan before his wife delivered an ultimatum. She'd found him at 3 AM, rigid on the kitchen floor, his fists white-knuckled against invisible enemies while their daughter watched from the doorway. The VA psychiatrist's prescriptions gathered dust on their nightstand. Only after Terry introduced the rhythmic eye movements of EMDR did John's hypervigilance begin to soften, his breathing steadying even when sirens wailed outside the clinic windows.

During a small pause in the session, Tessa took advantage of the lull to quietly exit the observation booth and find the women's bathroom. She splashed cold water on her face, hoping to wash away some small part of the pain she felt hearing this man's story. Listening to the various traumas that so many individuals have suffered through was... stressful—but long hours of training and years of working with patients had created a formidable shell of protection for herself, as it did for most therapists.

Turning her phone back on, she made her way to her office while musing on how badly she needed a break. Just then, all her messages came through, including a couple from Jax. She'd remembered he had called earlier, but didn't leave a message. He had sent a follow-up text asking if she could get away for a long weekend. With no hesitation, she replied.

"You, sir, are a mind reader! Give me an hour or so to wrap things up here. I'll swing by the house to pick up our stuff, then meet you at the Center. God, I really need this!"

5

Weekend Vacation

After Tessa cheerfully accepted his spur-of-the-moment invitation, Jax let her know he would arrange accommodation for their trip to Colorado Springs. Although his wife always enjoyed the opulence of the Broadmoor Hotel in the southern part of the city, Jax preferred a hotel closer to the middle, which was closer to both his dad and his favorite hiking spot. Their compromise was a suite at the charming Marriott.

Although he held a valid license, Jax hated driving in traffic. Therefore, letting Tessa drive her bright red Honda Pilot was the obvious choice. Unlike Jax, Tessa didn't mind driving in the least. In fact, her having lived in London for most of her life made Denver's traffic chaos seem trivial to her.

Throwing together an overnight bag for herself and one for their dog, Bear, Tessa grabbed Jax's prepacked duffel from the closet and was gone. Growing up in a military household since preschool, Jax kept a go-bag always tagged and ready.

Her only other task was picking up their 85-pound Malinois Shepherd from the neighbor's house, and she was ready. Arriving at the Center in under thirty minutes was a tribute to both her organizational skills and her enthusiasm at the thought of escaping for the weekend.

As she pulled in front of the entrance, Jax was waiting for her on the Center's steps— sans his bike. He placed his backpack in the rear seat and greeted Bear with a kiss on his nose and a scratch behind the ears.

"Oh, sure," Tessa quipped, "Bear gets a kiss but not your wife?"

"You're absolutely right, honey." He then made a big show of kissing Tessa on the nose and scratching her ear.

She softly smacked his shoulder as Jax strapped in. They made it to the southbound freeway in record time, and once out of the metro area, Tessa exhaled loudly. Both of their shoulders seemed to relax in unison. When he looked over at his wife, she grinned like a fool. Getting away seemed to be exactly what they both needed.

The hour passed quickly, with most of the drive spent listening to classical music, with the French composer, Erik Satie, her favorite for longer journeys, with his gentle touch that settled her thoughts. The lack of chatter seemed to give them both time to embrace the music while mentally locking away thoughts of work. Bear was content to lie in the back of the vehicle, his head resting on the seatback, eyes closed.

They passed the Air Force Academy's expansive 18,000 acres of land, stretching from the freeway all the way up into the foothills, an indicator they were approaching the northern part of Colorado Springs. The evening traffic was starting to build as they headed toward the correct exit. They pulled into the parking lot of the red-bricked hotel just as the sun began its slow descent behind the western mountains, known as the Front Range. Jax took Bear out to relieve himself, while Tessa got them checked in. With the Memorial weekend still several days off, the throng of tourists had not yet descended, and they were quickly processed at the front desk.

After settling into their room, Jax suggested a glass of wine at the hotel bar. Ensuring Bear was fed, they made their way downstairs to the cozy tavern with its tantalizing aromas filling the air. They made their way to an empty table that provided a nook of privacy while offering a full view of the darkening foothills. Jax ordered for both, making sure to include a particular appetizer he knew was Tessa's favorite.

"When I took Bear out, I called my dad to let him know we were in town. He invited us to dinner tomorrow night if that sounds okay. I told him I would talk with you about it and let him know later."

"Jax, you know I love your dad's cooking. So does Bear!"

With a smirk, he said, "I told him we were going to go for a sunrise hike and probably want a quick nap before heading over."

"So, you already told him we'd be there? What happened to checking with me first?"

"I know you like my dad, so I was certain you'd say yes. And if for some reason you did object, I was fully prepared to tell him you simply refused to see him."

"You, sir, have no shame, you know that?"

"Agreed. You know, my wife keeps telling me that."

"Maybe then you should listen to her more often?"

"What, and ruin my reputation?"

When their food and drinks arrived, Tessa held a small bruschetta in front of her to get Jax's attention. Then she slowly rubbed the bread over her lips as she looked longingly into her husband's eyes.

"You, madam, do not play fair."

"And?" she said coyly, as she glided her bare toes up and down his leg. "What, sir, are you going to do about it?"

He could feel her body's warmth through his slacks as a blush grew in him. "Let me take care of the check, and I'd be happy to show you."

Leaving the bar, they made their way into an empty elevator. Allowing his wife to enter first, Jax stood close enough to catch the scent of her skin. When the car began to rise, she leaned back slightly until her shoulder blades brushed against his chest. His hand found the small of her back, fingers tracing slow, deliberate circles. At their floor, the elevator doors opened with a soft chime. Jax's normally steady hands trembled slightly as he pressed the key card against the scanner. Inside their room, Tessa turned to face him, her eyes holding his as she stepped backward, one finger hooked in his belt loop, gently pulling him along. The door clicked shut behind them.

Sunrise through the massive Kissing-Camels rock formation was so much more than picturesque. Quietly perched on his self-proclaimed throne of boulders, the rising sun warming his face, Jax immersed himself in the majesty that was the Garden of the Gods.

The couple silently absorbed the otherworldly feeling surrounding them. The stone spires that rose like giant fingers reaching through the ground, and the billowing clouds, a theatrical curtain illuminating Pikes Peak. This spray of reddened clay was where he instinctively found himself whenever he felt the brutality of life collapse atop him.

Tessa handed him a small cup of coffee from the thermos they had obtained at the hotel. The taste of the hot, dark beverage on his tongue was the perfect balance to the crisp morning air, which held a hint of sage. He gazed over at his wife with her wholesome face and her lush blonde hair pulled back into a high ponytail. Tessa's pale skin reflected the morning light flawlessly on her cheeks, her deep blue eyes looking into and through him.

"Tess," he whispered, "something's happening at work that I want to share with you. I needed this separation—I had to regain my balance before I could talk about it objectively. That, and I wasn't going to mess up a perfect evening with you last night."

"Jax," she whispered back, "it's been so long since we've had the chance to just talk. And yes, last night was wonderful, even if we did scare Bear with our antics."

Jax smiled at her comment as he studied her smile against the blanket of sky. He took another sip of coffee, feeling its warmth run down his throat. Energized, he looked back lovingly at this amazing woman and continued his narrative.

"Steve pulled me into his office yesterday. He told me that they're turning off the funding tap by the end of summer. I'm going to lose the lab, Tess. The team."

Gently looking into his eyes, she squeezed his hand. "Jesus. I'm so sorry, Jax. And he just told you? Without any warning?"

"You know, at first, that's how I felt. Now that I've had time to think about it, I have to admit that a part of me expected something like this. More of a feeling than a rational thought. It's like we hit a stone wall this past year. I don't know. Maybe my heart isn't into it anymore."

“Sure, that can happen to anyone. I get that sometimes myself. But if you’re honest with yourself, do you think this is something you can, or even want to, continue for the next few months? More important, what did your team say when you told them?”

“I never got that far. I had just gotten the word, and then things kind of fell apart between us at the lab before I got to the bad news. Surprise—welcome to Colorado Springs!”

Tessa leaned closer, her eyes softening as she brushed her thumb across his knuckles. “Jax, honey, I know how much that lab means to you, but remember, you don't have to stay somewhere that's hurting you. Your work deserves to be valued.”

Her voice dropped to that gentle tone she often used. “And if that means another lab somewhere else, I'll be right there beside you."

“Tessa, sweetheart, I don’t...I don’t think I have an answer right now. It’s not that I don’t want to share my thoughts about this, I simply don’t know what I can tell you. I feel like I’m driving on empty right now. Maybe later?”

“Good enough. So, are we still on for dinner at your dad’s tonight?”

“Yeah, I owe him dinner. Also, he mentioned he’s invited over a friend of his, so that should be interesting.”

“A friend, huh? Okay, just let me know what I can do to help. Okay, the sun is up. Do you feel like walking the trail for a bit?

I think Bear is feeling left out, just wandering around by himself down there sniffing out rabbits."

"Why, yes, Mrs. Beck. I do believe getting off my ass is most definitely called for."

"Well, it is a fine ass now, isn't it?"

"That's what my wife keeps telling me."

6

DINNER AT MARK'S

RETIRED LT. COLONEL MARK Beck had spent the final ten of his twenty-five years in the Air Force as an instructor at the nearby Academy. Earlier in his career, he'd served as a fighter pilot during the initial years of the war in Afghanistan. After sustaining an arm injury, he was reassigned to teach aeronautics and related subjects to cadets.

It was during that transition that Mark moved his family from Chicopee, Massachusetts, to Colorado Springs, Colorado. Jax, then in his late teens, completed his senior year at Air Academy High School on base—the same year he lost his mother.

Standing at the front door, Jax suppressed the familiar jab of anxiety that always accompanied returning to the house where his mother had lived. Elena had been a vibrant, optimistic woman who saw the good in others. Tessa gently grasped his arm in a gesture of support.

The door swung open to reveal Mark's smiling face. Though shorter than his son, his gregarious nature made him seem larger. Now in his mid-sixties, Mark maintained a disciplined regimen of exercise and diet, giving him the healthy glow of someone much younger. Although his hair was mostly gray, he was—as always—clean-shaven.

"Jax! Tessa!" Mark beamed. "It's so good to see you. Come in!"

After retiring, Mark remained in the home he and Elena had purchased decades earlier. Nestled in the foothills, it suited his lifestyle perfectly—close enough to the airport so he could fly his Cessna, affectionately named Cloud Dancer—yet still enjoy the spacious, fenced backyard where his older Golden Retriever, Bravo, could romp freely.

Following family tradition, they both removed their shoes and stepped into the expansive living room. A woman with red hair and a freckled nose rose from the couch and approached them with an outstretched hand.

"Hi, I'm Molly," she said warmly. "It's so nice to finally meet you both."

"Well," Mark said, "obviously this is my son, Jaxon—Jax, and his wife, Tessa. Oh, and that's Bear. This is Molly Green. Molly is an old friend. Excuse me. Molly is a friend I've known for a long time."

Tessa was first to reach Molly and embraced her warmly. It was evident that Molly was several years younger than Mark, but Tessa did not care about such things.

Jax first hugged his dad, then closed the gap and shook Molly's hand with both of his, not quite sure what was appropriate for their first meeting. He noticed she had the scent of an expensive perfume his mother sometimes wore.

Mark took the harnessed Bear to the back door, where Bravo eagerly awaited his canine companion, then closed the sliding glass door behind him. "What can I get you two to drink?" Mark said from the kitchen. "Tessa, I have your favorite wine out, but I also whipped up a pitcher of my famous margaritas if you dare!"

"Thanks, Mark," Tessa said, "I think I'll stick to wine so I can drive us back safely."

"I have no such problem," Jax said, "so I'll go with your tequila concoction. Dad, do you still have those glasses you got in Mexico from your last trip?"

"Absolutely!" Mark said. "Coming right up."

The living room was set up with two matching sofas facing each other, and a large wooden coffee table situated between them. A magnificent floor-to-ceiling stone fireplace capped off the sitting space. Tessa sat next to Molly, while Jax chose the opposing seat, giving him the best view of the exchange between the two women.

"So," Tessa said, taking Molly's hand, "how long have you known Mark?"

"Okay," Mark said loudly from the kitchen, "so, that's how it's going to be? No small talk, just right to the interrogation?"

Chuckling, Mark entered the room and set a bulky tray on the coffee table. The platter was filled with drinks, bowls of chips, salsa, and guacamole. He held out the gold-lined glass of wine to Tessa, then giant goblets of margaritas to Molly, and Jax then claimed one for himself. He held his glass in the air as he sat next to his son. "To family and good friends!"

They spent the next hour enjoying the refreshments and the warm fireplace as Mark regaled them with his latest exploits from an air show in Arizona. He'd raised Bravo since he was a puppy and had flown with Mark on nearly every trip around the country. When the group adjourned to the dining room, he allowed the well-behaved canines to accompany them for the meal.

Over a dinner of fajitas and salad, the group began to share each other's backgrounds. "I was a nurse," Molly said, "assigned to the hospital near Ramstein Air Base in Germany at the same time Mark was there recovering from his wounded arm. I oversaw the physical therapy of soldiers, airmen, and marines injured in battle."

Jax noticed the two of them looking at one another when this information was divulged. From the small glint in his dad's eye, he was sure their relationship had been more than just patient-nurse.

Jax stared at his father, realizing that Mark would have still been married to his mother during that time if his suspicion was correct. He turned to Tessa and clasped her hand. He couldn't imagine a life without her—or any variation where he had to share her.

After dinner, the four refreshed their drinks and stepped into the backyard, settling around a stone fire pit beneath a crisp, star-strewn sky. The spring air still had a bite, prompting Tessa and Molly to gratefully accept the camp blankets Mark kept on hand for nights like this. Jax and his father, warmed by the tequila and the fire's glow, were content. The dogs basked in the heat radiating from the stones.

"So, Molly," Tessa asked, "are you still in the service? Still in nursing?"

Molly nodded. "Still a nurse, but not in uniform anymore. I left the Army shortly after my deployment in Germany. I moved to Michigan and worked at the VA Medical Center for a while. About a year ago, I was offered the position as Clinic Director here in Colorado Springs. I manage to run that show now."

"Damn," Tessa said. "That's a hell of a résumé. Are you involved in anything beyond the administrative side? I hope I'm not prying, it's just that your work sounds so familiar to what I'm involved with myself. I see a lot of veterans dealing with PTSD and the challenges of transitioning to civilian life."

"I know, Tessa. Mark and I have talked about your work, as well as Jax's research. There are a lot of overlaps. PTSD is more widely recognized now, which helps. But we also focus on patients who've lost limbs, sight, hearing... sometimes all three. There's no shortage of trauma, but there's also resilience."

A quiet settled over the group. Each stared into the fire, lost in their own thoughts. The flames crackled softly, casting flickering shadows across their faces. Tessa looked to Jax, who seemed lost in his own thoughts as he surveyed the house and yard where he had spent the better part of his youth—and where he'd lost his mother.

Mark stood abruptly and walked into the house. "Stay put. Molly brought something to show you. Nothing crazy, but I want you to hear this, now that you're here."

A few minutes later, he returned, carrying what looked like an oversized pair of glasses, connected to a tangle of wires dangling down. He placed the device on a table between his and Molly's chairs and sat down again. He smiled at Molly, as if it were Christmas and he had a gift to unwrap.

"Maybe it's the tequila," he said quietly, "or maybe it's just the right time. Either way, I want to share something that's been hard to talk about...well, until recently."

He drained the last of his drink, eyes fixed on the fire, and began to speak. "Molly has been helping me deal with my own stress-related disorders for the past year. Honestly, for much longer than that, but what she offered me—what has made a noticeable difference is...well, unique."

Molly reached over to the small table between them and picked up the item he had just brought out. She patted his hand affectionately before continuing.

"Tessa," Molly asked, "I assume you've worked with EMDR therapy?"

"Yes, quite a bit. It's been around for years now and has helped many of our patients. Of course, it's not a universal solution."

"Exactly. It was never meant to be one-size-fits-all. Every individual brings a unique set of variables, which is why we integrate a range of therapeutic approaches."

"So, you have something new to add to the mix?"

"We've partnered with a local tech company to develop a tool that complements traditional therapy. As you both know, EMDR relies on the patient identifying and engaging with the trauma they've stored in memory. This visor helps eliminate external distractions and allows the patient to engage more directly with the memory. I guess you could say it's to help them see it more distinctly."

She paused, then continued with quiet conviction. "We think of trauma—especially persistent, unresolved trauma—as a kind of injury, like a broken arm. It needs to be set and healed properly for the person to function in the present. Otherwise, flashbacks or what we call mental paralysis can block progress, even with conventional therapy."

Jax raised an eyebrow. "So, what is this? A psychological lobotomy? Some kind of memory wipe?"

"No, Jax," Molly said gently. "It's not about erasing anything. It's about clarity. People misremember events all the time, adding or omitting details. This device helps them revisit the memory as if it were happening in real time. It strips away the filters and safely guides them through the process of re-filing that memory. Not erasing it but integrating it. It's so they can live in the present."

Jax stood and cracked his neck, a familiar ritual to release tension. He paced briefly behind his chair, scratched Bear's belly, then sat again. It was apparent to everyone that he had something to say, and they waited until he was ready to speak without interruption.

"Look, you all know I'm a scientist first. I believe in the physiology of memory. What we call a memory isn't stored in one place but rather a network of sensory impressions encoded by dendrites and synapses. Sight, sound, smell—they're all processed in different regions of the brain. But together, they form a single experiential imprint."

Molly leaned forward slightly. "Jax, would you be open to seeing what we're working on? Just a demonstration. Nothing invasive. Would that be okay?"

"Jax. Tess." Mark said, his voice firm but measured, "You're both doctors. You believe in scientific inquiry. This isn't voodoo or some fringe pseudoscience. It's an established therapy. It's just been taken to the next level."

"Dad, what about the risk of implanting false memories? What about the long-term psychological effects? You can't just amplify a treatment without considering the fallout."

"I'm with Jax on this," Tessa added. "Molly, I'm not trying to shut you down, but has this been through controlled studies? What evidence do you have that this kind of leap in trauma therapy is safe—or at least free from conflicting outcomes?"

"Stop," Molly said abruptly. "Just stop for a minute. No, I'm not a doctor, but I'm not an amateur either. I appreciate your concern for Mark, but we've been working on this for over a year. Trials have been conducted. We've gathered and analyzed the data. So far, the results have been consistently positive. We've done thorough follow-ups and haven't seen any harmful effects in patients who've chosen to use the device."

Tessa leaned forward. "Okay, but what are you telling us? What's your sample size? How long after treatment are you conducting follow-ups? Do you include spouses or family members? Anyone who can help assess the patient's overall well-being?"

Mark stood, exhaled loudly and rubbed his hands together. "Maybe we need to let this go for tonight. This was just supposed to be a friendly evening. I think we've drifted way too far off course."

"No, Dad. I think it's time for a demonstration. I want to see what you and Molly have been working on. I need to be sure you're not being misled—or worse, exploited."

"Enough!" Mark snapped. "Molly is my friend. A dear friend. And I won't stand here while you insult her or dismiss her work because your fragile ego can't handle something unfamiliar!"

"Mark, please—" Molly began, reaching for his arm.

"No. No, he's right," Jax said. "I don't understand this. So, let's fix that oversight—right now."

7

VyzR

"Okay, Jax," Molly said, "why don't we have you sit in this side chair rather than the sofa. In a minute, I'll have you place the EMDR visor, spelled V-y-z-R, on your face. Tessa, do you want to look over the visor before we start?"

Stepping closer, Tessa took the VyzR from Molly and turned it over in her hands. Then she held them up to look through the lens.

"It looks and feels like hipster sunglasses," Tessa said, "except the lenses are opaque and a bit larger. It reminds me of something out of *Star Trek*. And are these little headphones on each side piece?"

"Yes," Molly said. "Using the microphone, the patient hears the therapist's voice more clearly than just talking. In addition, there is a binaural sound set at 40 Hertz to block out background noise, but it comes across as more of a hum. The same principle applies to the lenses as well. After putting them on, the patient presses that small button right above the bridge of the nose. The background sound will begin, and a gentle blue light will trace back and forth in the wearer's field of vision."

"So," Tessa said, "the light replaces that part of the original session where the therapist's finger would move back and forth, having the patient trace the movement for focus?"

"Correct. The research I conducted with the manufacturer of VyzR concluded that therapy sessions that limit external sounds and visual interruptions help the patient concentrate more deeply. This makes the experience more effective overall."

"I get that, but isn't this just a high-tech form of hypnosis? Can I see your data?"

"EMDR itself has some of the same qualities of hypnosis, but it doesn't cross that threshold. As for the data, the specifics are proprietary and closely guarded. I know that sounds like an excuse, but this is a very competitive field, and with an NDA in place, I can't tell you too much. Just know that in addition to my work at the VA, and my one-on-ones with Mark over the past several months, the experience has proven to be very effective, and more importantly, quite safe."

"Hey guys," said Jax, "can we skip the mechanics of this for now and let me try it out? I feel like you're talking about me, while I'm just sitting here."

"Sorry, Jax," Tessa said, "the therapist in me got swept up in talking."

Handing the headset back to Molly, Tessa relocated to the far side of the room and sat next to Mark. They were positioned so she could observe the process without interfering with the demonstration. Mark patted her shoulder and nodded gently.

"He'll be fine," Mark whispered. "I've done this dozens of times, and I think I still have all my marbles."

"Sorry, Mark," Tessa said, "it's just new, and I'm both excited and nervous for Jax."

Molly began settling in, dimming the room's lights and finding a comfortable spot on the edge of the couch. She smiled at Tessa and began.

"Again, Jax, I will be speaking directly to you through these speakers to help guide the process. This is just a basic demonstration to let you understand the patient's point of view. We are going to search for any random memory that pops into your mind and not attempt to focus on any specific trauma you may have experienced during your life."

Turning on the VyzR, Molly handed the device to Jax, who looked at it for a moment, turning it over in his hand. Satisfied, he placed it on his face.

"You will immediately notice two things," Molly said through the speakers. "The first is the low hum, and the second is the soft blue light before you."

Jax settled back into the chair and kept his focus directed straight ahead. Tessa sat on the edge of her chair, hoping to catch everything going on.

Jax had experimented with similar therapies during his exploration of migraine treatments, so it was not difficult to calm himself and get comfortable. He couldn't see anything but kept looking straight ahead in anticipation of what was to come next.

"Now," Molly said, "take a few deep breaths and try to relax as much as possible. As you listen to the sound of my voice, I want you to keep looking forward and focus on the blue light as it slowly moves from left to right. As you get more comfortable, I want your thoughts to form without judgment or bias. Let whatever images you see take shape, but don't try to force anything."

Jax felt an unpleasant tingling run up and down his spine and squirmed a bit in his seat, trying to get more comfortable. His fingers began to tap nervously on his knees. At first, it was a slow, regular beat matching his pulse as blood flowed through his temples. Then it increased in speed and ferocity, its pace matched by his labored breaths.

"The light," Jax mumbled, "it's here—the storm is here."

Jax found the pulsing blue light irritating enough, but now a flicker of an aura began to form. Just beyond it, a rainbow starburst was growing, with a white light filling the gap. The light slowly morphed into an image. It was confusing, but also...intriguing.

"I see," Jax began in a faltering voice, "a large green board right in front of me. I—I think I'm standing at a chalkboard. I'm in a classroom, and I've got a piece of chalk in my hand."

Molly turned around and looked at Tessa and Mark. Her face held a puzzled expression, as if they could provide some insight into what Jax was saying.

"Alright, Jax," Molly said calmly, "we can forget this image and find your way back to your father's living room. We've gone far enough for tonight."

"I just started middle school. I can see my shoes. I can see out the windows."

"Jax," Molly said, "it's time to stop. I can't remove the visor until you've separated yourself from this memory. You need to stop now, Jax."

"Oh my god, it's the morning of the terrorist attacks. It's the day Uncle Walter dies!"

"Jax!" Molly said firmly. "Jax, I'm going to turn off the visor. I want you to take a deep breath and close your eyes."

Molly turned off the unit, then quickly removed it from Jax's face. Tessa rushed over to her husband and knelt by his side. His eyes were tightly shut, but he appeared asleep or in a deep state of meditation. Tessa grabbed her purse and rummaged around until she found a little plastic container. She pulled out a single white pill and returned to kneel in front of Jax.

"Jax, honey," Tessa said quietly, "I need you to hold out your tongue. I have your medicine, but I need you to open your mouth so I can give it to you. Okay, sweetheart?"

Jax lightly shook his head, silently telling her no. Molly retreated to the end of the couch to give the couple some space, and Mark joined her with his glass still in hand.

"Here, Molly," Mark said, "take a couple of sips to calm your nerves."

"My nerves are fine, Mark," Molly said crossly. "I just need to know what the hell happened. I didn't plan on this." Leaning forward on the couch, she asked quietly. "Tessa, how are his vitals?"

Tessa pulled out a penlight from her open purse and ran the light over her husband's eyes. She ran a couple more cursory tests, then turned back to them and shrugged. "His pulse and breathing seem fine. His pupils are a bit sluggish, but not abnormally so." When she turned back to her husband, Jax didn't look at her—just lifted his hand for her to stop.

Tessa stood up and pointed toward the kitchen without looking at Molly. Molly followed. Mark began to rise, but Tessa stopped him with a single raised finger, not breaking stride. In the kitchen, Tessa turned on the faucet, then turned it off. She put both hands flat on the counter and stood rigidly for a moment before she finally turned around.

"What," Tessa said through gritted teeth, "the holy hell was that?"

"I honestly don't know," Molly whispered. "This has never happened before. I get that he might have been in the middle of a migraine episode, but I have no idea what he saw or was experiencing. Do you honestly believe I would let him use that machine if I knew that would happen? I'm as confused by the whole thing as you are."

"That wasn't a migraine, at least not like anything he's had before. He doesn't need a hospital, but I think the best thing I can do now is to take him back to the hotel and let him sleep off whatever the hell this was. But damn it, Molly, this isn't over. I want answers!"

"Well," Mark said from the entranceway, "you can start with what he just told you. Elena's brother was serving at the Pentagon on 9/11. We found out later that afternoon that Walter was one of the casualties."

"Mark," Tessa said, "Jax has not—he's never mentioned any of that to me."

"I know," Mark said. "Hell, you're the shrinks with all the degrees, does shit like this really surprise either of you? Damn, Molly, you talk about the psyche nearly every time we're together. I think this is just my son's shit, but now he'll have to find his own way through it. He has to process what happened."

"I'm not dismissing what you're saying, Mark," Molly said, "but something is different here. The machine shouldn't be able to dredge up suppressed memories. Its purpose is to help people deal with identified traumas on a conscious level."

"Well, I must tell you, knowing my husband as I do, we just opened up a can of worms. Yes, he may want to talk about his uncle's death. But he's also a scientist, so you'd better be prepared to describe this technology in greater detail. That little unit lit up my husband's brain tonight, and if you don't allow him to explore this to his satisfaction, you'll never hear the end of it. Am I wrong here, Mark?"

"No, kid. Once Jax has his sights zeroed in on something, he's relentless. You could dangle distractions, throw curveballs, or try sweet-talking him off course, but once his target's locked in, it's game over. He doesn't just chase the goal—he lives inside of it."

"Tessa, I know tomorrow is Saturday, but I'm scheduled to be at the VA. If you and Jax feel you're up to it, I'll carve out some time to go over the details of the VyzR with you. I even have a second unit at the facility that I'm sure I can convince VRMX Technologies to loan to both of you. If there are other applications that he discovers which we haven't explored, they may even want to bring him deeper into the fold."

Tessa nodded her agreement, then stopped and turned to look through the doorway at her husband. Jax was sitting motionless in the chair—eyes now open but vacant.

8

THE VA

"YES," TESSA SAID, "I'LL hold."

"What?" Jax said. "Who are you calling at this hour?"

"Shh. Why don't you try to drink some coffee, okay, honey?"

"God, yes. Coffee. Is there any food?"

"Yes. Hello Molly, this is Tessa. Yes, he's doing better. Can we still come by?"

"Molly? Honey, when did we get back to the hotel?"

"Actually, that would be best for us as well. Yes, he needs to wake up a bit more. Lunch sounds great. Okay, we'll see you then."

She closed her smartphone and turned to look at Jax. The sun had already crested the eastern horizon, and the subtle thrum of traffic could be heard from the streets below. Bending over the bed, she kissed her husband's forehead. She was fully dressed in what she called business casual attire. He slowly rolled out of the bed and shuffled his way to the room service cart parked a few feet away.

"Okay, I got most of that. So, we're going to meet Molly for lunch?"

"She's going to give us a tour of the VA Clinic first, then we'll catch lunch at a restaurant she knows that's close by. How are you feeling?"

"I'm groggy as hell—and there's this kind of gap in my memory—fragments. I know I drank too much tequila, but damn it, I can't even remember leaving my dad's place. Maybe all of that celebrating on top of recovering from that beast of a migraine the day before...but no, this isn't a hangover. I think I know what caused it, but I can't seem to find the right words. On top of that, I had the weirdest dreams..."

"After you get some coffee on board, why don't you jump in the shower. I laid out your slacks and the sports coat you wore the other day. I'm going to check my emails on the laptop for a few minutes, then we can head out. Okay?"

Without responding, Jax picked up the three ibuprofen tablets Tess had thoughtfully laid out for him and threw them down his throat. He filled his mug with coffee, picked up a slice of toast, and staggered into the bathroom. He knew he would start to feel a little better once the meds kicked in and he got some hot water on his body.

An hour later, Tessa and Jax entered the modern glass-and-stone building's lobby and checked in with the receptionist. While they waited for Molly, Tessa sat in a nearby chair, while Jax stood and looked back out through the two-story glass entrance. Even feeling a bit off, he was still amused at how it seemed like every building in this city always managed to face Pikes Peak—America's Mountain—nature's Disneyland. After a short wait, Molly walked out of a door to the side of the receptionist's desk.

"Hey, guys," Molly said, walking up to them. "I'm glad you could make it, especially after what you went through last night, Jax. I am truly sorry for what happened to you."

"Yeah, sure," Jax said, a bit confused. "The whole thing was a little odd, but everything's good now. So, Tess tells me you have some new technology you think I might be interested in seeing?"

Molly turned to Tessa, puzzled. Not saying a word, Tessa just smiled at her and nodded ever so slightly.

"Yes," Molly said. "Yes, I do want you both to see that. But first, are you up for a quick tour of the facility?"

"That would be great," Tessa said, "right, Jax?"

"On the ground level, we have our primary care facilities for routine checkups, chronic condition management, and preventive care."

Glassed-in exam rooms lined the corridor, each one lit in clinical white and crowded with rolling stools, medical posters, and hand sanitizer dispensers perched at every doorway.

"In the back of the ground level is the audiology department for hearing tests, then we have speech therapy, and the VA compensation exams. The physical therapy department takes up half of this floor and offers rehabilitation and mobility support for injuries or chronic conditions."

The trio walked through a set of double doors and continued down a long hallway, passing exam rooms. There weren't many patients or medical staff in the hall, which seemed odd. They rounded a corner and came to a see-through plexiglass wall that revealed a large room filled with a variety of machinery and peculiar apparatus. A half-dozen men were using the equipment, each with an attendant directing them. One man was missing a leg, another both legs.

"Molly," Tessa said, "you have this large, relatively new building, but you don't seem to have that many staff. Your lobby seems full of patients—am I missing something?"

"Veterans Affairs," Molly said, "has always seen lean budgets. With the recent cuts, our wait times for these services have certainly increased, but we adapt as best we can. It sort of comes with the territory, and most vets are used to these conditions."

"Plenty of money for ammo and bombs," Jax said contemptuously, "but never enough to take care of the people who put their lives on the line in the field."

"Every government agency is politically motivated, Jax. It would be naïve to think we would be any different. We have dedicated doctors, nurses, technicians, and specialists. Do they—do we get frustrated by red tape? Of course we do, we're human. We can stomp our feet about it, or we can do the best with what we have. Shall we continue?"

Molly directed them to a bank of elevators and, after allowing a couple of people in wheelchairs to enter first, rode to the second floor. Molly stepped off the elevator but only walked as far as the nearby railing that overlooked the entrance below.

"On the second floor," Molly says, "we have compensation & pension services to the left. It's here that our staff help with disability claims, pensions, and fiduciary services. There are also complete dental offices on the right. I thought we could skip walking this floor and go right to mental health services on the third floor."

Molly directed them to a bank of brushed steel elevators at the end of the corridor, their doors reflecting the fluorescent lights in warped rectangles. After allowing a couple of veterans in wheelchairs to enter first—one elderly man with oxygen tubes trailing from his nostrils, another younger with a thousand-yard stare—they squeezed into the cramped space. The elevator lurched upward with a mechanical groan, depositing them on the second floor with a soft chime. Molly stepped off onto speckled linoleum tiles but only walked as far as the nearby glass railing that overlooked the sunlit atrium below, then pointed behind them.

"Behind you are about a dozen offices dedicated to addiction treatment, but straight ahead is where we conduct individual and group therapy sessions, conduct psychiatric evaluations, and, of course, trauma-informed care. It is this last type of treatment that I was excited to share with you and continue our discussion from last night."

"Since we got here," Jax said, "I've been remembering a bit more from last night. I mean, about your visor machine and me zoning out a bit. I'm sorry I left without saying goodbye."

"Don't mention it," Molly said. "So, as the name suggests, trauma-informed care recognizes that many individuals—especially veterans—have experienced trauma, whether from combat, sexual assault, childhood adversity, or other life events. TIC is less about what's wrong with them and more about what's happened to them."

"Hence, our foray into EMDR," Tessa said. "How often are you using the VyzR in your treatments?"

"Those sessions typically take place twice a week—more if the therapist believes the candidates are ready. We don't use the VyzR with everyone, however. Each patient has an individual treatment plan, so depending on where they are in their therapy, they may or may not be right for that level of intensity."

"May we discuss the specifics about the VyzR? After what Jax experienced last night, we would like to understand better how you're using it. Maybe even talk about some of your cases, if that's alright, of course."

"My office is just up one level. If you don't mind, I'd rather use the stairs. I've been sitting too long and need to stretch my legs."

Tessa and Jax followed Molly up a winding staircase, through a maze of cubicles, and arrived at a large, open space that led to the director's office. Molly smiled at her assistant and stopped to pick up the phone messages she'd gotten in the short time she had stepped away.

"Listen, I have to call this senator back. I have a video, produced by VRMX Technologies, all set up near the window. It provides an overview of the VyzR system that may help you understand the basics of the unit. Why don't we start by having you watch that, then we can talk more when I'm done."

After starting the video, Molly stepped behind her desk and buzzed her assistant to connect her with the senator. Jax glanced over and noticed that Molly's phone headset had noise-canceling earphones and, apparently, a special microphone that prevented her conversation from being overheard by anyone who may be listening.

The video's production quality made it apparent that the manufacturer was familiar with more than just the EMDR visor they were considering. Tessa typed the company's name into her phone's Google app as the introduction began. Looking down, she saw the search results list the company as the same one that made high-end gaming equipment and software. An adjacent article mentioned VRMX Tech's relationship with the military and DARPA—the Defense Advanced Research Projects Agency.

The company's partnership with the government included integrating drone users with high-tech equipment. Closing her smartphone, she looked up at the screen, which was showing an exploded 3D diagram of the VyzR and its parts. A female narrator spoke as the video proceeded.

"The state-of-the-art speakers embedded in the sides of the visor provide a clear, focused session between patient and therapist. The use of 40Hz background vibrations has been shown to stimulate regions in the brain associated with memory recall and higher learning capabilities.

"To help enrich the therapy experience, the large, curved lenses on the VyzR utilize the same material found in spacecraft and block out as much as 95% of extraneous light. When brought together, these technologies provide the user with an immersive experience unmatched by traditional methods.

“If you wish to be a part of the future in psychotherapy, or would like additional information on this medical device, you will find all contact information available at the end of this video to connect you with a representative. Remember, integrating VyzR can help you help thousands heal their psychological wounds. We are VyzR!”

“Shit,” Jax mumbled, “I feel like I just got through watching a high-end car commercial.”

“Yeah,” Tessa said, “but not something as boring as steel and plastic. They’re fucking around with people’s minds.”

“Molly, I get it,” Jax said. “This visor thing has promise. I’m a little put off by the DARPA thing, but anymore that’s true of almost all high-tech research out there. I need you to understand that I want to approach this through the context of my work with migraines—is that fair?”

“Yes,” Molly said, “but that’s not the point. I want you to run with this. Just know that other people are watching and want your results. Are you okay with that?”

"Wait," Tessa said. "What about the issue with what happened to Jax last night? Are you both ignoring the fact that, while using this—this tool, Jax somehow dislodged a deep memory, and probably sparked some bizarre sort of migraine in the process?"

"Yeah," Jax said, "that was weird. Even now, I'm still not sure what happened to me. I mean, the memory is still a bit fuzzy. Whatever caused me to experience that stuff came on quickly. I mean, I've had bad events, but even those took a little time to come on. This happened within a minute of activating that thing. You've got to admit, that's a little scary."

"Look," Molly said, "we're all professionals trying to understand how the brain works. I'm not forcing this on you, but I think once you get the opportunity to think about it, you're going to want to pursue this. Your wife and your dad agree with me on this, and in the short time I've known you, I think this interests you as well. I must admit last night seemed like something straight out of the Twilight Zone. Hell, I'm not totally sure I want you digging into this further. I don't want you to get hurt, that is my line in the sand!"

"Do I have the green light from VRMX Tech?" Jax asked. "I mean, I don't know what I'm going to do with this yet. I need time to examine the desired outcomes and weigh them against possible consequences before I even begin tinkering with this. Has your contact given me the freedom to take this where I see fit? If not, this is going to be a very short discussion."

Molly reached into her lower desk drawer and pulled out a black case, roughly the size of a briefcase. She laid it down in front of her, so it sat between Jax and Tessa.

"I was told that whatever decision I made would be supported—again with the caveat that your results are documented and that all data are shared with the company. Are we clear on the one point?"

"Thank you, Molly," Tessa said, "I know you don't have to do this. Where are you keeping that NDA? I know you must have one in your desk somewhere—am I right?"

With a smile, Molly opened her side drawer and rifled through her folders until she found the one she was looking for. Reaching down, she pulled out a stack of stapled legal-sized paper.

9

HIKE

THEY PLANNED TO SPEND the next morning hiking with Jax's dad, and with both of their dogs in tow. As they were removing their gear from the SUV to begin the hike, Jax stopped and sat on the open gate.

"Look, I get it. Metaphorically, there's an elephant in the room, and I guess I'm the one holding it. So, I need to talk with both of you about what happened the other night."

"Son, you don't have to say anything if you'd rather not get into it. We can just walk."

"Jax, naturally, I'm concerned about you, especially about what happened to you the other night. If that had something to do with your uncle's death, I'd rather you share it with your father and me."

"I think I do need to talk about it, and you are the two people in the world I trust most. First, you have to understand something. Dad, you were deployed somewhere in North Carolina when 9/11 happened, and leave had been canceled for all active-duty personnel. It was just Mom and me, and I was just a pre-teen at that. Grandma had passed away just about a year prior, so when Mom found out her brother had been killed—well, shit, I didn't know what to do or what to say to comfort her."

"Jaxon, I'm sorry it played out like that. Unfortunately, shit happens in real life whether we like it or not. I had a duty to protect this nation's skies during that period. We were holding our collective breath on base. We didn't know if it was a one-off or the opening salvo to a much larger attack. No one knew who was involved in the attack. Some generals even believed the Russians could have been players, which created even more paranoia. I couldn't get home for a month, and although I tried, I wasn't much help to your mother. I wish for your sake I had been able to do more. I certainly didn't mean for you to be the one carrying the emotional load at home."

"That doesn't explain what happened to you at dinner, honey. What about that?"

"I don't buy the narrative that Uncle Walter's death was some suppressed memory or some such crap. You both know me. I never felt the necessity to dissect my feelings about that tragedy. As for my reaction, think about it for a minute. I had just gone through a powerful migraine, and my body was nowhere near recovered.

"Then there's the stress level at work, which is through the roof. So, I come here with that shit floating around in my head, and I get to Mom's house, with all the smells from my childhood still hanging around, and I end up having way too many drinks. There we are having a serious discussion about treating trauma, and Molly whips out a fucking machine that was made specifically for treating that specific thing.

"There must have been a subconscious suggestion somewhere in all of that, and wham! The next thing I know, my mind shifts to Walter and all the emotional junk that surrounded his death. I think the light in the visor must have sparked the beginnings of another migraine and then—well, I don't know exactly, but an educated guess was that my brain simply got overtaxed."

"Do you still feel you're up to this hike? You know this trail isn't that easy?"

"Thanks, Dad, I'm okay. I think the exercise will do me good before I go back and sit on my butt for hours on end. Besides, Bear would not forgive me if I bailed now."

"Although we don't get the chance when we're in Denver to be out like this, as your wife, I'm going to have to throw the bullshit flag on the other stuff. You've done a nice job of wrapping everything into a nice little package, but I know you too well. You're not telling the truth, or at least you're not telling us the whole truth."

"Hey, guys," Mark said, "I came out here to hike and breathe some pine-filled air. Do you think you can put a lid on this for the moment and psychoanalyze your issues later?"

"Of course. I'm sorry, Mark, I didn't mean to stir the pot. It was a reflex from what we learned from Molly. My apologies...to both of you."

While Mark donned his daypack and grabbed the dogs' leashes, Jax just sat and looked into his wife's eyes. He saw the genuine concern behind her accusation, but he had never been comfortable getting too emotional around his father. It just wasn't done. He patted her arm, closed the vehicle's hatch, and began the slow walk up the dirt path.

Most of the three-mile hike up Blodgett Peak was steep with a difficult gain in altitude. This physically limited idle chatter, allowing their lungs to adapt to the ascent.

Neither Jax nor Tessa spoke of their dealings with Molly the day prior. Jax was still mulling over everything he'd heard about VyzR, VRMX Tech, and DARPA. Although unspoken, he was also trying to get a better handle on the glimpses of memory surrounding the incident at his dad's place.

Tessa wasn't wrong that what he had laid out for her and his dad was laced with bullshit. If he were being totally honest with himself, he'd have to admit he was a bit scared of what he experienced. But he was taught early on that you faced your fears—you didn't whine about them.

They each had their own reasons for avoiding any mention of the device they were given. Tessa didn't like Jax's blatant dishonesty with her. Jax didn't like what the fear he felt said about him as a man. Nor what kind of husband it made him by keeping that from Tessa.

The drive back home was much like their hike—casual conversation punctuated by long stretches of silence. The Beck men were never ones to offer their opinion about much beyond local politics and sports. So, keeping private thoughts private was the favored norm. Jax had learned that it was best to keep your feelings to yourself. It was much harder for Tessa to cope with such rules.

Although an only child of parents still living in England, she shared her feelings openly and often. Jax loved this trait about her and, aside from certain innermost feelings, felt secure communicating his thoughts with her as well. The few times he was quiet, though, she knew not to push.

Arriving home, they wordlessly unloaded the SUV—Jax carrying the luggage and Tessa walking Bear to the backyard. The intimacy the couple had shared during their short trip had dissipated by the time they unpacked. Once settled, Jax told her he just wanted to sit and read for a while before heading to bed. There had not been any talk of dinner, so Tessa reheated some leftovers and poured herself a glass of wine.

As she sat at the kitchen island with a goblet in one hand, lazily tapping the keys on her laptop, Jax came in, poured himself a tumbler of wine, and sat down across from her. Throughout their few years of marriage, they had an unspoken agreement not to begin serious conversations until both were ready. Each understood this wasn't some silly game but rather a mutual respect for each other's mental processes.

"I want to use the visor," Jax began in a hushed tone. "However, I don't want you to be there. I need to remain as objective as possible, and I don't think I can do that with you in the lab. Does that make any sense?"

Setting her wineglass on the counter, Tessa looked at her husband, nodding but not in agreement. "I don't agree with your logic. Especially after what happened at your father's. I am a trained physician, and no one on your team has that level of experience."

"I get that, I really do. But I'm not sure I can relax around you. I need to study this—whatever this is. And with the people I work with day in and day out."

"If I agree, would you at least consider an EMDR therapist to sit in on this? One we have on staff? I wouldn't feel right if something happened like the other night without someone trained to handle such situations being present. Are you at least okay with that simple request?"

"I guess so. Who'd you have in mind?"

"Terry Adler. You met him last Christmas, remember? He would need a quick lesson on the use of the technology, but he has extensive experience in this type of therapy."

"Babe, you understand this doesn't have anything to do with you, right? This is new territory. I don't know what I'm going to experience."

"Don't ask for my blessing when I've made one concession. I was reviewing our online calendar before you walked in. I see that Terry is free on Tuesday. If he agrees, will that work for you?"

"Actually, that will give me a day to brief the team. Then, explain what I think happened to me, and what I hope to accomplish in a clinical environment. So yes, if he's free, then that would be good. I'm going to stay up a bit longer to do some reading. Don't wait up for me if you want to turn in."

"I do have just one question, so please answer honestly."

"Of course. What's on your mind?"

"Will Amy be a part of this experiment?"

10

The Plea

"But you are my advisor, Dr. Mason!" Amy said. "The work I've done—my dissertation involves so much more than just Jaxon Beck." She was standing in front of the closed door of the Director's office with both hands on her hips. The older man was seated behind his desk, but equally agitated.

"Ms. Taylor," Dr. Mason said, "I am well aware of my responsibilities regarding your work for the Center and the research contained in your dissertation. I am telling you, as your advisor and someone who truly cares about your future, that you need to suck it up and stay with Dr. Beck for a little while longer. I can't give you specific details at this time, but you need to trust me on this."

"Please tell me. What exactly am I supposed to do with that? Sometimes I really think Jax is going to sink my career before it has a chance to take off! He's off on some tangent that has nothing to do with the work I've already done for him. The papers I've written. The classes I've taught. The crap I've put up with! Why is remaining as his assistant so critical to my graduating?"

"You're not listening to me, damn it. What I am saying is that you need to finish your research, write up, and submit your findings, and get through the next few months! My God, if you are unable to do that, then maybe you don't have what it takes to make it on your own. Nothing, Amy—I mean nothing is going to be handed to you. And that is coming from a Black man who has had to learn when to fight and when to keep my mouth shut.

"What I am honestly trying to make you appreciate is contained in this simple inspirational message I keep hanging right there."

He pointed to a small picture frame dangling crookedly on the wall behind him. "I often read this when I need to get past something or someone. 'Weak people take revenge, strong people forgive, but intelligent people ignore'. You've done really good work so far, but sometimes I wish you would control yourself a bit more. Please, Amy. Try to ignore the slights you feel, be they real or imagined. Do you think that's possible?"

Amy's shoulders relaxed, and she sat in the chair she had been hovering over. "I've listened to you for the last four years. Yes, I can get through the next few months. I'm not thrilled about where this is going, but I can get through this. For my sanity, Dr. Mason, there must be an end to this."

"You'll see. I have a plan for you. But, please, manage to have a little faith in the process and in me for just a bit longer."

Returning to the lab, Amy walked into the middle of what appeared to be an intense discussion Jax was having with Gabriel and Sita. All three became instantly silent when she strolled into the room. After her blow-up last week, the tension in the room was profound, as if they were waiting for an eruption to occur. All three seemed surprised when she quietly sat down and opened her computer.

"Hey guys," Amy said, "I'm sorry about my little meltdown. I guess I'm under more stress than I realized with trying to complete my dissertation. Dr. Beck, would you mind catching me up on what you were talking about?"

"Sure, Amy. I was describing to the crew what I experienced over the long weekend. I have some ideas I want to follow up on, and we were discussing what I hope to accomplish. Do you mind if I fill in the major gaps with you later?"

"Of course. I'm sorry to interrupt, it's just that I needed to talk to Dr. Mason about my graduation requirements."

"Well, basically, I'm going to be our next volunteer for a different type of experiment. Let's say I believe I'll be in an altered state of consciousness while some tests are done on me."

"So, you're going ahead with the use of psychedelics then?"

"Not quite that, but that's not too far off base."

“Boss man is going trippin’ with technology,” Gabriel said jokingly, “but without the physiological effects of LSD or psilocybin.”

“Well, hopefully nothing as crazy as all that, but I am hopeful we can come away with some solid readings. We’ll have a guest from the hospital's psychology department. A Dr. Terry Adler.

“Gabe, would you see to setting things up for tomorrow—the lighting, video recordings, and the like. Sita, we need to calibrate the EEG. Okay, I’ll let you two get going on that while I bring Amy up to speed on our Frankenstein-like experiment tomorrow morning.”

Although he stated the last bit in air quotes, Amy questioned whether Jax had gone off the deep end. Conducting experiments on yourself was always the act of a desperate scientist, even though such individuals were often extolled as heroes.

“So, you’re pursuing the psychological slant to your research?”

“To our research, yes. There’s so much more to this, Amy. You will just have to see for yourself. Between us, I think there may be more we’re going to discover than just a treatment for migraines, but I won’t know until tomorrow. Now, here’s the catch. I don’t want you to be a part of our little experiment tomorrow.

I am going to require your expertise with brain scan comparisons when we’re done. But what I don’t want to do is to introduce any possible bias by you being actively involved in the experiment itself.”

"Wait. It's our research, but I'm not going to be a part of it. Are you serious?"

"Just for tomorrow. If it comes through as I hope, you will have plenty of work just reviewing the video and scans. I spoke with Tom next door, and he could really use your help tomorrow with translating his data on epilepsy and Parkinson's into a narrative. Trust me on this one...okay?"

"Trust you? Trust you! What the fuck, Jax?"

"I get how this might look to you at the moment, but yes, trust me. Please."

"Okay, sure. I'm only your senior lab assistant, but I get sent packing while you do—you do God knows what. But why the hell not?

"One last thing before I clear out. Was this really your idea, or was this Tessa's?"

Jax turned his back on Amy and picked up a clipboard. "Amy, do you really have to ask such a question?"

"Well, judging from your reaction, I don't! Geez, that was five years ago!"

11

TEST#1

JAX SHIFTED IN THE lab chair, his back flat against the padded cushion. Directly behind him was the electroencephalograph, or EEG, its scanning cap resting on his head. The electrodes touching his skull would show and record electrical activity in different regions of his brain as neural activity increased.

Sita sat behind him to monitor his brain activity, as well as his heartbeat and pulse. All information about the latter was transmitted from the small band Jax wore on his left wrist and index finger.

Gabriel also sat behind Jax, but on his opposite side. A small lighting and sound control board was placed on a tray where he now rested his arm. A large computer monitor faced him, the screen displaying four different images from small video cameras. Each camera was set back to avoid interfering with the process. Two of the cameras showed the chair and participants from the left and right sides, the third zoomed in for a close-up of Jax's face, and the fourth was set near the back of the lab to record the overall process.

Jax held the EMDR VyzR in his right hand and looked it over. He wished they'd had more time to construct the shielding Sita mentioned, which could protect the unit from any electrical interference the EEG might emit. It would have been nice to get images rather than just the graph this machine produced, but maybe next time.

Still, he was quite pleased that Sita had time to install bone-conduction microphones on either side of the visor so they could hear anything he might say during the experiment. He placed the visor on his face and waited.

Terry Adler had met with Jax the prior evening to explain how he would employ the Eye Movement Desensitization and Reprocessing technique under these unusual conditions. The older man spoke in a soft, rhythmic voice, even when not conducting a session. Tessa had told Jax that she had never known Terry to ever raise his voice, regardless of the emotional circumstances he encountered as a therapist—or perhaps because of them.

"Jax," Terry said, "we're going to explore that childhood memory of yours we spoke about earlier. The device will emit a gentle light to replace what an EMDR therapist would normally do with their finger or with a lightbar. I will also be using this device to speak to you directly through the speakers in your eyepiece."

"Got it. We've tested the extra microphones, so I can reply while Gabe records us. Gabe, Sita, let's run through our checklist so we can get started. Are we recording—good. So, for the record, it's

10:55 AM on May 20th. I have asked Dr. Terry Adler to guide me through this process and look for any adverse effects I might encounter during the session."

If he was correct, the VyzR would likely bring on a migraine attack, like what happened when he'd first tried it out with Molly. Terry had forewarned him that there were certain queues he would be watching for while undergoing this session. He made it clear that if Jax encountered any sign of extreme physical distress during this experiment, he was ethically bound to end the session immediately.

Jax tried to relax the best he could while Gabe went through their checklist, ensuring all of their equipment was working properly. When all had voiced their readiness to proceed, Jax reached up and switched on the visor. The blue light inside lit up and began its smooth horizontal movement from left to right and back again, compelling his eyes to track its journey.

For the first few minutes, Jax listened to Terry's prompts to ignore the hum in the background, breathe normally, relax, and focus on his childhood memory. After the first five minutes had passed, Jax became concerned that something he had done, or failed to do, may have interfered with the experiment.

Just as he was about to call the test a failure, the familiar rainbow starburst appeared before him. As he waited, the jagged lines did not dissipate into the typical tunnel vision that had come with his many migraines. Instead, he was struck with the distinct sensation of vertigo as he felt his perception shift. It was as if the aura was slowly pulling him out of the chair and drawing him up and forward. Unable to control this sensation, he tried to speak but failed to form cohesive thoughts to describe what he was experiencing.

"I'm entering the threshold of the aura...moving through... I sense a shifting... I think I'm passing...the other side...there's a white light."

After a moment, the white light receded, and Jax was once again standing in front of a chalkboard. He knew this was the same memory as the one from the other night. He heard his name being called, but it sounded as if it were coming from far away. He comprehended that this scene was from his past, but felt as if he were there—now.

He had the sensation of standing in front of a classroom, with early morning sunlight streaming through the window. Children were seated before him, and a woman in a long skirt was standing to the side and calling his name to get his attention.

"Jaxon. Jaxon Beck." She called. "Jaxon, are you alright? Do you need to sit down?"

Jax turned his gaze to the top of the chalkboard, where he saw the date clearly displayed. It confirmed his expectation—Tuesday, the 11th of September 2001. The clock mounted on the adjacent wall read 8:35 AM. He blinked a few times, then recalled that the woman's name was Murphy. Mrs. Adeline Murphy had been his homeroom teacher, and this had been the beginning of the school year at Chestnut Middle School in Chicopee, Massachusetts.

He knew this was the day his Uncle Walter died, which was why Terry wanted to start with this vivid memory. Overwhelmed by the lucidness of the scene before him, he crumpled into a heap. The children in the classroom began to giggle and laugh, but Mrs. Murphy told them to hush, then rushed to his side. He could feel her holding his shoulders, and he could smell her perfume. The children's laughter and Mrs. Murphy's words faded away as he fixated on the ticking sound coming from the wall clock. The minute hand clicked once. The time was now 8:36 AM.

"They just hit the north tower," he whispered. "They'll steer the second plane into the south tower in 17 minutes, then into the Pentagon in less than an hour. He dies there along with 124 other people, not including the passengers on the plane. The whole attack...almost three thousand dead."

Mrs. Murphy held him at arm's length. Her face showed confusion, then alarm. Turning and waving an arm at the class, the room grew silent once again. She turned back and stared intently into his eyes. All Jax could see in her eyes was fear.

Jax was aware that he, or rather the younger him, was crying, although he wasn't sure why. He continued to look into the eyes of this caring woman, who he knows will die of an aneurysm three years from now. He is telling himself this is just a memory. Terry is repeating the same words in his ear, but it's so damn hard to concentrate.

"Jax, this is all just a memory. Try to do the block breathing we talked about. Inhale for a four count—hold for a four count—exhale...hold...repeat. Hang with me, Jax. Jax...?"

Jax tried to follow Terry's instructions, but when he looked at a sunbeam shimmering through the window, he knew this wasn't right. Yes, his mother's brother was killed in that attack, but what he's experiencing didn't take place that morning. His mother didn't even know about the loss of Walter until that afternoon. *This isn't a memory.*

"Jaxon," Mrs. Murphy says, shaking him gently to get his attention. "I'm going to walk you down to the nurse's station so you can rest, okay? Just keep taking those deep breaths like you're doing. You'll be fine."

"The principal," Jax mutters as he is slowly led out of the room, "will announce the attack on New York City and the Pentagon later today. Did you know my Uncle Walt works for the Defense Intelligence Agency?"

He looked up at Mrs. Murphy, but the woman was just staring at him, as if he were sick or crazy. They made it past the principal's office and then the attendance desk. They arrived at a small room at the back of the main office. A plain-clothed nurse took hold of his arm and guided him onto a lumpy bed, then covered him with a thin blanket. Excited voices could be heard coming from the front desk. Through the open door, he could hear some of what was being spoken.

"I just heard a bomb went off in New York," a woman said.

"My husband just called," another woman said. "He told me they think a plane flew into the Twin Towers in Manhattan!"

Mrs. Murphy had stepped out of the nurse's station to return to her classroom, but turned and slowly walked back in, staring at Jax lying on the small bed. Without taking her eyes off him, she said to the nurse, "He just told me this happened. He told me before we got here."

Jax stares up at the two women, who are looking down at him curiously. Mrs. Murphy's perfume is still in his nose. Their faces begin to soften at the edges, features losing their definition, until they are two pale ovals ringed by the water-stained ceiling tiles of the nurse's station. Their voices stretch and overlap, the words no longer separate from one another. His body has gone distant—he doesn't feel the bed anymore.

Through the narrowing tunnel of his vision, the jagged rainbow starburst has reappeared above him in the corner of the ceiling...waiting. The vibration begins deep in his skull, then spreads outward. His next breath does not come, and he gasps for air. Then the oval faces and the perfume and the chattering and the rainbow all go dark.

12

EMERGENCY

"ALL OF HIS VITALS look normal," said the female physician.

"So," Tessa said, "Dr. Hintz, why did he lose consciousness?"

"Mrs. Beck—" Dr. Hintz started.

"It's Dr. Beck, and I have privileges with this hospital. So, let's say we cut the condescending attitude, and you and I simply talk. One professional to another."

"Fine. Sorry. Dr. Beck, we can't find any medical reason for what happened to him. All the tests we ran came back negative. I would like to keep him here overnight, but I'll let you make that call. Look, he's awake now, so I'll leave you two alone to discuss this. Maybe he can answer these questions better than we can."

"Tess, what's going on?"

"You know damn well what's going on! Using that flippin' machine on yourself—you knew it was a risk after the other night. It's a wonder your brain isn't scrambled."

"Well, you heard the doctor, the tests—"

Tessa slapped his shoulder a bit harder than one could call playful. "They want to keep you overnight for observation, and a part of me agrees with Dr. Hintz."

"No. I want to get back to the lab. What time is it?"

"A bit after noon," Tessa said. "You were out of it for about an hour."

She helped him get out of bed and put on his shoes. They had left him dressed, so she held onto one of his arms as they made their way to her car. When they stepped out of the whooshing double doors, Jax stopped abruptly and turned to her.

"Tell me we got a record of all that!"

"I don't know what you were looking for," Tessa said, "but Gabe and Sita have video and scans of your brain activity for the three or four minutes you were with Terry."

"Four minutes? That wasn't any four minutes, Tess. That had to be at least fifteen minutes—at least."

"Look. You can work all of that out with your team tomorrow, but right now we're going home, and you're going to bed. We are not going to discuss it further!"

"Okay, but at least let me call the lab to check in. Where's my phone?"

"It's in my purse. You should know that you really scared the shit out of everyone."

Ignoring her concern, Jax eased into the car seat and began rummaging through her purse. Finding his phone, he hit the speed dial for the lab's landline. Tessa started the car, pulled out of the hospital parking lot, and headed towards their home.

"Hello?" Amy said.

"Ah, yeah, Amy. So, I guess you heard?"

"Jax! Are you alright?"

"Yeah, I'm okay. Hey, is Gabe or Sita around? I'd like to discuss the test results."

"I'll get them in a minute, but I've already gotten my first look at the video and the EEG scans myself. Jax, are you sure you want to do this right now?"

"Let's start with an overview, then we can talk about the details."

"From the camera angles and what everyone told me, shortly after the session started, you mentioned an aura, then something about a light. Shortly after, you just stiffened up and pitched forward out of the chair. Fortunately, Terry caught you before you fell.

"The scan shows a burst of neural activity coinciding with your body going rigid. I've gotten the initial material, and I'm planning on reviewing the graph in greater detail, but it will take a while."

"So, what? They called you when this all went down?"

"No. Actually, Dr. Mason called me. Gabriel and Sita didn't know that I was in the building, so they called him instead. It seems you didn't tell them I wasn't going to be joining you there in the lab during this—whatever the hell you're calling it."

"Listen, Amy, Tessa's not letting me come back in today. But can you get everyone together for a video call in a couple of hours?"

"Damn it, Jax!" Tessa said. "I practically had to carry you out of the ER. You are not going to work!" Tessa grabbed the phone out of Jax's hand and yelled into the phone. "Amy, ignore what this maniac just said. All of you can wait until tomorrow to talk!"

Handing the phone back to Jax, he quietly asked, "Did you get all that?"

"Yes," Amy said, "and she's right. You know she's right. Get some rest and maybe write down some notes in the morning. Talk to you later...bye."

"Nice. She just hung up on me!"

Tessa stomped on the brake, and the SUV came to a shrieking halt. The van behind them swerved around them, missing their bumper by mere inches. The howl of horns filled the air around them, but inside the cab, there was an unyielding silence. The look of incredulity shrouded Tessa's face as Jax tried to melt into his seat. He closed his eyes, trying futilely to hide from his wife, but he couldn't escape the heat radiating from her glare.

13

More than a Memory

The next morning, Jax was the first to arrive in the lab. Both to get a jump on reading the test results and to avoid confronting his wife. He had stopped and left a note for Dr. Mason, saying he would contact him later after speaking with his team. He was just putting on a pot of coffee as Amy and Sita walked in the door. Gabriel showed up a minute later.

"Jefe!" Gabriel said. "Man, I'm glad you're okay. That was so weird."

"I don't think," Sita said, "that I've ever seen you make the coffee. Are you sure you're doing okay? You're still Jax...right?"

"Yes, and I know I've made the coffee before...well, maybe...occasionally? Nice little touch you added to your hair there, Sita. So, a purple streak, huh?"

"Well, thanks for the compliment, but you're about six months overdue."

"Maybe I'm just a little more attentive this morning. Look, I've got a lot to go over and a whole lot I still don't understand."

Seizing their coffee mugs, they all huddled in the conference room. Amy had not spoken a single word since she arrived, but Jax tried not to read too much into her silence.

"So, I heard from Amy about what you saw, and we can look at the video a little bit later if we think it's worth it. I'm more interested in what the EEG looked like. Then I have my story to share."

Sita rolled a cart from the corner of the room with a computer and monitor on it. She moved to one side, then pressed the *Enter* button. She pointed to the screen. "Everything looked normal when we started. Smooth rhythmic waves and normal spikes. Then, you start to get a little Beta activity from the frontal leads about the time you see the aura.

"When it gets really interesting—would be about here. Your BP starts to climb, and Terry tells you to breathe in that special way to stay calm. Then, out of nowhere, your brain activity just jumped. I'm not talking about a bit of activity here or there, but everything spikes everywhere all at once. Then you just, like...passed out." Sita shuts off the monitor and rolls the cart away.

"I went back to get a closer look," Amy said, stretching a printed form of the graph out on the table. Reaching over, she tapped her finger on one spot circled in red. "I wanted to see if I could pinpoint the areas that were affected initially.

"It appears that the hippocampus and amygdala engaged first, which is normal when accessing a memory. But what is most interesting is that your prefrontal cortex and all sensory cortices seemed to engage almost immediately thereafter—it was as if all your senses switched on soon after your migraine aura started. It's like Sita said, there is almost no buildup. One minute nothing, then the next—everything."

Gabriel said, "That must have been one hell of a memory to get your neurons spiking like that. Do you think you just overloaded your senses, and that led to your fainting like that?"

"First of all, I didn't faint—I don't faint. The second thing, and this is the really strange part, is that it wasn't a memory. I didn't learn about my uncle's death until I got home from school that afternoon. What I went through was something else. I was in my morning class as a kid, and I interacted from that perspective while going through this...session. And when I say I interacted, I mean all my senses. If it was just a memory, even a traumatic one, then why remember it in that way and hours before I found out about it?"

"Damn," Gabe said. "So, what about your head. You still got a migraine going through that, right?"

"Yes and no. I definitely got the aura phase, but I don't recall getting the pain that would normally come with a full-on attack. But here's the strangest thing. I started experiencing the aura halo in my vision, right? But instead of it just being a visual manifestation like with others I've experienced in the past, this time I got—well, I got pulled through the aura into a bright white light."

"What? Like, you were dead?" Gabe asked.

"No. That's not how I would describe it. Nothing like that. It was only after that light faded that I experienced the memory, or whatever it was, that I just shared with you. I know how all of this sounds, but I need you to humor me."

"No, Jax," Amy said caustically, "we don't have to humor you. You went into this without any controls, and you come back with a fantasy you want us to accept blindly? Like you got touched by God or something?

"Damn it, as a scientist, you sure as hell are not acting or sounding like one. You know that stimulating the brain, either chemically or electrically, causes visions and hallucinations. You just said it yourself. It wasn't a memory, but more of a jumble of things that you remembered about that day and put together in that twisted brain of yours."

"Amy, it was more than that! I'm telling you all this so that we can go back now and add in those very controls you just mentioned."

"Another trip into your memories? Are you fucking serious?"

"I'm completely serious. And I was hoping you could help me figure out how we can use what I went through to make inroads into better understanding the brain, and by extension, migraines.

I want us all to work from the premise that I accessed some form of remembering of a traumatic incident. I experienced the aura, but it never produced the pain. In a way, it...opened my mind. Now take that and find a way to use the VyzR with the MEG to really see what's going on."

"On it," Sita said. "Understand, you have to navigate interference from both radio frequency and magnetic forces. I'm gonna have to use non-ferromagnetic materials to prevent interference, like plastics, ceramics, or aluminum. We can shield it with industrial aluminum foil, or metalized polymer films if we have the budget to block RF interference around the electronics."

"Whoa," Amy said. "You've already begun designing this thing?"

"Well, yeah. I jumped on this right after Jax texted me last night. I have a close friend who's an electronics nerd, so he and I stayed up late identifying the issues and ways around them. We still need to swap out the traditional magnetic-coil-based speakers for other materials, but the technology to modify this thing is already out there. It also helps that the MEG isn't even close to being as powerful as a full-sized MRI."

"So," Amy said, dragging out the word. "You end up in the ER, and Tessa drags your butt out of there and tucks you into bed. Then you dismiss her concerns and stay up plotting next steps?"

"I took a nap, okay? When I woke up, Tessa had gone back to work, so yeah, I had some ideas I wanted to get down on paper...so to speak."

"But your brain got zapped! You don't know what part of that was memory and what was hallucination. Jeez, it could be as simple as that migraine hit you harder than you are willing to accept!"

"Look, we already know that magnetic and Vagus nerve stimulation, as well as other technologies, can cause a placebo effect that mitigates migraines. That placebo effect can even be used in conjunction with behavior modification to eliminate migraines. So, the worst case is that we use this technique as a multi-sensory behavior modification system. What do we have to lose?"

"Man," Gabriel said, "that is one giant leap. From having a wild-ass memory or dream, to this being a treatment for migraines? I don't know Jax. This doesn't seem like a logical course of action based on your physical reaction."

"And what," Amy said, "or better yet, who is going to act as your control with this? Gabriel? Sita? Or am I going to get strapped in that chair? How about we use some of the volunteers we have on record? Yeah, we pay them $50 to wear that visor and see what visions they have. Jesus, we'd be the laughingstock of the Center, not to mention the entire neuroscience field!"

"We can talk about controls later, but I need to know that the three of you are with me on this. Well, at least with me as far as exploring the possibility of using this technology to help us meet our goal."

Jax got up and began walking out of the room to fill his coffee mug. "I'll let the three of you talk about it. Again, I'm just asking you to come up with some ideas about this. Free association, or brainstorming, or something. Please, give it a shot."

Gabriel and Sita sat and looked at each other, while Amy just looked at the floor and shook her head repeatedly. Gabe went to the whiteboard, erased everything, then picked up a pen and drew a circle in the middle of the board with three lines extending from it. At the end of the three lines, he wrote each of their names, then tapped the pen at the larger circle a few times before writing *Jax.*

"I need to think," Gabe said, "and mind-mapping has helped me work through other problems before. I understand that this is a little batshit-crazy, but is it okay if we at least try to wrap our heads around what he's suggesting?"

"I'm down for that," Sita said, "as long as we don't go too far down the rabbit hole."

"Amy?" Gabe said. "Can we at least hear what you're thinking?"

"What I think," Amy said, "is that this is a waste of time...but, if you two want to start, then I'm willing to listen. I'm not sure my mind works like yours with this method of idea creation, but it might jar something loose in me just hearing you two talk about it."

"I'll take that as a yes," Gabe said. "Personally, I'd like to see what ideas Brainiac has in mind, just as long as he doesn't fry his brain. I think that's our number one priority as we look at how he can achieve this... whatever he's calling it. So, should we include Jax in our mental gymnastics, or just keep this between the three of us, and we play around with ideas first?"

"He's right there," Sita said, "so he might as well be in the room while we throw thoughts around—am I right?"

Gabe waved for Jax to join them. He didn't have the heart to tell them that he could hear every word they said. With the door open, the glass that enclosed the small room acted like an amplifier. He picked up his mug and, with a big smile, joined his team.

"So," Dr. Mason said, "is Dr. Beck actually on to something with all of this, or has he completely lost it?"

"I think," said Amy, "and what the other two members of Jax's team think, is there's something worth looking into with these types of results."

"Ms. Taylor, I don't give two shits about what you think! I'm asking for an educated yes or no answer as to whether this Center should expend any additional funds in pursuit of this—this so-called treatment!"

"Dr. Mason, there simply isn't enough data at this point to make that type of conclusion...sir! Yes, there is an argument that Jaxon has lost it. That this was a hallucination. There is an equally strong argument that what he is proposing has strong scientific merit. Something beyond having Americans pop yet another pill.

"My God, Dr. Mason, tell me what you want to hear! Do we look at a potential cure, or do we say screw it? Do we keep allowing the pharmaceutical industry to continue making billions of dollars treating symptoms while graciously sprinkling a few million around to support research that will never—"

"I think it's time you leave, Ms. Taylor. I expect you to keep me up to date one way or the other. If you want me to sign off on your work, and you get to wear that doctoral hood over your shoulders any time soon, you will check yourself and provide me with facts. Tangible facts! Am I making myself clear, Ms. Taylor?"

Rising from her chair and stiffly moving towards the door, Amy uttered a simple, "Crystal."

14

Lecture

Enjoying a more cautious ride to work, Jax arrived at his classroom a few moments before his class was to start. Completing his normal routine with his bike and riding attire, he walked to the podium. Pulling out his note cards from his backpack, he laid them on the small wooden platform to quickly review. He slapped at his coat trying to locate his glasses, but found the pockets empty, then just shook his head in defeat.

Jax waited for Amy to finish her discussion with several students who were huddled around her in front of the rows of desks. After a few minutes, she nodded and then joined Jax at the podium.

"Some of the students," Amy said, "are upset you're making them come in on the day of the finals. They argued that no other professor on campus is forcing them to resort to the archaic practice of writing their finals by hand. They were hoping you'd reconsider using an online testing app like everyone else."

"Thanks for the update. What did you tell them?"

"That I'd talk to you and see if I can change your mind—like that's ever happened."

"Let me think about it. With everything we're trying to work on, not having to deal with them in person may not be such a bad idea."

As Amy turned to leave, she said, "Yeah, you're such a people person. I can see how broken up you are by that thought."

Not responding to her dig, Jax turned to the auditorium and said, "Picking up where we left off last week. Let's talk about migraine triggers and treatments."

The slideshow displayed a faded image of pills, with a list of medicines superimposed. This was not the right picture—they were out of order. After staring at the image for a few seconds and hearing murmurs from the class, he decided to begin from this point. He shuffled his notecards, then moved to stand just under the large screen. Reading off the list, he plunged into his lecture as if this were his intention.

"So, there are a few medicines that have been effective for some individuals suffering from this condition. On the low end, we have over-the-counter or prescription-strength pain relievers, such as aspirin or ibuprofen. Also, there are specific migraine pain relief meds that combine caffeine, aspirin, and acetaminophen."

Taking a deep breath, he felt more confident and walked to one side of the screen. Feeling more poised, he kept the momentum going.

“Moving up the scale, we have prescription drugs like Rizatriptan and others, which block pain pathways in the brain. Then there is Lasmiditan, but it can have a sedative effect and cause dizziness.”

Jax moved away from the screen and stood in front of the desks. He looked thoughtfully at the students before continuing.

“There is also a group of medications that are supposed to act with the body to prevent onsets. These include beta-blockers, antidepressants, and anti-seizure medications. But now we are looking at only partial successes, along with the added risk of more serious side effects.”

He pressed the control, and the screen turned dark green with white lettering that spelled out *Triggers*. He continued pacing slowly back and forth in front of the group.

“Okay,” he said, “now it’s your turn to be put on the spot. Who can name some of the known triggers of migraines?”

“Caffeine,” said a male voice from the audience.

“And alcohol,” said another.

“The lack of sleep,” came a feigned whine from a male in the front row.

“Yes,” Jax said, “as well as too much sleep. Okay, what else?”

“Hormonal changes, especially in women,” came an equally whiny voice of a young woman.

"Stress," called out another.

"I'm not sure if I'm saying this right," said a cautious male voice, "but stimuli, like flashing lights and maybe sounds?"

Pointing at the young man, Jax said, "Yes, but don't forget the impact that strong odors can have, and supposedly pleasant smells like those from perfumes or cologne as well."

A female voice added, "Can someone please tell this to my boyfriend? His nasty male body spray gives me a headache!"

"Okay, moving on. Anyone else? No? Alright, then we have the weather, food additives, certain foods themselves, and of course, medicines. Even some of the meds we just listed as treatments can be the cause of migraine onset themselves."

He returned to the center of the room and slowly shifted his head from left to right until he heard a satisfying crack along with a small release of stiffness in his neck. He turned back to face his students, and from the raised hands, he took a deep breath and sighed. He realized too late that his long pause in the middle of his lecture had given rise to unwanted questions.

A disembodied voice from the back asked, "How bad are your migraines? And how bad have they been in the past?"

Jack nodded, understanding he brought this on himself. "For me, I like to use the analogy of earthquakes and the Richter Scale employed to measure their intensity. Sometimes the symptoms are a two or a three, and with some ibuprofen, I can ride it out, but other times it's been a five or a six."

A woman from the middle row asked loudly, "Have you ever had like a seven or even an eight on the scale you just mentioned?"

Her shrill voice made Jax's head throb just a bit. He shut his eyes for a second, then walked to the podium and rapped his knuckles on the wooden surface three times and forced a weak smile.

"I have not, and just hope to whichever deity controls such things, that I never do! This is one of the big reasons why I believe so deeply in my work, and the work that my team helps me conduct at the Center."

He dipped his head down a bit before looking up again at the sea of faces. They all looked so young, even though he was only a decade older. Gathering himself, he continued.

"Unfortunately, there are many individuals out there who do get that elevated degree of pain and discomfort. Some even have it every time they get a migraine."

He recognized he'd lost control as several hands from the audience suddenly popped up in further query. Hoping to make it through his lecture a bit further, he tried to ignore their questioning waves and plowed onward.

"So, we have talked about the migraine itself—how it may present and some commonly prescribed meds for controlling the symptoms. Now, tell me what makes an individual susceptible to migraines?"

After no one responded, he said, "I know this was a part of your reading assignment, so please tell me what was in the research?"

Again, no one answered, and the room was quiet. Jax moved in front of the screen, holding up a hand and pointing at it with noticeable irritation.

"First," he said, "is your gender. Again, women are three times more likely than men to have migraines right off the top. This tracks with what we already said about hormonal changes being more likely to manifest in females.

"Moving on, we have physiological maturity. We've already stated that anyone from any age group can have migraines, but data show that migraines tend to peak during one's thirties and then gradually become less frequent as one gets older. Again, I am referring to averages, and we realize that some people have them well into their golden years."

As he walked away from the podium, he raised his hand. With his index finger pointing up at the screen, he lightly shook his fist.

"Lastly, one of the variables that my team is looking at closely relates to family history. Having a family member with migraines means you have a higher chance of developing them yourself."

Jax scanned the room again and abruptly stopped when he saw a man's silhouette standing in the back. Was this someone he knew? Without his glasses, there was no way he could make out any features, just a shadowed form.

"Let's move on to the more experimental. What's being studied, and what is the medical community discovering that we need to examine more closely?

"Your readings should be talking about Neuromodulation, especially devices that focus on transcranial magnetic stimulation or TMS, and Vagus nerve stimulation. By the latter, we are referring to non-invasive electrical stimulation through the skull. This includes devices worn on the forehead and others worn on the ear or around the neck. The idea behind these gadgets is to disrupt the pain coming from the nerve externally and make it less sensitive over time."

A young woman raised her hand and said, "What about psychedelics? I've heard these are being used in psychological therapy."

"Yes! Good point. There have been some small studies done, mostly in Europe and Japan. In today's political climate in the U.S., the experimental use of restricted or illegal drugs has gotten better, but it still isn't very popular. Without proper research, we can't speak to the efficacy of these with any confidence. We'll have to wait until politicians stop dictating the limits of scientific inquiry based on their own biases."

"That sounds pretty woke," a male voice stated loudly from somewhere in the back.

With a dismissive wave of his hand, Jax returned to the podium and slid the remote into its holder.

"Sure, whatever. The research in my lab and the work presented in this class are about real science and the world of medicine. I'm not going to get entangled in any political discussion."

As Jax turned to face his accuser, he saw bewilderment on his students' faces. Gazing towards the back, he had the distinct impression that the snipe might have come from the mystery man in the rear of the room. But, as he stepped forward, he realized the man was gone.

Did he really see someone back there, or was his mind playing tricks? He could have sworn that he heard a man's voice. Yet, judging by the students' expressions, he doubted whether they had heard the taunt. What the hell was going on?

15

Lab Work

The next day, the team was scattered across the city, working. Sita had driven out to Leif Thorsen's workshop, where the two of them were bent over a circuit board, trying to harden the VyzR's electronics against the electromagnetic interference the MEG would produce.

Gabe had buried himself in research publications, hunting for any precedent—any study, however tangentially related, that might sharpen their approach before they went further.

Jax and Amy had completely taken over the lab's conference room. Printouts and diagrams covered every inch of wall space, and two additional whiteboards crowded the corners, both already dense with notation. They moved around each other in the narrow lanes between furniture, coffee mugs in hand, thinking out loud.

"What I want to know," Amy said, tapping the diagram nearest her, "is what exactly was firing in your brain when this happened.

Which regions were firing during the retrieval—and whether that's what set off the aura."

Jax walked over to the diagram Amy was pointing to. "That's a tall order. Pinning down specific activity during a migraine episode, with everything else we're trying to control for—"

"The new MEG can handle it. The Center's model—the upgraded one—uses detectors sensitive enough to localize actual neuronal firing. And this time we would have a full recording to work from. Hundreds of images, if we're lucky."

"Right." Jax rubbed the back of his neck. "I keep forgetting we have that thing."

"Tom's been running it on his epilepsy cohort. I sat in on a few sessions—I know how it works. I can reach out and get us on the schedule."

"Do that."

At that moment, Sita walked into the conference room, followed closely by Gabriel.

"Hey guys, what's going on?"

"I was working with Leif," Sita said, "when Gabe here called and said I should come back to the lab. We were on our way to lunch, so I just brought Leif along since it involved him. He's out trying to find a place to park and should be here soon."

"Alright, Gabe. Obviously, this is important, so what's got you all hot and bothered?"

The short young man was rocking on his heels, grinning. "Okay. So I've been buried in publications all morning, and I think I found something. There's a new headset—consumer-available, clinical-grade—that could make the MEG entirely a non-issue for us. The MEG's already the portable option, sure, but it's still large, and runs on magnetic pulses."

"Which is exactly the problem Leif and I have been trying to solve," Sita said.

"Right, right, I know—that's what makes this so—"

The doorway darkened. Leif Thorsen had to angle his shoulders slightly to clear the frame, his blond hair nearly brushing the top of it. Sita glanced back at him and patted the chair beside her. "Leif, come in. Everybody—Leif Thorsen. That's Jax, Amy, and Gabe."

Gabe and Jax waved a greeting to him from where they stood, but Amy walked up and, literally standing in his shadow, shook Leif's large hand.

"Sita," Amy said, "why don't we move some of these whiteboards out of the way so we can all sit down. There's a pot of coffee in the corner if anyone needs it."

Once settled, Jax pointed to Gabe, signaling him to continue talking.

"Yes," Gabe said, "so the magnetic pulses proved to be the major obstacle, which you two were working on. But this new device, called *Kernel Flow*, is now available for clinical use and bypasses that by using light to scan the brain instead!"

"Slow down, Gabriel," Amy said. "Take a breath and tell us more."

"The older models," Gabe said, "that used this technique relied on shining a steady stream of light into the head, but the new model uses ultrafast pulses of TD-fNIRS—"

"Wait!" Sita said. "Hold up. We're supposed to be the nerds here, but even I don't know what that acronym stands for."

"Sorry," Gabe said, "I'm just excited, as I'm sure you can tell. The use of light to scan is based on time-domain functional near-infrared spectroscopy, or TD-fNIRS. So, the new model, called the *Kernel Flow 2*, uses this light in pulses, but it is now on the order of trillionths of a second. By measuring how these pulses scatter and are absorbed, you track oxygen levels in the brain and see how blood flow changes as someone thinks, moves, or learns."

"So," Amy said, "by tracking changes in hemoglobin levels and other brain activity signals, we can trace brain function at its source."

"Yes!" Gabe said. "Yes, that's it exactly. And best of all, it connects with our computers just using a simple USB cable. So, as far as the VyzR modifications are concerned—"

"—You don't have to shield the unit," Sita said, finishing his thought.

"And," Gabe whispered, "it's only slightly larger than a football helmet and weighs about five pounds!"

"I like it. I like it a hell of a lot. I will still need to upgrade the speakers and microphones in the VyzR. I want to be able to vocalize what I'm experiencing but not actually speak above a whisper."

"That is not problem," Leif said, "as we were in the process of changing the unit to hold military-grade components. You know, like the ones your—slick teams use."

"He means," Sita said, "the SEAL teams and similar special forces."

"Ja," Leif said. "They got the best thing. Not regular, but throat. So sharp it nearly hears your thoughts! I have extra from a project I did last month, so no cost."

"The last question, maybe the most important one, is the cost—and can we get our hands on one soon?"

"I knew you were going to ask that," Gabe said, "so I put a call into the company before we came in here. I don't know the Center's budget, but although pricey, this is still much cheaper than other scanning machines. Also, we could have one in a week—maybe even a few days."

"Before we go down that road," Amy said. "Jax, I have to ask again. You've stated that you've never had vivid memory experiences like these before using the VyzR. Are you still convinced that using it is a critical component of this process?"

"It is a valid question. I can tell you this. It's been what, almost a week now, since our first test? I've had two regular migraines in that week. Aura, light sensitivity, and neck pain. All the classic symptoms one would expect. So, I'd have to say yes. Yes, the visor is critical to the process."

"Okay, another question," Amy said, "is whether you think you can control the process any better than before. From what we saw, it seemed like you overloaded. Even if we can scan your brain better using this new unit, if you pass out again, then what's the point?"

"Yeah, I get your point. But I'm convinced that the first time was a surprise—it was so unusual—so illogical that it caught me completely off guard. I want to talk with Terry about how I can prepare better before we jump into the EMDR part of the session. I know what to expect from an aura phase of a migraine, but if I can brace for what comes after, I may have some control over the experience."

"Is Terry willing to work with you again?" Gabe asked. "He seemed pretty rattled the last time he worked with you."

"I honestly don't know. But I believe Tessa's right about having a psychologist present to talk with me before and during the memory recollection part of the session. I don't mind sticking my neck out, I just don't want it cut off!"

16

MOLLY'S HELP

"JAX, THAT'S A BIG ask. A really big ask," Molly said.

Jax guessed that he had caught her driving and had answered the call through use of her car's system. Not only was there a slight crackle in the connection, but he could also make out the sounds of traffic in the background.

"I am aware, Molly, but I wouldn't be bothering you or your contact at VRMX Technologies if I didn't believe this was important. The Kernel Flow machine promises to be a game-changer. Your guy has to understand that by acquiring this piece of technology, the applications for the VyzR would expand exponentially, not only across neuroscience but also many other disciplines.

"I've already sent them the data from our initial experiment, along with the diagrams showing how we've enhanced their unit for better therapist-patient communication. Have you gotten any feedback?"

"Yes, I spoke with my contact person just yesterday. The company is very interested in what you've accomplished and even more interested in what you are proposing. I also wanted to thank you for sending me copies of your work as well. May I ask that you not send any further communication electronically? Corporate espionage and all that."

"Of course, I get it. Well, anyway, I think you were right. If half of what I believe we can accomplish occurs, I'm going to owe you big time."

"You know, Jax, you got me thinking just now. These technology gurus have backdoor conversations with one another all the time. It's not that I think what you are asking can't get done—I think you just caught me a bit off guard when you mentioned the cost."

"Am I hearing that this ask is doable?"

"Let me look into this a bit further and get back to you. I should have an answer for you within a couple of days—but Jax, no promises, okay?"

Ending the call, Jax hung up the office phone, leaned back in his office chair, and removed his glasses. It was then that he noticed movement and looked up to see Amy standing rigidly in his doorway. Her arms were crossed as if preparing for battle. Her frosty stare was unwavering.

17

The Talk

Amy remained standing in his doorway even after he had gestured for her to enter and sit down. She didn't speak for several seconds, although her vicious glare had already pierced Jax.

"That guy, Bruce. The one who works in the dean's office. He just told me that funding cuts are happening all over the university. He said those cuts included the Neuroscience Center—is this true?"

"Amy, it—that is, I was..."

"Damn you, Jax. It is true! And what? You didn't even think to tell me?"

"I was going to tell you. I just couldn't find the right time to tell the team."

"I am not talking about the fucking team! I'm talking about me. You couldn't tell me?"

"Can we—can you just sit down so we can discuss it. Just us, okay?"

"Go to hell!"

Storming out of his office, she slammed the door behind her. Jax just sat staring at the glass panel for a moment, half expecting it to shatter. He drained the open water bottle from the desk in front of him, replaying what she had said. Then, hoping he wasn't too late to catch her, he quickly packed up his computer and left his office.

As he entered the lab, Jax was grateful that Amy had come here rather than leaving campus. He knew she was right and that he should have been more open with her and the team about the funding issue. He had acted cowardly by not leveling with them before now. It was time to lay all his cards on the table and hope for the best.

The three were seated around the conference table as Jax wordlessly walked in and sat down. He glanced uncertainly at each of his three colleagues, not knowing what to expect.

"We need to talk. I have something to discuss with you."

"Yes," Amy said, "I absolutely believe that you should talk."

"We're going to lose our university backing. I was told that the funding will end in about eight weeks."

"You're not serious?!" Gabe demanded.

"When did you find out?" Sita asked.

"He found out last week," Amy said. "Didn't you, Jax?"

Jax closed his eyes briefly, then nodded in agreement.

"I should've told you all sooner. I kept hoping I could fix it before it became a crisis."

"You let us keep planning for this big second experiment of yours," Gabe said, exasperation filling the room. "You pushed and pushed to sell us on this damn thing! We were working like we had plenty of time." He stood and leaned against a wall. "Man, that is not being hopeful—that's just cruel!"

"What Jax?" Sita asked. "You didn't trust us to handle the truth?"

"No. No, it wasn't that. I just didn't want to derail the work. Or the team."

Amy stood up and slid her chair into place under the table. She stepped forward and leaned her face so it was inches from Jax's, whispering. "You didn't want to derail me. I'm your lead assistant. I've been managing projections and coordinating with the ethics board. You knew this would hit me first—and hardest."

"I know. You're not wrong. But I wasn't trying to shut you out."

"But you did. I'm not just your assistant, Jax. I was—I was someone you trusted. Or rather, I used to be."

"You know that you matter—to this work, and to me."

Amy drew back, still standing above the table. Gabriel and Sita glanced at one another, then looked between Jax and Amy, sensing the emotional undercurrent in the air.

"So, what now?" Gabriel asked. "We scramble to make something happen and hope someone throws us a lifeline, or what?"

"In my perfect world, we'd keep going with setting up the experiment. Sita and Leif are almost done with the VyzR modifications. Amy has a great working outline for tracking what lights up in my brain. I'm still waiting to hear about financial backing for the Kernel Flow helmet, but I'm pretty sure it's a go.

"I still need help with my preparation before the trip, and then a guide to get me through the process while I'm in the chair. We could really pull off something valuable here, guys. If we do this right, maybe even something that keeps us funded."

"So," Gabe said, "Terry was a no-go for round two?"

"He hasn't returned my calls. But we'll work something out."

Jax looked over at Amy and tried to read the expression on her face. He couldn't tell if she was still hurt or really pissed off at him—or both.

"It really comes down to one simple question. Can I count on your support to help me finish the work on this second experiment?"

"No, Tessa. I'm not going to go through that again."

"But Terry, you're the most trained person we've got. I trust you on this."

"Look, you have Valerie. She has been doing EMDR therapy for over a year now. She's young and would probably enjoy working with your husband on his project. But I'm having a real problem with the ethics involved in bastardizing this respected form of therapy to fit with—well, in all honesty, it's not really therapy—just a babysitting job!"

She was quiet for a moment, sitting behind her desk and staring out the glass window into the psychiatric unit of the hospital. Everything he just said was the cold, hard truth, and she couldn't escape it, even for Jax.

"That's quite all right, Terry, this is on me. I truly apologize for trying to push this on you—that was not my intent. I fully respect your position regarding this matter. Please forgive me if I crossed a line professionally between us."

"You didn't cross any line with me, Tessa. You know I enjoy working with you. Thank you for taking the time to talk with me openly about this issue. And for the record, I really do hope this works out for you—and for Jax."

The older man stood and left Tessa's office. Alone with her thoughts, she ran through the point Terry had made. Could she ask another psychologist to do this? Did she even have the right to put someone in an awkward position by asking? Terry was correct. This wasn't a proper use of EMDR. Jax was using the process's outward structure, but it wasn't therapy.

After debating with herself for another few minutes, she turned to her bookcase and pulled out the EMDR handbook. Returning to her chair, she spent the better part of an hour rifling through the pages and illustrations. When she was satisfied with what she'd read, she shut the book with a snap.

"Damn it," she said aloud, "I've got more than enough training to do this. All I have to do is convince Jax. Oh, the hell with that! I need to convince myself!"

18

PREPARATIONS

JAX COULD BARELY CONTAIN himself. This was the last day of his classroom commitment to the university—*finals day*. He had readily agreed to the request to hold the final as an online exam. He found it hard to give a crap about how any of these students performed. This class had always kept him from his real interests, and now he could move on.

Molly had called him back less than a day after he had called her. VRMX Technologies had agreed to purchase the Kernel Flow brain-scanning unit, but there were conditions. Jax was used to compromise, so he had not been surprised. The company requested oversight of the machine's installation in Jax's lab, followed by observation of the experiment. The company's liaison would meet with a Kernel Flow technician, who would then show team members how to set up, operate, and interpret the unit's readings.

Leif Thorsen had affably volunteered to act as a proxy participant while the team members got step-by-step instructions from the Kernel Flow representative. As it turned out, the VRMX Tech representative was a young pale-skinned man named Mikey, who, although in his mid-twenties, looked like he belonged in high school. Jax later found out that he held two PhDs—one in physics and the second in software engineering.

Jax laughed to himself when he thought about trying to fit Leif into the helmet, as they had come to refer to the high-tech scanning unit. Luckily, the manufacturer had understood that patients came in a variety of sizes, so the helmet was built with adjustable plates to fit nearly anyone. The bigger issue was Leif's hair. As thick as a rug, Leif had to flatten out his mop for the machine to fit snugly and provide accurate readings. The operator then had Leif perform tasks such as finger tapping and memory recall to ensure precise calibration.

For data collection, laser pulses were directed into the participant's scalp at picosecond speeds. The picosecond laser pulses would measure how photons scatter through brain tissue, enabling precise mapping of blood oxygenation. The system would track changes in hemoglobin concentration, or more simply, show how and where the protein in red blood cells responded to brain activity.

When Jax casually asked how fast the light would be moving using layman's terms, the technician flatly stated that to best understand what he was asking, Jax would need to wrap his head around a different perspective. What one picosecond is to a second, a second is to approximately 30,000 years! Jax didn't ask any more questions.

19

HYPNOSIS

"JAX," TESSA SAID, "WE'VE both undergone hypnosis sessions before, so nothing I say about this will be new to you. I'm just going to repeat the steps involved so we can agree on the best way to integrate this into the EMDR structure."

"I get that. Go ahead and start. If I want to add or modify anything, I'll interject."

"Good. Just as a reminder, hypnosis isn't about losing control—it's about gaining access. So, first, I'll guide you through a grounding exercise. Breath work, sensory orientation, and then establish a physical anchor—something that brings you back if things get too intense. I suggest we use my voice, but we'll come back to that.

"After the grounding, I'll lead you into a focused state or trance. Once you're in that state, I'll deepen it gently. Some methods involve counting, a metaphor, or rhythmic cues. The goal is to quiet the analytical part of your mind so we can access the sensory and emotional layers beneath."

"I think that counting is best. When I am at the dentist's office, I imagine riding down in an elevator and visualize watching the floor indicator light go from the tenth floor to the first. I have been doing it so long that I enter a light trance almost immediately. Do you think we can do all of this while I'm already wearing the VyzR? It would make the transition to the EMDR process a bit easier for me."

"I don't know. Is there a way to leave the visor light off? If you're right, that light seems to act like some sort of trigger that initiates the migraine aura. You said that you wanted to spend more time preparing before we jump into that—correct?"

"I'll ask Sita if she and Leif can modify the on-off switch so that the light stays off during the initial stage of hypnosis, but the speakers and microphones stay on. Then slide the switch back on as I enter the EMDR stage. I'm sure that won't be a big challenge for them."

"Moving on, then, here's where your migraine comes in. Once you are in a focused and relaxed state—say, between five and ten minutes—we'll turn on the pulsing light in the visor, as you just said. If what we believe is right, then the aura phase will start shortly thereafter and rapidly intensify."

"I'll probably have you turn on the visor light for me when we're ready. That way, I can maintain the relaxed state and not have to think about it. Are you good with that?"

"Sure. Once the memory surfaces, I'll continue talking to you as if in an EMDR session and guide you from there. Ideally, you will be able to vocalize what you are observing without too strong an emotional reaction to the memory. We'll also track any shifts in heartbeat and pulse just in case."

"I don't know how long I can hold on to the...let's just say memory. The last time, it didn't feel like I had any influence over the duration—it arrived the way a wave does, and then it receded the same way, with me not having any say either way. I hardly remember the return at all, really. There was a numbness, like the feeling of a foot that's fallen asleep, and something like floating—the way you feel in the seconds before you actually fall asleep. And then I was just back, the way you're suddenly back when a dream ends. If possible, I'd like to find a way to control that exit myself, to be the one who decides when I've seen enough."

"When you think you've reached a natural pause, I'll work on guiding you back with my voice. Maybe we can work on controlling your exit, so it won't be as drastic as before. We'll try to reorient you to the present, awakened state slowly. But you need to give me a signal—some cue when you want that to happen."

"So, you're telling me we need like a safe word. A word that is rare enough to stand out from normal conversation. Okay, how about using Bear?"

"I think our pup would be quite happy if we used his name as the means to bring you safely back to us."

20

Test #2

Jax sat partially reclined in the padded chair, the room dim, the soft weight of the visor now snugly fitted across his eyes. The Kernel Flow scanner cradled his head much like his bicycle helmet, its sensors beginning to map the blood's whisper through his cortex.

Tessa sat beside him, her hand resting lightly on his shoulder. Her voice had already guided him down—slow breath, softened limbs, the gentle descent into a deeper trance.

"You're safe and relaxed," she said, her voice now piped through the tiny microphones embedded near his ears. "I'm going to turn on the light in the VyzR. I want you to remain relaxed and just let your eyes follow the light."

She flicked the switch, and the visor lit up with its slow, rhythmic pulse of blue light—left, right, left—like the tide rolling in and out. EMDR phase one. Jax allowed his eyes to open as he tracked the motion, his body slack, his mind open.

Then it began. The rainbow aura appeared—first a shimmer, then a spike. It bloomed outward, jagged and radiant, like stained glass caught in a storm.

Jax felt the slightest pull forward. The aura grew, its edges vibrating with impossible color. Reds that hummed. Blues that chimed. He was rising from his chair.

Drawn up and through the aura, his body tingling. The white light ahead beckoned. Tessa's voice was still there, distant now, like ripples through water.

"Let it come. You're doing fine. Keep breathing deeply and just relax."

Jax reached for the light—not with hands, but with something deep inside of him. A siren's song without sound, and then...

...the Mustang's engine purred like it always did—low, confident, a sound Jax had grown up with. His mother's fingers tapped the steering wheel in rhythm with the radio, some old '80s track she insisted was the only 'real music' worth playing. The sun was barely up, casting long shadows across the dashboard.

Jax sat up straight. He was in the passenger seat, his backpack in his lap. What the hell was happening? He wasn't supposed to be here. Not this day. Not this memory.

The radio playing, *"You can't always get what you want, but if you try..."*

"Big test today?" she asked.

Without thinking, he mumbled, "Chemistry...no biggie."

She smiled, but it faltered. Her hand went to her temple.

"Mom, are you okay?" Jax was gradually becoming more aware of when and where he was. He was in a memory from when he was seventeen, but his thoughts were slow to adapt to those of a man twenty years older. He looked at her. Drops of blood were running from her nose.

"Just a headache," she said, blinking hard. "It—will—pass."

But it didn't. By the time they hit the stretch of road coming out of the foothills, her knuckles had gone white on the wheel. She winced, eyes fluttering.

The song continued, *"...you just might find, you get what you need."*

"Mom—Mom, listen to me, you're having a migraine—a big one. You need to pull over right now. Stop the car!"

"I'm...fine," she said, but her voice was tight, clipped.

Then the Mustang blew through a red traffic light and veered up against the curb, scrapping the hubcaps against the concrete with a squeal.

Jax saw the red pickup too late—it was backing out of a driveway.

"Mom! Stop the car!"

She didn't respond. Jax reached across the seat and grabbed the steering hoping to miss the truck, but it was too late.

The impact was brutal. Metal shrieked. Glass exploded. The world spun.

When the car came to rest, Jax found himself hanging upside down—the seatbelt cutting into his chest. He tasted blood in his mouth—the odor of gasoline filled his nostrils. The Mustang crushed like a soda can—the front end embedded in the back of the pickup, the windshield shattered with pieces scattered over the car and street.

Wiping a rivulet of blood from his face, he turned his head, pain lancing through his neck. He knew what he was going to find.

"Mom? Mom, come on, don't do this to me. Mom, please don't die. Not again!"

She wasn't moving, but lay crumpled on the car's upended ceiling. By the time the police and paramedics arrived, Jax was free from his restraint and standing by the destroyed door where his mother lay, blood coating that white, flowing blouse she loved.

"Son," a woman said quietly, "it looks like she died on impact. She wouldn't have felt any pain. Can you tell me your name?"

Instead of answering her, Jax numbly pulled out his wallet from his hip pocket and handed it to her. He felt someone try to lead him away, but he refused to leave her. He felt his hand being wrapped in a bandage, and his head patted with something that smelled medicinal, but it seemed too far away to really care. He couldn't take his eyes off his mother's crumpled body. At some point, the woman, a policewoman he now knew, walked back up and stood between him and what was left of the Mustang.

"Jaxon, we got a hold of your father, and he's on his way. He should be here soon."

"I could have saved her," Jax whispered. "Why did I arrive this late? Five minutes—even two minutes earlier, and I could have saved her. Why now?"

"Jaxon," the policewoman said, "you've just been in a major accident, and you're still bleeding pretty badly. I really need you to let the paramedics treat you to stop the blood loss. I'll wait with you until your dad gets here, but then you'll need to go to the hospital and get fully checked out."

He looked at the officer as if she were speaking a foreign language. What was she talking about? What hospital? He glanced down at his left hand wrapped in a bandage. Even through the blood-soaked gauze, he could tell he was missing his pinky finger. When had that happened? That never happened.

"I think it's time I go see Bear."

He could hear the lilt of Tessa's voice but couldn't make out any words. The shimmer of the aura appeared in front of his 17-year-old body, summoning him back to his rightful time and place. But it wouldn't let him enter and stayed just beyond his reach. He was having difficulty breathing normally and began to hyperventilate.

His focus returned to the ruined body of his mother as the aura stayed on the periphery of his sight. Was this thing mocking him? He wanted to leave this memory—now. He needed to get away. She's dead. Again. He thought he could have—should have stopped this from happening! He wanted to stop this. He should be gone!

Through slitted eyes, he could just make out his wife standing over him, gently shaking his shoulders. Then, sparks radiated from the aura as she slapped his face. Once. Twice. Harder. The pain felt right. Justified. He was given a second chance, but he blew it. He'd imagined saving her thousands of times over the last twenty years. Here, he had been given the chance—but he failed. A fucking failure!

"Jax, come on, damn it. You need to wake up!"

21

DATA COLLECTION

DURING THE EXPERIMENT, AMY stayed in the control booth behind the glass partition. Her eyes remained fixed on the live Kernel Flow output as a cortical map of Jax's brain was displayed on the large monitor above the console—each photon echo being plotted with picosecond precision.

"Baseline's clean," she murmured. "Prefrontal's stable. Default Mode's quiet."

From the speakers connected to the VyzR and transmitted to those in the booth, she had been listening to Tessa's hypnotic induction, then to her words as the EMDR phase began. For the first few seconds, all readings were neutral.

Then it hit. She could see that Jax was rocking his head back and forth, most likely an indication that the aura phase of a migraine had begun. Then she registered a sudden flare in the precuneus, the section of the brain that helps reconstruct past experiences.

He had jumped from migraine onset to memory recall almost instantaneously.

A moment later, the display showed erratic spikes in the posterior cingulate and parietal cortex, areas of the brain that indicated Jax was in the process of retrieving intense, emotionally charged memories. She looked at the digital clock on the wall and saw that it had barely been a minute since Tessa switched on the visor's light and had begun prompting Jax to access his memories.

The brain scan continued to display a heightened emotional state for another thirty seconds, then something unusual caught Amy's attention. She leaned in closer to the monitor to confirm the machine's readings.

"What the hell—photon arrival's off-pattern—latency's drifting. It's as if the photons are hitting two timelines. He's not just recalling, he's re-routing!"

Amy was aware that during a normal EMDR process, when a memory is recalled, it temporarily enters an unstable state. During this window of instability, new emotional or sensory input can alter the memory. The memory would then be reconsolidated—rewritten with the new associations. But this was more, much more.

She tapped the mic. "Tessa, can you hear Jax speaking right now?"

His head pitched under the visor. Tessa looked over her shoulder at the control booth and nodded, but with a deeply worried look on her face.

Amy froze. Was something wrong with the system? The data she read off the monitor wasn't right...was it? What she saw in the feed shouldn't be possible.

"He's not following the process anymore," she whispered, "he's rewriting a second memory in parallel with the older one. Is he...rewiring his brain?"

She flagged the timestamp, then looked once again at the monitor's feed. The system had just labeled it, 'Temporal Displacement'.

Amy turned her mic on again. "Tessa, we're not just triggering a memory. The scan's showing a bleed—like he's cross-indexing two separate memories."

"Is he okay?" Gabe asked from the doorway.

"This can't be remembering," Amy whispered. "It's something else. Something more."

Tessa had brought a small medical kit with her to the lab. She had found a stimulant vapor ampoule and broken the capsule under Jax's nose. She waited for a beat, but he still was responsive. She gestured at Sita to raise the helmet completely off his head, while she lifted the visor off his face. His eyes remained closed. She leaned over his prone body and slapped him once—twice. "Jax, damn it. You need to wake up!" She raised her arm to strike him a third time when Jax caught her hand.

He opened his eyes and smiled at his wife. Pulling her hand to his face, he gently kissed it. He closed his eyes and softly shook his head in a futile attempt to rid himself of the remnants of the agonizing imagery he'd just lived through. He felt Tessa stroking his beard and hair. "God, my body feels like crap. Even my ribs hurt. Tess, she died...again.

He sat up abruptly. "Her death—and my wound!" He held up his left hand. Where once were five healthy digits, now there were four—and a stump where his little finger had been. He took a few deep breaths to calm himself, then held up his hand to show Tessa.

"My finger. What the hell happened to my finger?!"

"Jax, honey, you've just gone through a major trauma. It's natural for you to be a little groggy for a while. Take your time. We can talk about everything you went through in a few minutes, okay?"

"Tessa, I lost my finger. Sita, Gabe, can't any of you see that?"

"Shh. It's okay. Yes, from what we could tell, it seems your brain decided to jump to the traumatic accident that killed your mother. I'm so sorry, hon."

"But my finger," Jax said, almost to himself. "Why don't you understand?"

"I know, I get it. You told me once that losing your finger reminded you of losing her. Now, try to relax for a minute. You need some time to relax. Let your body and mind heal."

At that point, the others slowly approached him. "We got it," Sita said. "Amy is looking over the data right now with Mikey."

"Mikey?"

"Mikey. The VRMX Tech representative you met two days ago?"

"Okay," Tessa said, "I really think Jax needs some time to just relax. Can we continue this a bit later? He needs at least 30 minutes, maybe more."

"Yeah, boss," Gabe said, "take your time—don't push it. Can I get you a coffee?"

"Yes, thank you. That sounds good right now."

"However," Dr. Mason said, "if that won't cut it, I have scotch in my office."

Tessa slowly led her husband to his private office and closed the door behind them. After having him sit in the chair, she handed Jax the coffee Gabe had poured and then leaned against the bookcase and just stared at her husband. "I'm not sure I can go through that again," she said quietly, but forcefully. "And I'm not convinced you should put yourself through it either. Remembering that kind of trauma without any safeguards..."

"It wasn't a memory, Tess. I was there. I can't explain why it happened without any time for me to do anything to prevent it, but that's why I lost this. I didn't lose my finger in the first accident. I mean the real accident. Damn it, you know what I mean!"

"Sweetheart, you put your mind and your body through a terrific strain. You of all people must recognize what such pressure can do to jostle up your memories."

"This isn't that! Don't you think I would remember if I lost a finger or not?!"

"Honey, please stop yelling. What I need you to do right now is relax and show yourself the smallest bit of charity. Just allow yourself time. Things will sort themselves out. There doesn't need to be a definitive answer right now—am I correct?"

"God Tess, I'm on the verge of losing it right now. I'm really...confused, and I need you on my side here. My dad used to tell me that my actions have consequences. Well, there I was...again. I should have done more when I had the chance. What the fuck is wrong with me?"

Tessa bent down and hugged her husband. No more words, just the soothing touch of her fingers as they stroked his hair. She kissed his forehead, then stood back up.

"It is my professional opinion that you, sir, need to go home, have a drink, pet your dog, and maybe kiss your wife. I'll let your team know that you'll be back first thing tomorrow. Then and only then can you trouble yourself about what happened. Deal?"

"Yeah. Deal. Who am I to argue with my doctor—Doctor?"

"Yes. I'd hate to have to kick your arse, but I will if you make me!"

22

Temporal Anomaly

Jax got into the lab early so he could pore over the session logs uninterrupted. His hands trembled slightly as he scrolled through the neural trace data. The Kernel Flow helmet sat on top of the console beside him—seemingly mocking him. He read Amy's notes on the scan from the day before, but she must not have had the chance to edit the narrative because some of it was nonsensical.

A technician's note flashed on the screen, reading, *To Jaxon Beck from Mikey Z. - Confidential.* Jax quickly typed in his personal password, and a video of the young man appeared on the screen, obviously nervous. "A-hem. Excuse me. Dr. Beck, it appears the system detected a temporal displacement anomaly during yesterday's experiment. To eliminate any possibility of a malfunction, the company is having me remove the VyzR and the Kernel Flow unit for further study in our labs. I appreciate that this is abrupt, but it's also totally necessary for legal and health reasons. I apologize, but please ensure the equipment is ready for pickup tomorrow. Thank you."

The screen went blank, and Jax stood looking at it a moment, trying to understand what the implications were of what was said. "Temporal displacement? That's not supposed to—that's the stuff of science fiction."

He pulled up the Kernel Flow data from the computer and displayed it on the main monitor. A 3D map of his brain activity during the session bloomed across the screen—color-coded bursts of light in the hippocampus and amygdala.

"This isn't right. The timestamped memory shows that the data is conflicting. This pre-scan shows me with five fingers. The post-session scan only shows four."

A voice came from the doorway. "And you think the system rewrote it?" Amy asked.

"Oh, hey. Didn't see you come in. No. According to this printout, my memory actually changed after the scan. Well, maybe not exactly changed—the memory was accessed twice, but in a slightly different way. So yeah, I guess the more accurate term would be rewritten or even overwritten."

"I've been thinking about this all night, but I can't nail down a plausible explanation for these readings. Jax, what if during the experiment, you didn't just unlock that traumatic memory, but your brain layered neural connections? One version or memory of the crash where you lost your finger, and another one where your mind believes you didn't. That might explain the reading I got yesterday."

"The Kernel Flow doesn't just read, it maps. If the brain stored both versions, maybe it's less like a—a Mandela effect, where I'm misremembering, and more like an insertion, where the older memory is disregarded and replaced with a new one. That leads to only one logical conclusion. I think my brain triggered a temporal anomaly. Holy shit!"

He leaned back, staring at his hand. The absence of the finger felt more real now. Not painful. Just...inescapable.

"Did Mikey make it by the lab yet?"

"Yeah," Gabe said. "He came by just before lunch. He didn't say much, just something about you knowing all about it. He loaded up the visor and helmet hardware and printed a copy of the test data, then took off."

The whole team had gathered once again in their cozy conference room. Jax and Amy wanted to run the results by Gabe and Sita to debrief them, but also to plan next steps.

"Sita, do you think Leif is up for some more work on our behalf?"

"Sure. He's a giant geek when it comes to building stuff, plus we got his ass fired up when he got to see what we were doing. What do you have in mind?"

"I think we should build our own technology to continue this work. I don't trust VRMX Tech to come rushing back with the visor and helmet. They're going to want to take both units down to their core components and test the crap out of them. It could be months before we see that equipment again, and as you all know, we don't have months."

"Sure, but we don't have a budget either. I'm sure Leif will work for free as long as we continue to include him in the testing phase, but some of those—hell, most of those components would cost a year's salary. This isn't anything we can cheap out on. Not when we're talking about your brain. One last thing, that tech is proprietary, and we all signed their NDAs. Couldn't we get our asses sued or worse if we copy their work?"

"First things first. I need you and Leif to focus on how to make this thing. Move into the planning stage and let me worry about how to pay for the equipment. Second, I don't have any intention of violating any patent or copyright laws here. I have some ideas that won't involve their stuff. As long as we aren't trying to sell what you build to anyone else, then we won't violate their non-compete clause either."

"Can we discuss the results first?" Amy said. "I mean, before we get all worked up about building stuff we can use—or should be using?"

"Makes sense. Amy, do you want to do the honors and explain to the group what you got from the Kernel Flow data?"

Amy walked to their ever-present whiteboard and erased everything scrawled on it. She then wrote two words on the board and underlined them.

"What do either of you know about temporal anomalies?" Amy asked.

"You mean like time travel stuff?" Sita asked.

"I'm not talking about *Star Trek* or *Dr. Who*. I'm talking about irregularities or disruptions in the timing of brain activity. You know, the boring neuroscience stuff we're doing here."

"So," Gabe began, "along the area of the brain, you would... No, I've got nothing."

"Let's look at it from another perspective. You both are familiar with disorders like OCD or PTSD. These occur when certain neural circuits lock in and replay traumatic or compulsive thoughts. Technically, this is called pathological looping."

"I see that," Gabe said. "Temporal denotes time, specifically chronological sequence, as in yesterday is history, today is happening, but the future has yet to occur. So, if I'm catching your drift, what you'd be referring to is when the timing and coordination of neural signals are disrupted—repeated or looped."

"Exactly. So, in Jax's case, his brain looped, but in so doing, it created a second pathway on top of the original. According to the scan, he actually has two copies of the same memory. I believe this most likely occurred deep inside the midbrain, just behind the ears. We were—"

"Excuse me for one second. Do you guys understand that we have two hippocampi—one in each hemisphere of the brain? Each memory is a network of neurons that acts like a switchboard linking different parts of the brain."

"We were able to detect this," Amy continued, a bit perturbed at being interrupted. "Because the Kernel Flow machine tracks changes and essentially deduces patterns. I know you heard all of this when we set up the unit, but it's worth restating."

"So," Gabe said, "are you telling us that you did a sort of time travel bit when you were recalling that memory of your mom's accident? Oh, hey—I'm sorry, Jax, I know that whole experience must still be kind of raw for you."

"Thanks, Gabe. Yes, and it's even more painful due to what Amy and I are trying to lay out for you here. For me, it was more than just recalling the memory, like with PTSD. What I believe is that I was essentially back there, reliving the incident while it was occurring."

"That is," Sita said, "the scariest shit I have ever heard. Are you trying to tell us that your consciousness traveled back in time? Not your physical body, but your mind? How exactly does that work? Are you still you when you go back or what?"

"Okay, that is where Jax and I disagree. Strongly disagree. Most neuroscientists believe that consciousness is related to brain activity—patterns of electrical signals and neural networks. I think Jax experienced a re-remembrance, which provided a sense of interacting with people and his environment. Decidedly vivid, but not actually reliving the moment."

"Which is where our philosophical paths differ. In my original recollection of that time, I didn't know what was happening to my mom, so I was just sitting there in the car, oblivious to everything one minute and upside down in this wreck the next. But this time, I almost instantly recognized that my mom was having a massive migraine and grabbed the wheel, trying in vain to stop the collision. I'm certain that one small act led me to lose this."

Holding up his hand and showing the space where his fifth digit should have been led the group to be quiet with their own thoughts. It was a lot to absorb, and the ramifications of either Jax's or Amy's assessment of what took place were overwhelming. The room was silent for several minutes.

"I don't know," Gabe said finally. "The idea of you changing things in your past is not like having an altered memory. I know therapists sometimes instill different memories in trauma patients, but that's to blunt the intensity of the trauma. Right?"

"I kind of agree," Sita said hesitantly. "Couldn't it have been something to do with the machines and how they interacted? I mean, the Kernel Flow is just a measuring device, and the VyzR is just a modified version of a light bar, but maybe the confluence of the two...?"

"Both are excellent questions. That's why I want to build our own visor and test it again in a more controlled manner. I need to know if I'm having amnesia about losing my finger in that accident or if my hypothesis about reentering that time is correct."

"Regardless," Amy said, "what does any of this have to do with your work here at the Center? Are you going to shelve everything we've been doing and move on to this experimental outing in what little time is left on the money clock?"

"Another good point. Knowing what we do now, what are the applications? I believe one avenue is the replacement or overwriting of a traumatic event, much like PTSD. We may also be onto something here that can treat OCD, depression, or even more serious neurological ailments like Parkinson's."

"Yeah," Gabe said, "but do we have the time to demonstrate whether those applications are viable? I love you guys and all, but I have a little girl at home who I have to take care of. I need this job—or I need to start looking for another one with a bit more security beyond the few weeks you told us we have left."

"For the moment, we may be close to our goal of migraine control or perhaps even a cure. If we accept the theory that migraines are neurological in nature and not psychological, we may be able to override the very neural activity that cascades into the pain receptors."

Amy's gaze dropped to the floor. "Jax, I need to tell you something." She took a deep breath, fingers fidgeting with her lab coat button. "Director Mason wants me to head up data analysis for the entire Center, starting Monday." Her voice softened. "I'll still be in the building, just working across all the labs, helping teams make sense of their research." She finally met his eyes. "I'm sorry, but I'm out."

23

DISCUSSION

"STEVE, ARE YOU HEARING me?!"

"I'm hearing you all too well," Dr. Mason said, "and if you keep yelling at me, Jax, I'm going to have to ask you to leave my office! Now, damn it, sit down and let's walk through this—well, I guess this is a proposal, am I right?"

"It's an offer. I'm offering to make the Center, and by extension you, the shining star in the neuroscientific world."

"Oh, please cut the bullshit. We've known each other too long to have you try and blow smoke up my ass. Get to the part where you want more money, then tell me why I should give it to you."

Jax took a minute to collect himself and purposefully sat in the chair furthest from the Director's desk. He was aware that it was getting late, and he wasn't going to risk a bicycle ride in the dark.

"Are you still hiding that scotch in your bottom drawer?"

While Dr. Mason ritualistically pulled out the decanter of 20-year-old scotch and two crystal glasses, Jax texted Tessa to pick him up when she was done for the day. Dr. Mason gently pushed the half-filled glass across his desk to prevent any of the precious liquid from spilling. He held his glass in a wordless toast, then took a deep sip from his glass.

"I found something. Something that came out of our experiment, which could be a turning point for neuro-based diseases and conditions. I need a tad more time and enough capital to keep Gabriel and Sita with me through the end of the year."

"I've already shuffled positions and closed out all peripheral contracts to extend you as far as what we've already discussed. Amy is now on board as my number two as of this week. What the hell do you want me to do? Please, elaborate!"

"We have evidence of a temporal anomaly arising from our test."

"You have what?! What the hell are you talking about, Jax?"

"When I accessed that memory in my brain about the accident that killed my mother, another—a secondary memory was created. It also seemed to take precedence over the first. As an aside, I also believe it resulted in a change in present-day reality."

He held up his left hand as he took a sip from the glass he held in his right.

"What in God's name are you talking about? You lost that finger years ago—at least as long as I've known you."

"Exactly. That is exactly what I'm trying to tell you. That whole line of truth versus fiction changed when I was in that last test. I'm telling you it's true, Steve, because it happened to me! It also seems to have affected the memories of everyone around me!"

"Show me," Dr. Mason said quietly.

Jax reached into his backpack, pulled out a stack of documents, and placed them on Dr. Mason's desk. As the Director started leafing through the mound of papers, Jax reached over, picked up the decanter of scotch, refilled his glass, then topped off the Director's. Mason kept reading but reflexively picked up the glass and drained it.

"Well, this appears remarkable. You're positive that all of this is accurate?"

"Yes, it is incredible. I'm so sure it's accurate that VRMX Technologies, which sponsored all this latest research, took back their equipment to test for a malfunction. A fucking malfunction, Steve. Why would they do that if what you're reading didn't happen?"

"But you don't have anything to base the other supposition on other than what you remember to be the truth, as you put it?"

"It's a catch-22 situation. I was both observer and participant, so when the change occurred, I was an integral part of it and have a memory of both before and after. The bitch of the thing is that no one else remembers that duality. I need to test more so I can prove this type of thing really occurs when I'm doing this."

"Let's leave that alone for now. I'm more interested in the part where you state your neural network was overwritten. If the data back that up, then the implications..."

"Are wide open. Yes, I've tried to think of ways this type of work couldn't be used. There are none! Every project you have running right now can utilize this—a damn cure for Epilepsy, for Parkinson's, OCD, depression, you name it, we can use it!"

"Please stop yelling—I can't think when you act like this. I need to read through this more carefully. Leave this with me, and we'll talk more about this later. I hope what you're telling isn't just the ramblings of a brain-damaged lunatic."

"Okay, I'll check with you tomorrow. But Steve, understand that the Center will need to get its own Kernel Flow helmet. Keep in mind that the cost will be a small fraction compared to what the Center can command with this discovery."

Jax's phone vibrated with a text telling him that his wife was downstairs waiting for him. He placed his empty glass on the desk, stood, and left without another word.

When the door closed, Dr. Mason picked up his phone and typed in a number. When the call connected, he said, "We need to talk. Yes, it looks like things just changed—in a big way."

24

Build It

"So, this is the prototype?"

"Yes," Sita said, "with the emphasis on prototype. We still have a long way to go, but we needed a launch point, so we have this unit to start us off. We took regular off-the-shelf VR glasses and added the same extra-sensitive microphones we used to modify the VyzR. Neither VRMX Technologies nor the company that makes these glasses holds a patent for the microphones, so we don't have any legal issues there."

"Ja, so the biggest difference you'll notice," Leif said, "was getting that little EMDR light and the background sound, to act just so. You see? These glasses—they're built to plug straight into a computer. So, we just write a small program, or find one that mimics the light bar, ja? Like Sita say, this tech—it doesn't belong to one company or group. It's open, more or less. But you should buy that special sound. It's not expensive—maybe a dollar from a music app, or something like that."

"This is really great work, you two. I'm anxious to try it out as soon as we can. Sita, can you research the light bar and sound app? You already have my credit card information from before, so you could use that."

"I already did. No, you do not look at me like that! I know you, and you made it clear that you wanted to get something up and running as soon as possible. Well, now we're halfway there. This unit will do the job until we can construct an actual working model—so, when you're ready, it's a go."

Jax just smiled at her, then patted Leif on his shoulder. He had always prided himself on keeping in shape, but Leif's muscles felt like slabs of rock. At his request, they had met in Jax's private office. With Amy leaving the team and the lukewarm reception he'd gotten from Dr. Mason, he thought it best to conduct any additional tests privately.

"Where's Gabe?" Sita asked. "I didn't see him come in this morning."

"He had a job interview, so I told him to take the day off. I'm not saying he's unimportant to the research, but I understand the need for him to protect himself and his family. Just so we're clear, that goes for you as well, you know?"

"I'm not worried about that shit," Sita said, "I can get a job tomorrow at any of a dozen different tech companies right here in the Denver area. Plus, I don't have kids to worry about."

"Ja, so Jax, how will you run these tests now, without your team? You had to give back the monitor. What will you do about measuring your brain... neurals? Neurons? The word misses me, but you get what I say. The activity inside. You need to show the signals, or it's only theory, no?"

"Leif, you never cease to amaze me with how smart you are. Thank you, my friend, but I don't believe that we need to measure anything related to the brain at this stage. Our last test showed us enough to make some educated hypotheses about what is going on up there. I need to play around with this new device behind the scenes. I have some things in motion to secure the funding to buy our own Kernel Flow device for monitoring, but that may take a little time. What about you? Doesn't your job miss you being there? I mean, I appreciate everything you've done—and continuing to do for us, but I don't want to screw things up for you too."

"Ah, no stress. I finished the other projects already—maybe a week ago, maybe more. I just tell them I'm still working, so I send in the reports like always. As long as they see the work, they don't care if they see me, you know? I'm glad to be working with you—and with Sita, of course. This kind of project...it's good. Feels more real."

"Thanks. Really, thank you both. Look, it's a beautiful day out there. Why don't you two take off and enjoy each other's company someplace—well, someplace that doesn't include these stone walls.

Okay? I'm going to grab a cup of coffee and try to clear my head a bit myself."

As they left, Jax picked up the visor they had brought him and put it on. It wasn't nearly as light as the VyzR, but neither was it uncomfortable. He turned on the unit and felt the electronic hum start to vibrate in his head. He yanked off the visor and just looked at it for a full minute. He recognized that he needed to be more careful in planning out his next steps for testing his theory.

"Okay," he said to the empty room. "What if I really can evoke a memory and change some aspect or outcome? Can I do that without hurting myself? More importantly, not hurt anyone else?"

25

THE DIRECTOR

DR. MASON CAUGHT JAX a bit off guard by suggesting they meet in his lab instead of the man's office. Something about getting out from behind his desk and remembering the character of a laboratory, or some such story. It slipped Jax's mind that Dr. Mason had once been the leader in his own lab and had conducted his own research. He had always thought of him as an administrator, not a scientist.

"I believe," Dr. Mason began, "I may have found a sponsor for your work."

"Don't leave me in suspense here. Who are we talking about, and how serious are they about ramping up our research in this area?"

"Why don't we talk about that once we get a bit closer. After all, I've only had this data for less than a week. I would like you to draft a more formal funding request and break down the anticipated expenses, including the equipment you believe you'll need and the personnel required to make this happen. At the moment, all I have is an idea of what this can do. I don't even have a solid theory to make a case to get you what you think you might need."

"I know what you're saying is reasonable, but I already lost Amy—to you, I might add. I might be losing Gabriel soon, too. The deadline you originally set, and which I was obligated to share with my team, is ticking closer every day. I'm going to need a few days, basically working alone, to put all of that into a comprehensible report."

"Let's proceed methodically. Write up a narrative of what you believe took place. Reference the test data you already have, and what you think the implications could be for neuroscience and neurodegenerative diseases. I know you're capable of delivering that in a few days—again, broad strokes only."

"So, what I'm hearing from you is that we may get funding, but only if I can put this into a storyline that someone else can understand. Can I at least assume whoever is going to read this has a scientific background?"

"It might be best," Dr. Mason said, "if your narrative stayed away from the jargon and acronyms we use around here. That would provide me some room to fill in the gaps when needed and not...confuse anyone."

"Do you still have Amy's analysis that I gave you yesterday? I don't want to weed through the raw data if you want to turn this around in a reasonable time."

"It's on my desk. "So, just pick it up on your way out. I'm under the impression you'll want to work on this in private, so feel free to work from home for the next few days."

After gathering up the stack of papers from Dr. Mason, Jax went to his office and loaded everything he thought he would need into his backpack. He began rolling his bike towards the exit, then remembered he might need some of the data they had pulled from their first test. As that information was still in the laboratory's mainframe computer, he propped his bike against his door and walked quickly to the lab.

When he got there, he found the door was slightly ajar, although he was certain he'd locked it shortly before. Slipping past the doorway, he noticed all the overhead lights were off, but the computer was running—something he definitely wouldn't have forgotten. Turning, he spied Amy typing away at her old station with just the desk lamp softly illuminating her face. Obviously engrossed in what she was doing, she hadn't noticed Jax enter.

"Is there something I can help you with?"

"Jax!" Amy said. "Jesus, you scared the shit out of me. Yes, I mean no. It's just that I have some files here that I was going to use during my dissertation defense. I saw the lab shut down and didn't think you'd mind me accessing them. Was I wrong?"

"No, Amy, you know you can take whatever you need. I was just surprised to see the lab up and running after I'd gone, that's all."

She looked up at him as he approached and turned to face him. The low light illuminated his face in a way that softened his eyes.

"Mason gave me a card for the Center. Mimicking a line spoken in the movie, *The Fifth Element*, she said, "Mul-tee-pass. I have a multi-pass."

Jax just grinned at the reference. It was a movie they had once enjoyed together a long time ago.

"Tessa did really well by you during the test. She's good for you, Jax. I mean, she's a good partner for you...now."

"Yes. Yes, she is. Look, Amy. I—I recognize that I must have hurt your feelings with all of this. I mean, the choices I made. About us—the lab—the budget cuts. Tough as it was, I believe I made the right decisions."

"Well, everything seemed to work out in the end...right?"

"But you and I. We're still friends?"

"Friends. Yeah. Sure."

26

EPIPHANY

READING, THEN EDITING, THEN rereading. Jax finally gave up. He groaned and massaged his back as he stood from behind the coffee table. Before him were all the reports and notes from the experiment, his laptop holding down the heap of paper.

He walked to the kitchen, where he found the remnants of the cabernet he and Tessa had started a few nights before. A part of him wanted something stronger to kick his mind into gear, but he was concerned that being too relaxed might mean producing a less-than-professional synopsis of his work. But in a way, wasn't that what Steve had asked of him? Just identify the cause that resulted in the effect. Which meant...?

"God, enough already, Beck! It's not as though you're writing your first term paper. You know what happened. You saw the results, both in printed data and with this—this physical manifestation. Yeah, but what about the applications? Are there not enough, or are there too many to list?"

He downed the glass of wine he had absently poured for himself, then reached into their built-in wine cooler and grabbed another bottle without reading its label. It was only early afternoon, but Jax was starting to feel a buzz from his indulgence.

"I'll be damned if I can't get my brain to come up with something concrete to send the Director soon. What is the best way to describe a practical concept?"

Reaching blindly into the refrigerator, he grabbed a container of leftover pizza and proceeded to eat its contents cold. He had no idea how long that slab of dough and tomato sauce had been sitting there, but it was of no consequence—it was just fuel to keep the fire stoked inside him.

By the time Tessa arrived home, Jax was completing his first draft of his proposal. He had finally decided that he just needed to put words in an organized manner and be done with it. He would read it once more before sending it to the Director. Nodding at this wife's presence, he held up a single finger to indicate he was almost done. Satisfied, he gently closed the lid of his computer.

"Everything okay?" Tessa asked tentatively.

"Fine. Everything is fine."

"I would ask if I could pour you some wine, but judging by that empty bottle, I'd say you're way ahead of me."

"You're not wrong. Do you feel like getting out and grabbing some sushi?"

"Babe, if you really need to, I'll try to rally, but it is nearly seven. To be honest, I could really just use a long, hot shower and some sleep. Are you alright?"

"Of course. I'm sorry, I just lost track of time writing this proposal up for Steve. But I'm done for the night. So, what can I make you—assuming you're hungry?"

"I'm just going to munch on some carrots and hummus. Did you eat? We can get something delivered. Do you feel like pizza?"

"Oh, hell no. Thanks, I'll dig up something."

"So, tell me about your day. Did you get to talk with Dr. Mason?"

"Fuck him. Tell me about your day. How are you doing?"

"You're sweet to ask, but I really don't feel like replaying all the crap I had to deal with between clients, staff, and reports. I'm just done. Maybe we can grab breakfast together and talk more then?"

"Sure. You go ahead and take your shower. I'm going to kick around for a while more, so don't wait up. Please, take care of yourself. I'll be fine. Love you."

Something was nagging at the recesses of his mind. He hated the draft proposal he had written and was making another attempt to explain himself better, or at least more organized. He tried laying out the process and what might have been the foundation for the effect—machine, biology, or the mixture of both. He had gone through one complete yellow note pad of notes and additional questions about the test and had just started writing on a second pad.

"Shit. I've nearly rewritten all our notes as well as the entire print-out from the monitor. I just don't see..." He stopped writing and restarted his computer. "I didn't see."

Browsing through the various files, he found the videos from the first and second tests and played them in separate windows on the monitor. He let each video play out, then stopped each at the same time in the experimental process—the conclusion. "What is it that I didn't see in these images?"

"My migraine—specifically the aura phase! I've been so caught up looking at the data that I've forgotten that I never entered the attack phase either time." He rose from his seat and walked to the glass doors overlooking their backyard. Staring at his reflection, he continued. "It's true, I did pass out the first time, but it's like Gabe said, my brain was just overloaded from the stress of the experience. But afterward... Afterward, there wasn't any pain and no hangover symptoms either. Those always presented right after the aura phase, but not now. Not with these!"

He sat back down and replayed both videos again to confirm his conclusion. A short period of disorientation, but then he just snapped right out of it. No head or neck pain. No fatigue or brain fog, and no sensitivity to light or sound. He stood to stretch his back and to pace—he always thought better when he paced.

A whine came from beside him, and he saw Bear sitting in front of the sliding door. Jax opened it and followed his dog into their backyard. "So, Bear," he said as the dog sniffed out the right spot to conduct his business. "What is your conclusion? I was able to overcome, or more precisely, bypass the worst parts of a migraine. So, can this be replicated? But why now? I've had migraines with an aura for years. It can't be as simple as this stupid visor that's causing me to experience this effect...can it?"

Bear let out a small bark, knowing he was being spoken to, but not understanding the words. Jax held his hands in front of his face, making a circle with his fingers and focusing on the full moon so his fingers blurred. "The aura phase began like every other one I've ever had, but it didn't morph into semi-blindness or anything close to that."

He extended his arms, altering his perspective. Now, his fingers came into focus as the moon blurred. "So, am I saying the visor allowed the aura to create a focused mechanism that enhanced the recall of a memory? No, damn it. This was much more than that! The visor must have altered the aura, turning it into some kind of conduit. My mind—my consciousness enters, and the brain's synapses create new connections over older ones, replaying—no, reliving the memory."

He followed Bear back into the house and closed the door. Walking through the kitchen, he returned to the living room, gesturing as he went.

"In both of those tests, a traumatic memory became a focal point for the brain. I didn't have any control over where my mind went, it just...went. What would happen if I could consciously control some retrievable memory fragments and intentionally isolate a single memory by choice? Is that even possible? Of course it is. People do it all the time."

Settling back on the couch, he stretched his legs and tucked a pillow under his head. For several minutes, he watched the abstract swirls on the ceiling, letting his thoughts scatter and churn. He shut his eyes to still the chaos he felt rising in him.

"I've already lost a finger to this process," he mumbled. "That fact is undeniable. Well, at least it is to me. Does this mean I could reshape reality by deliberately altering a memory from my past? The more challenging question is, should I even try? Will I cease to exist?

"Man, I have got to stop watching reruns of the *Twilight Zone*. Either that or give up drinking. Nah, I'm afraid I'm going to have to ditch my old collection Rod Serling CDs. That's all there is to it."

27

Going Solo

Confiding in Sita and Leif about his plan for the next experiment, he obtained their help in setting up the visor they had created. He did need one more thing from their expertise in dealing with anything and everything electronic.

"What I'm looking for is to use the hypnotic and EMDR techniques Tessa used on me last time. I'm thinking of taking her voice from the video and running it through some sort of AI program, where she—her computer-generated voice that is, can talk me through specifics that I have laid out beforehand."

"Jax, just so I'm clear, ja?" Leif said. "You want to use a simulation of your wife's voice to help trigger a hypnotic state. Then have her—or rather, the computer—guide you through a specific memory. A kind of structured recording meant to support the experiment without another person involved. That's the setup you're aiming for, eh?"

"It sounds creepy when I hear someone else say it, but yes, that is exactly what I want to set up. Also, can we use Tessa's voice for multiple variations after this and not just this once?"

"We're just starting to appreciate what AI can accomplish," Sita said, "but I know what you're looking for exists already. I mean today and not some future B.S., but I have to be honest with you. I'm not entirely comfortable with you doing this in isolation. Can't we at least observe you so you have a backup if something goes sideways?"

"Look, I trust you—both of you. I honestly don't know what is going to happen. What if your proximity to me while I'm under impacts you in some awful way? I couldn't handle it if that happened, so I must take this first step on my own. Think of it like taking a new car out for a test drive. I want to know what I can and cannot do before I involve you any deeper. Does that make sense?"

"You're an honorable man, Jaxon Beck. I trust you—and I'll support whatever you think is needed to make this work. But I want your word. When this first solo test is finished, we're more involved. Not just watching, but part of it. Do you agree?"

"Thank you, Leif. That means a lot, and you will definitely be a part of this as long as I know this will not be detrimental to either of you. Sita, you got quiet there."

"No. I get it, Jax. I'm just worried that you're jumping out of an airplane without a parachute. I like being there for you—I'm not comfortable with how you're going about doing this, that's all."

"Yeah, I care about you, too. That's why I have to do this my way."

It was eerie knowing that the words being spoken were not actually coming from his wife, but so be it. His little speech to Sita and Leif also applied to Tessa. If something went wrong and if having her anywhere near him brought harm to her, then he wouldn't be able to live with himself. No, what he had set up was a close second, and he left everyone he cared about as far from it as possible.

"I want you to put the visor on now," Tessa's voice said. "But please leave the EMDR light off for the moment. I want you to relax as much as possible, so we're going to have you concentrate on your breathing while you focus on the sound of my voice."

Jax had spent the better part of two days outlining a specific memory in such a way that he could determine if an effect had actually occurred, yet innocuous enough that nothing critical would happen either way. He decided to concentrate on the day of his wedding reception.

After their wedding ceremony, they returned to his father's spacious backyard. He had written in detail about the small episode where the dogs, Bear and Bravo, had gotten overly excited and knocked the wedding cake onto the ground. Nothing important as far as he and Tessa were concerned, but still, something he might be able to establish if he could, in fact, change an autobiographical outcome.

"Your breathing is excellent," Tessa's simulation said. "Now let's take a ride down this comfortable elevator in front of you. You are completely safe and are becoming increasingly relaxed as we continue.

"As you enter the lift, you notice a small light above the doors that indicates the floor levels. As you settle in, the light shows you were on the tenth floor, and now it gently descends to the ninth, breathing deeply and relaxed. Now the eighth floor, and then the seventh, going deeper and deeper. Passing the sixth floor, then the fifth. You are totally relaxed and enjoying the elegant comfort of the elevator's interior. Now you pass the fourth floor...then the third, going deeper and deeper as you get closer to the ground level. Descending past the second floor, the lift gently stops on the first floor. The doors silently open, and you walk out to a stylish yet comfortable grand entrance room. As you glance around, you see the comfortable sofas and chairs where people are gathered, laughing and enjoying themselves."

Jax had purchased several induction downloads for self-hypnosis over the years. But whether it was due to the comfort of his wife's voice or just his state of mind, these instructions felt like something at a much higher level. The experience felt more personal, more relatable. He was being guided by the voice of someone he loved, and he felt the induction process was proving a complete success.

"I'm going to have you switch on the light and background audio on your visor and begin your journey to a time in your past that was happy and deeply fulfilling. Let the aura come and carry you away. You recognize that the rainbow starburst is there to guide you and means you no harm. You move up and through towards the white light."

"You are at your wedding reception," Tessa's voice continues, "in your father's backyard, and you have just finished off a glass of champagne from a crystal flute. You are at the house where you graduated from a youth to being an adult..."

As the white light retreated, Jax looked all around him at the gathering of friends and family. He could feel the warmth of the late summer afternoon and the beginnings of perspiration under his tuxedo. His head was swimming a little bit from the wine, but he was overwhelmed as he stood looking at the face of his new bride.

When the DJ invited the couple to come up in front of the crowd, Jax noticed the dogs playing too close to the table holding the three-tiered wedding cake and remembered his mission, which was to invoke this memory. He started forward, shooing the dogs back into the yard, but in his haste and slight intoxication, struck the corner of the table with his hip. He tried to catch the collapsing table, but his effort shook the cake off its stand.

While the crowd of guests gasped at the disastrous accident, Tessa sat down next to her husband and was quiet for a long moment. Then she smiled at him and picked up a handful of the ruined cake. Laughing, she daubed it on his lips. All he could think about was how glad he was she agreed to marry him. When he accepted that his visit had concluded, he whispered the name *Bear*, and the aura returned to his vision. Regaining the feel of the laboratory chair on his back, he gently stirred.

Removing the visor, he sat on the edge of the chair. He was confused about what had happened. His head was spinning, and he had a loud ringing in his ears. His vision was a little blurry, and for an instant, he could swear he saw his little finger fading in and out of existence. Taking a deep breath, his hearing calmed down, and his vision returned to normal. Holding his hand up, his little finger was still missing.

Standing and shaking off the effects of the strange return, he realized that in some backhanded way, he'd accomplished the objective of his test. He had changed the remembered event from one in which the dogs caused the accident at the reception to one in which he was the one who caused it. Taking a few steps towards the lab doors, he had the sensation as if he were a little hungover. That, and he could swear he still held the distinct taste of champagne on his tongue.

28

Confirmation

As Saturday was Mark Beck's 65th birthday, Jax convinced Tessa to join him once again on a trip to Colorado Springs. This time, he had sweetened the deal by arranging a room at the Broadmoor Hotel. Although the rooms and service were top-notch, what Tessa loved most was walking the grounds of the five-star hotel, especially the private Cheyenne Lake with its elegant swans and other waterfowl.

He owed her a real vacation after what had transpired in the past weeks. He admitted he could use a complete change of pace in his own life, if for no other reason than to escape the technical carnival he had constructed. He also had an ulterior motive.

Jax kept things light on the drive down the I-25 and focused on simply enjoying his wife's company. He had made the arrangements to take his father and Molly out to one of their favorite spots just outside the hotel proper, the Golden Bee.

It was an upbeat atmosphere in the style of an English pub, with sing-a-longs, yards of ale, and a higher quality of food than one would expect from a local bar. Jax also welcomed the level of noise and the pub staff's playful antics, as they prevented any potential conversations about work. He would talk with Molly later.

After the two couples said their goodnights, Tessa persuaded Jax to take a stroll around the hotel grounds with the pretense of walking off dinner. Even though it was well into the evening, the lighting and innocuous security provided a bubble of safety that only affluence could provide.

Neither Jax nor Tessa would consider themselves part of the upper crust of society. They did, however, acknowledge they were fortunate enough to have reputable positions that afforded them these getaways every so often. The fact that these stays always put his wife into a romantic mood was just a side benefit.

When they reached the privacy of their room, Tessa coyly undressed, revealing her lacy black lingerie. Jax couldn't help but let his eyes roam over her body before stepping closer and pulling her into a passionate kiss. Their hands roamed each other's bodies, exploring every curve and crevice as the intensity between them grew. Not just the sexual satisfaction, but also how such intimate time together always blocked out the rest of the world. Finally spent, they enjoyed lounging in the king-sized bed, wrapped in each other's arms and lazily talking.

"My folks called me today," Tessa said quietly. "They want to come out for Christmas festivities and thought we might be up to going skiing and the like."

"I haven't been on skis for at least two years. That sounds good."

"So, my mum asked again if she's going to be a grandmother anytime soon. She thinks I'm getting a bit long in the tooth for babies now. I told her we're working on it—mostly so I wouldn't have to do that whole chat again. Honestly, she's relentless."

"Well, in her defense, we are coming up on our fifth anniversary soon, right?"

Smacking him lightly with a pillow, Tessa said, "Fifth! It's only been three! Or do I need to remind you once again that I still consider us newlyweds?"

"I think I need to be reminded at least a few more times. On a different subject, I was thinking that I kind of miss not having Bear around. It seems strange not to take him with us on a road trip."

"I know, but he's in good hands with the White's. Plus, I think he has a crush on their poodle. Good thing he's neutered."

"Is that a hint that you want me to get snipped?"

"We really haven't talked about having kids in a long time. Any thoughts on the subject?"

"That would mean a big change. I'm not against the idea, but I'm not sure I'm quite ready for sleepless nights and diaper changes."

"You poor boy. I think you'd adjust if we did decide to go down that road."

"Oh, I'm not concerned about me. I was just thinking how tough it would be for you, handling all that baby stuff and still being able to do your job."

"You are a stinker, you know that, Dr. Beck."

"So my wife keeps telling me. Hey, do you remember at our reception how the dogs knocked over the wedding cake?"

"What are you talking about?"

"You know, just before we cut the cake, how Bear and Bravo were wrestling and took out the table leg."

"You are starting to lose your tolerable sense of humor. You know you nearly tripped on the way to the dogs and knocked the cake onto the floor. God, what a laugh! I don't think I loved you more than in that instant. The brilliant scientist with a boy's heart."

"Shit, you're right. I am a brilliant scientist."

"Sir, if you are making fun of me again, I shall have to report you to my husband."

"No. I just remember how happy I was that day. So, are we ready for sleep?" Turning off the lamp, he lay on his back and gazed at the ceiling. The textures shifted as he let the pieces fall into place.

"I did it."

29

CHALLENGINGDAD

IN ADDITION TO MOLLY, Mark had invited several dozen people to his party, including buddies from the service, a few neighbors, and a couple Jax didn't recognize. Keeping with tradition, Jax was relegated to grilling duties while Mark tended bar. Both Tessa and Molly engaged the other guests in conversation, but always circled back to their men to offer their assistance when needed.

When everyone had had their fill of food and drinks, a trio of Mark's Air Force buddies played some easy jazz, which quieted the conversation and inspired several couples to enjoy the impromptu dance floor on the back porch. This was also Jax's cue to corner his father to help settle his internal doubts about the restructured memories he had attained through his last test.

"Hey, Dad. Great party."

"Good friends and family, what more could a man ask for?"

"Would you mind if I ask you a couple of questions? I promise not to keep you from your party for too long."

Without saying a word, Mark led the two men to his private den across from the living room. Mark gently shut the door behind them.

"Okay, son, what's on your mind?"

"First, and I know this sounds stupid, but do you remember the dogs nearly knocking over the wedding cake at the reception we had here?"

"Well, I remember Bear was still a puppy, and Bravo didn't know how to deal with all of that energy. Unfortunately, your clumsy attempt to keep them from hitting the table resulted in you knocking it over yourself. Lucky for you, your wife has a great sense of humor. Most women would have gone ballistic over that. So, why don't you get to what's really on your mind?"

"I've just been having difficulty with my memory lately, so it helps to have you as an anchor, that's all. I do have just one more question, but it's a bit more serious."

"Sure, but let's not abandon the party for too long, okay?"

"It's about Mom's accident."

"Shit, Jax. That's a lot more than serious—that's depressing."

"I know, Dad, and I wouldn't even bring it up if it wasn't important."

"Go ahead—ask."

"Did you know that Mom suffered from migraines?"

Mark nodded and looked at the ceiling before framing his answer. "She didn't want you to know. She thought it would worry you—distract you."

"Dad, I was seventeen when she died. Don't you think that distracted me?"

"You were grieving for your mother, Jax—I was grieving for my wife. I didn't see the point in adding more weight to an already fucked-up situation."

"But it wasn't just grief. It was confusion. I thought she was fine. Healthy. That her accident came out of nowhere. But she was in pain, and I didn't know anything about what she was going through. If I'd known, maybe I could have done something—I don't know, maybe not die?"

"Well, she had them for as long as I knew her. Some were worse than others, but she tried to downplay them around you—even around me to an extent."

"Did you know... Did I tell you after the accident that she was having a bad migraine when she crashed the car?"

"You were in shock—and honestly, I was too, so I don't recall. I just remember the EMTs bandaging your hand and then trying to take you to the hospital. You wouldn't leave until the other ambulance took your mother's body away... to the morgue."

"So, you just let it be? It's been twenty years, Dad. Were we ever going to talk about it, or were we going to keep a stiff upper lip and ignore that fact? I fucking needed you, Dad, and you weren't there. Then I find out all this shit about Mom that you knew about, but didn't think—what, I wasn't ready to talk about it?"

"She was stubborn and proud. It was her strength as much as her weakness. You want to stand there and whine because I didn't hold your hand the last twenty years—Dr. Beck?"

Jax turned and ran a hand through his hair. When he turned back to face his father, a single tear was forming in his eye. "Shit. You're absolutely right. It's bullshit to bring this up now. And on your birthday. I didn't mean to blindside you with this. It's a fucked-up thing to do, and I'm sorry."

Grasping his son's shoulder, Mark spoke in a near whisper. "Look, Jax, you were always brilliant. From the earliest time I can remember, there wasn't a puzzle you couldn't figure out or an equation you couldn't solve. I guess... Well, I guess I thought that brilliance meant you were aware, that you already knew what the score was with her, but didn't want to talk about it.

"You seem to forget how much you withdrew into yourself afterward. You didn't have any friends, or at least none I knew of. I love you, son. I'm sorry if it didn't seem like it to you, but sometimes you can be a little cold and intimidating—even to me."

Jax wiped the tear from his face, then hugged his father tightly. "Please know that I am very grateful for all you've done for me over the years. And I'm sorry that hasn't been said or made apparent to you in some way." He broke away but still held his father at arm's length. "At the risk of sounding even more like a selfish ass, may I ask you one last question? Not about Mom, but about how I lost my finger?"

"Nice transition there, Doctor. Well, yeah, that was a bit strange. They looked, but no one ever found it. Not the police or the EMTs. The hospital docs said they may have been able to reattach it. But, no, we never got an answer to that. Does that information help you in any way?"

"Yes, it does...somewhat. I didn't mean to get all dark and gloomy on your birthday."

Just then, there was a light knock on the door, and Molly entered. She looked at the somber faces of the two men. Mark walked over to meet her at the doorway.

"Is everything alright? Mark, they want you to cut your birthday cake."

"Sure. I believe we were just finishing up. I'm on my way out now. Jax, feel free to stay in here as long as you like. No rush."

"Thanks, Dad, I'll be right out."

As Mark left the room, Molly lingered for a moment, holding the door to purposefully block his exit. She was smiling, but it wasn't a pleasant smile.

"We haven't had a chance to talk, Jax. There's something you should know about the findings from VRMX Tech and the equipment. It will just take a minute."

"Okay—shoot."

"After running tests and not finding any malfunction, management had Mikey run the same test on volunteers that you had performed when you had your little...dream. Mikey took the exact steps as you, using twelve different individuals. Males and females between the ages of 25 and 40. All migraine sufferers."

"Don't keep me hanging here, Molly. I need to freshen my drink. Please get to the point and tell me what they discovered."

"According to the data, not one person had the same temporal episode as you. Also, not one recalled having even close to the level of distinctness with their memories that you experienced."

"Did they at least come up with a working hypothesis about why I had all of that, but they weren't able to replicate the same effect?"

"According to what they were willing to share, the working theory is that it has something to do with your specific biology, or rather, your neurobiology. Other than that, it's anyone's guess."

30

FRIENDS

HE STOOD FOR A long moment just looking at the dent in the thin metal locker. He raised his hand, acknowledging his bleeding knuckles, and nodded. "Stop whining and do something about it, you fuck!"

The metal scrape of the lab doors closing caught his attention, and he turned at the sound. Sita and Leif stood staring at him, still and silent. Their witness to his tantrum was...humiliating.

"So," Sita said casually, "was that some manly ritual thing, or did that cabinet do something to piss you off?"

Jax didn't answer—he couldn't answer. Instead, he turned his head and licked the small drops of blood from the back of his hand.

"Yeah, I thought so. Look, I saw you called a few minutes ago and figured... Well, I just thought it would be easier to show up in person rather than call you back. So, what's really going on with you, boss man?"

Collecting himself, he turned to face them. "Yeah, I'm sorry about that. I was trying to get a handle on things. I didn't mean to do...that."

"Mm," Leif muttered. "You are struggling with all that has happened, I can tell. And you feel alone in it—no door open, no one you trust with the heavy thoughts, ja?"

Jax tapped his nose with a finger and pointed at Leif. "You nailed it. Yeah, so here I am beating up this helpless cabinet because I need... I need to... shit!

"Look...seriously, I need to tease out the significance of what I've found, but I just can't seem to do this alone. I've racked my brain trying to make the pieces fit. To find some rational reason for all of it. I guess I want—no, I need you to help me make sense of this—and keep me from losing my friggin' mind!"

"I give my word," Leif said, "Whatever we can do—we're here. So, point."

"He means shoot," Sita said, "but... oh, hell, never mind. Go ahead and lay it out for us."

Jax spent most of the next hour explaining what he considered facts versus speculation. He told them about the solo visit he'd taken and filled in some gaps he hadn't told anyone else about.

"First, my mother did suffer from migraines, which I now know was the reason behind the car wreck that ended her life. I don't know what kept her from telling me about her condition. Maybe I was just a self-absorbed teenager. I don't know.

"Second, the formal experiment I undertook resulted in an amputated finger. Not that it's a big deal in my life at present, but still—where did the severed digit end up?

"Third, VRMX Tech wasn't able to produce the same test outcomes that we got. They concluded that these phenomena are due to my neuronal distinctiveness. Does that indicate that one's brain composition is unique, like fingerprints? Does that mean it's just me, or are there still others out there with this ability, and we just haven't found them yet?

"Lastly, my father and my wife remember my reception identically, specifically regarding the threat of the dogs and my graceless face-plant. In my original recollection, it was the wrestling dogs that ruined the cake, not me. Am I the only one who can tell that a change has occurred, or have we not asked the right questions?"

"But...nothing happens with Sita and me?" Leif asked. "We're still da same, ja? I mean—just so I know. It hasn't changed, has it?"

"Well, yeah, except the purple in Sita's hair isn't there anymore."

"Wait, my what? Hey, not to mess with your head further after everything you just said, but Jax, I've never had purple hair, even during my teen rebel days."

"Well, there you go. I'm just glad the change wasn't something more serious. So, let me add that every time I recall a memory in this fashion, something changes. It can be innocuous or more serious, like with my finger. I don't have a rulebook to follow here."

"Okay, let's talk about the changes when you return, or wake up, or whatever. Is this a weird quantum physics thing? Like, are you the thing that's affecting the world around you? You know, the observer effect, where things change when you look at them?"

"Dere is something that has been, eh... gnawing at me," Leif said. "I did not mention it when we first spoke. but—what if dere is a multiverse? And when you go into these, eh, trances, you are not just shifting yourself but stepping sideways—into a parallel timeline. Maybe dat is why only you remember how tings were before."

"That, my friend, was the first thing I thought of when I started to experience these memory do-overs. What keeps me from accepting that is the fact that the only things that have changed have been confined to my personal timeline. Hell, this can't even be explained away as some damn Mandela Effect thing, like with *Captain Crunch* or the *Monopoly* guy's monocle. Everything that changes...it just happens to or around me. No one else notices the change."

"You can't disregard what Leif just laid out, though," Sita said. "The full multiverse theory also talks about branching timelines. For example, when you do your interventions, you could be creating a new timeline where things change around you but not to others."

"My gut says no, but I promise to keep that as a possibility. I'll try to find out more through research or by talking with a physicist who is more knowledgeable about such things. Just out of curiosity, where were you two when I took my solo trip last week?"

"Ah, that day of your solo test? Sita and I—we were in Fort Collins, ja. Visiting a friend at Colorado State University. We didn't even realize it was the same day—not until later."

"So, Tessa's memory, your dad's memory, and our two memories all align, but your mind remembers distinct differences each time you...do your thing. The first memory, or original memory, gets wiped and replaced by a duplicate, or separate memory. And that happens regardless of physical distance.

"Damn it, Jax, we need a common vocabulary for this shit. If for no other reason, so that I can keep track of what the hell we mean when we talk to each other."

"I've given that some thought. I know it isn't grammatically precise, but for simplicity, I want to call the initial memory the 1st Iteration. So, the new memory, or rewrite, I've designated as the 2nd Iteration."

31

Warning

Annoyed by the self-imposed confinement of the lab, Jax suggested they all grab an early dinner. They ended up at a tiny hole-in-the-wall restaurant two blocks from the university, and Sita ordered for everyone. If nothing else, the establishment's featureless exterior provided a degree of insulation from the Center and any curious onlookers.

"After you've laid everything out," Sita said, "I have a rough understanding of the changing memory thing. But now, I have some questions, or at least topics for discussion. Think about this. You clearly remembered the accident with your mom, so why don't you go back again and try for a different outcome?"

"Actually, I have considered that...seriously. In keeping with our parlance, going back again would be a third Iteration of the memory. I must admit I have concerns because I don't know enough about what's actually happening when I am in the moment. I...we have talked about this as an accessed memory in my brain. Honestly, I'm no longer sure that's an adequate explanation for what's going on with me."

"Ja," Leif said, nodding slowly. "You are remembering... or you are reliving, eh? Because dere's a difference, you know. Remembering—dat does not change the world. But reliving? Ah, that can. It can twist things, make them worse... second time, third time, ja—even fourth. So... is this what we are saying now?"

"Yes. I think you summed up precisely what I'm stuck on regarding that issue."

"Are there markers," Sita said, "that we can use while you are living an iteration? Hang with me while I use a hypothetical. For example, you're in a diner, and a server spills a drink right before a man enters and begins shooting people. Is the spilling of the beverage a marker that tells you what is about to happen?"

"I've spent the last three days playing with this hypothetical. Going with what you just laid out, what would happen if I stood up and rushed to the door when I heard the drink spilling? Would that prevent the shooting from occurring? Would I be able to stop the shooter? Or, what if a person was supposed to be killed, but I prevented that? What if that person ends up committing a worse crime because I intervened?"

"In keeping with that line of thought," Sita said, "you mentioned you grabbed the steering wheel to prevent the collision. Is the accident a fixed point in time, where no matter what you try to do, no matter how many times you go back, the outcome remains the same? I'm not trying to be pessimistic here, but is that a possibility? Are some things unfixable, inflexible, or unbending...shit, this stuff messes with my head!"

"Welcome to my world. And remember, this is only about the timeline of my life—an autobiographical limit, if you will. I can't jump into my eleven-year-old body and prevent the 9/11 attacks from happening. I'm still eleven years old. What would I do if I bounced back to when I was one or two? Even having the cognitive abilities of a man my age, I'd still be a toddler—I couldn't do shit!"

The food arrived, and the trio focused on consuming the spread before them, partly because they were all hungry and partly as a respite from the mental exercise they were engaged in. After most of the food was eaten, they resumed their deliberations.

"I mentioned that VRMX Technologies tried testing this on other people, but came away with the notion that I have a unique brain and am unable to recreate this ability in others. Do we take their word for it, or is this something worth exploring further?"

"To what end?" Leif said, tilting his head. "You must look at what you can do... and what you cannot, ja? This thing—this ability you speak of—it is like Spiderman, no? You understand—a great power equals great responsibility thing. You know this. But do you know how to control it? I think... not yet. First, you must find your limits. Then, maybe, you can bring others in on your efforts."

"Good point," Sita said. "So, what is our next step to get you the information you need to answer some of the questions we just voiced?"

"Part of what I've already beat myself up about is that I did my solo thing without fleshing out the entire experience in greater detail. I need to lay out some memories that are solid enough so that when I do a 2nd Iteration, I have as much knowledge about the time I'm in, so, if it's possible, I can make a change—a measurably positive change."

Sita started to say something in response, but Jax held up a hand to stop her when he noticed a man wearing a dark suit and shaded glasses at the entrance to the small restaurant. He acted casual enough as he stepped up to the counter and read the menu posted to the side. There was just...something about his movements. Something that deeply bothered Jax when he glanced at him.

Jax's hand gestured to gain their attention. "We need to get out. Now."

Sita's head began to swivel toward the entrance, but Jax laid his hand on her forearm, his eyes drilling into hers with such intensity that she froze. Abandoning their meal, they slid from their seats in unison, Sita taking point through the cramped tables while Jax's heart hammered against his ribs.

Just before reaching the exit, the suited man caught Jax's eye and raised two fingers—barely anything. Jax stopped and turned. The space where the man had been standing was empty, the menu still swinging on its hook. Jax pushed into the door hard. A voice came from somewhere close behind him, low enough that only he could hear it. "You think you know what you're doing. You've no idea the cost."

32

Short Steps

Dr. Mason just stared at Jax from across his cluttered desk. He had the habit of chewing on the end of pens when he was contemplative, and one was currently dangling from his lips. For his part, Jax sat perfectly still, permitting the silence to convey his position.

"So, Dr. Beck," Dr. Mason said, "what does all of this have to do with your work on migraine research?"

"I'm not completely sure. Which is why I want the freedom to explore it further."

"And you want me, the Center, and the University to pay for this fantasy?"

"Well, let me ask you, what became of the proposal I submitted to you? I'm about to have all my funding end, and you haven't said shit to me in the past weeks."

"I'm still waiting for a response. Please remember, you work for the Center and for me. You have conveniently forgotten that I provided you the professional courtesy of telling you I needed something concrete from your research. What have I gotten instead? Some unsupported pitch about how you can get neurons to rewire themselves. It's horseshit!"

"What if I'm right, and my findings end up being published by some other research center? What do you think the Chancellor will think of his Center Director then? And what the hell happened to you being a scientist? Now you're just a damn accountant!"

"Fuck you! I've done a lot of good here. The other labs have produced solid neuroscience research. You want to play around..."

"...because you were too cheap and narrow-minded!"

"Get out of my office! And remember everything in that lab is the property of this Center, including all your data. If you ignore that fact, then you will be stuck in lawsuits until you're an old man."

Dr. Mason just stared at Jax from across his cluttered desk. For his part, Jax sat perfectly still, permitting the silence to convey his position. A pen dangled from the Director's lips as it often did when the man was planning his next move.

What Jax saw himself doing was totally strange, even by his standards. He literally was just here minutes ago, and he and Mason had started this conversation in exactly the same way as the first.

But now he had returned using a 2nd Iteration bump in his memory. To support his theory, the result this time needed to be different.

"So, Dr. Beck," Dr. Mason said, "what does all of this have to do with your work on migraine research?"

"I'm confident we will have the answer to that question soon. Which is why I want to explore it further."

"And you want me, the Center, and the University to pay for this fantasy?"

"Well, Amy and Gabe haven't been on my payroll for a while now, so I was hoping you could use those unspent funds to give me an extension. Also, may I ask if there's been any movement regarding the proposal I submitted to you?"

"I'm still waiting for a response. You know these things take time."

"Certainly, Steve, I understand that. This is one of the reasons I am requesting some leeway. By continuing to investigate a variety of methodologies, we increase the likelihood of identifying crossroads with the research conducted by the Center's other two laboratories. Furthermore, demonstrating practical applications for various conditions may enhance our prospects for securing external funding."

"You surprise me, Jax. That is very sound reasoning and a very good way to frame your work. Okay. I'll see what I can do to push that deadline back to the end of the year. If you come up with other uses that can be shared with your peers here, then we can talk more about a long-term solution. Is that acceptable?"

"Thanks, Steve. One more small thing. You met Leif Thorsen during our last experiment. Leif would like to work with us as a part-time intern—unpaid, of course."

"That can be arranged. I'll see that he gets a security pass for the building."

"Thanks for your help, Dr. Mason. I'll plan on talking with you later."

When he exited Dr. Mason's office, Jax stood still in the hallway. He waited for the rainbow aura to appear, then beckoned the kaleidoscope of colors to envelope him. Once the usual tingling in his body dissipated, he became aware of his body lying in the chair in his lab. He removed the visor and immediately cupped his hands over his ears. That same loud ringing in his ears that he'd experienced before was back, making his eyes ache. He saw Sita trying to talk to him and held up a hand signaling he needed a moment to collect himself. After a minute, the sound faded, and he exhaled loudly.

"Jax, are you alright?" Sita asked.

"Yeah. I just hit a little turbulence landing, but I'm fine now."

"So, were you able to get what you wanted?" Sita asked.

"Yes, my short-term memory test was quite successful."

Sita pointed at Jax. "Boss, your nose is bleeding a little."

Jax reached up and wiped the droplet from his face. "Sinus issues. No big deal."

"But I don't understand, no," Leif said. "You didn't do the first part before the EMDR, ja? You just took some deep breaths, a minute goes by, then—puh—you exhale, and you take off the visor. Tell me, how is this a success, then?"

"He's right, this time compression thing is really weird. Are you sure you're okay?"

"Well, I can tell you that the meeting with Dr. Mason during this 2nd Iteration allowed me to convince him to extend our funding for a few more months. Also, Leif, you are now officially a part-time intern with our team."

"I know you said we were going to test that theory, but you never told us it was with Dr. Mason. Short-term memory mostly involves hearing and seeing, but it's also fragile. Long-term memory, on the other hand, is highly structured and involves a multitude of networks and associations."

"As you said, short-term memory is fragile, so I made a recording of the 1st Iteration to help me hold on to the first few moments of our meeting. I used a marker, like you suggested, Sita, to give me a prompt and to help me focus—it was Dr. Mason chewing on his pen. I don't see myself using that little trick often, though. There isn't much benefit to what we are trying to accomplish."

"Do you still have it? The tape recording, I mean—I love ancient technology."

Jax pulled out the micro-recorder and rewound the tape. When he pressed the play button, there was only the sound of static, but no conversation.

"Well, that tells me that without the helmet, any proof I possess is just in my brain."

"Okay. So, what kind of test are we talking about now, then? You've got a plan, ja? Something with... specific outcomes, maybe?"

"I have a concept of a plan. I need to work with the two of you to help me literally map out my history and match that to events or incidents I may want to alter. It seems that using this technique has accomplished two things already. The first is that I haven't had a serious migraine in a while. Secondly, my comings and goings through the aura phase into the 2nd Iteration are a bit easier and more controlled."

"You're forgetting," Sita said, "that we still have to submit weekly reports to Dr. Mason. If you don't want to share what we're working on with your 2nd Iteration visits, then we need to have another project that's running in parallel. We will at least have something substantial to show what we're working on while in the lab."

"Why don't we go with what Gabe mentioned a few weeks ago. Let's set up Vagus nerve stimulation units and maybe some biofeedback devices that Tessa told me about. Using the data we already collected with the TMS machine, we research whether it's possible to train the brain to stop migraines. Behavior modification at its best."

"I like it, boss. And this equipment is relatively cheap. We just need to sign up more volunteers. The new semester starts in about a week, so fresh meat."

"We must do this mapping of your life somewhere else, ja? Not here. If Amy or Dr. Mason walks in on it—poof—they blow da whistle, and then we are finished."

"I can start by creating dedicated e-mail accounts for each of us. Jax, you start the process by developing a rough outline of your life, then you'll share it with us, and we'll ask probing questions to help fill in important details about that period. You should limit the range, though. As you said before, your adult consciousness placed into the body of a six-month-old won't do you any good other than as an observer."

"When does self-awareness begin? Do we know that?

"Give me a minute to run a Google search here, and—okay, self-awareness can occur as early as one and a half to two years. But one attains a stable self-concept and theory of mind around five. I think that might be too young if you're looking at interacting during a 2nd Iteration, don't you think? You'd probably scare people."

"I was eight, you know, when my papa took me hunting," Leif said softly. "I still see the face of the deer I had shot—but not killed, no. She looked at me. Papa said I must finish it. So, I did. I slit the throat, as he told me. I don't forget the look in her eyes."

Sita's eyes widened. "That's... just awful, Leif. No child should have to do something like that." She wrapped her arms around his waist and gave the large man a gentle hug. He bent down and kissed the top of her head. The image of their affection made Jax stop and think of Tessa. He knew they loved each other, but they rarely showed their feelings publicly. He asked himself whether that was due to their positions or a harsher commentary about him as a man.

Shaking his head to refocus on the conversation, he picked up a pen and a tab of paper from a nearby desk. "Yes, rather brutal. But it does provide an answer to the question. I don't know if five is too young or not, depending on what I would need to do. When you're eight, you remember things better and have a bit more mobility. Jeez, thirty years of memories I need to sort through.

"Well then, what I will need from you two is a list of events going back roughly the last thirty years, so we can do a comparison. High-profile events with a lot of information. That will not only allow me to fully prepare but also give us something to better compare the 1st and 2nd Iterations. That way, I have something more concrete to verify that my intervention worked."

Jax started to walk away, then thought for a moment and turned back, leaning closer to the couple. "Look," he whispered. "I know this may sound morbid, but this event we're looking for—people should have died."

33

Camouflage

"Jeez, Sita, I am totally impressed! So, tell me, what exactly am I looking at here? I mean, the abstract for this paper is very well written, but can you break down the essence of what it's saying?"

"No problem, boss. I'll try to summarize. The research from the last year studying transcranial magnetic stimulation, or TMS, was focused on two applications. One was an acute treatment, and the other, a preventive treatment. We've seen success with acute migraines by calming the excited membrane, and the preventative treatment has helped with reducing migraine frequency and intensity. Amy wrote about this, and it was published two months ago.

"I contacted research centers studying Vagus nerve stimulation, or VNS, and cited their work to support our study. I called back as many volunteers from our TMS project as possible to test the VNS and then compared treatment effects. By the way, the only cost of all that work was me losing so a lot of sleep. I submitted the final paper to the same journal where you published two articles last year. This one's under review, but the editor was optimistic about it being included in next month's publication."

"Also. Sita—she's already written one popular online article, ja? I think the plan was to spark interest in... neryo—no, neuro—eh, those brain things, you know? But I'll admit it—she's got a way with words. Very sharp. Very dramatic. Clever, ja?"

"Stop it, boys," Sita joked, "you're making me blush." Remember, Jax, all these articles are being written under your name. If there's any blowback, it's not my ass on the line...it's yours!"

"Well, that clarifies why we've had all the people coming and going through here. Have you come across anyone else who's undergoing the same type of study? At least that you're aware of? I don't want to be accused of plagiarizing anyone."

"When I wrote this up for you, all I could find were researchers looking at the effects of either TMS or VNS. A few others are in the middle of comparing the effects of magnetic versus electrical stimulation, but no one is conducting head-to-head studies. Although our sample size isn't large, it's still the first of its kind."

"So, what I'm showing to Dr. Mason is that we are continuing to contrast the effects of the two different treatments here in the lab. And if we secure funding to increase our sample size, we'll improve the validity of future test results. Yeap! I think that should satisfy him."

"Jax, now that I have your attention, I need to bring up another subject. Look, having us work here in the lab is perfect for this study for sure, but I have to tell you—I'm glitching when it comes to the other thing. I mean, we can't openly discuss our...extra research here."

"Ja, I feel the same. I can't let myself explore those possibilities—not here. Doesn't feel secure, ja?"

"I don't disagree with what either of you is saying, but where else can we talk about this freely? I don't think my tiny office is going to be much better."

"You know, I bet Tessa probably has access to empty rooms at the hospital. Do you think she'd be open to us working on this if you asked her? Especially knowing that she's already worried about your health from the last major experiments."

"If I had to speculate, I would say yes. But damn, I'd really hate to put her on the spot like that. Realistically, you're right. I don't have a better alternative, and it needs to be someplace that's close to the Center in case Dr. Mason or others try to reach me."

"You've talked with her about your 2nd Iteration work, ja? I mean... she already knows what you've been doing. I'm right—or no?"

"I haven't found the right time to talk with her about it. Plus, she's been at a conference in Los Angeles this last week and just got back. Aside from my solo trip to our wedding reception and the test of short-term memory a couple of weeks ago, I haven't tried experimenting with it again."

"I, for one," Sita said, "think that is a smart idea. We really need time to plot out when you want to revisit and for what purpose. I like having a plan, even if it's just a stronger outline to follow. You know, something we have agreed to among ourselves."

"There is one other thing I haven't mentioned to you. My migraines have come back. So far, they're not major, but I can't help but draw a connection between the interruption of migraine events and the 2nd Iteration visits. Just in the last two weeks, I've already gotten three, just like before."

"Well," Sita said, "we just need to add that as one of the hypotheses to be tested."

"Look, Fridays are usually an early day for Tessa at the hospital. Why don't I arrange a small gathering at our place? Having you as a backup will let me explain the process more objectively. Plus, there's less chance she'll throw something at me!"

Amy Taylor lingered by the cracked lab door, thumb hovering over her phone's recording app before pressing stop. She slipped away, her footsteps silent on the polished floor. "Damn it, Jax,"

she breathed, barely audible. "Are you trying to get thrown out of here?"

Halfway down the corridor, she froze, glancing over her shoulder and back at the lab doors. She pulled up Mason's contact and stared at his name. Her finger drifted to it once, then away. If she called him now, she was the one who'd handed over a colleague—her finger on the trigger. She locked her phone and kept walking. There was a right moment for this to happen. She needed to think this through.

34

RELUCTANTCOMMITMENT

"LOOK," TESSA SAID TENTATIVELY, "I know I've been busy at the hospital and then gone for a week in LA, but I feel I've missed a year's worth of news from you guys. The last thing I heard was that Steve extended your work for a few more months."

"Tessa, that's still correct. What I haven't told you is that the work I've done—well, what mostly Sita and Leif have done—is just a distraction. What we've really been trying to do is study what happens during a 2nd Iteration visit."

Through squinted eyes, Tessa prompted, "And what exactly do you mean by that, Jax?"

"You got a hint of it," Sita said, "during the last experiment when you were with us at the lab. We all heard Amy talking to the VRMX Tech guy about how the helmet registered a temporal anomaly while Jax was in his trance. What happened during his remembering of his mother's accident... that's what we call a 2nd Iteration."

Stiffening her back, Tessa crossed her arms and raised her chin. "Clearly, but all I heard was a bunch of techno-babble about over-writing his neurons. Are you saying you've been screwing around with this—this whatever without telling me about any of it?!"

"Tess, I haven't done much of anything so far. Part of the reason we're asking if you could carve out an unused room or two at the hospital is so we can plan it...safely."

"You honestly believe that screwing around with your brain like that is safe? And, what the fuck do you mean when you say you haven't done much? How much is much?"

"Remember our trip to the Broadmoor? The night I asked you about our wedding reception?"

"What about it?" Tessa said, running her hand through her hair.

"I asked if you remembered the dogs crashing the table and, as a result, our wedding cake. You told me that wasn't what happened. That I was actually the one who crashed the table and not the dogs."

"Is this like the finger thing that you said happened when you remembered the accident?" Now Tessa was twirling a loose strand of hair through her fingers. "Jax, are you able to put this into simple words that I can digest before we go any further?"

"I'm really sorry, hon. I understand that I'm throwing a lot at you at once, but things have been moving at what seems like light speed. I haven't been trying to hide anything from you. It's just that we're trying to preserve the inroads we've made, and we—that is, I haven't had the time to sit you down and explain it all to you."

"So, it was really the dogs? And you somehow... what, you changed that?"

Tessa brought the glass of wine to her lips as she surveyed the three faces now sitting around her in their living room. Jax had sat in front of her when he started speaking more seriously after dinner. She had an inkling that something was afoot when Sita placed herself in Tessa's direct line of sight, although Leif had retreated to the far end of the room, observing rather than participating.

"You do know that, as a trained psychiatrist, what I hear you telling me just now could be classified as standard delusional behavior?"

Jax got up and sat by her side. He lightly stroked her arm with his fingertips. "And you know," he said tenderly, "that I am your husband. Before being an MD or neuroscientist, I am your husband. I know how this all sounds, I do, but you have my word... What I'm telling you is real."

"What we don't have," Sita said, "is the equipment like before. If I hadn't seen the printed results from that experiment, I would probably have to agree with you. But I've come to trust what Jax says. With any luck, and a lot of ass kissing, we may get the helmet back and then have demonstrable evidence that such occurrences are real and not some form of Mandela Effect."

"I am painfully aware," Tessa said, "when our brain reconstructs memories, it often fills in gaps with assumptions or associations. Add on social reinforcement where many people share the same incorrect memory, and it feels validated. The fucking Internet has only made our collective concept of reality worse with misquotes, memes, and viral content... Everyone's questioning what is and isn't real anymore!"

Jax took her free hand and gave it a gentle squeeze. "Tess, try not to lock me up, but there's another thing that's been going on for a while. There have been people showing up on the edges of my world who I don't know and who don't belong on campus. One guy showed up in my classroom when this was all just getting started. Then, the other day, another guy shows up when the three of us are having lunch and warns me in an odd way to back off."

The harsh ringing sound of her wine glass landing on the coffee table stopped the conversation. "Oh great, so you are delusional and paranoid? What the bloody hell, Jax?"

"He is not wrong, Tessa," Leif said low. "Jax—he has not shown signs he's off his rocker. He's someone I trust. Is he... any less to you?"

Tessa broke from Jax's embrace, rising from the couch and going into the kitchen. She stopped at the wine cooler, grabbed another bottle, and pulled the cork. No one spoke. Sita retreated to sit next to Leif and nestled into his embrace.

After a pause, Tessa brought the bottle back with her to the living room, reclaimed her seat, and filled her wine glass. She placed the bottle where the others could reach it, but no one dared move.

"Damn you, Leif," Tessa sighed. "If anyone else had asked me that, I would have thrown them out on their arse. No, you are correct. I trust what Jax is telling me is true. But that doesn't mean I have to agree that what he is doing is right in any way.

"You two didn't have to pick him up from the emergency room. You didn't have to steer him out of his father's house like some comatose patient. You didn't have to slap him back to consciousness while he was lying on that chair, scared to death that your love might be dying or brain-damaged!"

As she turned to face her husband, her voice tightened. "But you, Jax. You just want me to smile and go along for the ride like none of that ever happened. Well, it has happened! And it didn't just happen to you. It happened to me as well. It's happened to us, damn it! How am I supposed to just say, la-di-da? And of course, please bring on the next round, dear?

"And while I have your attention. Have the three of you stopped to fully consider the ramifications of your actions? Have you taken a breath to consider if this course of action could result in some form of permanent injury to your brain? And then there's the issue of whether your paranoia is a real threat. What about the physical danger you are placing us in by staying on this path?"

"Tessa, my sweet Tessa. I have been a selfish bastard. You're right that I have been seeing this through my own lens. Please forgive me. I hope you understand that, because you are the only person on this earth that I trust with my life, I put you in that position. I didn't mean to be a thoughtless ass about it. I guess it just came naturally." Jax turned to Sita and Leif. "Hey guys, I'm sorry, but I think it's best we call it a night."

Sita and Leif stood to leave, but Leif stopped, his head slightly bowed. "Tessa, Jax, I am but a guest in your home, ja? May I please be allowed to speak? I will be quick, and then I will go, surely."

"Of course, Leif," Tessa said sadly. "I'm sorry to chase you off. Please know that."

"I speak only from deep respect for both of you. Tessa...I hear you truly. You love this man, ja? And you are afraid of losing him. Anyone can see that. You are not wrong to worry. If I had a partner doing what Jax is doing, I would worry too.

"But I have seen what this does to him—not just the danger, but the meaning. Some people are born with a thing they cannot ignore. Jax is one of them. In my country, we say the gift and burden are often the same thing. Jax has both. And this world... I am believing, it may need what he can do."

Tessa was still, looking at Leif, then at Jax, then back to Leif. "God, I hate that I know you're right. It's just...I love him. Jax, you can still... We can just keep having a life together, right? I know you think this is important, but if I lose you—" Tears showed in her eyes, threatening a storm.

"Tess," Jax said, voice cracking. "You know me better than any other person on this planet. Honestly, how would you answer that question if the roles were reversed?"

"I know. Oh, I know." Tessa stood and walked towards their bedroom. "I'm exhausted," she sighed. "I'm going to call it a night. I'll think about what you said. Just give me some time, that's all I ask." She nodded her head to each person, then retreated into the bedroom and softly closed the door.

35

DECEIT

LATE AFTERNOON SUNSHINE SLIPPED through the blinds, casting striped shadows across Dr. Mason's desk. Amy stood just inside the doorway, arms casually folded, her ID badge swinging slightly. Dr. Mason gestured to the chair opposite him, his expression impatient as he continued writing.

"Amy, you said you wanted to speak with me privately. Something to do with the migraine study that was making you uncomfortable? Isn't that what you said?"

Rather than sitting in the chair itself, Amy chose to perch on its arm with her legs still planted on the floor. She waited until she had his attention before speaking. "I believe I used the term uneasy."

"Amy, I have a meeting with the Chancellor in half an hour, so please get to the point."

Amy pulled out two stapled sheaves of paper and held one up. "This is the proposal Jax wrote to you a little while ago about his experiment using the Kernel Flow data, detailing a temporal anomaly and how he posits that with adequate backing, he has a serious chance of mitigating, if not eliminating, migraines, OCD, and PTSD. He further states the possibility of treatment for more severe neurological conditions, such as Epilepsy and Parkinson's."

Amy lowered the paper to see Dr. Mason's expression, but he was just staring at her. "What is your point, Ms. Taylor? It is a proposal that is, after all, based on data you yourself interpreted from that experiment."

"Amy lowered the first report and held up the second. "Fine. Then, if Jax and his team are preparing to jump into curing neurological ills, why are they conducting experiments on TMS and VNS and publishing papers on those results? What is the real focus of that lab and his team?"

Dr. Mason pushed his chair back from his desk, never taking his eyes off his young protégé. He chewed on his pen for a few seconds before a large smile spread across his face. He removed the pen and pointed it at her. "You're jealous. Jax's down there without you, and without Gabriel, I might add. And he's kicking ass."

Amy was shocked into silence. She slid into the chair and just stared at the Director. "Jealous? Jealous?! You don't even know what the hell they're really doing down there. Sita wrote this article, not Jax! A damn technician with a bachelor's degree. Jax is busy playing around with memory stuff he's calling 2nd Iteration or some such thing. He's convinced himself that he can time-travel.

That proposal he wrote is so he can measure the changes when he does these activities or whatever he's calling them.

Dr. Mason sat forward, placing his elbows on the desk. "That's a rather serious claim. So, there's nothing to what he said about treatments for OCD and the like?"

"Well, there may be. Hell, I don't know how much is truth and how much is fantasy with him. The temporal anomaly could possibly overwrite the looping found in OCD and PTSD patients, but there's no way we can say there's a causal effect with this."

"He never claimed there was one. He is merely suggesting there is enough evidence to research it further. I'm getting a little frustrated by your reaction here, and I'm going to be late for my meeting. You have enough to get your degree, and I'm not going to block you from getting it. Just decide if your future is here or somewhere else. Okay?"

Dr. Mason stood, clearly expecting her to leave. Amy didn't say another word but collected her things and quickly left his office, obviously shaken to her core. After the room was empty and the door closed, Dr. Mason sat back down at his desk and lifted the phone to his ear. He dialed the number by memory, and it connected on the second ring.

"You asked me to inform you if there were any promising results that might prove to be advantageous. I believe if you're going to do anything with what we discussed earlier, you'll need to do it soon.

No, that didn't seem to have slowed him down. Yes, I think that's a fair assessment of the situation. If I find out anything more, I'll get back with you."

36

SurpriseVisit

The lab doors opened noiselessly as the Director walked in and casually headed straight for Jax's cubicle. He glanced at Sita and Leif as he made his way across the large room, but did not offer them any form of greeting.

"Hey, Dr. Mason. To what do I owe the honor?"

"Jax, I've been wanting to witness what you've accomplished these past weeks, but haven't had the time until just now. I was hoping you could show me around and give me a firsthand account of the results from your work."

"Well, I'd be happy to show you what we have so far. I take it you've read the journal article on the magnetic and electric stimulators and their efficacy in reducing migraine events and serious headaches?"

"Yes, as a matter of fact, I have. I must admit, I was a bit surprised by how quickly you produced the results of that initial research.

So, what are you doing with the volunteers I see coming and going through here?"

"That published paper detailed some of the results from prior TMS tests and compared them to new tests specifically utilizing Vagus nerve stimulation. Our current work is focusing on the use of this treatment on a few of Tom's Epilepsy patients and some of Jane's OCD volunteers. We've even had a few patients diagnosed with PTSD who were referred by therapists from the hospital. As I suggested when we last met, I'm hoping to determine if these treatments have applications to other neurological conditions."

"That's very ambitious. May I see the results you've gotten from these examinations thus far?"

"We've only been on this for the past two weeks, so we only have the raw data. The sample sizes for each group are still too small to provide a clear picture. I can provide you with a rough table showing the results from each group of volunteers we've had so far, but we've had very few migraine sufferers volunteer, so we don't have the big picture. As you're aware, the new semester for the university doesn't start for another week, and most volunteers with migraines are students."

"Alright then, why don't we plan on revisiting this discussion at a later time. I take it you're not teaching this semester?"

"No, I'm not. I am trying to use the limited time you gave us to deliver concrete results for each of the Center's three laboratories.

We're doing our best to fulfill our part of the agreement to secure continued funding for our project. If the program is still robust in the new year, then I'll put my name down for teaching during the Spring semester."

"Fair enough. Jax, may I ask you another question—off the record?"

"Steve, I'll try to answer any questions you might have about the work we're doing."

The older man smiled at Jax and nodded his agreement while absently rubbing his shaved head. He looked around to ensure that Sita or Leif would not overhear their conversation. Then, he pointed to the coffee machine a few feet away. Jax waved a hand in that direction and followed the director to the beverage cart.

Nothing was said while Dr. Mason poured himself a cup of coffee, then opened two packets of sugar and stirred them into his drink. Jax could tell that his superior was deliberately taking his time in an attempt to use the pause as a tool to rattle him. Since he started exploring the 2nd Iteration, nothing much upset him, and certainly nothing the Director had to say was going to change that attitude.

"Jax," the older man finally said after sipping from his mug. "I'm worried about you. Just a couple of months ago, you were gung-ho about measuring neural networks as related to migraines. You got some interesting readings from the helmet monitor...then nothing. Whatever happened to that research? Or did you discover something that moved you away from continuing down that pathway? Maybe even something you don't want to discuss with me?"

Jax took a moment to interpret if there was a deeper meaning behind the question. He was also trying to get any clue as to whether Dr. Mason knew of his underlying work and, if so, how much of it he knew.

"Aside from waiting to hear back from you about some actual funding streams, I've been keeping busy. As you can see for yourself. Beyond this, if I thought there was anything worth sharing with you, Steve, I would." Glancing up at the wall clock, then back at Dr. Mason, Jax smiled at the Director. "Look, Steve, I don't mean to be rude, but I'm supposed to meet Tessa for lunch here in a few minutes."

"By all means," Dr. Mason said frostily. "Don't let me keep that beautiful wife of yours waiting."

37

PHILOSOPHY

"SCREW IT. WE ARE going to sit here and finish this excellent bottle of tequila. It may sound stupid, or juvenile, or some such thing, but damn it, we need to talk about this without any constraints. Are you in—are we ready?"

"But," Sita said, looking at Leif. "What about feeding my cat?"

"What cat?" Leif asked, confused. "When did you get a cat?"

With a coy grin, she said, "That was just my first toss at a fuck-it-all start to this discussion ...Namaste, my friends."

They threw back the shot glass that sat before them. Lifting the bottle, Leif filled everyone's small glass again and gave his own salutation.

"To my ancestors. May we all meet again, ja? One day, somewher e... we shall sit together once more."

Tessa chose that moment to arrive home. The team had put together a meal of finger food and set it out on the kitchen island.

Obviously exhausted, she gave a half-hearted wave and walked over to Jax and gave him a short, gentle kiss. He held up a shot glass for her, but she held up a hand refusing the offer. "I need some food first—I missed lunch. Thank you all for this, it looks amazing."

Tessa filled a plate and took a seat at the table. The others were already animated, their voices overlapping, riding the particular energy of people who had been drinking long enough to feel invincible. She poured herself a shot but left it sitting in front of her for a while before finally bringing it to her lips. She did not throw it back the way the others did. She was not quite there yet—not with the tequila, and not with any part of the topic being bandied about.

"Remember that scene from the original *Matrix* movie?" Sita asked. "The one where Keanu Reeves is in the kitchen with the Oracle, and she says, *'Don't worry about the vase.'* Then he turns and knocks over the vase. Then she asks him, '*Would you have still broken it if I hadn't said anything*?' That's where my head is right now."

"Ja, are you really changing parts of your past, Jax? Or did doing this... 2nd Iteration visit cause the thing that was meant to happen, eh? Maybe you think you're rewriting. But maybe you're just walking the path that was already laid out. Like the fjord—it curves, but it always leads to the sea."

"Wait. Wait. Wait. I'm going to have an aneurysm trying to keep track of this very heavy conversation. May I suggest we approach this as scientists and expose the overarching questions first, then discuss the peripheral issues?"

"And what," Sita said, "oh mighty guru, is the ultimate question here and now?"

"Let's start with what we know. For example, I possess this... Well, this ability that we call the 2nd Iteration. We have physical data showing that a temporal anomaly occurred in my brain, which, in effect, overwrote a memory that I posit changed the current day's reality. I have also shown I can replicate this... Or, at least I've proven this to myself.

"Lastly, before we get into the moral and ethical pros and cons, I believe that these visits I take provide relief from the attack and prodrome phases of my migraines. When I stop doing these visits, the full spectrum of the migraine returns, but I can't prove that at this point. The aura phase seems to be an integral part of the 2nd Iteration, acting as a sort of doorway to relive the memory and then, like a revolving door, becomes an exit back to the current time."

Everyone was quiet for a moment, digesting what Jax had just detailed. Leif stood and filled each shot glass. While he was busy with this task, Tessa pulled out a small pad of paper and intently wrote something on the page.

"Listening to you describe your experience," Tessa started, then stopped. "Well, the best way to state this is that what's happening to you—it's a kind of fusion, really, between neuroscience and metaphysics. Where it becomes more complicated is in what you choose to do—or not do—with that ability. That's where you start treading into moral philosophy, and the ethical questions around agency and responsibility."

Jax smiled lovingly at her and laughed softly. "I knew inviting a psychiatrist to this discussion was a great idea."

"I am having a strong belief, ja, from how I was raised—that we are here, you know, to serve. If you are calling my quasi-Christian faith something... metaphysical, then okay, that is fine by me. But this word you say—agency—can you tell what you mean? I am not quite catching the use, no."

"Agency in this context," Tessa said, "means to make decisions that reflect your values, desires, and reasoning. It implies ownership—not just reacting to conditions but actively choosing how to respond or intervene. Not to sound overly judgmental, but I believe Jax has already displayed this to some degree, but he has not yet fully grasped what his actions may produce in return. Either consciously or unconsciously, any future activity will cause a ripple effect that you will own."

"So, wait a second," Sita said, reaching across the table and clasping Tessa's hands. "Are you talking about a butterfly effect here? That if he visits himself at age seven and crushes a spider, then he causes a war in Greenland?"

Gently releasing herself from Sita's strong grip, Tessa continued. "Well, that's a touch more dramatic than what I was getting at. I do believe it's something that ought to be considered properly when you three are planning a visit. Who's present in that memory? Is there a clear sense of what you're hoping to achieve? And if a change does take place, are there consequences you haven't accounted for? From what you've told me, the things altered so far aren't terribly serious... Except for your finger, of course."

"An excellent point, which is why I wanted to be more cognizant of the when, where, and what before jumping back in for another visit. I've been trying to build a decision tree around the different periods of my life and see if there is something that happened around a certain age that I might be able to influence for the better."

"You know," Sita said, "my parents are practicing Hindus, and although I don't share most of their beliefs, there are basic philosophical teachings that transcend religion. What Tessa just said about ripple effects arising from altering fate is one. Another asks if the past is fixed or fluid. In Jax's case, that one hasn't been fully tested yet. The most interesting question for me is, should we act to undo pain, ours or another's, or accept and learn from it?"

"As a therapist," Tessa said, "we do make use of the ability to revisit and reshape traumatic memories—to treat PTSD, phobias, even persistent pain. Reframing the past can give someone back a sense of control over their personal narrative. There is, I'd say, a sound justification for that. I'm not quite sure you could apply the same reasoning if the aim were to benefit oneself."

"What about saving someone's life? Would I violate some cosmic or karmic law if I could find a way to keep my mother from dying in that car wreck?"

"I don't claim to be the keeper of all truth and knowledge," Tessa said, "but you did want to begin with what's known, so let's start there. This is something you've mentioned a few times before. When you went back—why didn't the memory begin just a few minutes earlier? Why precisely at that moment? It suggests there are some rules you just haven't been made aware of yet. And forgive me for putting too fine a point on it, but your brief intervention did cost you your finger. What if next time it's something more serious...or fatal?"

"Collateral damage also," Leif said. "To change a memory, ja, to save yourself—or someone you love—it might bring harm to others. Say you manage to avoid that accident, but then another person dies instead? Then I ask you...Who must be carrying the moral responsibility?"

"I've noticed we've stayed away from the topic of consciousness," Tessa said, challengingly. I understand that, within neuroscience, you tend to focus more on the physiological and chemical conditions of the brain. Our conversations often skip over that part where we talk of the mind.

"When I work with a patient, yes, I recognize that there are some physical elements to their condition, but I work with the person. That person has a consciousness that must want and accept the changes in themselves."

"Tess, that's a very difficult question to answer. On the one hand, I would agree that my consciousness is traveling back in time. However, as a neuroscientist, I have come to understand that consciousness is directly related to brain activity—even if the exact mechanisms remain elusive."

"Cogito, ergo sum," Leif said. "I tink, derefore I am. Descartes. He believed de mind and body are...how you say...fundamentally different dings."

"Damn, Leif," Sita said, throwing a strawberry at him. "If you're going to start speaking Latin, then I am definitely going to need more tequila."

"So, what is it? Do I have an obligation, whether it be to God, the universe, or some antique clock, to continue this work and try to do some good with this gift? Or do I just turn my back on this and walk away, never looking back...figuratively and literally?"

"May I suggest, dearest, that you take things one step at a time. Carry on with your planning, and when you feel ready, try answering some of the questions we've raised this evening before you actually...visit."

"So, here are the last questions I have for this group tonight. First, who still wants to follow me? And second, am I naively putting all of you in jeopardy if we go forward?"

"Well," Sita said, "I've always had a flair for questionable decisions. So, count me in."

Tessa was quiet for a moment, turning her pen over in her fingers. "You're giving us a choice," she said finally. "And I'm still choosing you." She set the pen down. "I just want it on the record that I'm also terrified, and that I reserve the right to revisit this decision if things change."

Leif stood and laughed, "Hoo vants to live forevah? I am right, ja?"

38

SPECTERS

"DAMN IT, CURTIS," MOLLY yelled into her phone, "what do you want me to do?"

"Molly," Curtis said coldly, "it was your original recommendation that persuaded us to invest serious resources in this matter. You need to find a way to corral him."

"What does that mean...exactly? I want to be clear about what it is you are asking me to do here—now? In this moment?"

"The work that Jaxon Beck has undertaken is something that we want to pursue. From what we can tell, he doesn't yet have a firm understanding of its full potential, but by all indications, he is close. We would prefer to have him working with us on this, but if we can't get him on board, we can't afford an adversary. We would, at the very least, want the data he's collecting."

"The last I heard, you forced VRMT to take away all of his toys. The gossip I heard was that Jax may be sidestepping that entirely and continuing this process completely on his own."

"We need to know what he's doing at a more significant level. Have you read his results for yourself? That should give you some idea of how best to exploit this unique aptitude to further the larger project. I am not going to connect all the dots for you over an unencrypted phone line. You should be able to take what you know along with the influence you have in place to make that happen."

"You sure know how to charm a girl, you know that?"

"Oh, do grow up! You knew what this was all about decades ago. Jaxon was always a good candidate to help the project evolve. You just happened to stumble onto something that helped advance him to the next level. It's not as if you're losing out on anything by positioning yourself in his work or personal life. At the very least, you'd be securing capital for the VA. Of course, that is in addition to your retirement plan...clear?"

"Curtis, I've had the displeasure of knowing you for over twenty years. I understand what's at stake without your subtle threats about my future. I just think we should let Mason and his friend run with this for a while longer and pick it up when they get it into a working model. Let's not rush it ourselves and do all the grunt work—let them do it. Get a firsthand account of what Jax is trying to do with the system he's created and see what he develops."

"No. We need more control of the outcomes. I want you to find a way to get closer to his work. That should be your primary focus, and the sooner the better. Find a way to spend more time in Denver and learn what boundaries he's been able to establish thus far. Mason is too close to Dr. Beck to be an objective player in this matter—plus I've never fully trusted that team to see this through to the end. You already have a well-established relationship with the Beck family, so why are you hesitant about using that?"

"Sure. But why don't we start by having you press VRMX Technologies to return the equipment they confiscated from Jax? On the one hand, the act would serve as an inducement to gain his cooperation. But we can also devise a way to pull data directly without relying on Jax or his crew to hand it over. That should be easy enough for you...right?"

"Honestly, I'm getting pushback from that little pissant mole. They've been stonewalling me for weeks now. Apparently, they've gotten a taste of the potential of this project and want to capitalize on it, which, I guess, is the nature of the tech business."

"Well, start there. Fuck your little insider. They really aren't relevant any longer, are they? Just make sure Jaxon Beck has the tools to move this project forward so we can see the potential. Then you can determine who else you want to get involved in the process. Am I wrong?"

"I'll work on that end. In the meantime, do you think his father could be of any further benefit? Maybe spending more time with him will loosen Jaxon's tongue a little. Dr. Beck is smart—strike that—the man is brilliant. However, my gut tells me he's not going to be completely straight with anyone with whom he doesn't trust 100%. Wasn't it his old man who originally brought him to your attention? Do you think Lt. Colonel Beck is still a team player—being retired and all that?"

"Mark's loyalty to his son has nothing to do with the man's patriotism. While he was recovering from his wounds in Germany, Mark showed me a sample of Jax's capabilities. Jax even wrote a paper early on in high school that could have been published in a science journal if his teachers had any imagination. Mark was just proud of what his son had done at such an early age, and that was his way of... bragging, I guess. I just recognized his talent and flagged Jax's name for future consideration. Mark wouldn't do anything he considers to be a threat to his son. On the other hand, if he believes he can assist his son, he might be of some help."

"He's been like that since his wife died, hasn't he? Being overly protective of his only child after her death. But that's been what, twenty-some-odd years now, hasn't it?"

"Mark is a father. A very caring father who's done a great deal to ensure his son has made it into the best schools and has had the best mentors. He may help our cause, but you cannot bully this man. No. He may be able to assist us in obtaining information, but only if he is nudged—gently nudged."

"I will get VRMX to play ball, but I'm expecting to see results on your part very soon. If we're not able to get what we need from Dr. Beck subtly, then I'll be forced to use more persuasive measures."

39

THE CONFESSIONAL

AFTER ANALYZING THEIR OPTIONS, the group determined that attempting to communicate with one or more individuals in 1995 Oklahoma City would be a good use for a planned 2nd Iteration excursion. The hesitancy Leif had expressed regarding Jax's chronological age during that period was echoed by both Sita and Tessa. Jax had proposed multiple methods he could use to convey a warning, taking into account the real limitations he would face at that age and with the technology of that time.

Tabling the discussion, Jax returned his father's missed call. Mark left a message asking Jax to come back for another visit. As Jax was always open to an excuse to visit his old stomping ground and let Bear act the heathen, both he and Tessa agreed to another trip down to Colorado Springs. This time, however, his father insisted they stay with him, offering any of the three guest bedrooms in his expansive house. In addition, Mark had extended his invitation to both Sita and Leif, who showed sincere excitement at the thought of a real weekend vacation.

After finishing the week and ensuring all foreseeable emergencies had contingency plans, the group of four drove down for a weekend of mindless relaxation and anticipated overindulgence. Eager to be allowed to drive, the quartet of explorers and the ever-eager Bear all loaded into Leif's 4-wheeler. As was befitting his personality, Leif's massive vehicle could have easily seated six large adults with room to spare for multiple bags.

After arriving at Mark's home and exchanging introductions, Jax and Tessa placed their overnight bags in his old bedroom. To no one's surprise, one of the larger guest rooms was claimed by Sita and Leif. Once settled in, Mark brought out a large tray of prepared food and his renowned margaritas. As Sita had overindulged during their last tequila venture, she chose to stick with sparkling water and fresh lime slices, while the rest of the group eagerly enjoyed the mix of booze, salt, and fruit. To a person, there was a collective sigh of relief at getting away from the lab, the Denver area in general, and the mind-bending work they had explored over the last few weeks.

Halfway through the second pitcher of margaritas, the front doorbell chimed, and Mark ushered in Molly Green. Although his dad never mentioned inviting the woman, her appearance was not entirely unexpected. While Mark introduced his guests to one another, Jax noticed a significant change in the room's atmosphere—much like the comfortable bubble that had been swelling had abruptly burst. Eagerly taking a proffered drink from Mark, Molly made her way to the front of the fireplace and stood facing the group. Although it was still 70 degrees outside, the gas fireplace seemed to offer the woman a subtle warmth.

Being the effervescent host, no matter whose home he occupied, Leif stood and lifted a glass in a toast to all gathered before him.

"To good friends!" Leif bellowed, his voice full of cheer. "To good times, ja? And to the memories—we keep them close, always!"

Although unintentional, the last bit of Leif's toast left Jax unsettled. It seemed his whole life at this moment was centered around memories. Old memories, rewritten memories, unfixed memories. He knew his friend did not mean to cause any unease, but his words remained…resonating throughout the house.

"Jax, I got some good news today," Molly said casually. "It seems VRMX Technologies has completed their diagnostics and wants to give you back the Kernel Flow helmet and the VyzR. That is, if you still want them. They would also like to discuss partnering with you. From what little I could tell, they're willing to fund your work for the remainder of this year and the next."

At this announcement, all conversation ceased. The room fell completely quiet. Jax looked around at this team and saw reflected in their eyes what he felt in his gut. The team had all been under the impression that this weekend would be free of any work-related discussion. Now, the peace they had been savoring vanished—washed away in silence.

"That's good news, isn't it?" Mark asked, confused by the group's reaction. "Won't that kind of backing give you a lot of breathing space for continuing your research...or am I missing something?"

"Yeah, Dad, under normal circumstances, this would be good news. But something here isn't right. It's like I stepped in something...bad."

Leif slowly rose from his chair and smacked his chest with an open palm. He glared at Molly then and stated in a low, ominous fashion, "Maybe I look like a fool to you—and to most, ja? Growing up, I gain the sense of the wolf. Smell friend from foe. You cannot tell me I do not know a trap when I see one...or hear of it."

"Whoa, tiger—ah, wolf," Sita said. "Let's hear what the lady has to offer before we turn her over to the hounds. Okay?"

"Leif isn't wrong, though. I've been walking a tight rope for too long. The hairs on the back of my neck are sticking straight up right now. So, I need to know if what VRMX Tech is offering here, and by extension, you, Molly, is going to help me find my balance...or push me over the ledge."

Molly was visibly shaken by this verbal rebuke and by the physical emanations of two large men threatening her with physical violence. "I want to..." Molly started, then stopped, her voice choking up. She was backed up against the fireplace, with nowhere to turn. "Damn it all, Jax, I care about you—I want to help you, I really do. But I can't honestly say I have the slightest sense as to what that might sound or look like to you." She sat on the tiles in front of the crackling fire. "Shit, she cried. "I am...so tired of this act. What if I declared that I actually come in peace? Would that make you or any of your very loyal crew feel any better about what I'm trying to do here?"

Jax remained standing but lowered his voice. "Your timing is the thing here, Molly. Why now? After ignoring all my requests, why do they want to give it back—no, not give it back—they want to partner with me! And why you? Who are you to them? I mean, why not send a company representative? Or did I miss the part where you informed us you were a part of the company? I've got to level with you here. It is solely out of respect for my father that I don't show you the door this very minute."

"Ah-mehn," Leif said. "I bounce her like a ball, ja, right here—right now. I trust her same as a snake in boot. I am not wrong. But I do nothing until Mark says."

"I don't know what the truth is, Molly," Mark said, "but when I think about it, I'm afraid I must agree with my son and his large friend here. I think this whole setup has been just too damn convenient. You have some explaining to do...so do it now."

"Mark, this was supposed to be a gift. The cost of that helmet alone is more than what you make in a year from your retirement."

"When you're in combat," Mark said, speaking slowly into his glass, "you learn to rely on your instincts to stay alive—to keep others alive. I haven't seen this side of you before—more accurately, I've not allowed myself to see this part of you. I always hoped what we had was real, but now..."

Molly stood still, meekly staring at Mark. She gently placed the glass she held onto the table before her. She tilted her chin to keep tears from spilling down her face, then stated in a very casual, friendly manner, "Hey, would you all mind if we continue this discussion out on the patio? I would really like to hear the crackle of your fire pit while we continue discussing this subject."

Mark and Jax immediately understood her meaning. It took Leif another few seconds to grasp the implication of her request—they couldn't talk openly in this room.

"You know, darlin'," Mark purred as he stood. "I think getting some fresh air would do us all a world of good. Whatcha' think, Jax, are you in?"

"Damn, Dad. I thought you'd never ask. I need to check on Bear, and I think everyone needs their drinks refreshed. Am I right, Leif?"

"Ja," Leif murmured, drawing a slow breath. "Glorious air, this. And I'll need more of your drink, Mark—stronger, if you keep it."

Within a few minutes, the group had reassembled on the patio surrounding the blazing fire pit. Ensuring everyone's drink was refilled, Mark took a seat near his son. Jax just glared at Molly for a full minute before any words were spoken.

"Molly, I need to understand what you know, how you're involved, and who you're working for before we have this discussion. This is your only chance to make this right."

"I still think," Tessa said, sitting forward, "for all of our sakes, Leif should just throw her out on her lying ass."

"Look," Sita said, "I believe I'm the only person here who is not impaired by Mark's liquor-heavy brew. So, let me say this may be the best chance to get answers to a few questions that've been hanging over us. That is, if we can all throttle this down a notch."

"I'm not going to defend her," Mark said, "so get that straight. However, I do agree with Sita about this. Let's hear what Molly has to say and then make up our minds, okay?"

"Okay then, you have the floor, Molly. Please enlighten us about what the hell has been going on here. Can you do that?"

"I always admired the depth of your intellect, Jax," Molly said, taking in a deep breath. "Okay then, shall I start at the beginning or jump to the conclusion?"

"My guess is that all of this shit started in Germany," Mark said stiffly. "Am I right?"

"It's true that I've worked for some government agency or other since that time. But Mark..."

"No. I don't want to hear it—not now. Answer my son, please. I met you for a short time while I was at the hospital. You were exactly what I needed then. And it's just some coincidence that you end up working in the same city where I live? And you just happened to have the visor with you the first night you met Jax and Tessa?"

"Listen to me, please! They have something on me—something I did that I'm not proud of, but I can't get out from under. I couldn't then, and I can't now.

"I've known Jax, or more accurately, I've known about him, since he was fifteen. Jax, you wrote a paper for your AP Science course while you were still in Massachusetts. Mark shared a copy of it with me while he was recovering from his wounds. It was his way of showing how proud he was of you—how brilliant he thought you were. I—well, I shared a copy of that paper with some people to whom I answered during that time. That's what put you on several agencies' radar."

"I was fifteen fucking years old! What lit a fire under all these people?"

"Your paper posited the concept that we—humans, could see things and do strange, wonderful things despite what the best minds of the time said was impossible—just a fantasy."

"What I remember about that stupid paper addressed some of the Defense Intelligence Agency projects from the 1970s, '80s, and '90s that were trying to use psychic—parapsychology to spy on other governments. I wrote about how the final public article on Project Stargate declared the work tantalizing but lacked valid data. I think all I suggested was some alternative methods for remote viewing...and similar things."

"Yes. You essentially sketched out some ideas for a machine that could do that work for you. Do you remember that part of your paper?"

"Not really. I think I gave those and other papers to someone at my high school, my guidance counselor, I think, to help me get into college. We ended up here a few months after that, and I haven't given them another thought...until just now."

"Jax, what was your first impression when your dad showed you the VyzR that night? Did it seem familiar to you at all? The better question is, would it surprise you to know that the original idea behind that visor was presented in your papers?"

"I had some fuzzy feelings about that, but I had just experienced a major migraine a couple of days prior. I was still recovering. I do recall being particularly concerned for my dad and whether it was safe for him to use it in therapy—that's as much as I recall."

"Are you trying to tell us," Tessa said, "that Jax had an idea when he was 15 years old and that his idea became the VyzR? What happened to those original papers of Jax's from his high school years?"

"Mark was an officer. And as such, all his documents technically belonged to the government, including work he obtained from his son. I assume the packet Jax submitted for college admission got... lost, shall we say.

"After I sent a copy of his original papers to my people, there was a lot of debate about where he got them. You have to understand the panic I heard from these people. Some of those component ideas hadn't been created yet. Others that did exist were highly classified.

"At first, the DIA was concerned about Mark being a spy or something, but that idea was quickly dropped when they looked at the breadth and depth of Jax's school work. Although I never saw them myself, I heard that there were dozens of papers and diagrams written by Jax at that time. It was just sheer luck that your high school science teacher wasn't smart enough to exploit those ideas."

"But what about now? Does this have something to do with these guys I've run into around campus? Am I under surveillance? Is that why we're out here away from my dad's house, because he's being bugged too?"

"Don't you get it, Jax? Everyone's scared shitless. They don't know if the work you're doing now is going to solve cancer or be the next atomic bomb."

"So, spying on him—on us is acceptable?" Tessa asked.

"You still haven't told us who you work for," Mark said. "Or what the relationship is between you and VRMX Technologies."

"I'm not exactly sure who I work for," Molly smirked. "Only that VRMX is just one of many such companies that have ties to my handler. I suppose, whichever agency owns him, also pulls the strings at these companies."

"Ja, this is fine tale for children," Leif said, teeth bared. "But you haf told us not'ing, not one true t'ing tonight."

"For example," Sita said softly, "are we in danger?"

Molly wrapped her thin sweater more tightly around her shoulders. Then she gently stroked the fur on Bear's back, attempting to avoid the glares that now bore into her.

"The truth is...I don't know."

40

Wine & Dine

"Do you know why you're here, Ms. Taylor?"

"No. All the Dean said when he called was that an important person wanted to meet with me to discuss the future of the Center."

The server arrived at their table, patiently waiting out of earshot until he was certain they were done talking.

"Will the gentleman and miss be having any cocktails this evening, sir?"

"I'll have my usual, Claude. Amy, may I order for you? Well then, a generous glass of the Cloudy Bay Sauvignon Blanc for my guest, if you would. They have a wide variety of pescatarian, vegetarian, and vegan offerings here. This New Zealand white pairs exceptionally well with any of those choices."

"So, you know my dietary habits. What else did the University tell you about me?"

"Excuse me for sounding crass, but I'm not impressed by the people working there. No. Any information I gleaned about you, I did so honestly...I bought it."

"Then you also know I have a low threshold for bullshit. Could we please forego the pleasantries, and you tell me why I cancelled another weekend with my parents to meet with you? The Dean was quite insistent that we meet...tonight."

"Jaxon Beck."

"Of course, this is about him. It couldn't have anything to do with the multiple articles I have written, or the work I'm doing for the Center. This is all about the inescapable question as to what the fabulous Dr. Beck is doing now. Well, I don't know, and I find it hard to give a fuck what Jax is doing. Oh, I'm sorry, was that too crass?"

"Your disdain for the matter is noted. That does not dismiss the fact that you, above all others in that little building, know more about Dr. Beck, especially the work in which he is currently engaged."

"So, why me, why now, and why for the love of God in this place do we have to have this discussion?"

"Because, my dear, I simply don't trust anyone else to tell me what I need to know to do my job—to complete my mission, as it were. I've lost confidence in my last connection to Dr. Beck."

The server arrived with their drinks. He then turned to the unnamed man, who nodded as if to acknowledge a shared secret. The server then gracefully departed.

"So, I assume you're a regular here. Is that because it's a few hundred feet away from the capital and those who hold the real power here, and probably beyond?"

"I knew you were perceptive. It was in your profile, as was your desire to take charge of your own research laboratory. And if my instincts serve me, perhaps more than that?"

"Big surprise there! I have my PhD—well, almost. And I have seen that the fucking men who run the various research grants in that stupid little building are either close to senility or so enamored with having their name on a door that they have forgotten how to be innovative, bold, explorers in the scientific world. Was that adequate for you, or should I continue?"

"You do not disappoint. You are everything that I have heard or read about you, which is quite complementary, I might add. No. I want to be your...benefactor, for lack of a better word. I see your potential and want to help you get there."

"Listen, whatever the hell your name is. I'm not fucking my way to the top here, okay. I don't need or want a sugar daddy to save me from the mean old men. I will make it there on my own merit, thank you."

"You misunderstand my intentions, Amy. May I call you Amy? I fully understand that you would cut the balls off any man who stood in your way of professional recognition and success. That is an attribute in my book, not a detriment. I am simply offering you a partnership in which we both benefit. This has nothing to do with any distasteful sexual arrangement. I simply need you to work for me—with me, if that sounds more palatable to your sensitivities."

"Well, Mr. Mystery Man, why don't you start with who you are, who you work for, and what you want?"

"You may call me Mr. Curtis, and who I work for is inconsequential. What I want is to know if Dr. Beck is breaking any laws, be it the laws of man or the laws of physics."

41

ENTANGLED

THE NEXT MORNING WAS...INTERESTING. Molly had spent the night in the separate guest bedroom, not with Mark. Jax wordlessly congratulated him for not trading his ethics for sex or surrendering to the imaginary romance the two had going on. After Molly's revelation in the backyard, each couple had silently retreated to their rooms.

After the requisite coffee and breakfast, Tessa announced there was an emergency at the hospital and that she had to get back. Supporting her strategy for creating a plausible reason to exit, the other three stated that they might as well head back themselves. When they finished loading the vehicle, Mark hugged his son goodbye and whispered in his ear, "Stay strong."

Back on the road, no one spoke. Whether it was the stress or paranoia, idle chatter didn't seem appropriate. As they reached the outskirts of Denver, Sita opened the passenger side window and took a deep breath. Then, she started banging both fists against the truck's ceiling multiple times and screamed out her window, "This is such bullshit! You don't have the right to do this to us—damn you all!"

"Hey, hey—listen now!" Leif said gently. "I am de scary monster, ya? Dis is just anudder churn of the life, and you are supposed to be de peaceful, passive Hindu princess...you remember, eh?"

"Oh, fuck off—oh no, not you—I'm so sorry, my love, I didn't mean to say that. This shit has just really gotten to me, and my Gods, it's starting to feel like I can't breathe anymore."

Although Sita's outburst initially jolted everyone, no one could disagree with her sentiment. Jax looked back down at the small piece of paper nestled in the palm of his hand. He had read it and reread it a dozen times over the past hour. Before exiting his dad's house, Molly had slipped Jax this note. In it, she warned Jax not to trust anyone at the Center, including Dr. Mason. She didn't know exactly who could or couldn't be trusted, but she knew the Director still played some part in this mess.

Jax hated the idea that the man he once thought of as a friend had turned into an obstruction, if not an outright foe. He had already lost faith in Steve for trying to derail his work, but this raised a deeper concern.

"I want to move forward with our work on Oklahoma City," Jax declared soberly. "I need to see how deep this shit runs and who's a part of it. I need to know what the fuck I'm dealing with. We have this visit charted out as far as we can go. But I need you all to listen to what I'm about to say next and hear me out...completely.

"I also want to get the helmet back from VRMX Technologies. I'm sure I can play along and get it back through Molly. We need to—"

"Jax, what the hell?" Tessa said. "You heard what that woman said. They want to use you and your work to possibly create some damn weapon! You can't put yourself and us through that."

"Tess, please just hear me out. I have prepped on the Oklahoma City attack, and I will memorize every possible phone number of people I may be able to help. When I do this, I want to demonstrate scientifically that the brain can alter aspects of reality. I'm not proclaiming that the mind is a manifestation of the brain. That would be too arrogant, even for me. I am saying that there is something worth exploring here.

"Additionally, we need to let the rat find the cheese. Let me be the bait, follow through with the experiment we've been planning, and see what rats show up."

"You miserable bastard! And then what? We're just supposed to sit back while they lock you up—or worse? How fucking selfish can you be?"

"Sweetheart, don't you see? They're already aware of me—of us. They already have the helmet data showing it was a temporal anomaly. We can't take that back. Our only alternative is to plow ahead and see this through. I know I'm not the only one feeling the stress they've put on us, and damn it, we need to get a semblance of control around what we're dealing with."

"What if you do nothing? I can't be the only one who's thought of that as an alternative. Am I correct? If you don't do anything more with this crazy venture, what can they do?"

"Tess, I love you, but we don't have the luxury of doing nothing and hoping they'll leave us alone. As I said, these people, whoever they are, have seen the effects of the experiment. Undoubtedly, VRMX has the data and probably sent it to their contacts, which at least demonstrates neurological changes.

"Furthermore, as Molly told me, I seem to be the only individual they have yet identified who can do this...work. If I don't act on this voluntarily, they will come and make me do it, probably by threatening any of you or my dad."

"You are not alone, Jax, ja?" Leif murmured. "We cannot be inside that memory, no... but you do not carry it by yourself."

"Just tell us the plan, Jax," Sita said resignedly. "We're in this with you till the end."

"My God, you are surrounded by fools!" Tessa said, still facing the window.

Jax reached over and put his hand on her knee. She didn't move. "Tess. I'm not going to push you."

A few seconds passed. A highway sign for Denver slid by.

She turned to face him. “Do you really think I’d just—” She stopped. Looked at his hand on her knee, then back at him. “You think I’m just going to let you do this alone?”

“No matter what you decide, I would never—”

“Stop.” She held up a finger, then turned to the others. “I have conditions. Do you all hear me? I have conditions, and they will be met.”

42

Molly's Connections

"I'm actually quite surprised to see you again, Jax."

Sitting in her office at the VA clinic, Molly looked across her desk at a man who had noticeably aged in just the few days since her confession to the group. After decades of working clandestinely, she could tell when a subject was starting to panic. Jax was close to the edge, which would be bad news for them both.

"Truth be told, I'm a little surprised myself. I thought a lot about VRMX's offer to return the equipment. We need the helmet, if for no other reason than to keep a record of what's happening with our research. And, if we do decide to continue to test other theories on volunteers, then we can use the VyzR for that as well."

"Management has just been waiting for me to get back to them with your answer. I've been avoiding their calls since last week. Mr. Curtis, on the other hand, is expecting a call from me today or tomorrow, and he's someone I can't stonewall."

"Do they know what you revealed to us?"

"I can't be entirely sure, but I don't think so. At least nothing has been said or done overtly to indicate otherwise. Curtis is a slippery SOB, and before you ask, I've swept my office for bugs yesterday—an old habit, as you can imagine. I'm sure they still keep tabs on me—and you as well. But this meeting will look to them like you came in person to accept my offer, so I think we're good."

"Do you have a sense of what the next step will be with these people?"

"Curtis will probably insist that I bring you the equipment personally and gather more information about how you're going to use this in your experiments. Keeping me in the loop may have the benefit of giving you a heads-up if anything radical changes."

"And what precisely are we talking about when you say radical? Is Curtis going to hold us hostage and force us to work for him? Should I be looking at moving to Costa Rica?"

"He will probably want to expand your research to see what your limitations are and how he can use your...skills. At the same time, he'll keep trying to find another subject like you, so he has more control over the project. At the moment, you are an anomaly with a unique talent. But there must be a few other people who share your brain makeup, probably someone from the military who has already sworn an oath of allegiance. He will always use national security as an excuse for manipulating compliance."

"What a bastard. And this is coming from our own government?"

"My limited view of things is that there are overlaps in the interests of most elected politicians and their big donors. Things have only heated up with the new administration. For all we know, other governments may even be a part of this now. Curtis has his own set of handlers, so I would guess some committee in Congress already has a rough outline of what's going on with you."

"If I do accept VRMX's offer to take back the equipment, does that automatically mean I'm partnered with them? Could that be a separate conversation for another day?"

"The way it was presented to me, returning the equipment would be a gesture of good faith on both sides, as they would still have access to your results, just like the first time around. The offer and acceptance of any funding would be the hook. If you take that, then you, meaning the Center, and VRMX Technologies would be partners—the paperwork that needs to get signed will no doubt stress that point.

"I need to clarify one thing that I said the other night, Jax. There is obviously some connection between VRMX and whoever Curtis is working for, but I can't say with any certainty that the company works for him directly. Sure, the VyzR plans were most likely given to them by some agency. Just keep in mind that they could have just been serving as a contractor working for the government and not the government itself."

"Okay, that's as clear as mud. So, how are you going to swing being the director here at the VA and running up to Denver to act as their liaison?"

"Although not part of the government, the VA is a government-funded organization. If our overlords want to get this done, I'll be made available. I do have a deputy director and assistants here, so I'm guessing I'll be up there by Monday."

"Have you spoken with my dad since that night?"

"I really don't want to get into that with you. Let's just say we're all adults and leave it at that. I won't be involving him any further, but that doesn't mean that Curtis wouldn't use him, Tessa, or anyone else he thinks can help him meet his goals."

"That is so fucked up. How can you work for this man?"

"As I stated the other night, I put myself in a position where they use me to get what they want. If that arrangement ever changes, I'll probably be in prison...or worse."

"I think I get that. I don't like it, but I understand where you're coming from. So, can I expect the equipment you bring us to be bugged? Even if we voluntarily share our data."

"Probably. But as you said, you'll be handing your printed and recorded data to them anyway, so ensure that whatever you need to keep private stays that way."

"Well then, onward to glory... or whatever."

43

Equipment Restored

"Jax," Leif said, "you are sure you can trust her, ja? I am afraid for the meddling, what she and VRMX might do, and this—it is your life we are speaking of, you know?"

"No, my friend, I don't trust her, or anyone else entirely at this point, except, of course, you, Sita, and Tessa. But we're running out of options...and time. That's why I need you to take a close look at the helmet to see if any small alterations have been made. I don't care as much about the VyzR, as the one you created is superior for our needs."

"We haven't established exactly what our next step is going to be," Sita said. "Are you certain about the target date we've set?"

"Yes, it's a go for 1995. Were you able to find any more information about the people from Oklahoma City? It would help to know as much about them as possible."

"I have those three individuals confirmed. There were only a dozen or so people in that entire place whose phone numbers weren't classified—being a federal building and all.

"Also, you are going to have a credibility issue with anyone you try to contact. There has to be some motivating factor other than an ambiguous threat to get a person to act. These three are the only ones I've been able to identify that meet those criteria. I think you have everything possible, but I'll give it one more pass before you go."

"Then that is our plan. I'll inform Molly and Mikey of our aim and include Steve and Amy as well. Before I do, Leif, have you made any headway with modifying the visor to allow others to view what I see during a 2nd Iteration?"

"I yust started on that, so it is hard to say, ja? We don't want to be invasive, like—eh—drilling into your head, so it's not a simple ting like receivers, you know? Even then, we can only hear and record your voice, not anyone you may speak with."

"I get that, it's just that I don't have any proof. It boils down to the scan, and my word, that things changed. So, Sita, keep probing, and Leif, check the recording devices.

"And, in the meantime, I need to practice my painting skills."

Needing to refill his mug, Jax sauntered over to the coffee cart and started making a fresh pot. A minute later, he was joined by Mikey, who just stood there looking at him.

"What's on your mind, Mikey? I didn't even know you liked coffee."

"I don't. Listen, Jax, maybe this isn't a good idea. Undertaking this again, I mean."

"Thanks, Mikey. But I have to do this...for multiple reasons that I can't explain."

"Just remember," he said quietly, "the past isn't the only thing that can break you."

"Thank you for meeting with me on short notice, Jax," Amy said warmly. "It seems like ages since I've been back here in the lab."

"We're always happy to see you, Amy. How's the new position working out? I see Steve is still the Director, so you haven't implemented any type of coup... yet."

"I always admired your dry wit. No, nothing as evil as that...as you said, yet. It's just been a little over a month since I took the assistant job with the Center. I have gone through everything the other two labs have been doing, but haven't made it down here to see first-hand what your devious mind has been up to."

"Devious, eh. You've called me a lot of names in the last four years, but I don't think I ever heard you use that one before. Was there something in particular that's drawn your attention in our direction? I'd be glad to fill you in on whatever it is you're looking for."

"To be honest, I was a little thrown off by the fluff piece with your name on it. What was the title, heralding the benefits of magnetic and electrical stimulation or some such thing? I seemed to have detected Sita's distinctive writing style infused in that article. I was hoping for a more meaningful discussion about what you're really working on here."

"I have no idea what you are suggesting. Was there something specific?"

"Yes, but I really don't feel comfortable talking about it out here in the open. Would you mind if we continue this discussion in a more...neutral environment?"

"Please. Just show me where that would be."

"Thank you. Take a short walk with me then?"

"Of course, lead the way."

Jax was certain that Amy would direct them to her office or even to the Director's. Surprisingly, she continued walking until they crossed over the central pavilion of the building and paused in front of a wooden door to an office in the opposite wing. She produced a key from her jacket, looked up and down the hallway, then unlocked the door and entered.

As Jax followed Amy into the room, she gestured for him to close the door. The office was completely empty, but its built-in bookcase and wooden wainscotting matched that of every other office in the Center.

Amy crossed to the opposite side of the room and leaned against the wall. The afternoon sunlight spilling through the window provided a wispy curtain between them.

"Are you in some kind of trouble, Dr. Beck?"

"That's a hell of an opening line. In trouble with whom?"

"Jax, I've known you a while now, and even though things didn't work out between us, I always respected you. I'm asking for some of that same respect to be shown to me in return. I overheard you and your little team plotting some work stemming from that temporal anomaly reading we both observed.

"In addition, I had a very unpleasant conversation over dinner with a Mr. Curtis the other night. He seems to think you may be breaking some laws, both physical and metaphysical. He made me quite a generous offer if I were to inform him of any progress you might make in the course of your experiments. He gave off the vibe of someone from the government, although that fact was never established."

"I'm sorry, Amy, I'm confused. Are you trying to find out what I'm doing so you can run and tell this individual what a bad boy

I've been? Offering me up so you can get in good with the powers that be and really be handed Steve's job?"

"I admit I have a temper and have been impatient with the way things are run around here, but I just thought I was dealing with another good-old-boy network. This isn't that. This has some serious people sniffing around you, and somehow your stink has gotten on me. I know I can accomplish a lot of good things in this field, and I plan on making that happen. What I'm not going to do is be a lackey for anyone—you or them."

"Let's say I believe what you're telling me is true. How do you see this little drama playing out? I have Sita and Leif to consider as well as myself."

"You failed to mention your wife. Do you really believe Tessa won't suffer from—"

"Are you threatening her...?"

"Oh, get over yourself! Tessa may not trust me around you, but whatever we had is in the past—I moved on a long time ago. I'll ask you again, what are you experimenting with? It has to be something dealing with the readings we got from the helmet. I don't expect trust, but I already know enough to make trouble for you if I really wanted to. Why don't you just fill in the blanks to this little mystery?"

The empty room was quiet while the two just stared at one another. Small bits of dust glittering in the waning daylight were the only movement for a long moment. Jax finally broke the silence. “We call it the 2nd Iteration. And just so you fully understand, I’m putting my life on the line here.

“That’s not me being melodramatic. I don’t mean my job or any of that—I literally mean my life. I think I’m on to something that someone wants to misuse. I get the strong impression, from what little I do know, that if I don’t choose to play for their team, I’ll be taken out of the game completely. That, and I’m trying to ensure no one in my life gets hurt.”

“Well, I’m not stupid. I can extrapolate what you’re probably doing, but after talking with this Curtis clown... I mean, the guy reeked of a cheap spy novel. Honestly, does any of what you're doing have to do with treating migraines anymore?”

“At first, I genuinely thought it might be something we could use, and I wanted to keep it quiet until I got a better handle on how to proceed. But now I’m not so sure. I think I may have unlocked... Well, something entirely different, and I’m having a hard time seeing a way out.”

“Please, just tell me what’s going on.”

“Amy, you were my star pupil, which is why I wanted you in my lab in the first place. You’ve seen the results firsthand, and I still believe this work may have applications for healing the brain, but we just don’t know enough, yet. At the moment, it’s taken a left turn, and we're going to look at those other applications I proposed earlier within the next day or so.

"If it's okay with you and Steve, I would like you back with me in the lab to oversee the readouts. You're the best at interpreting the nuances."

"Of course." Amy paused, running her thumb through the dust along the windowsill. "You know what I keep thinking about? You've been so focused on going back in time. Has it even occurred to you to go in the other direction?"

Jax looked at her sharply. "What do you mean?"

"I mean forward." She let that thought sit for a moment. "Far enough forward."

He was quiet. His brows pinched together curiously.

"Forget it." She smiled, pushing off the wall. "Perverse scientific curiosity."

Jax opened the door and spoke over his shoulder as he was leaving. "No. I haven't."

Amy nodded slowly, as if she had already known his answer. "Too bad."

44

SELECTED TARGET

"THE OKLAHOMA CITY BOMBING on April 19, 1995, remains one of the most devastating acts of domestic terrorism in U.S. history. It also occurred a week after my grandfather died—on the very day of his funeral. I'm intending to target that day to remember during this demonstration."

Jax had invited Molly and Dr. Mason to view his next experiment, and they were now being introduced to the process and anticipated outcomes. Amy had just finished calibrating the Kernal Flow helmet. Mikey from VRMX Technologies was also present in the crowded control booth, more to keep him out of the way than to serve any real purpose.

Tessa sat on the short stool situated next to the reclined examination chair where Jax would conduct his 2nd Iteration visit. Her medical bag was at her feet, and an AeroSyn wand was taped to the side of Jax's chair. If she had difficulty reviving him again, passing this wand beneath his nose would release a cool oxygenated mist that would make him gasp awake. Just one of her conditions for continuing to work with the team.

While Tessa was focused on interacting with Jax, Sita was charged with tracking his vitals using standard equipment, and Amy would focus on the readings received from scanning Jax's brain. Leif stood against the wall behind Sita, overseeing the audio equipment and ensuring the physical safety of his friends.

"But you were, what, four or five years old when that happened?" Molly asked. "And weren't you living in Massachusetts at that time, some fifteen hundred miles away? So, what is it you're hoping to accomplish?"

"Sita, would you remind the group? What are the stats surrounding that attack?"

Sorting through a pile of papers, Sita pulled out one and skimmed it before answering.

"The attack happened at the *Alfred P. Murrah Federal Building* in downtown Oklahoma City, a bit after 9 AM Central time, or 10 AM in Massachusetts. There were 170 people killed, including 21 children from a daycare center, with over 680 other individuals injured.

"Timothy McVeigh and Terry Nichols were the domestic extremists convicted of the largest terrorist attack before 9/11, using a rental truck full of explosives parked in front of the building.

They were supposedly motivated by anti-government ideology. The children's center was called *America's Kids Day Care Center.*"

"My folks," Jax continued, "thought I was too young to go to my grandfather's funeral. They had a neighbor come over to watch me and babysit a cousin's toddler. I found a photograph of that day, along with several others, on an old CD I came across while piecing together my history.

"Although I don't remember the neighbor's name, I recall her making us pancakes for breakfast. If that's true, then it should be around that same time of day."

"And what, Jax?" Dr. Mason said. "What do you think you're going to do here? Remember, I read your proposal. Do you truly expect to interact with someone while you replay this memory? Hell, even if you could, what are you imagining you would achieve? You said yourself you can't control when this 2nd Iteration starts after you access this vivid memory, so what happens if you wake up hours after that attack already took place?"

"The idea Sita and I have been working with involves parents who worked in the same building as that daycare center. We recognized that it would be difficult to motivate someone even if it were to protect themselves. But, when you tell them their children are at risk, wouldn't they be more apt to move the children out, if only to be certain?"

"The building," Sita said, "was primarily staffed by employees from federal agencies and military recruiting offices. We obtained limited information about those people because that information was secure. There were only two companies besides the daycare that non-federal employees staffed, the credit union and the snack bar."

"You still haven't answered me," Molly said. "What do you think you could do even if your timing is perfect? You were a child. You think maybe you just go and tell the neighbor who's watching you to call someone? Why would she believe you? Why would anyone?"

"The credit union," Sita said, ignoring Molly's interruption. "It had an employee working the customer service line who had a child in the daycare center nearby. The Bureau of Alcohol, Tobacco, and Firearms, or ATF, had a civilian operating the public line that morning who also had a child in that daycare. A third individual who worked at the snack bar also had a child at that daycare. Ideally, one of those three would get the daycare center to evacuate, but that's unlikely given the number of children and the few daycare workers. We also know it is improbable that anything Jax might be able to do will stop the bombing itself."

"I'm hoping that my 2nd Iteration visit will be able to save some or all of these three people and their children. I'm also hoping that the person at the ATF will have a good enough relationship with the agents there to be able to do something, but there are too many unknown variables at this point. Aside from my personal goal of making a historical change, this will also be a proof-of-concept experiment with Amy looking for any indication that another temporal anomaly took place, just like the first time."

"Are you still claiming, as you did in your written proposal to me, that this can be used in some manner to treat neurological diseases? That by overwriting neurons in the brain, it can perhaps even cure some ailments?"

"Steve, we haven't gotten far enough into the research for me to make that claim with certainty...yet. That's one of the reasons we are conducting this research today and using the Kernel Flow helmet to provide evidence of physiological changes occurring in the brain. I can tell you this, when I carried out the last 2nd Iteration visit, the frequency and intensity of my migraines were substantially lessened. I wasn't cured from experiencing them, but that may be because several sessions like these are needed to establish enough new pathways to overwrite the ones that cause the migraine to begin with."

"It's damn ambitious," Dr. Mason said, "but as long as you're the guinea pig in your own experiment, then I'm willing to sit here and review the results. I can't make promises, but if you're able to show this, then you may get enough backing to see it through to fruition."

"Speaking on behalf of my company," Mikey said from the control room, "if there are demonstrable outcomes today, there's a good chance we can discuss a partnership with plenty of capital to explore this more fully."

"Well, it's always good to hear that there are still people interested in the pursuit of true science. All joking aside, I understand that it takes capital to keep the lights on, so thank you.

"During the first few minutes, Tessa will help me relax deeply through a hypnotic induction, just like the first time we did this. My only request is that you not say or do anything that would disrupt the induction portion of the session. The headphones and visor on this unit should block most extraneous noise, but I'd rather not have to start from scratch because someone got up to use the restroom.

"You will be able to follow along with most of the 2nd Iteration visit due to the throat mics I'll be wearing, and the connected speakers behind my team and behind your seats. For obvious reasons, we can't have the volume too loud, but you should be able to catch most, if not all, of what's going on. Unfortunately, the ability to share what I'm seeing isn't viable. So, if there are no more questions, let's begin."

45

Oklahoma City 1995

Jax arrived to find himself in the old playroom in the basement of his parents' home in Chicopee, Massachusetts. He recalled the high-set windows had faced south—that the morning sun always lit up the white walls and made the linoleum floor shine like a waxed car. He looked down at his arms, which were quite small, and although at first, he thought he was sitting, realized he was standing. Welcome to age five.

Trying to orient himself, he looked around the room and saw a crib set to the right, just next to the minibar his father had built when they had moved in. To his left was a collection of mismatched couches and recliners, all facing a television mounted on a wooden console. In one of the recliners was a brunette teenage girl, Jax guessed to be around 16. She was watching some music videos while the baby quietly slept in the crib.

"Is everything okay Jaxy?" the young girl asked. "Do you need to go potty?"

For the life of him, he could not remember this girl's name. He just knew she lived in the house next to his and had watched him a couple of times over the years. She got out of her chair and loomed over the five-year-old Jaxon Beck.

"Hon," she said, gently holding his shoulders. "Can I get you something? Maybe some juice?"

"No," Jax answered, "I'm okay."

His voice sounded so strange to him. He had discussed at length with his team about what he would experience coming here and interacting as a child. Seeing the world from this perspective and hearing his young voice, however, was not an intellectual exercise, and it took him a moment to adapt.

"Well, just remember Jenny is sleeping, and we don't want to wake her. So, if you think of anything you need, let me know."

"Where's Mom and Dad?"

"They're with your grandmother, remember? They'll be back in a little while. Probably after naptime."

Jax nodded, and the girl returned to her chair. He saw he had been reading from a Dr. Seuss book in front of one of the sofas. Near the girl was a purse, which he assumed was hers. Dangling from the long handle was a ceramic unicorn with the name Mary written across its body.

"Mary. Of course, now I remember."

“Did you say something, Jaxy.”

“Mary, what time is it?”

“The clock is on the wall over there. Can you remember how we worked on telling time by looking at the big and little hands? Think you can tell me what time it says?”

“It’s 9:14. I still have some time.”

“Very good, little man! That was wicked awesome. You have time for what? Is there a program on, like Sesame Street or Barney the dinosaur, you want to watch?”

“Not now, thank you.”

“Wow, you are sure growing up fast.”

“Mary, can I do some painting?”

“Sure. I’ll set up your stuff on the counter, so we don’t mess up the furniture. Is that okay with you, sir?”

“Yes, ma’am.”

“Jeez, Jaxy, look how all polite you are and stuff.”

In a matter of minutes, Mary had put out a small jar of water, a set of watercolors, brushes, and several pieces of thick legal-sized paper. Jax sat on a booster seat atop a leather barstool.

"If you need anything," Mary whispered, "just raise your hand, and I'll come back over."

The first thing Jax did was write down the phone numbers he had memorized before slipping into this 2nd Iteration, just to ensure he would not forget them. He had not yet mastered the dexterity of his hands and fingers, but was managing to make the numbers legible. Then he flipped the paper over and began drawing a large box, rotating it to depict the image in 3D. He tried to convey that the box's center had collapsed, and wisps of smoke were emerging from it. His work wasn't the correct dimensions of the Murrah Federal Building, but the general concept was there. He finished by writing Oklahoma City at the top of the page.

Half-turned in his chair, Jax raised his hand to get Mary's attention. Not surprisingly for a teenager, she had a phone cradled between her head and shoulder and was talking animatedly. This wasn't a smartphone, but a regular cordless phone with an antenna sticking from it. A glance at the clock showed 9:28 here, which made it 8:28 in Oklahoma. He had about 30 minutes to convince Mary to make one or all three phone calls.

Grasping the drawing, Jax slowly wriggled his way off the stool and plopped to the floor with a smack. He stood perfectly still to see if his escape from the seat had awakened the infant—she was still quiet. However, the noise alerted Mary, who quickly hung up the phone and walked over to him, obviously a little peeved at the trouble he might be causing. When she started to gently pull his arm, leading him back towards the couch, Jax decided he didn't have the time for subtlety.

"Mary, I'm sorry to do this to you, but I need your help."

"Wha...Jaxon, why are you...what are you talking about?

"I'm going to need you to trust me for the next few minutes. In about half an hour, there's going to be an attack on a Federal Building in Oklahoma City. A lot of people are going to die, Mary. I'm hoping with your help we may be able to save some of them."

Shocked by what she was hearing, Mary said nothing. Jax held up his picture so she could see what he'd been painting. Now a bit scared of the child before her, she backed up until she tripped and plopped down on a large ottoman, a hand covering her mouth.

"Mary, I understand what I'm telling you is bizarre, but I'm not possessed by some demon or anything like that. This attack is a fact. It is going to happen, and you just might be able to be a hero to someone. I need you to call these numbers I've painted and tell them there's a bomb threat and they need to evacuate as soon as possible."

"They'll think...I'm crazy. I must be crazy. Or that son-of-a-bitch Willie Birch put some drug into something I ate, and I'm hallucinating? This can't be real!"

"Mary, please try to calm down. Look, the phone is right there. Call this first number and see if someone named George Marshall answers. If I'm right, then this will tell you what I'm saying is true. Can you do that?"

Seeing Mary was still in shock at this small child talking to her like an alien from another planet, Jax walked over to where she had laid the phone. He picked up the handset and punched in the first numbers by memory. When the other end of the line began ringing, he placed the phone near Mary's ear.

"ATF, can I help you?" the man on the phone said. "Hello, is somebody there?"

"Is...is this a Mister Marshall?" Mary squeaked out.

"Yes, miss, this is George Marshall. How can I help you this fine morning? Miss, are you still there?"

"There's...there's a bomb in your building. You need to get people out."

"Miss, are you aware that it is a crime to make crank calls like this? Especially to the ATF? I should call the police on you right now!"

"No, wait. This is real, I wasn't sure before, but now I know. You only have a few minutes before your building—the whole building blows up. Please listen and get out!"

"This is a federal building, no one would dare do that. Besides, I've got my boy in daycare here and getting him out will be...wait, are you...you for real?"

"Yes! Please go get your son and get away from the building."

Jax gently took the phone from her hand and started to dial the second number, this time relying on the numbers he'd written in watercolors.

"You did great, Mary. Let's try this again, and this time it will be a person named Susan Sear. Now this part is important. Susan also has a child, a little girl in that same daycare. As soon as you can convince Susan that your call of a threat is real, you need to tell her to get her daughter and get out of that building."

"...ederal Credit Union, may I help you?"

"Hello, Mrs. Susan Sear?" Mary said.

"No, I'm sorry, hon, Susan just stepped away from her desk. This is Judy. May I help you with something? You know the credit union's not open yet?"

"Please just listen. There's a bomb in your building that's going to explode in a few minutes. You need to tell Susan she has to get her daughter and leave. You too, Judy. You and anyone else you—"

"Listen, miss. That is not funny. Take your sick little joke and stick it. For God's sake!"

Jax could hear the line disconnect from where he stood. He reclaimed the phone from Mary's hands, dialed the last number, then held it up to her.

"This will be Anna Toller at the snack bar. She also has a daughter in daycare. Just do your best, Mary. That's all we can do. Here, it's ringing."

"Snacks 'n' Stuff, this is Anna, may I help you?"

"Mrs. Toller—Anna, please listen to me, and for God's sake, don't hang up. You have a daughter in daycare. There is a bomb almost ready to go off in your building. Please, please grab your child and get away from there. You must leave now. Please, I am begging you, please get your child and save yourselves."

"I...I can't just leave. I have customers, and I'm here by myself. You sound so sure that this is true...are you...sure?"

"Yes. You must leave. Please believe me!"

The phone disconnected, and Mary set the phone by her on the ottoman. She just stared at Jax, then held up his painting and shook her head as she let a tear run down her face. She looked unsure of her actions. She let another tear fall, then another.

"You did really well, Mary. I am so sorry I had to have you make those calls, but I don't think anyone would have listened to my small voice. We may never talk about this again, but I want you to know you're a real hero in my eyes. You did what most people would laugh off or dismiss outright. Do good things with your life, Mary."

It was at that moment that the baby, Jenny, awakened from her nap and began crying loudly. Jax looked at the clock. It had just turned 10:02. As Mary went to tend to the baby, he took his painting into the small bathroom and closed the door behind him.

He stood over the toilet as he ripped his artwork into small pieces and let them fall into the water. Flushing the toilet several times, he left the bathroom and returned to sit in front of the couch. He quietly called out for Bear, the code word he and Tessa had devised to conclude his 2nd Iteration session. The sparkly rainbow expanded in front of him, and he closed his eyes, allowing it to surround him. A moment later, young Jaxon happily picked up his book about a funny cat in a silly hat and let out a small giggle.

46

The Return

PUSHING UP THE HELMET and removing the visor from his face, Jax felt a weight lift off his being. He sighed deeply at the thought of having that teenager allow herself to be swayed by the pleadings of a five-year-old to act on behalf of others. Embracing the aura made his comings and goings easier on his system, but his head was still vibrating, and he could feel a regular headache just behind his eyes.

He could feel Tessa's gentle touch on his arm, helping him sit up. "Are you sure you don't want something to help with discomfort? Anything at all?"

"Thank you, sweetheart. I think I'm good. So, did you guys get the recordings?"

"Ja," Leif said, "hell ja! I just played back a small bit, where you are talking with someone—having, eh conversation. You got this Mary person to listen to you, which is bloody fantastic, ja?"

"That is most assuredly bloody fantastic!" Tessa said.

"Let me pull up the record," Sita said, "so Jax can compare iterations. Okay, we didn't expect to be able to prevent the explosion, so let's not go there. Jax, this shows that there were 168 people killed, including 19 children, with over 680 injured."

"So, nothing really changed then?" Dr. Mason said. "From the printout Sita gave us while you were being hypnotized—all the numbers are exactly the same. The identical number of deaths and injuries."

Jax gently rubbed the palms of his hands over his eyes. His face was blank as he slowly rose from the chair. He smiled at Leif, then Sita, and finally his wife. The vibration in his head finally subsided, and he walked over to where Dr. Mason and Molly were seated. He just stood in front of them for a few seconds, then grinned stupidly at them.

"Four people—we saved four people. The calls Mary made kept two adults and their two children from dying that day!"

"It's too bad," Sita said, "that the rest of us can't see the change when you 'iter it. Damn it, Jax, that still sounds like a fantastic outcome. Good work!"

"Ja! This is a success," Leif said, bright with pride. "You are glorious, ja? 'Iter it'. I like this odd word very much, Sita. Gives what Jax does a real punch. I vill buy all the drinks tonight, I tell you!"

"I don't understand Jax," Dr. Mason said. "What is it that all of you are celebrating?"

“Let me check out a few things first, and then I’ll come back and answer all your questions.” Huddling with his team, he turned to his wife. “Tess, how long was I under this time?”

“Not including our hypnotic induction session, you were in the chair for just under 15 minutes.”

“That’s a start for future work. I know I was visiting for about 60 minutes.”

“Extrapolating that reasoning,” Tessa said, “If you were to be under for an hour by our clock, that would translate to visiting in another time for four hours—correct?”

“I don’t think we can make that kind of blanket statement at this point. Let’s talk more about all of that later. Sita, were you able to trace what became of those four souls we saved from the bomb? And if possible, the full name of that neighbor girl, Mary? I want to get a better sense of any ripple effect our work might have had.”

“I’m waiting on the search results as we speak. Their names were queued up before the session, and the recording during your visit confirmed that group. Let me see what the records tell me now. You know, if I had Mary's last name, I'd be more likely to find her. Honestly, tracking who she is will be pretty tricky.”

Jax stuck his head up and called to the control booth. “Amy, how about the readings from the helmet? Have you gotten those up yet?”

"Yes," Amy said through the speaker. "The helmet showed the same temporal anomaly readings as those from your first experiment. But Jax..."

"Okay, Jax," Sita interrupted. "I've tracked down some preliminary facts on the people you saved, but you're not going to like it. George Marshall died of a massive coronary four months after the bombing. Anna Toller was divorced and moved to Washington right after the Oklahoma City attack. She died along with her daughter, Sally, during a school shooting in February of the following year.

"George Marshall Jr. grew up with his mother and joined the Marines right after high school. He died in Afghanistan in 2006 during the rescue of a U.S. pilot who was shot down. George was posthumously awarded the Silver Star for saving two fellow marines during that operation, who in turn rescued that pilot."

"What you're telling me is that the deaths of these people were inevitable. All I did was postpone it from happening. A few months for most, a few years for the Marine. Was all that a waste of our time? Are deaths fixed points in time?!"

"Jax, wait!" Sita said. "The pilot who was shot down and suffered shrapnel wounds to his arm. His name was...Major Mark Beck, USAF!"

"What, the...? Wait, that was my dad? That was my dad they rescued?"

"Jax," Amy said through the intercom. "Please just listen for a minute! There's an important detail from the Kernel Flow readings. You need to check the monitor. Look closely at the corpus callosum area of your brain. Something's...really off."

47

Corpus Callosum

"What do you mean, off? I see a little..."

"Jax," Amy said, "look at the image we just pulled off the helmet. Now compare that to the same image spot, but from the first experiment. Your brain is...different."

Jax had retreated to Amy's old desk and pulled out the computer monitor's swing arm to look at the computer-generated images while he stood. He inched his face closer until his nose nearly touched the screen, then backed away to see the whole picture. Tessa came up to look over his shoulder.

"Amy, I see it. Can you overlay the second image onto the first?"

"Give me a minute. The computer needs to translate the request—okay, it's up now."

"What the hell is going on?" Dr. Mason said, standing in the middle of the room. "Jax, Amy! Someone, please tell me what the hell has you all excited?"

"Steve, come over here so I can show you on the monitor. I'm sorry, Tess, why don't you stand here on the other side of me? Now, you see that blurry mass right in the middle, right there? Okay, watch when Amy displays the images to show the older and newer images side by side."

"Is that neural connections...growing?" Tessa asked.

"Yes. My brain has enhanced the connectivity between the two cerebral hemispheres."

"You're sure it's not a growth or something else?" Dr. Mason asked

"No, just look at it closely. See the tissue, almost like webbing, stretching between left and right. Those are neural networks. New neural networks. Hundreds of them!"

"Excuse me, gentlemen," Molly said. "I am aware that the connection between the hemispheres balances spatial awareness and logic. What I don't get is the implication of having greater connectivity. Is this a good thing, or does this jeopardize Jax's health?"

"Good question," Tessa said. "Also, is this continual growth, or does it only occur with a 2nd Iteration visit? I think you need a complete physical to determine if other systems in your body have been affected or if this is isolated to the brain."

"Tess, slow down. I don't feel any different, and I still have questions that need answering. Amy, was that as much information as you pulled from the helmet?"

"Yes. Well, just the same notification about the temporal anomaly, but nothing else seems out of place."

"Okay, everyone, keep looking at the data we got to ensure we didn't miss anything. You all need to excuse me. I have to go and call my father. This can't wait."

"Jax, you need to speak up. I'm at the airport prepping the Cloud Dancer, so I can hardly hear you. What about Marines and Afghanistan?"

"It's about the time you were shot down in Afghanistan. The Marines who rescued you. Do you remember those men?"

"Yeah, in the Zabul Province near Kandahar. We talked about this once when you were in college. It was a key corridor for the Taliban, and we were charged with taking out supply caravans. A tactical with a 50-caliber took out a section of the left wing on my Thunderbolt and damaged the hydraulics on my landing gear, so I had to make a belly landing. I got out a Mayday and found a small valley in those mountains to put it down. It was close to winter at that altitude, and I found a patch of snow. That's what kept me from flipping. That area was cold enough to freeze the balls off a brass monkey.

"I was waiting for nearly three hours when I saw the Tali' coming down the far ridge. My arm had a lot of damage and blood loss, and I was barely able to get out of my bird with my back to the hills. I almost gave up hope until I saw that helo coming from the south. I don't think I've seen a prettier sight than those boys fast-roping just yards from my position. The enemy started laying down fire almost as soon as our guys landed. I saw one go down and limp away as they were returning fire.

"When a couple made it to me, one did a quick wrap of my bicep while the others stood guard. As we stood to run for the helo, we saw the flash of an RPG. At first, I thought they were aiming for the chopper, but they were really trying to take out a couple of our guys in a rock formation who were causing serious damage to the advancing group.

"One of our boys, though, just started running at the bad guy with the RPG—I mean, straight into the fight. He must have thrown in a couple of frag grenades because after the initial explosion, everything went quiet. When the boys in the rocks came down to help, one grabbed my arm, and I started bleeding again and passed out.

"Marshall. PFC George Marshall. Is that the answer you were looking for? A young jarhead. He was the one who charged the enemy and saved his brothers. A boy not much older than you were at that time had sacrificed himself for his crew and me. I wasn't able to attend his service as I was still in the hospital. He's the only one whose name I remember. His life for mine. Hardly seemed fair."

"I'm sorry to bring up that time for you, Dad. Yeah, I just came across that name in some background we were doing here in the lab. I saw your name on the report and wanted to see what you remembered."

"Was he a student there, or a patient?"

"No, we were looking at records of his father and saw the connecting information about you and George Junior. It was just a coincidence, but it made me think of you and everything you went through. I'll let you go. Where are you flying?"

"Just up to the Colorado Air Show near Fort Collins for the weekend. I have a couple of old flying buddies doing an exhibition. Did you need me for anything else?"

"No, that's it. Stay safe—and Dad, I love you. I hope you know that."

"Yeah, but it's always good to hear. I love you too, Jax. Talk soon."

48

Scientific Inquiry

When Jax returned to the lab, the room was empty except for Sita and Tessa.

"Where is everyone?"

"Leif had to go into work," Sita said. "Dr. Mason left for his office with Molly and Mikey in tow. I don't know where Amy went—she just left without saying a word."

"The thing about George Marshall being killed saving my dad can't be a simple coincidence...can it? I mean, what are the odds the two are unrelated?"

"Is he doing alright?" Tessa asked.

"Yeah, he's good. He just confirmed that he remembered him as the lone member of his squad to be killed that day. George Jr. wasn't more than three years older than me at that time. Yet, he had the balls to run into enemy fire to save the mission, his comrades, and my dad. What kind of cosmic joke is it that we save him, only to have him turn around and save my father?"

"I wouldn't use the term joke, sweetheart. What would have happened if you hadn't saved him in 1995? Would someone else have taken his place on that battlefield? Or is it like Leif keeps saying that it's a connecting circle where you saving him was fixed? That this was always going to happen? That he would grow up to become the hero in this story?"

"Well," Sita said, "so much for free will, eh? It goes back to that *Matrix* thing again—did we do it because it was always meant to be?"

"We can't stop and dwell on it too long. Sita, for right now, I need you to prepare a list of possible candidates for our control tests. I want to start next week—that is, if Tess can make it?"

"We have our regular Monday meetings at the hospital, but I should be able to free up a day or two to assist you here. Will that work?"

"I want to say yes, but I need to confirm that with Amy. She's the best one to be here in the control room. That way, we can have consistency in our comparative studies. I got a tentative agreement from her, but I want to be sure she's still on board.

"Look, I'm sure Dr. Mason is going to want to speak with me before I can call it a day. Tess, would it be possible to have Sita and

Leif over for dinner to discuss how we want to proceed from here? Say tomorrow night?"

"As long as you're not counting on me doing all the cooking, then I think we can manage. Look, I have a patient waiting and need to get back. We'll talk more later." With that, Tessa exited the lab.

"Sita, you know what you need to do to get ready for the next phase of this study? If you have any questions, just text me. So, before I head off to Mason's office, I'm going to see if I can track down Amy and tie up all the loose ends regarding her part in the control tests."

"You won't have to look too hard," Sita said, pointing. Jax turned and saw Amy entering the lab carrying a small stack of printouts. "I'm going to get moving on all this stuff on my to-do list so I can get out of here. Is that all you need?"

"Yes, and thanks again, Sita. Today was quite the day."

As Sita retreated to her office space, Amy walked up to Jax and motioned him towards the conference room. Once Jax entered, she closed the door behind him and sat in a chair facing him.

"The thing with your neural connections growing really freaked Mason out—as well as Mikey. I think they wanted to talk about partnerships, money, and all that. We, however, need to talk about the science."

“Sure, but first, did Mason give you the go-ahead to continue working the scans for our control group?

“Yes, he did. You must have convinced him that this is a priority, so I’m back in the booth for the next couple of weeks. I was able to line up our first volunteer. She’s pre-med here at the university, so it's a double bonus for us. Her OCD is fairly strong, which is making her studies difficult. And before you ask again, she can be here any morning next week at nine.

“Sorry, I forgot I already asked you that earlier. Yes, if she’s here on Tuesday, Tessa can make it, so we have that first hour to prepare her about the process and what we hope to see happen during the experiment.”

“Okay, now the science part. I was really curious about why we didn’t see any change after your first scan with the helmet, so I went back to the older records and zoomed in on the images we had stored. I did find a small group of cells in the region of the mid-brain that I hadn’t noticed earlier. I missed it primarily because there was very little difference on that initial scan, but the growth between that test and this last one was so much more pronounced.”

Amy pulled out several pages showing various images of Jax’s brain, each with timestamps in the upper corners. She selected one and slid it across the table so Jax could view the computer-generated scan. She used a pen from her pocket to point to a spot on the picture.

"This magnification is ten times normal. You can see it's a cluster that's just beginning to form. It's also vibrant, so the cluster has a certain iridescence that can only be seen when viewed at a slight angle. Obviously, your very first test didn't have the means to measure the granularity of your brain, so we have no way of knowing whether there was an initial spark at that time. I think we can assume that something did happen, although as a scientist, I will deny that I ever used the term, assumed."

"So, a seed was planted. Then we have...what? Cell proliferation—cell growth and division leading to an increase in neural quantity?"

"Growth, yes, but not hyperplasia—division, which is consistent with healthy neurons. That's good because it allows us to rule out cancerous development. This clearly shows the expansion of your neural network is in play. Now, the big question—the one Tessa mentioned—has this growth been continuous when no 2nd Iteration visits take place, or does this growth only occur when you engage in this activity?"

"What you're telling me is I need to be scanned again."

"I think you need to be scanned multiple times. As a control, it should be when you are just sitting in that chair and not 'itering it, as you've all come to call it."

"Let's see what next week holds. Maybe we'll get lucky, and something will show up in the volunteer's scan."

"To keep this as an honest control, we also need to have her scanned at various periods as well. We should do one before the start of the experiment, during, then say one or two more a few days later for a good comparison."

"So, Amy, are you saying you don't want to be scanned as well?"

"Oh, please," she said with a snort. "Someone has to be the adult in the room."

Amy squared her shoulders and set the stack of brain scan printouts aside, arms folded as if to resist the temptation of further debate. Jax felt her steely gaze boring in—appraising him.

"So, Tuesday. You and Tessa will run it, and I'll do the post. Now, can we talk about the real weirdness? Your temporal parietal junction is lighting up like Christmas. It's not just new cells—it's the connectivity. You're literally seeing with more bandwidth than before."

Glancing back at her, he nodded in agreement. "Yeah. I am—seeing more that is."

49

ZANE

As Jax walked up to the closed door of the Director's office, he could hear a loud conversation coming from within. He knocked once, then let himself into the room. He expected Dr. Mason, Molly, and Mikey to be present, but was surprised to see another man seated in front of Steve's desk—one whose face was quite familiar.

"Mr. Zane," Dr. Mason said, "this is Dr. Jaxon Beck. He would be the best person to answer your questions."

Jax stepped into the crowded office and stood alongside Mikey, who was leaning against the bookcase.

"May I know who Mr. Zane is before we have a conversation?"

"A fair enough request," Mr. Zane said, rising to his feet and offering Jax his hand. He spoke with a slight accent, but one Jax couldn't place. "Leo Zane, CEO of Zane Enterprises." Zane stood somewhere around five and a half feet tall, but his gripping energy made the man's presence seem twice that size.

"I own several companies in a variety of fields, but all specialize in the development of new technologies. VRMX happens to be one such company, and the one that owns that very expensive equipment currently being used for these experiments of yours."

"So," Jax said, accepting the handshake, "you're a wealthy tech enthusiast who has personally come to interrogate us? I would have assumed you'd send one of your minions."

Zane just smiled, a flicker of amusement in his eyes. "I heard you have a sharp tongue, Dr. Beck. Please, call me Leo. May I call you Jax?"

"Sure, Leo. So, what questions can I answer for you that Steve and Molly haven't been able to satisfy up to this point? And I guess that includes Mikey as well?"

"I'm certain you haven't been properly introduced, but Dr. Michael Zane is my son and the President of VRMX Technologies. To answer your question, yes, he should be included in our discussions."

Turning to the thin man beside him, Jax gave the younger Zane an appraising look before commenting. "Damn, Mikey, now that is something I wish you'd shared a while ago. Anyways... Leo, please proceed."

"Of course. First, am I clear on the point that, up until now, you are the only one who notices when a change is made to what you call reality?"

“I’m hoping this isn’t just my reality. But to answer the question, aside from the Kernel Flow data showing temporal anomalies, I am the only one who...remembers aspects of my life differently.”

“Then you will appreciate that I am cautious about investing in something that we only have your word for having succeeded.”

“You stated you are the type of person who likes cutting-edge stuff. We have indications that ripples from my actions may become measurable. Today was the start. This is where people hop on the train to see where it leads. I see this as an invitation to help us discover this project’s possibilities.”

“Just so, Jax. And what would a ticket for a ride on your train cost me...exactly?”

Before speaking, Jax studied Leo's face. Something flickered across the man's features—a slight tilt of the head, a momentary twitch at the corner of his mouth that vanished as quickly as it appeared. Amy's words about extended bandwidth echoed in his mind.

"Look, Leo," Jax said, leaning forward slightly, "I'm not here with my hand out. This project is still in its infancy. But I'm curious—what price would you put on technology that could revolutionize our understanding of the brain? Information that could potentially heal people? I'm asking genuinely. What's that worth to humanity... and to Leo Zane personally?”

“I’m growing weary of this bantering, Jax. Your proof of concept is weak, which even a man with your obvious ego can appreciate.

Typically, a small venture like yours requires about a million in startup capital to become profitable. I want a 70/30 split from all proceeds arising from your patents and related intellectual property. I think that is more than fair."

"I'm sure you do, but I'm not going to agree to anything final today, and I doubt Dr. Mason would be so inclined either. In the meantime, we have work to do in the next couple of weeks. That would only require using the Kernel Flow helmet for accurate measurement. Why don't you make ownership of that unit a gift to the Center—as a gesture of your willingness to reach an amicable arrangement?"

"And Michael will continue to oversee your work as your small gesture of good faith?"

"Sure. I like Mikey."

"Then, consider it done. Also, I would like to see your setup firsthand. So, give Michael advance notice before you do your little trick again so I can be there."

"You might find being a spectator boring, but that's not a problem. Give me a week or so to run control tests. I wouldn't want you to rely solely on my word."

50

DINNER TALK

"I GET IT! I get it! We've already talked about the philosophical ramifications of my work with the 2nd Iteration. But we have a couple of new pieces of information I need to know where to put in this puzzle box I'm living in. Okay?"

Sita reached for the pie plate. "Mind if I finish this off before we dive in? And thanks for cooking—you two outdid yourselves tonight."

"Two things that were mentioned before ring true," Tessa said, sitting back and sipping from her wine glass. "The first was from Leif, who talked about the possibility that the visit to your past and saving George Marshall Jr. was always meant to happen. Sita voiced the second regarding the Hindu question of whether the past is fixed or fluid. Do any of those things sound factual to you as the causal agent in this story?"

"That implication leans into the single timeline possibility, where everything happens as it must. If that is what's going on here, then my intervention was always part of history, and George Jr. was always destined to die saving my father. So, I can't change the past—only fulfill it. That means there's no free will, and I'm having a hard time buying that. My Dad was alive before I started this experimentation. I have to believe that if I had never pursued this work, he would still be alive—according to my memory of original events."

"Might I shift gears a moment," Tessa said, "to speak of the other people? The other three you saved from the bombing...they died not long afterward, didn't they? To my mind, that rather supports the notion of fixed points in time. They may curve, perhaps, but not be wholly undone."

"If you put what happened to all four," Sita said, "it seems to be a blend of both fixed and fluid. Maybe you're giving yourself too much credit—or blame here, Jax. I know you are an atheist, but what if there really is a higher power involved in all of this...reality?"

"So, we should be seeking out a priest or a...Sita, what do Hindus call their holy men?"

"There are a few different ones, but in this case, I think you'd ask an Acharya."

"Okay, people of faith, then, each having a different interpretation. Or would running this by a tenured philosopher at the university be of any help? Am I the only one who thinks we covered almost every philosophical perspective already?"

"As your wife and a trained psychiatrist, I would recommend you keep thinking about these issues and even journal your thoughts as they arise. We, humans, are rarely given absolutes in life, so we must learn to navigate uncertainty—and yes, make peace with ambiguity. Otherwise, you'll drive yourself nuts. That happens to be a technical term, by the way."

"Thank you, Dr. Beck. Switching gears again. Let's talk about Leo Zane and his desire to become a controlling partner in this work. On one hand, the man has deep pockets, but I don't like the idea of giving up control."

"Big surprise there," Sita snickered.

"Jax is not wrong, you know," Leif said. "He gave you the helmet—that is really all you need to carry on by yourself now, ja? What would his money give you that you don't already have, eh?"

"How about my salary, Big Guy?" Sita said. "Not to mention Jax's and anyone else we need to run more experiments. Then there are the costs the Center incurs when we use the lab, equipment, and even utilities. Would Mason even allow you to turn down Zane's money machine?"

"My gut says no. I think Mason has been trying to get me to monetize my work for some time now, and I have come to believe that's why he cut off my funding. He wanted to push me into producing some migraine-related product. The fact that Steve was even able to get a man of Zane's status to show up on our doorstep tells me this arrangement has probably been in the works for a while."

"So, what if you simply decline to participate?" Tessa asked. "Will the Center close down your work?"

"I tried that once before, and yes, I believe that is exactly what Mason would do. I'm sorry that I never mentioned that to you, but it didn't get to that point, so I didn't say anything. And just so we're clear, it is the Center that was given the helmet. That's a critical piece of equipment for any future experimentation."

"We'll talk about what you just shared when we are alone. For now, could you clear up one point for me? Molly told us straight away that she had concerns about VRMX Technologies working for the government. The original plans for the VyzR came from a younger Jax. So, wouldn't that mean that Mikey, and likely dear old dad, Leo, have some form of shadowy connection to at least one government agency?"

"I would have to agree that if that were the case, we'd be partnering with both the Zanes and some agency like the CIA. We've already confirmed that they are working with DARPA, but that is merely where the sorting begins. Who knows what they will want from us—now or down the line? I don't know if my working with Leo will provide any more clarity as to motive."

"You think they could turn what you do into a weapon?" Leif asked. "Maybe just carry on with their, eh—secret squirrel business—like dat Project Stargate thing, ja?"

"I think that would be a good assumption considering who we're dealing with. Zane himself already has a small personal army of robots. Granted, they probably work as well as the cars he builds, but that's not to say the man isn't dangerous."

"What you're telling us," Sita said, "is that we're fucked. You either work for the guy out in the open and probably get misused, or you cross him, and he buries your work and maybe you as well—professionally, I mean. He could make it so you wouldn't be able to work in this field again."

"Well, thank you for that visual, Ms. Singh. I must say, I no longer believe my husband to be safe—regardless of which path he takes. This conversation has been growing darker by the minute."

"Well, once we're through the control trials, maybe we'll have a clearer picture of what our future with this man would look like. We still have time to work out a possible third alternative. But for the moment, we need to be careful about whom we share these kinds of thoughts with. Zane wants something from me beyond any partnership."

"What makes you so sure, sweetheart? Did he say something to you that you haven't mentioned before now?"

Jax thought back to his meeting with the man and the microexpressions he saw. “No, nothing in his words, but there was something in the way he spoke that bothered me.”

“Maybe,” Sita said, “we could all just move to Norway?”

“Nei, not with your music!” Leif said. “You’d scare off all the birds in Trondheim, I think.”

51

TEST& RETEST

"PLEASE STATE YOUR NAME," Amy said.

"My name is Mina. Mina Takahashi, and I'm twenty-one years old."

"Thank you. Please tell us where you were born."

"Here in the Denver area. I'm, that is...my grandfather was from Japan."

"And Ms. Takahashi, you are a student here at the university, correct?"

"Yes, I'm a sophomore studying Pre-med. Um, I should be a junior, but..."

"Are you comfortable stating why you are being seen here at the Center?"

"Yes. Well, it's kind of embarrassing. I've been diagnosed with OCD. Uh, Obsessive-Compulsive Disorder. I'm having a hard time finishing my work. It's never right."

"Thank you for volunteering that information and for agreeing to allow us to run some tests on you today. For the record, do you feel that we've explained to you thoroughly enough what today is going to look like and what you can expect?"

"You're going to scan my brain using the Kernel Flow monitor, which is so cool. I've read all about it, but I've never seen one before—will I be able to see the results? The printouts after we're done, I mean. Do I need to change my clothes? I just wore my sweats because I wasn't sure if I was going to have to wear a hospital gown...or whatever."

"No, Mina. What you wear makes no difference. However, I will ask you to remove any earrings or any facial piercings to prevent inaccurate imaging."

"I don't...I'm not allowed...I don't have any piercings, and I left my earrings at home. Oh, what about my hair? I didn't think I needed to do anything with..."

"No, that's fine. You have very beautiful hair, and because it is straight, it will allow the helmet to fit securely on your head. Maybe take a few breaths and try to relax. We're going to do an initial scan, which will take about 10-15 minutes. Then we're going to have you wear the EMDR visor while we run a scan of your brain a second time. Do you recall why we are going to have you undergo the EMDR session?"

"Yes. You want to look at the neural activity in my brain during the session to monitor for increased electrical excitation while in a hyper-relaxed state and focused on the therapist's voice—is that right?"

"Perfect. I understand you know who Dr. Beck is from your classes. Are you familiar with his wife, Tessa? Excuse me, this is the other Dr. Beck. She will act as the therapist during the EMDR session and be responsible for turning on the visor's light after the initial relaxation period. Do you have any questions? No? Okay, then let's begin."

The young woman tried to see around her while the Kernel Flow helmet was placed over her head. During their earlier prep session, Sita had adjusted the helmet's plate segments to match Mina's smaller skull. It was unclear whether Mina was agitated because she was in a reclined position, because of the procedure itself, or because she was trying to study everything everyone was doing at once.

After the initial scan, Mina ran to the restroom but was back in the chair within ten minutes. Tessa held Mina's right hand gently and explained how they would proceed.

"Mina, we are going to start slowly so you get used to the sound of my voice. This part of the process is merely to help you attain a level of relaxation, and I am not going to do or say anything that hasn't already been explained to you. If at any point you need me to stop the process, just hold up a hand, and I will end the session."

The visor was placed on Mina's face with the light still in the off position. The goal was to help the young woman relax after Tessa's brief hypnotic session. She wasn't going to try to induce a deep state, just enough to transition to the actual EMDR therapy.

"The most important thing that can happen right now is for you to trust that I will not do anything that may harm you. You can answer yes to any of my questions simply by nodding your head gently. So, I am going to have you start by taking a deep breath and holding it for the count of four, then exhaling gently for another four seconds. Good, now go ahead and keep breathing like that while you visualize descending an escalator."

It had been decided beforehand that Tessa would not use Jax's imagery of riding down an elevator, as closed spaces made Mina nervous. Tessa's relaxation session seemed to calm the woman noticeably, so she reached over and switched on the EMDR light in the visor. As agreed, Tessa began a calm exchange about one of Mina's pleasant childhood memories, sidestepping anything that might inadvertently upset her. The goal was to purposefully avoid any traumatic event that may cause Mina to have an unexpected reaction or any after-effects when they were done.

When they had finished, Mina returned to her animated state. "Oh...my...God. That was so amazing. That visor and the sound of your voice coming through the speakers around my ears made me feel like I was really, really focused. Can we do that again?"

"Not today," Tessa said, "but soon. Sita will schedule a date for a second round."

"Can I go see the Kernel Flow printouts now? And do you have any of the company's handouts about the machinery itself? I heard the infrared lights are wicked fast."

After they had satisfied Mina enough to continue with their analysis, Amy and Jax looked over her scans. The cortico-striato-thalamo-cortical loop was evident, which was the basis of OCD episodes. Nothing extraordinary showed anywhere else in the brain.

They had been able to scan Mina once more the following week, and Sita had delivered three other student volunteers who had each undergone one session. Jax also underwent an additional scan while refraining from any 2nd Iteration visits. His migraines had started to creep back, with a mild incident occurring just the day before.

"I've read your reports on Mina and the others. It looks like they all have gotten something out of the sessions with Tess, but so far, nothing like what I've gone through. Do you agree with that assessment?"

"We still haven't made it through the second round of testing on these other three, but if Mina is any indication, then no. Nothing like your results. It's still fascinating, Jax," Amy said. "See this shift in prefrontal activity? That showed up in Mina after her second session with Tessa. It shows her executive function kicking in—behavior indicative that she is no longer stuck in that obsessive loop.

"Before the sessions, her orbitofrontal cortex just above the eye sockets lit up like a warning flare. Now? It's quieter with less compulsive noise. Her brain's reprocessing, literally rewiring. The old memory trace isn't gone, but it's been...softened."

"But not the temporal anomaly caused by having two memories coexist. I mean, I'm glad it's helped her, but I guess I was hoping for a more comparable effect."

"The data don't lie. The theory that your situation is still unique remains unchallenged. But keep in mind, having just these four control subjects limits us from making any substantive claim either way.

"On the other hand, we do have a strong argument regarding your neural network between the hemispheres. Laying the newer scans over the older ones shows growth has neither weakened nor increased since your last 2nd Iteration visit."

"Let me guess. The only way to establish that my visits trigger additional growth is for another full-on experiment?"

"I believe that is necessary for a couple of reasons. Mason has been adamant that I stay with you during this testing. He's practically salivating about getting funded by Zane's fortune. The problem is, we don't have anything to offer the guy right now."

"I've started looking at other possibilities. But for now, we've just started working with migraine sufferers, so we're at least a month away from having any data on that."

"It would seem your ability to vividly recall long-term memories is the only thing we have at the moment. I'm hoping you and your team will come up with some practical ideas that we can demonstrate soon."

"And that concerns me, Amy. Mikey was here for both experiments. He saw the anomalous readings from the helmet. Is there a more corrupt use of this ability that would be valuable to a man like Zane—or to others?"

"You've picked the wrong scientist to have that discussion with. I understand you and the rest of your little gang have been talking about something Einstein would deem spooky action. My expertise is not in quantum mechanics, nor am I religious or into new age crazes. I will admit that something is going on with you during these sessions, but I'm not ready to accept that you can alter things in time. That's a bit too far for me."

"I'm sorry. You've made your position clear in that area. I guess I was thinking out loud. But, as a scientist, you have to concede that my neural network has grown?"

"We have evidence to support that position, yes."

"Then what acceptable theory do you have for that physiological change occurring?"

"I wouldn't call it a theory, but I believe when you create additional neurons during your remembrances, you stimulate growth in adjacent parts of your brain. As we've seen, most of what is taking place is in and around the mid-brain, and that is where the expansion of networks is also taking place."

"Then why am I the only one who is developing these extra neural pathways?"

"I'm not saying you are. What I am saying is that the only trials here and at VRMX Tech have had very small sample sizes. There still may be others who are similar to you, but our ability to test a significant cross-section of individuals is extremely limited."

"Not to Zane. You stated that after you met Mr. Curtis, he seemed to be with the government. We also know for a fact that VRMX Tech is working with DARPA."

"So what? Zane, Inc. must be collaborating with the government?"

“Why not? It’s not that big of a leap. He could be their front man for funding scientific and technological discoveries that can be used...”

“...in defense of the nation?”

“I was going to say as weapons. The claim of national security has been overused as a justification for controversial actions since Nixon. Our hands aren’t clean.”

“Did I forget to mention that in addition to not being religious, I’m not political either?”

“If things go sideways, Amy, you may not have a choice.”

52

VISITORS

THE FOLLOWING WEDNESDAY, LEO Zane showed up at the entrance to Jax's lab. He was accompanied by his son, Mikey, Dr. Mason, and a man who, judging by his appearance and demeanor, had to be Zane's personal security. Walking directly up to Jax and warmly shaking his hand, his intense gaze spoke of sincerity, honesty, and ruthlessness all at once. Zane wielded a command of people that one might attribute to a wizard.

"Dr. Beck—Jax. It is so damn nice to see you again. I apologize for just dropping in, but I had business in the area, and I hadn't heard back in a couple of weeks, so I...." The man took a step back and placed his hands on his hips. "Damn. Here I am blabbering on like a schoolgirl, but I guess I'm just eager to be working with you!"

"Well, thank you, Leo. I—I mean, we're still in the middle of our control studies. As a matter of fact, that's all I have to show you at the moment. We have a volunteer here now and were about to start a session."

"Don't let me get in your way. I just wanted to look around and get the flavor of what you and your gang are up to. Michael has told me a great deal about your process, so I guess I'll find a spot out of the way and watch a bit. Will that work for everyone?"

"Sure. I'll have Dr. Mason set you up in a spot out of view of our test subject. A quick introduction of my team before you sit. That's my wife, Tessa, who will be conducting the session." Tessa raised her eyes at the sound of her voice, then refocused on the young woman lying in the patient chair.

"Then, there's Amy in the control room who will be tracking and interpreting the readings from the Kernel Flow helmet. That's Sita, my technician. She is currently monitoring the patient's blood pressure and heart rate as a precaution. Lastly, Leif over there in the corner is recording the session, both from the therapist, my wife, and the patient."

"You see, right there. That quick mind and succinctness of thought. That's what I've come to see. I want to observe the people behind the ideas."

"I'm not much of an entertainer, Leo, especially when we have all these other performers doing their shtick."

"Just so. Steve, would you and Michael join me while we watch? And Carter is a quiet sort. He'll stay near the door, so you won't even notice him after a bit."

Returning to his position on the opposite side of the volunteer, Jax raised his hand and twirled his index finger in a wind-up motion, signaling for his team to begin the procedure. Tessa stole a worried look at her husband, then focused on the hypnotic and EMDR induction process.

After the better part of an hour had passed, Tessa gently removed the visor from the woman's face and calmly claimed, "All done. Take a few deep breaths, Jean, and when you're ready, you can leave. No rush. We have water, soda, or coffee if any of that would help." The woman shook her head, declining the offer. Then she swung her feet off the chair, dropped to the ground, and hurriedly left the room—eyes downcast the whole time.

"Jax," Leo Zane asked cautiously, "what was the purpose of all of that?"

"Give me a minute, Leo. Let my people finish their work, then I'll be able to talk with you in private."

Jax turned to the control booth and found Amy staring back. She shook her head, then turned back to the printout of her measurements.

He turned to his wife, who was busy gathering up her things. "Tess, thank you for all of your hard work on this. It really means a lot."

"Sweetheart, don't take this the wrong way, but I'm exhausted. Two weeks of this and now I'm starting to wonder if the hospital pays our therapists enough. I'm headed home. Don't judge me if a wine bottle has gone missing when you make it back."

"Understood and understandable. Again, you have been an integral part of this, and I can't thank you enough."

After Tessa exited the room, Leo and Michael Zane walked up to Jax.

"Well," Zane said, "that was...interesting. That wife of yours is an amazing woman."

"Yes, and she's a hell of a doctor to boot. I guess I'll keep her."

"Right, right. Point taken. She is amazing, period. Would this be a good time to have a quick conversation?

"Sure. Let's talk in the conference room."

Jax led the way, and the two Zane men followed closely behind.

"Nick," Leo said to his security man, "you can wait for us outside in the limo."

Once the door shut behind them, Leo immediately jabbed a finger at Jax.

"I don't appreciate being put on ice while you do your little jig out there. I do have places to be, you know!"

"Leo, I understand you're a man who's used to getting his way, whenever he wants it, but this is science. Real science. And that comes with a lot of downtime waiting for answers that can't be produced on demand. I can't be the first person to tell you this!"

"That is such complete bullshit. You said you'd get back to me in two weeks. Those weeks came and went, and I didn't hear shit-all from you. That is not how you conduct business."

"No, you dipshit. But it is the way you conduct science. What the holy fuck did you expect when you waltzed in here, waving the promise of money under Mason's nose?"

The senior Zane's face reddened at this retort. "You bloody wanker, I ought to..."

"Dad, stop, just stop!" Mikey interjected loudly. "This is legit, don't you see? Jax is legit, and the things he has claimed to do when he's the one in that chair are real!"

Jax stared in puzzlement at the young man, then returned his gaze to his father. "Leo, I am honestly confused by your actions right now. You claim to be involved in all things technological, and your own son is neck-deep in it. Do you actually believe you can have breakthroughs in tech without having the science to make it work? And, Mikey, what did you mean just now? What are you not saying?"

"I have...that is, I remember what took place before you iterated back to 1995. I also remember the time when you relived your mother's accident and her death. You were right. Before the experiment, there was nothing wrong with your hand. But, when you exited the session, your finger was just...gone."

"So, although you ran all those tests at VRMX, you never conducted one on yourself?"

"No, of course I did. I just didn't have the same vivid memories as you. However, when I was here as an eyewitness, I recalled the differences, including the number of people who originally died in Oklahoma City and then afterward. At the time, it scared the hell out of me, but I didn't know what I was supposed to do with that information."

"How about telling me?" Leo snarled. "After all, I am your damn father!"

"It's because I knew you'd act like this. You don't talk with people—you talk at them— forcefully. Cruelly!"

Zane Sr. took in a long breath, then straightened his tie and looked back at Jax. "Okay then, what about this other thing? This capacity to heal certain neural conditions, like the lass who was just in here. What about that?"

"Okay." What about it? We've had some limited success, but nothing to write home about."

"So you haven't had any success with the brain rewiring to help with OCD patients or with you growing extra neural networks in your own brain?"

Jax was a bit shocked by this revelation. The only other person he had shared these results with was Amy. He looked out at the control booth to see her staring back at him with a slight smile on her face. "We... We've just started to collect these results. You must know that those numbers—"

Just then, there was a loud knock at the door, and Leif entered, a scowl on his face. "Jax... there is a man here. Curtis, he calls himself. He says you were probably expecting him. I do not like him. And I like even less the man who walks with him."

Jax turned to face Leo Zane, expecting to see some acknowledgment regarding this development in man's expression. The man just raised both hands in surrender.

"Don't look at me, Beck. I don't know this guy, but I imagine this has something to do with us trying to work together. Regardless, don't think we're through talking about this situation. I need more answers. Straight answers from you...and from my son."

Stepping out of the conference room, Jax's eyes locked onto a stone-faced man built like a linebacker, his shoulders pressed against the wall beside the laboratory entrance. Mason fidgeted in the center of the room, and next to him, looking frightened, was Tessa.

Leif and Sita stood together on the other side of the conference room, both looking uneasy about what was transpiring. Jax shot a quick glance at the control room window and caught a look of confusion in Amy's eyes. She just shook her head and stood at the control room doorway.

He turned back towards the lab's entrance when he heard the doors close. Jax froze as Molly entered the lab and stood silently by the beefy man. Molly cocked her head at an older man who was standing by the coffee cart. His grey suit and silver hair made him blend in with the steel walls and chrome equipment.

The man was unnaturally still, as he fastidiously sipped from Jax's personal mug—the one with Tessa's lipstick still marking the rim. The man's eyes never left Jax's as he raised the mug in a toast. "I'm Mr. Curtis," he said, his voice a dry rasp that filled the sterile lab air. "And you, Dr. Beck, are the great and powerful wizard of...this." He waved a gloved hand around the lab contemptuously.

"Your research file, Dr. Beck—all seven hundred or so pages—makes for fascinating bedtime reading. You may not believe it at the moment, but our interests are greatly aligned. I am genuinely looking forward to introducing you to my work. You see, this country's security largely depends on the work I do. The work I hope you and I will soon be doing...together."

"Jax," Zane said, "I have lawyers in this city. I can have them here in minutes. Just say the word."

Initially, Jax thought Zane might have been behind all the sneaking around these last few weeks. Aside from Amy leaking him some minor research details, it was actually Molly who was setting him up—again—still. He didn't know why that would surprise him. She told him what type of person she was. She confessed so she could keep playing him right out in the open.

Curtis flicked his wrist dismissively. "Lawyers." He didn't bother looking at Zane as he spoke. "Mr. Zane, your visa expired." He checked his watch. "My, my, that was thirty-seven days ago."

He nodded toward the linebacker without turning his head. "Mr. Smith, there is with Homeland Security. One word from me, and you'll be sampling airplane food on your way to Johannesburg before you finish whatever tedious protest you're about to make." He sighed, as if explaining simple concepts to a child. "Or you can spare us from all the theatrics and just leave."

Leo turned to Jax. His expression was a contorted mix of anger and sadness. "I'm sorry, Jax," he said, deflated. "Perhaps we will be able to continue our discussion at some point...later."

Curtis set down Jax's mug, the soft clink against the counter like a distant warning bell. "Dr. Beck," he said, his voice slicing the air as he approached Jax. "Tomorrow at precisely 10 AM, I'll need you to explain your little time-travel trick to some interested parties who will be waiting in your old classroom. In the meantime, you'll be my guest for the evening." His eyes flicked to Tessa and lingered there. "For your safety, of course. Mrs. Beck, I'll arrange for one of my people to drive you home."

"Ve vill drive her," Leif said in guttural tone, "to make sure she gets home...safely."

"What about our agreement, Mr. Zane?" Dr. Mason asked, reaching for the man's arm as he was leaving. "We were going to talk about your endowment to the Center."

"Steven," Zane said, "there are bigger issues in play here." He turned to look at Jax once more. "Unfortunately, it seems I am needed elsewhere. I'm sorry, Jax. I hope this all works out for the best. I really do."

Curtis leaned close to Jax. "Dr. Beck," he said, "We've made arrangements for the night. Nothing extravagant, just...secure." His fingers brushed invisible lint from Jax's shoulder. "Why, we even packed you a change of clothes. Mr. Smith will escort you."

"And what if I tell you to just fuck off?"

Curtis's voice dropped to a cold, smooth tone. "Just one night, Dr. Beck." His eyes never left Tessa as he straightened his cufflink. "Nothing sinister, I assure you, but it's my job to ensure your assistance." The corner of his mouth twitched upward. "I trust you're sensible enough not to make a fuss. For everyone's sake."

"Vat if I vant to make a fuss?" Leif growled.

Mr. Smith pushed off the wall and took two steps forward. His hand remained in his jacket pocket, but it was obvious he was grasping something...ominous.

Jax caught the man's movement and quickly planted himself in front of his large friend. "Leif," he said, putting a hand on the man's shoulder. "I need you and Sita to watch over Tessa. Can you do that for me?"

"I vill protect her. You have my word, ja, as your friend and brodder," Leif said.

Curtis tapped his watch face with a manicured fingernail. "Time waits for no man, Dr. Beck," he said, his voice like ice as he gestured towards the door. "Shall we?"

53

On Display

"Yes, yes, I understand, Dr. Beck. You have explained what is physiologically transpiring in your brain when you undergo these... 2nd Iterations, as you so quaintly call them. But would please clarify for the unwashed among us as to how exactly this is advancing the treatment of neurological diseases."

Jax hated this—this whole shit show. Curtis was unyielding in his insistence that he be here today. So, here he was. Back in his old classroom, but this time the roles were reversed, and instead of asking the questions, he was the one being asked. More precisely, he was being grilled—and grilled by a room full of strangers. There were dozens of them. Some wore suits, some lab coats, and others—so unnervingly many others—were wearing military uniforms.

"Our data to this point indicate the probability that the process which I just described can potentially heal the brain. Rewire broken or misfiring neural connections. Calm nerve receptors to neutralize pain. And if we are fortunate, maybe even find a way to extend life by allowing damaged cells to regenerate through directed conscious thought."

Almost to a person, the audience began vocally objecting to one or more of the points he had just detailed, with small debates breaking out among them. He looked around to see if Dr. Mason had shown his face, but evidently, the director had not been invited to this meeting.

"Dr. Beck," came a voice floating in from nowhere, "far as I can tell, the only solid proof's comin' straight from you, sir. You ain't been able to pull off this memory-rewritin' trick on nobody else and judgin' by what I've read and heard from the folks in this very room, don't look like anybody else has had much luck neither."

Jax waited a beat before answering. The man asking the question probably held some degree of clout with this group, but he wasn't the top dog, of that he was certain. He would play along with this stupid game until the real holder of power made themselves known.

"Sir, with all due respect, your line of questioning prompts an additional inquiry. One which I earlier put forth to my director, and through him, I imagine, his overseers as well. Isn't it likely—statistically likely that other individuals with my rare characteristics exist? And if so, shouldn't we continue with this research to seek them out?"

"Don't you mean hand you a blank check?" another man asked loudly. Laughter erupted throughout the auditorium, then slowly died down. Jax observed that some sophomoric idiots never grew up, just grew older.

"Let me ask you all a question, and this one is rhetorical. What is the purpose of conducting research—any research? Is it to find cures for horrid ailments that afflict millions? Is it to build a better weapon, as if our generals don't have? Or is it to discover more about ourselves as a unique species, one that is still stumbling around in the dark? Judging from your faces, I'd say each of you would have a different answer."

"Just what are you trying to imply by that, sir? Came a gruff voice, obviously offended.

"That will be quite enough," came a strong, feminine voice. "Dr. Beck and I need to talk, and I believe the rest of you have other duties that require your attention."

Oddly, with no further command and as soundlessly as humanly possible, the entire auditorium emptied of all its occupants. All, save one person who sat in the back row center, and was motionless as the throngs of people exited around her. When the last person had gone, a man stuck his head in from the doorway and announced, "All clear."

Then, and only then, did the woman rise and slowly but methodically make her way to the front of the room. Jax remained standing, motionless but undaunted.

"Jaxy, it's been a very long time."

He smiled when he heard this pet name. It had only been spoken by one person in his entire life, and he had heard it again just recently during a journey to his past.

"Mary?"

"I'm better known as Senator Braxton nowadays," the middle-aged woman stated cynically. "But yes, it's me...Mary."

"How? So, you've known about all of this? What a special perspective you must have."

"Yes, I know. What a kick in the pants, eh?"

"I tried to find you, but there were no records to trace."

"Well, in all fairness to you or whoever was trying to locate me, Braxton is the last name of my second husband. So, I wasn't trying to hide from you. What I was trying to do was to live up to what you said to me the last time we met. To do good things with my life. I've got to tell you, that's not as easy to do as it is to say."

"Mary. Rather, Senator Braxton, it's good to see you again."

"Jaxy—Dr. Beck, you may not feel the same after we finish our little talk. You see, I've been part of a committee that's been following your work. Oh, not just you, but a collection of people engaged in this special type of work similar to what you do. You, and people like you, scare the bejesus out of a lot of powerful people."

"I just love ominous warnings like that. No. No, I'm sorry. Please excuse me—continue."

"You were right just now that a whole lot of people see a potential weapon in you and the work you're doing. But they weren't there in that basement playroom thirty years ago when a five-year-old boy convinced me to try and save people neither of us had ever met. I know your intention with all of this has been to do good. To do the right thing. I guess I'm here to tell you a terrible truth, which is that most people, at least those in power, don't give a damn about doing the right thing anymore."

"One question, Mary? Do I have an alternative that hasn't been presented?"

"I would have to answer that by asking, are you as clever a grown man as you were a young boy? If so, you need to think your way past that man who's currently waiting up in the hallway for you to come out—that Curtis fellow. Heck, I don't even know who he works for. But what I do know for sure is that he's one dangerous SOB.

"It is my understanding that he wants to lock you away in some lab until he gets better answers about how your time thing works—in a way, dissect you, Jax. What he wants is to find out how our government can exploit your gift to protect us from—well, from whomever."

"Thank you for telling me, Mary. You're still my hero."

"No, Dr. Beck. It is I who owes you my thanks. You shook my world when last we spoke. You made a malleable young girl realize the world is more than she imagined—more than what the people in control want us to believe. If they had their way, I'd still be believing that life is about all the shiny new stuff we can buy. All the while, instilling in us a sense of insecurity that we are not good enough, that we have to keep running on the hamster wheel to get more. It's crazy, but this is what we've created—this is what we're fighting to protect.

"What's even crazier is this fantasy surrounding free will. I have come to see first-hand that people want to be told what to do, how to vote, even how to think. That goes for both sides of the political spectrum—the tune is just a little different."

"I've tried to keep my work focused on helping people. That's why I got into medicine to begin with. I've tried to make this 2nd Iteration about helping people, either through its medical uses or through whatever small changes I can manage."

"I get that, Jax, I really do. Maybe sometimes it's best not to change things. Looking back at what you've done, it just seemed to get you into trouble. Unfortunately, there's just so much I can do to help you. I've watched you, but I can't protect you from this man or whoever he works for."

"I have other people to think of. My wife, my dad, my friends."

"Your wife is with an individual I trust and who will protect her for now. These people don't care about your dad or your friends. Tessa is a different story. They know they can use her to make you behave. I've arranged for her to meet you. You need to link up and go somewhere that's safe... at least for a while until you can come up with a plan that's more permanent. I'm asking you to run, Jax. Please...run!"

54

The Getaway

Jax asked Senator Braxton for one last favor—that she linger in the auditorium as long as possible and have her security detail stall Curtis if they could. She agreed without hesitation.

Instead of leaving through the upper doors or the side exit he often used when teaching, Jax vanished behind the projection screen. He dropped into a chair and beckoned the aura, calling the name once again of his faithful companion, Bear, to herald the return to his present time. Another short leap—hopefully to save his ass and that of his wife.

Removing the visor, he shoved it into his backpack beside his computer. Rising, he shook his head to clear his thoughts. His head was still vibrating violently, and he urgently grabbed a handkerchief from his pocket to catch the blood oozing from his nose. Through double vision, he managed to shove his arms through the backpack straps and slipped through a forgotten emergency door whose alarm had been disconnected. Staggering down three short steps, he righted himself and pushed aside a stack of cardboard behind stinking trash cans. As his vision sharpened and his head cleared, he saw the gleam of metal from his bike and yanked it from the surrounding debris. Strapping on his helmet, he jumped on the pedals and began careening through the back alleys of the campus.

Ten minutes from his objective, he fought to stay ahead of the chase. The harder he pressed on the pedals, the more blood flooded into his muscles, and the stronger his will to reach Tessa. The long hill that had nearly wrecked him coming down months earlier now loomed before him, needing to be climbed. Not hesitating, he sprang atop the pedals and pushed, driving more adrenaline into his system. His thighs burned as he forced himself up, rising higher, higher, then cresting the peak. Once at the top, he stopped and stole a glance down the hill. The roar of a large black SUV startled him, as the beast was just beginning to charge up the incline. "Hang on, Tessa. I'm coming."

A few minutes prior, Jax had been about to follow Mary out of the auditorium when Mr. Curtis entered. He was followed by a broad man with the feel of menace—not the Mr. Smith from before, but still the same. The older man smiled as he stepped aside to allow the senator to leave. As she departed, Mary turned to Jax, a look of fear on her face.

"Dr. Beck," the man said, "would you be kind enough to accompany us, please. We have a few more questions we'd like to ask—in a more private setting."

"Of course. Just let me collect my computer, it has a lot of sensitive information on it."

Jax didn't wait for permission but purposely slid behind the large projection screen. The man accompanying Mr. Curtis casually began to walk down to the side exit, ready to cut Jax off if necessary. After a long moment waiting for Beck to rematerialize, Curtis signaled his companion to find him.

When Jax had made it behind the screen, he pulled the visor from his backpack and placed it on his face while sitting on a folding chair. Skirting the slow induction process, he took three deep breaths, switched on the EMDR light, and was promptly met by the shimmering rainbow aura. The light blossomed around him as he genuinely welcomed the white light waiting just beyond its edges.

He remembered back to the hour before his presentation. Originally, he had been speaking with Sita and Leif outside in the hall. This time, he paused mid-sentence, then explained his 2nd Iteration visit using short-term memory and the reason for this action.

He laid out his plan for escape and their role in it. Nodding in agreement, they left to complete the tasks assigned to them. Calmly walking behind the projection screen, he placed his open backpack on the floor next to the padded chair, then began sending texts. The first was to his father, asking him to collect and watch Bear—the second was to Tessa, urgent and detailed. Then he shut off his phone and deposited it behind a stack of folding chairs.

After reenacting his performance and feigning surprise at Mary's arrival, he asked her to delay Curtis. Slipping behind the screen, he sat and emerged from his short-term 2nd Iteration visit. Grabbing his pack, he gracelessly exited through the disabled fire door and recovered his bike, which Leif had hidden. He rode until he crested the hill—just as the SUV appeared.

Pedaling onward, Jax gave a quick wave to Sita, who was fervently driving a very large rental truck moving in the opposite direction—straight down the steep hill he had just traversed. Jax smiled at the unmistakable blare of a car horn signifying the successful roadblock the moving truck had caused. There was still much to do.

Turning right at the next street, Jax found Leif waiting in his large vehicle. He jumped off his bike and tossed it into the truck's open hatch. As soon as Jax's butt touched the seat, Leif gunned the engine, and they erupted from the curb, straight towards the freeway onramp that lay ahead.

Opening the glove box, Jax pulled out grooming shears and a small towel and began shaving the beard from his face. When he was done, he stuck the towel out the window, and his shorn hair disappeared into the wind—symbolic of his life at the moment.

A short time later, they screeched to a stop at the Denver Airport. They shook hands, and Jax sprinted inside to the TSA choke point. Frantically trying to see through the throng of people, he finally spotted Tessa sitting on two carry-on bags. Weaving around wheelchairs and luggage, he gently squeezed her arm as he reached her side. She handed him a ticket, a new phone, and a Massachusetts driver's license in the name of Julius Axelrod, to which Jax laughed. The late neuroscientist he had so admired had become his alias.

The senator's contact told Tessa that their IDs had been electronically cleared to help expedite their departure. Using a credit card in Axelrod's name, Tessa had bought them first-class tickets an hour earlier. Now, as they entered the queue to get through security, Tessa handed him a baseball cap and tinted glasses to hinder surveillance.

Standing before the TSA agent, Tessa was told to remove her cap and glasses. After a back-and-forth look, the agent handed back her ID and waved her past. Seeing this, Jax removed his hat and glasses before being told. The agent scowled when he looked at the license Jax provided.

"When did you lose your beard, Mr. Axelrod?"

"My wife had me shave it this morning. Said I needed to get more sunshine."

"Would you mind stepping out of line, please. This agent is going to clear you. Next!"

Jax began to sweat. The tall TSA agent waved him into a screening area. Jax turned to watch Tessa pass through the screening arch as the agent turned and gave him a series of commands.

"Please raise your arms and spread your legs a bit. This won't take long. I'm now going to pass my hands over your body. Do you have anything to declare, Mr. Axelrod?"

"No. Nothing. I have nothing to declare."

"Okay, sir, please take your bag and place it on the scanner. Would you please place your accessories in that separate tray and walk forward?"

"Why was I searched, officer?"

"Just standard operating procedure when a picture is dramatically different from how you look today. Some people try to use the identification of others to travel illegally."

Jax bobbed his head in agreement as nonchalantly as he could. He then stepped into the advanced imaging scanning arch, which promptly lit up with a red light.

“Sir,” the TSA agent asked, “are you wearing any metal on your waist or wrists?”

“Oh shit, my watch. I forgot I had that on.” After placing his timepiece in another tray, Jax walked through the machine with no further complications.

“So, I’m good to keep going?”

The agent looked him in the eyes for a full five seconds, then said, “You’re good to go, sir. Have a pleasant flight.”

A shaken Jax caught up with Tessa near the escalator. They rode down to the train and then to their terminal. Walking briskly, they reached their gate just as boarding was beginning.

Fifteen minutes later, they were seated, champagne in hand, nerves taut. Jax kept glancing over his shoulder, half expecting Curtis or one of his minions to appear. When the plane finally lifted off the tarmac, a flood of relief washed over them. Only then did Jax lean close and whisper, “I love you.”

55

MAUI, HAWAII

JAX NEEDED TIME TO sketch out his next steps on this twisted path that lay before him. Days after their hasty retreat from Denver, he was starting to feel the warm embrace emanating from the island of Maui. He spent every morning snorkeling in the warm water alongside giant sea turtles and a multitude of fish. He tried to let the anxiety that gripped him drift away with the current...but it was a futile effort at best.

Their bungalow gave them plenty of space to move around without the claustrophobia that often comes with a traditional hotel. As their room faced due west, the sunsets viewed from their full-length windows or their slow walks along the beach made every evening seem like a waking dream. With the local economy reliant on tourism, the resort was even more welcoming than usual, offering accommodations to patrons willing to pay full price—and more discreet about their guests' privacy.

The first few days away from home found the couple behaving like newlyweds, which seemed only right, considering it was close to their third anniversary. At lunch on the third day, Jax thought he spotted a man who seemed out of place on this island. The stiff, muscular man was showing a piece of paper to the bartender and the waitress, who both shook their heads. The staff went back to work, and the man moved on.

Pulling his cap lower, Jax sat further back in the shade of the restaurant's porch. Closely scrutinizing the man, Jax noticed how his clothing looked too formal for a tropical paradise. When the man turned to continue down the beach, Jax casually led Tessa out through a side door. If Curtis had been able to track them, they were fucked. There were only so many ways to get off this island.

In the following days, Jax stopped swimming and ordered food delivered. Empty bottles accumulated on the kitchenette counter. He slept through sunsets that had once pulled them both to the window.

One morning, Tessa watched him push eggs around his plate and found herself thinking, unbidden, that she had told him. She had told him, and he had not listened, and now here they were on a beautiful island with nowhere to go.

"I'm exhausted," Jax said. "I need to rest."

She looked at him for a moment. "Fine," she said, folding her napkin. "I'll find something to do." She picked up the rental car keys from the counter without looking back.

She drove their rental car to the Nakalele Blowhole, located at the island's uppermost point. Strolling out to the cliff overlooking the rocky beach, she passed several couples who were smiling, laughing, and holding hands. Normal things couples should be doing. Things she and Jax may never have again because of the choices they made.

Finding a flattened spot to sit on the rough volcanic rock, she took in the expansive view of the ocean—water that seemed to go on forever. The crash of massive waves mirrored the churning of her thoughts and emotions. The gentle spray from the surf trickled down, anointing her face. The vastness of it all humbled her.

Staring down at the jagged rocks below, she contemplated the ease with which she could stop this incessant feeling of hopelessness. Just a few steps—then oblivion. She drew in a breath and closed her eyes. Agnostic about any one religion, at her core, she believed in a higher power, and there she prayed for forgiveness for her selfish thoughts.

Lifting her face to the warm sun, she pleaded for salvation. Deliverance for herself, but mostly for Jax. She stood, gazing out once more at the endless sea, then turned and walked briskly back to her car, away from the seduction of a fragile lie.

Once alone, Jax dropped his laptop and his DIY visor on the bed within easy reach. Closing the blinds and shutting off all the lights, he turned and scowled at his shadowed reflection in the mirror.

"This has to happen," he said to his darkened image. "You've known for a long while now, but you keep running away. Stop hiding and do this. You—Fucking—Coward!"

He turned and stretched out on the bed—their bed. He tried to make himself as comfortable as possible given the circumstances. He stared at the ceiling and let the patterns float freely through his mind, taking deep breaths to carry away the bite of his self-rebuke.

Once he had settled a bit, he reached out a hand and turned on the computer-generated audio recording. He gently placed the visor over his face and continued breathing deeply. He pressed the button on the visor to begin the gentle oscillation of the blue light and the soft background hum.

With an acceptance born from a paucity of options, he exhaustedly accepted the shimmering aura as it encased him—his mind submerged in the hypnotic rhythm of his wife's mechanically recorded voice.

56

Chicopee, Massachusetts

He surfaced from the aura-induced trance to the beat of Metallica's "The Memory Remains", blasting through foam-padded headphones, "...you can't stop me once I started, can't return me once I'm sent out..." Jax jerked off the earphones, wincing as they snagged a few strands of hair, and set them on his cluttered desk beside a half-empty can of Mountain Dew. After a few seconds, his old bedroom came into sharper focus—the faded navy walls, the twin bed with rumpled sheets, and Merlin, the family's orange tabby, curled on his pillow. Crooked Nirvana and Pearl Jam posters clung to the walls with thumbtacks, Kurt Cobain's hollow gaze seeming to judge him. Outside, amber September light filtered through thinning sugar maple branches, striping his algebra textbook in shadow. The dog-eared calendar on the pine bookcase read September, its generic beach photo giving no hint of the actual date. The digital clock on the end table displayed 4:15 in angry red digits, but offered no clue about the day of the week.

He got up from the desk chair and slowly turned to face the full-length mirror on his closet door. Long, scraggly hair framed a thin face above a lanky teenage body. He wore jeans and a T-shirt bearing a cartoon picture of lips and a large tongue.

What stuck with him most from this time was the news that his dad had been wounded while flying a sortie in Afghanistan. For a teen taught to keep his emotions in check, cranking this band's music at deafening volume was the only way he knew to keep his real feelings tucked deep inside of himself.

His memories of this time of his life were a jumble of images and scents. The posters had faded to washed-out pastels where the sun hit them daily. Mountain Dew gone flat mixed with the musty scent of unwashed sheets and the faint tang of cat litter that Merlin tracked in on his paws.

The music, though... It was the pounding bass and the feel of his old desk that Jax had focused on while lying on the bed in Hawaii. He had approached this visit with some preparation, but the specific uncertainties remained uncomfortably significant. Although he knew this time was generally correct, he couldn't be precise. Whenever this was, it just happened to be the day when he showed up.

Making his way to the kitchen, he was reminded of his mother and all her cookbooks and crockery on the counter. Warm air hugged his skin, thick with the fine grit of flour that always managed to settle on the surfaces, no matter how often his mother wiped them down. He flashed on an amalgam of images of her dancing around in the kitchen while she cooked and baked. She liked to crank up her stereo while she was doing such chores, sometimes banging out a drumbeat with wooden utensils.

He started to move into the living room to find a newspaper or something that could tell him the date, when he stopped and turned back. Had he really heard it? Yes, the distinctive sound of a car's engine rumbling in the garage. Then the slow tick-tick-tick as the car was turned off and the metal cooled down.

He was frozen, just staring at the plain white door with painful anticipation. On an intellectual level, he knew he would see her and had tried to prepare himself. But now, as he was struck by the reality of the situation, he found it difficult to breathe. When she opened the door that connected to the kitchen, all Jax could manage was an audible gasp followed by a dull whimper. His knees felt weak, and his stomach tightened.

"Baby," his mother said, "what is it? What's wrong, Jaxon?"

She propped the paper sack on the counter and hugged him tightly, rubbing his head softly. It took all the strength he could muster to gain even a semblance of control. He had forgotten what her embrace had felt like. The lilt of her New England accent. The smell of her shampoo in her long, dark hair and the hint of her perfume. God, he had forgotten that touch—her smell—her warmth—her essence.

"I...I've just missed you, Mom. I guess I just needed a hug from you, that's all."

Holding him at arm's length, Elena Beck smiled. "Well, any time a boy asks his mum for a hug, that's worth celebrating. Feels good to hug you, too, sweetheart. You're sure everything's alright?"

"Yeah, sure. Hey, can we sit down for a while and just...talk?"

"Sure, hon. Lemme put the milk in the fridge, and I'll be right there. Kitchen table, alright?"

"Of course. That's a good idea... I guess."

"Okay, I'm all yours. Now, tell me—what's on your mind?"

"Mom," he said, letting that sound resonate in his head. "Mom, I know you've been getting migraines. Bad ones sometimes. I'm worried about you, and I guess I don't understand why you never talked to me about it before..."

"Yeah, Jax, I do get migraines. But before we get into all that, let me ask you something, alright? Are you starting to get them, too?"

"I think they started when I was seventee... I mean, yes, I get them sometimes."

Elena sat back, straight in her chair, staring at her child. She gently stood and walked slowly to the sink. She filled a kettle with water, then placed it on the stove to boil, all the while keeping her back to the table and Jax.

"I'm having some tea. Want me to make you a cup?"

"That would be...really nice, thank you."

In a light tone, she asked, "Do you travel often, Jaxon?"

"I'm...what? I'm not sure what you mean. I've only lived where Dad was stationed and where we've had a home. So, I pretty much never traveled out of New England."

Continuing to face the stove, she spoke in a low voice. "You know, I've traveled quite a bit through my adult life. Looking back, I'd say it started when I was around the age you are now—maybe a bit younger. Your grandmothah showed me how to move about by using our family's ways. And you know...sometimes I'd hear her talking to you when you were little, about having these...experiences."

"I'm sorry, Mom, I don't know what you're talking about. I go to school here in Chicopee, and Dad will be temporarily stationed at Westover until his wounds fully heal. What do you mean when you say traveling?"

Elena turned and smiled at her son. He felt her eyes peering into his soul, her love almost palpable. The kettle began to boil, so she turned off the stove and poured the water. She opened a canister that sat on the counter, extracted two tea bags, and placed one in each cup. Returning to the table, she placed a mug in front of Jax, then sat back down with her own cup in hand.

"It's clear to those of us who travel. You're speaking with a young man's voice, sure, but your eyes... No, those eyes carry a kind of pain that belongs to someone much older. If you need to keep some things close, I understand. But don't ask me to pretend you're just my fifteen-year-old. It doesn't really matter how old you are—just respect that I can see that you're more than the boy you look like right now."

"I don't...I don't know how to talk to you about this. I don't remember ever having this conversation."

"That's perfectly understandable. And clearly, you came here with a purpose, so let's at least talk about that, alright? What do you need to get whatever this is done, and how can I help you along?"

"I thought this visit was entirely about some school papers I was working on, but now I think maybe this has more to do with you. I think you can help me with more than just some damn writings I need to complete."

"I see. So, these papers must get in the way of your life somewhere down the road, and you're trying to shift that by changing something now, in this part of your life."

"Yes. That was my goal originally. But the way you... The way you recognized what I'm doing is really messing with my head. You get the auras as well? I mean, you get them yourself when you get migraines?"

"It might be a little different from what you go through, but... yes, I have them. Your grandmothah had them, and her mothah before her. I think they go back pretty much as far as our family line. On my side of the family, of course. It's rare that a male has this ability, but not unheard of."

"You never told me anything about this. Shouldn't you have told me?"

"Yes...I should've, Jax. Something must've happened before yours started that kept us from having that talk. I'm sorry I wasn't there to help you through that shift. You must've felt so alone, not knowing what those headaches meant or how to find your way through them."

"I have migraines, not just headaches. But you could have found a way to tell me all of this before now. Especially before we move to Colorado Springs, and you..."

"No, Jax," she whispered, "we can't change that—not if you're talking about life and death. I'm sorry this is all so new that you haven't quite seen that yet. But that's one thing that can't—it won't—change. No more talk about that, alright?"

"But I have changed things. Why can't that be changed?"

"I don't have a perfect answer for you. You're right—some things in your past can shift your future, or even your present. It gets tricky trying to keep the tenses straight when we talk about all this.

But dying...that's kind of a fixed thing. For me, for you, for all of us I suspect."

"That doesn't seem fair."

"Few things in this life ever are. What we do control is the way we let it shape us...who we choose to be inside. That's the part we can hold onto. Now, tell me, how much time did you give yourself to be here, in this moment?"

"I'm not clear how that works, really. I have about eight hours in the present I left, but I don't know what that means in terms of how long I have here."

"Yeah...that one always caught me off-guard, too. Once, I traveled back to a younger age for just an hour—and when I came back, a whole day had gone by here. Then, another time, it flipped on me, and I was my younger self for two full days, only to return and find that just three hours had passed. Your fathah had a hard time making sense of that part of me. We don't talk about that so much anymore."

"Wait. He knows about this?! Then why hasn't he..."

"Shh, sweetheart. Let's talk about something else for a bit, alright? How are you traveling these days—or whatever you've started calling it?"

"A machine I was using affected me to the point where I discovered my memories can be overwritten. I call it the 2nd Iteration because it repeats an already established memory. My experiments led me to see that the aura before a migraine can act like a doorway to a memory, so I use a visor, kind of like large sunglasses, to prompt the modification in my neurons."

"Neurons, experiments, machines...sounds like you really did become the doctor you always said you would. Good for you, sweetheart—I'm truly happy for you."

"I've missed you, Mom. There's been this gaping hole in my chest since you..."

"I'm so sorry, Jaxon. You were always so bright—so quick to understand things most folks would struggle with. I wish I could've been there for you more, my sweet boy. But we're here now, and we'll face tomorrow when it comes. Right now, tell me what you need. How can I help you while you're here with me now?"

"First, I need to ask if I've sent anything to Dad in Germany. Maybe an envelope or a large letter?"

"No, nothing like that. You wrote a short note, and I tucked it in with a letter I sent him about a week ago."

"Good, then I think I still have time. There are some ideas, some concepts I've written that I need to collect—some scientific papers. The most important thing I have to change is to ensure that they don't get out until I'm ready to read them again. Not for several years from now. I can't let those papers get out. Certain people want what I wrote in those papers, and bad things will happen if we can't find a way to keep them from being shown to anyone—even Dad. No, I mean especially dad, not because he did anything wrong, but someone else will. Someone who betrays him."

"All of that sounds pretty serious. But... you don't seem to remember that your fathah's still over in Germany for a few more weeks. He's planning to finish his physical therapy once he's back, while he's stationed here at Westover. I don't think he's been given any new orders yet—not until his wounds are fully healed, and that could take a year."

"Okay, so that means this is still the first week of September, and school started just a couple of weeks ago. Is it okay if I stay home for a few days so I can make sure I get all of my notes? I'm not sure exactly where I left them, but I'm pretty sure they're in my room. Afterwards, I would appreciate it if you could help me understand a bit more about this ability, which I now realize I must have inherited."

"It's Friday, so... take whatever time you need. I'll let the school know you've got the flu or something, so that won't cause any trouble. What we do with these papers once you're done with your project—that's a little trickier, but I'll find a way. And I'll tell you what I can about the traveling."

"Thanks, Mom. I really do love you. You were always...you are terrific."

"Then I guess I did what I was meant to do, to have the privilege of being your parent. We can't always see the road ahead… but when we take a moment to look back, we can see how we ended up right here. Don't you think so?"

It took Jax the rest of Friday and most of Saturday to gather his scattered notes and sketches from around his room. He had to search through the closet and even under a loose floorboard to find all his secret hiding spots, but eventually managed to compile over two dozen pages. He added an additional sheet with information he had learned, or would learn, over the next twenty years. Once sealed in an oversized envelope, he handed it to his mother, confident she would keep it safe as promised.

During their dinners, Elena shared what she could about the ability she had called traveling. "I was a child of the '70s," Elena started, "so I just thought my mothah—your grandmothah—was just a bit odd. Then one day, when I was about fourteen, I got what I thought was the worst headache ever. I remember that day clearly. We were sitting in the dining room of our place in Marblehead, just south of Salem.

"Anyway, that morning, my head felt ready to explode. Mum gave me a cup of her special herbal tea she kept hid way in the back of the cupboard. It settled the throbbing a bit, and it... opened my eyes to something extraordinary.

"Mum held both my hands and started asking me questions about when I was eight. Told me to keep my eyes closed, relax, and tell her what I remember. You probably don't recall me talking much about it, but that was the blizzard of '78.

"That storm was a monster. It hit all of New England hard. Our little town got over two feet of snow, with winds gusting to 80 miles an hour. We couldn't get out for more than a week with the cold and the snowdrifts...and I was there, Jaxon. I'm sure you know what I'm getting at. I traveled right back into that same living room—my parents, my brother, Walter, all of us bundled up in blankets by the fire—but I was in my younger body.

"New Englanders are a hardy bunch, always prepping for storms like that. Mum had shelves of canned food down in the cellar, so once we finished what was in the fridge, we lived off all that. But we had this one neighbor family who weren't so lucky.

"The Randalls had just moved to Marblehead from New York a few months before, and they hadn't really settled in yet. They ran through all their food and most of their firewood after the first week. They had two children—a boy about my age, Ben, and a baby girl, Beth. I remembered that the parents and the boy made it through... but the little one didn't. I went back to that time because my mum had guided me there to help that family. That's what she wanted me to see—to live through again.

"She wanted me to help convince my fathah and Walt to dig their way over to the Randalls' place and bring them back. She'd tried herself once, but she couldn't get them to go. So she brought me into my first experience, into my younger self, and together we told the men that either they went… or we would.

"Her plan worked, kind of. The baby—Beth—she lived. But…the boy, Ben… he ended up dying from a fever a couple of weeks later. It was my first time traveling, but I learned a hard lesson anyway. When we step in and change things during a visit, there's almost always a heavy price to pay. And it's usually one we don't see coming."

"But, Mom, there's something I don't understand. You said to me that we can't really save someone if it's their time to die. So, why did Beth live? Or did she end up dying soon afterwards anyway?"

"Well, I lived with my parents in Marblehead right up until I left for college, and Beth was still alive then—thriving, really. The best I can tell you is that the rules around death are slippery. My Mum told me we couldn't go back to the exact day when she'd first tried, so we ended up going together the day after. It had to do with not being able to overlap your traveling. That's something I learned more about later. Anyway, she swore that if we could have just gotten to the family a day earlier, things might have been different.

"There's that, and then sometimes a person might have their death delayed to fulfill a purpose. You know, they stay around to provide a service or critical information. Kinda like shuffleboard, where you slide a disc, and it hits another, and then that disc is pushed into a scoring triangle, or off the court entirely. That's the best I can explain it. Things have a meaning we can't always see. Some call it God's work. I don't know."

"Did you ever get an answer as to why you were able to do this traveling? And, why I'm able to do this 2nd Iteration thing?"

"No. Not a direct answer about the why or the how. Just the stories my Mum passed down about her mothah and her grandmothah. My fathah wasn't a religious man, even though his folks were active in their faith. Mum was agnostic, though she did things we'd call mystical—she just called it nature's way. Regardless, she knew her herbs. She was quite familiar with all that business."

"So, you were given your mother's recipe for that tea. You use that as a means of traveling? Is it a type of hallucinogen?"

"Jaxon... please believe me, I want to answer every question you've got. But, son, this isn't something we can sort through in an afternoon—a week—or even a month. And yes... I've got all of Mum's notes on the right mix of herbs for the tea. I'll pass them on to you when the time's right."

"What about Uncle Walt? Did he travel as well?"

"As I said, men don't seem to come to this type of thing as easily as women. Mum told me Walt could only travel when she guided him... but didn't like it. He never got that aura that you mentioned, and he ended up declaring that the whole thing was just some silly game Mum and I had cooked up.

“Anyway... I think this is where we ought to leave it, at least for now. Listening to you, I can tell you’re starting to see—how it’s both a gift and a burden. I just hope you’ll move with care if you choose to travel more often. Every action has its consequence, Jax. It always wants its due...always.”

57

Return to Maui

Jax awoke from his trip to Massachusetts. Back from an emotional time with his mother. He hoped his efforts had stopped Curtis and his goons from chasing him, but he was still uncertain whether they were safe now. He reached to remove the visor from his face, but his hand came away with an ordinary pair of sunglasses. The visor was just...gone.

The bungalow was dark with only ambient light coming from outside. Jax shifted so he was sitting on the edge of the bed. He glanced at the digital clock on the nightstand—6:58. He had spent four whole days away, but only nine hours had passed here. His mother was correct when she said there was no pattern to follow.

As a parting gift, Elena said she would leave him with a large bound photo album filled with pictures and detailed summaries of the events each image portrayed. She explained that he would get it at some point as an adult. Having as much information as possible about a specific time would make it easier for him to travel. She wasn't sure when he would get it, but she would try to make it easy for him to find. Then he was gone.

Easing back into his adult body after being in his adolescent figure took a couple of minutes to get used to. Although not complete, he felt he had a better sense of where he stood on his continuum. The aura had shown up on his last day in Chicopee, just materializing in front of him. When he explained this to his mother, she encouraged him to recognize such signs as calls to travel and to know when to return. In her words, ignoring these markers would make his 2nd Iterations... disagreeable.

As he stood from the bed, he felt a warmth dripping into his mouth. He grabbed a tissue and dabbed at the blood trickling from his nose—and over the hair covering his lip. Discarding the tissue, he ran his fingers over his face. When he lay in his bed just hours before, he had been relatively clean-shaven, with just a few days of growth. Now, his beard was back—more sculpted than his favored style—but back, nonetheless.

Looking around the darkened room, he was struck with a sudden realization...Tessa! Seven at night—where had she gone all day? "Tessa!" His voice cracked as he snapped on the lamp. No bag. No sign of her. His chest tightened. His breaths coming in shallow bursts.

Slipping into his sandals, he flicked on the wall switch. His fingers wrapped around the doorknob as he took one final scan of the empty room. He flung the door open and stepped onto the balcony, his eyes sweeping across the resort grounds now bathed in soft evening light. Only strangers wandered the paths below.

"God, no," he whispered, his voice breaking. He patted his body to ensure he was clothed, then pounded down the stairs toward the hotel bar. Nine hours away—plenty of time for her to have gone for dinner or cocktails. She had to be there.

The bar was packed when he arrived, making it hard to see through the crowd. The live band was playing a blend of Hawaiian and soft rock music, making it nearly impossible for him to be heard. He walked up to a bartender whom he recognized from the first few nights. His name was Kaleo...no, Keanu, like the actor.

Leaning into the bar rail, he raised his voice to be heard by the man busily mixing drinks. "Keanu? Keanu, it's me, Jaxon...I mean Dr. Axelrod. Do you remember me from the other night?"

"Jaxon. Yeah, man. I remember you. You liked the good stuff. Get you a glass?"

"No. Not at the moment, Keanu. I'm looking for my wife. Have you seen her tonight?"

"No man. I didn't know you were married," Keanu said with a wink. "Not with the way you were acting with the ladies. You know what I mean?"

Jax opened his mouth to protest, but what could he say? Keanu turned to a server who placed her tray on the side bar. "I got to go, Jaxon. Good luck finding your lady."

Jaxon turned to the dozens of people gyrating to the sound of the band and sipping their drinks. "The way I was acting with the ladies? What the hell? Did I do something and upset Tess?"

Making his way out of the bar, Jax quickly strode up the connecting hallway to the hotel's registration desk. A lone young woman stood behind the counter. "Excuse me," Jax said. "I'm wondering if my wife might have checked out. We're in bungalow C, under Axelrod."

The young woman nodded to Jax, then turned to her computer. "Let me check."

"I'm sorry, sir, no one by the name of Axelrod is staying with us. You know, I was the one who checked you in a few days ago. I don't remember you using that name when you signed in."

Catching himself, Jax let out a small laugh. "It's a joke we use sometimes. Could you try, Beck? Jaxon Beck."

"Yes, sir. That matches the name I have on file for that bungalow. I only show one person registered...you. Did your wife join you later? I don't see any other name on your form. I'm sorry. I don't know what to tell you, Mr. Beck."

Jax thanked the clerk and started wandering back towards his room. Terrified by the implications of this information, nothing he sensed seemed real. It was as if someone had roofied him, and the world he now viewed wasn't to be trusted.

Once back in his room, he opened his laptop and found the website for the university's hospital. A search of the staff revealed no results under the name Beck, Tessa. Scrolling down the page, he found a Moreland, Tessa—her maiden name—listing her as the head of the psychiatric division. That much was the same as before.

Jax poured himself a full glass of scotch from a bottle he'd purchased days earlier. He sat on the corner of his bed and stared out the window at the moonlight as it illuminated the ocean waves. He found he was sitting on his phone and pulled it out. It wasn't the new phone that Tessa had bought him when they were on the run, but his old phone, the one he had left in his classroom auditorium. He turned it on but didn't find any listing for Tessa under his speed dial or by her name.

Walking back to the counter and refilling his glass, he gave the issue some thought. If he were successful when he returned to his younger self and prevented his drawings from getting out, then there would no longer be any issue with Curtis following him. But for some reason, he was no longer married to Tessa. On top of that, it would appear they didn't even have any relationship. Why else wouldn't she be in his contacts? Shit!

After pouring his third glass of the rich brown liquid, he stood and walked out of the room, not bothering to close the door behind him. Meandering the short way down to the beach, he found an isolated spot that butted up against the hotel's patio. He plopped down in the cool sand and leaned his back against the rough concrete foundation. He sat, mesmerized by the surf gliding to shore. "Tessa," he slurred, "what happened to us?"

He awoke to the sounds of a young couple running in and out of the waves, laughing and clutching at each other's wet bodies. The sun had not yet risen, but the clouds were ablaze with reds, pinks, and oranges. He didn't remember falling asleep, but his skin itched from fleas and the grains of sand that had found their way into various folds of skin. He stood and shook himself off the best he could. Picking up his empty glass, he headed back to his room to shower off and change clothes.

His head was pounding from the alcohol as well as the awareness that his wife was no longer with him. Not on this trip—and not in his life. He stayed under the shower's spray for half an hour, first cold, then hot, then he repeated the process twice more. After finding a clean pair of linen trousers, he picked up his laptop and tapped a key to bring it to life. When his screen stayed blank, he realized he'd left it running all night, draining the battery. Rummaging through the cabinet, he managed to make a small pot of coffee. When he had enough for a single cup, he sat at the kitchen counter and plugged the computer into the wall outlet.

While waiting for the machine to boot up, he downed the first cup of coffee, then poured himself a second. Opening an Internet browser, he pulled up his email account and scrolled through his messages. There were the usual ads, posts from colleagues at the Center, and a couple of very salacious notes from women he was not familiar with. Nothing from Tessa. Nothing from Sita or Leif. Nothing from...Dad.

His dad! Jax knew his father was an early riser and should be up. Finding his phone, Jax hurriedly looked for his father's number under contacts, but couldn't find any such listing. He typed in the number from memory and waited. After the call went to voicemail, a woman's voice came on. "Hey, this is Candy, but I'm not available. You know what to do." Candy. Who the fuck is Candy? Jax hung up the phone, not bothering to apologize for calling the wrong number.

He downed his second cup of coffee, then checked to make sure the number he called was correct. It was the right number, just not the right person. He returned to his computer and typed in a search for Lt. Colonel Mark A. Beck. The first two pages were entries for other Mark Becks, but finally, a hit came up on the third page from a Massachusetts Newspaper dated 2005. "Local Man Shot Down in Afghanistan."

Opening the link, the article showed a picture of his father from long ago with the story of Major Mark Beck, whose jet was shot down while on a combat mission. A squad of Marines failed in their attempt to rescue him, losing two men in the process. The article concluded that Major Beck was publicly executed by the Taliban a week after his capture. His body was later retrieved by the United Kingdom's Special Air Services and subsequently returned to the United States for burial.

Closing the lid to the laptop, Jax stood and glanced around the room, not seeing anything, not hearing anything, just desperately searching his mind for an answer—any answer. He tried to take a deep breath, but instead just gasped. There wasn't any air. The room began to spin, at first slowly, then faster, until everything turned into a blur. Stumbling towards the bathroom, he barely made it into the shower stall before his stomach lurched violently.

The stink of coffee and scotch emanating from the drain was too much, and he convulsed twice more in dry heaves. Finally able to catch his breath, he reached up and turned on the tap. The icy cold water beat down on his head. He could feel a massive headache forming behind his eyes, but he ignored it. The emotional pain he felt trumped any physical pain at the moment. Actions and...consequences.

It was several minutes before he managed to sit back against the shower wall. A sniffle escaped his throat, then tears started to flow out of him uncontrollably. His chest clenched with a wracking sob.

Desperately grabbing a towel off the rack, he clamped the folded cloth over his face as he let out a scream...then another.

Cautiously making his way back to the small kitchen, Jax poured a glass of water and sat back down at the counter. Even with the towel now covering his head, his dripping clothes had left a trail of water from his experience in the shower stall.

Sitting and sipping the water, it took the better part of an hour for Jax to clear his head enough to decide he needed to leave. He searched through his phone, found the pertinent information, then contacted his airline to arrange an earlier flight back to Colorado. His mind was still reeling, but he needed to be on familiar turf to get his bearings about what was real...and what wasn't.

58

DENVER

HIS PLANE TOUCHED DOWN just after six the next morning. He secured an Uber and rode to the address that he and Tessa had called home. When the car pulled up to the curb, he spied a small bicycle sitting on the front lawn and toddler toys littering the porch. This was not where he lived. This wasn't home anymore. The driver's voice brought him out of his fog.

"Mr. Beck," the driver said, "we're here, sir. Do you need help with your bags?"

"Ah, no. Please wait a minute." Jax pulled out his wallet and looked at the address on his license. It was the same little apartment complex he had lived in when he first met Tessa. He showed the driver the address and asked to be taken there.

"Mr. Beck, that's thirty minutes in the opposite direction from here. And that's not including the morning traffic. I do short airport runs, man, that's it. Not in town."

Jax pulled out a hundred-dollar bill from his wallet and held it over the driver's shoulder. "Look, I understand it's a pain in the ass, but I'm willing to compensate you for the inconvenience. I just got confused. I did live here...before the divorce, I mean. I moved a couple of months ago."

"Okay, man, I get you." The driver said, taking the extended bill from Jax's fingers. "Hey, I'm sorry that happened to you. I'm divorced myself. It sucks."

As the car pulled away, Jax stole a parting glance at the townhouse, a single thought crossing his mind. Yes—all of this sucks.

Jax sat cross-legged on his lumpy IKEA futon, trying—and mostly failing—to remember the last few months and all the changes this new reality had dumped in his lap like so much cosmic garbage. He'd gotten glimpses of this new life whenever a crossover memory ambushed his consciousness, but there were still enough gaps he could drive a semi through them.

His bare feet rested on the photo album his mother had given him, one of many items stacked atop his Swedish coffee table. He hadn't gone looking for it when he had returned to his apartment—it was just here, right in this spot. Now he didn't have the energy or desire to open it.

He had naively believed that once he'd returned from his visit to Chicopee, whatever changes had occurred to his chronology, he would be able to adjust like the genius he pretended to be. As Molly had informed the group just weeks ago, by his lone recollection, teenage Jax—that fucking idiot—had started this rollercoaster ride when he'd innocently sent his father his ideas and plans for scientific devices that caused the great minds of the time to freak the hell out.

To adult Jax, it was logical that a 2nd Iteration visit back to that point in time and confiding in his mother would have stopped all of that from happening. In a way, that logic proved true, but now he understood that the price he paid was...everything.

Jax squeezed his eyes shut, letting the fragmented new memories of this timeline surface—hazy and indistinct. Vague images of him in his laboratory, talking with Sita as she calibrated the equipment. It appeared that his research had focused on controlling migraines by applying...something—a neural circuit-breaker designed to halt the cascade of pain signals before they could flood the brain. Okay, but that look on Sita's face. Was that anxiety? Worry?

From the control booth, Amy is monitoring their progress, her face inscrutable. These images seemed different from what he remembered. He still wondered if she had actually gone behind his back to Zane, but there was no way to know for sure. She'd done so much for him, but what did he do to help her? In these flashes, he had taken her for granted and, in some ways, held her back professionally. This was another problem for another day.

When his thoughts wandered to his father, he could feel the man's absence like a phantom limb, and he had to choke back another tear. It took this to happen to make him realize just how much that man meant to him. Then that sadness gave way to another as he recalled another painful truth—he'd never married Tessa in this version of his life. The memory dissolved, leaving him grasping at wisps of this new reality that was and wasn't his.

Two days of mental gymnastics had left Jax exhausted and no closer to answers. He finally surrendered to the reality that these memories weren't a jigsaw puzzle he could force together. Whatever happened between that night at his father's place—the first encounter with the VyzR—and the here and now, existed in a fog that only time might dissipate. What terrified him most weren't the memories he'd recovered, but the ones still lurking in the shadows of his consciousness.

Holding up his hand, he stared at the five fingers on his left hand, trying to gain meaning from what he saw. All five digits. No missing pinkie from the time when he had relived his mother's accident. So, what were the implications? Was everything he'd done with the 2nd Iteration ability now erased? What about the people with whom he'd interacted during his visits? The accident? Mary and Oklahoma City? George Marshall?

Jax pushed himself up from his battered couch and plucked a blank index card from the stack on the coffee table. He scribbled a note, pinned it to the wall among the others, then looped a length of red yarn around the thumbtack and stretched it to another tack a foot away.

Withdrawing to the kitchenette counter, he poured the dregs of the bottle into his glass. Wine in hand, he stepped back and took in the entire display—an intense web of notecards and crimson string running from the entryway to the sliding glass door. It was a frenzied star map of his shattered timeline.

"George Marshall, Jr., damn it!" Jax said, grimacing. "When he and his father died in the Oklahoma City bombing, George Junior didn't become that Marine—he wasn't alive to sacrifice himself for his comrades—my dad wasn't saved. Fuck!"

The memory of drinking tequila with his wife, Leif, and Sita, and spouting philosophy, overcomes Jax, and one specific line from Leif resonates the loudest. "Ja, are you really changing parts of your past, Jax? Or did doing this... 2nd Iteration visit cause the thing that was meant to happen, eh? Maybe you think you're rewriting. But maybe you're just walking the path that was already laid out...laid out...laid out."

The empty wineglass clinked against the counter as he set it down. Jax walked slowly back to his outlandish diagram, his view zooming in on his last addition. He slowly raised a finger and followed the red thread's path across his makeshift timeline.

"If George Junior survives to become a Marine hero, Dad gets rescued. He's shipped off to recover in Germany, where Molly takes my papers at the hospital." He stopped and tapped a card. "But without him getting my research, Molly could never have pilfered it. No stolen research means no government interest."

The yarn looped in a wide arc, backward to the left, ending at the doorframe and the first card in his bizarre sculpture. "VyzR," he exhaled sharply. "The whole thing's circular. I needed the device to exist so I could travel back to 1995 and save George Marshall and his son. That sets off the chain—George Junior joins the Marines, heroically saves his squad, which enables Dad to be rescued. Dad is in Germany and meets Molly, who takes my papers. It's a fucking closed loop."

Jax takes a step back and raises his arms, as if conducting an orchestra. "I was always meant to send my papers to him. I was supposed to have my work scrutinized by the government, which gave the schematics to VRMX Technologies to build. Mikey or Leo Zane is told to include Molly in the testing process, and she sucks me in by using the device to treat my dad."

Jax moved to the far-right side of the wall until he reached the card for Chicopee. "I originally sent Dad everything, then went back and convinced Mom to intercept it all. I created my own paradox by fucking with the natural course of events."

He plopped back onto the couch and stared up at his creation. "But I don't need everything. I just need to get to 1995. I don't need the entire scenario to play out, just that part! Okay, you can do this, Jax. We can save Dad. George Marshall's destiny was to be in Afghanistan and save his comrades. But what the hell happened to the diagrams I drew when I was 15? If Dad died in this fucked-up timeline, then I never sent them to his hospital in Germany. Did Mom still save them? Did I even create them?

"Wait, wait, wait!" he said, smacking his hand onto his forehead. "If Mom had become a widow, then we wouldn't have moved out of Chicopee. She may not have even died in that car crash! Shit! My phone! Where did I put my damn phone?"

Digging under a pile of papers and empty food cartons, he found the device and scrolled through his list of contacts until he found one for his mom. He looked at the area code and was stunned to find it was for the Colorado Springs area. Tapping the number, he waited for an answer. "Pick up, pick up, pick up."

When the call connected, a man's voice answered. "Hello, Jaxon. What do you want now?"

"I—I want to...is she there?"

"You know damn well she's not. So, I repeat, what do you want?"

"Please, just give me a minute. Can you at least tell me where she's at?"

"Well, I haven't moved her, if that's what you're implying. She's still at the Morning Sun facility in Mountain Shadows. You know she's not allowed to take calls there."

Jax recognized the Morning Sun name as a memory care facility. "That's okay, I'll just go down and see her in person."

"Wait! Remember, you're no longer on the list of allowed visitors. Not after you got her so worked up last time."

"Please. I'm begging you, um...I'm sorry, but I'm drawing a blank on your name."

"Very funny. You know damn well it's Mark! I thought we were past that crap."

"Yes, of course. Mark, just like my father."

Yeah. The Marks Brothers of the 354th. Don't you think we've played this game a little too often? Ah, damn it, Jax, I know she's your mom and all, but... Okay, listen. Here's the deal. If I do this and get you on the list, you cannot get her excited. Do you hear me?"

"Yes. Yes, I hear you, Mark. I just need to see her...again."

59

Elena

Not owning a vehicle, Jax rented a car for the drive down to Colorado Springs. By the time he arrived at the facility, it was early afternoon, and he hoped that this other Mark had done as promised and added him to her approved visitor list.

When he entered the locked entry, the woman at the desk asked, "May I help you, sir?"

"Yes. I'm here to see my mother, Elena."

"And what's her last name?"

"I know this sounds stupid, but I forgot my stepfather's last name." Jax had hoped that he had played that correctly, not knowing his mother's married name.

"Well, we only have one Elena at the moment. May I have your name for a visitor pass?"

When Jax told her his name, a darkness clouded the woman's face. "Oh, yes. I remember you now. I see that her husband called and okayed your visit, but we can't have you upsetting her again. Do you understand what I'm telling you...Mr. Beck?"

Jax could tell that her not referring to him as Dr. Beck was her way of getting in a dig, but it was no big deal. "Of course," he replied. "And I wanted to apologize. For the last time, I mean. I was going through a difficult stage, but that's all in the past."

"So that you know, it took the staff an entire week to get her back to normal. Her normal, at least. It's difficult enough without her getting agitated."

"Got it. Can you please tell me which room she's in?"

"Same one, C-6." When she saw a blank look on his face, she continued in a huff. "Through the main door, stay to the right all the way to the corner section. Her room's on the left."

The woman handed him a printed name badge, then buzzed him through the heavy metal door that led to the living quarters. Jax was acutely aware of how the brain could betray the body that housed it. He wasn't sure which type of dementia his mother suffered from, but he knew she wouldn't have been placed here if it weren't serious.

When he got to her room, he found his mother seated in an overstuffed armchair, slightly hunched over and gazing blankly out of a single window that displayed the facility's courtyard. A staff member who was passing by his mother's room saw Jax in her doorway and leaned in to say with a soft smile, "I think she's having a good day."

Jax looked at the nameplate outside her room that read 'Elena Hawkins', then he entered the tiny room. "Hi, Mom," he said softly. She turned and stared at him with a bewildered look on her face, then turned back to look out the window.

"Mom, it's Jax—Jaxon."

"Jaxon. Jaxon. No, Jaxon isn't here. He's probably off traveling somewhere."

"You're right, of course. I have been traveling, but I'm back now. To see you. To talk with you, if that's okay?"

Elena turned halfway around in her chair and gave him a serious, scrutinizing stare. She would be close to sixty, but looked much older. "Jaxon...ayeh, I see it in your eyes. That look of pain. How long did you allow yourself to be here this time?"

"It's good to see you again, Mom. I'll stay as long as I can. Is that alright?"

"Saw you in Chicopee. Then in...Marblehead, I think... I don't recall."

"Yes, we visited when I traveled to our home in Chicopee. Do you remember our visit?"

"Ayeh...you were on a mission... Papers or some such thing. Oh, you were such a beautiful young boy. Didn't smile...and those same sad eyes."

Elena turned fully in her chair to look at Jax. Her left arm seemed to be tapping on the chair arm in a rhythm only she could hear. Her blouse hung on her due to severe weight loss, and she wore grey, stained sweatpants. The clinician in Jax immediately recognized the telltale signs of moderately severe dementia—Alzheimer's, if he had to guess by her behavior. She must be close to the later stage of the disease.

"So, tell me, what brings you here? I mean now. How old are you now? I don't...I don't know what I'm doing here. I should be getting home...and I've been waiting. Are you here to pick me up?"

"No," he said gently as he rubbed her shoulder. "I'm here because I need to ask you something—about the time you just mentioned. Mom, this is my present time, but things are very different for me. Not right."

The woman covered her mouth with her right hand to stifle a chuckle. "Oh...you must have broken a rule. It doesn't let you get away with much, does it? You were always a good boy, but then you... Oh, that cat." She bobbed her head and turned to look out the window once again. "I think that cat next door ate my roses. They were just here. I love my roses."

Jax clenched his jaw, fighting the urge to both weep and run. A withering brain had betrayed his mother's body, yet those eyes held fragments of the woman who'd made him tea just days ago in his timeline. The cognitive dissonance made his stomach lurch. How could he mourn someone sitting right in front of him? How could he not?

“Mom,” he said softly. “We didn’t get the chance to talk about the rules. I’m very sorry I couldn't have spent more time with you then.”

Elena's head jerked toward him, her neck moving before her eyes caught up. “But we did... during that...” She trailed off, blinking rapidly. Her gaze drifted to the wall, then snapped back. “The beach. Yes. The beach with the...” She tried to snap her fingers. “You kept... I couldn't tell what.” Confusion clouded her features, and she squinted at him, head tilting slightly. “Wait. You're not my Jaxon.”

Jax was startled by her insistence that he had traveled back to some other time to be with her. It took him a minute to fully register everything she said and to form an appropriate response. Abruptly, Elena tried to stand, pushing with one hand against the chair’s padded arm—twisting, but not standing.

“You’re not my Jaxon,” she said forcefully. “You need to leave this house. I’ll call the police, so help me.”

"No, Mom," he said, caught off guard by her reaction. "No, it's me. It's really me, Jax. I'm Jax!" Hoping he could put the words in such a way that they made sense to her. "Mom," he said in a conspiratorial tone, "remember when we lived in Chicopee?" Do you remember when I visited—when I traveled to see you? Do you remember that?"

Elena looked at him, then nodded slowly as she eased back into her chair. Her eyes drifted to the wall, then to the ceiling, then back to the wall. "Ayeh. Mark was still..." She paused, frowning, fingers plucking at her blouse. "Mark was...no, no, he wasn't. You said not to mail it. But he wasn't there anymore. They...they took him from me. They took him from me in the worst way. That was horrid, just horrid."

Elena stared at Jax. "Why'd you bring up that nasty business? Heathen sons o' bitches!" She was teetering between confusion and anger. Sundowning maybe? This was not what he'd intended to happen. He had to calm her down.

"Mom. Hey, Mom," he said animatedly. "Do you remember our talk about Grandma and the tea she made for you? I could really use a cup of that tea about now. How about you? Does that sound good?"

The older woman began to stutter, then seemed to collect herself. "I...I ca...can't. Ayeh...the tea, and the recipe I promised. I can't remember where I left the dang kettle—I think they stole it. I know I wrote it down for you...somewhere."

"It's okay, Mom. That's okay. Maybe it's with the envelope you were going to keep for me. Do you remember that? I was going to get it from you later."

"The envelope...yes, with the thick tape. I...I can't show it to Mark. Don't let your fathah know about those drawings, you said. Yes, I do believe the recipe's in there. Why don't you go look?"

"I would, Mom. The problem is, I don't remember where I left it. That's one reason I came today. I was hoping you'd remember where I left the envelope."

Elena began chuckling to herself. Then, she leaned over and spoke to Jax in a conspiratorial whisper. "I've got it, you silly boy. I hid it from the others because they steal my things. The papers...yes, your papers."

Elena got a look of clarity that Jax knew happened sometimes in these cases. She spoke calmly and clearly. "That must be why I'm stuck here...it must be. I hid it under my mattress, just there." She pointed to the small bed that would have been more appropriate in a prison cell.

Jax got up and peeked out of the doorway before returning and lifting the mattress. Lying between it and the thin boxspring was the very envelope he remembered handing to his mother just days before, from his perspective, but decades by hers.

He returned to the spot next to his mother and held out his hand, palm up. She placed her hand in his and gave him a big smile.

"So...you got what you came for? Good. Was there something else you needed to ask me?"

"Mom, I need to tell you that if I'm right—if I go ahead with my plan, then Dad will be alright. He'll be alive, I mean. But there's...a problem with that decision. Mom, it will mean that you...won't. You won't be here anymore."

"Oh, hush now, Jaxon. Look at the mess I've become. I'm...barely here as it is. Some days, well, some days I'm not here at all...no, not really, I'm just not me. It's not like traveling...but I'm supposed to be here for a reason. Got to be here, but it feels like...all of this is wrong."

Jax's voice caught in his throat. "I don't—" He clutched the envelope, knuckles whitening. "Mom, if I do this, I might save Dad, but I...I would lose you...again." His eyes burned as he looked at her familiar face, mapped with lines he'd memorized since childhood. "I love you so much. I need to know I'm not making everything worse. That I won't destroy what's left..."

"I love you, too, hon," she said, patting his arm. "You take care of your fathah and say hello for me...when you see him again. And...and... I'm still... If I can just help my son, then I...I got to talk with him. You go on now...go and get him for me."

Jax stood and looked down at the woman he adored, his throat tightening around words he couldn't form. Was he saying goodbye to his mother—again? Did she miss being in that car crash, but stay alive to pass on that information? Did she fulfill her purpose and can die in peace now—was that what she meant?

His hand hovered uncertainly above her shoulder before he finally bent down and kissed the top of her head, inhaling the familiar, faint hint of shampoo. "I will always remember you," he whispered, his voice cracking. "I will always love you."

Elena turned back to her window and looked out on the garden the facility had planted in the center courtyard. “Where are my beautiful roses? That dang cat...always getting into things.”

60

Back to Work

Jax's key scraped against the lock, catching twice before turning. He held his breath. The door swung open. His desk sat where it always had, the leather chair still tilted at that slight angle he preferred. The stack of manila folders remained in the exact crooked pile he'd left days ago. His eyes drifted to the windowsill, to the rectangle of faded wood where dust had gathered. His fingers twitched at his side. The silver frame with Tessa's half-smile and windblown hair was gone, leaving behind only the ghost of its outline.

He was still reeling from his visit with his mother. He was having a difficult time rationalizing how the woman he had been talking with in Massachusetts just a few days ago ended up like...that. By some miracle, he had gotten his schematics back for the visor and other devices, but at what cost? Had the universe punished his mother for his transgressions? Kept her alive, just to deliver that envelope to him?

Looking around, he knew he could not stand to be alone with his thoughts in this silent space for another minute. Retreating from his office, he made his way down to the lab at the end of the hall. He paused before entering, not hearing any sounds or voices. He gently pushed the door open and took a cautious step into the space he once thought of as his little kingdom. Looking around at the idle equipment and empty office cubicles, all he saw was a prison. A large, shiny prison.

A voice from behind him cut through the silence. “Welcome back, boss.” Jax's shoulders shot up to his ears as he stumbled forward into the lab. "Shit," Sita said, her eyes widening. "I didn't mean to spook you. You alright?"

His jaw unclenched, teeth no longer grinding. The knot between his shoulder blades loosened for the first time in days. His backpack slid from his shoulder and hit the floor with a thud. Before he could think, he was wrapping his arms around Sita, locking her in an embrace like she might disappear if he let go.

“What is this?” a deep, steady voice said, stepping up to the lab entrance. “You said this man was your employer. Is he something more for you that I should know?”

Jax released Sita from his unintended bear hug and turned to the large man standing before him. “Leif! Damn, it’s good to see you, my friend.”

Sita and Leif looked at one another, a confused, humorous expression on their faces. After patting Leif's chest, Sita turned and looked at Jax, not knowing what to expect.

"Dr. Jaxon Beck, this is my friend Leif Thor..."

"...Thorsen," Jax said with a wide grin on his face. "Close friend and electronics genius! Damn, it's good to see you both. I've missed you. And now that you're here," he said, turning and lifting his arms as if to embrace the lab. "I feel I am, well, it's not home, but...it's normal."

Sita and Leif just stood still, scrutinizing this crazy man before them. Sita finally broke the silence. "Dr.—Dr. Beck, I didn't think you knew Leif. But, hey," she said, holding up two white paper bags. "We have food. I mean, we just got back from the food truck, and we can share. If you're hungry, you know?"

"Thanks, but I'm good. Let me grab some coffee, and I'll come sit with you." He turned and paused. "I'm sorry, what I meant to say—what I meant to ask, is if that would be okay? The three of us sitting together, I mean."

Numbly, Sita nodded, then led Leif to the conference room and plopped down in a chair. Her face held the look of complete shock as she observed the man she knew as Dr. Beck making a cup of coffee on the old metal cart. "What the fuck just happened?"

"Nice man," Leif said, ripping open the paper sacks with his thick fingers. "Very open. Very warm. You never said he vas a friend of yours."

"He's not," Sita whispered out of disbelief rather than secrecy. "This is new. Weird. I mean, a good weird, but, shit, I'll take it."

Jax entered the conference room with his mug in hand. It wasn't the mug that Tessa had given him, but it had his name embossed on it, so he went with it.

Although Leif was eagerly engrossed in his meal, Sita sat staring at the man she had always referred to as Dr. Beck. She was debating whether to say something or just go with the flow. Jax settled the issue for her.

"Hey, would you guys be open to a thought experiment? It would be good to get a fresh perspective from someone other than myself."

"Sounds good," Leif said. "What is the subject that we vill discuss?"

"Reality," Jax said straight-faced. "How would you define reality?"

"So, nothing about the Broncos, or the best place to eat?" Sita said in disbelief. "Just right to what is real? I'm sorry, Dr. Beck, but what the hell? You take a trip, and you come back asking these actual, human-type questions? I've worked with you for over two years, and not once have you ever had lunch with the crew, much less made your own coffee. What is going on? Are we about to get fired, or what?"

Sita's words were like a physical blow. Had he really been that much of a prick? "Sita. Ahem, Sita, all I can think to say right now. All I can tell you is that I'm very sorry if I ever gave you the impression that I didn't respect you or your work. To answer your question, yes—I mean no, no one's getting fired. But, yes, something profound did happen to me. Something that sounds very bizarre when the words are spoken aloud, but I need you to maybe...trust me. I need both of you to trust me when I get to the point where I can lay everything out for you."

"You present yourself to be an honorable man, Jaxon Beck," Leif said. "I vill listen to your tale and will not judge you for your words and thoughts."

"Dr. Beck," Sita started, "I'm confused as to what..."

"Yeah. Confusion is a big part of this roller coaster I'm riding right now. And from now on, it's Jax. Not Dr. Beck, but Jax. Are you good with that?"

"Sure, just as long as I'm not going to get my ass chewed out when you come down off whatever drug you're on at the moment."

"Fair enough," he laughed. "But, just for the record, I'm completely sober and not under the influence of any chemical substance—legal or illegal."

"Well then, doc, I'm all ears. Some would say I'm all mouth, but you know what you're buying if you really want my opinion."

"Okay then. Reality. Is it fixed or pliable?"

Leif laughed a big, loud laugh. "You, doctors. You t'ink the brain is the beginning and end of it all. Your own inability to see beyond only de science...it keeps you from seeing that reality can mean many different t'ings to different people."

Jax shook his head and gave the man a big, genuine smile. "Damn, Leif. I've really missed your clear-headed way of looking at things."

"Dr....Jax, what the fuck is going on? You have never met Leif before today. You have never had conversations like this before! At least not with me, and never here! What the hell is happening?"

"I've tried to...I can't say what I want because it sounds crazy. Okay?"

"I get it," Leif said, his deep voice low, careful. He reached across the table and slapped Jax with the back of his hand lightly. "We have met before...just not like this. We know one another, ja? I felt it the first time I saw you." He shook his head and gave a small, rueful smile. "If I truly thought you vere making a pass at Sita, I vould have squashed you flat. You know this. So, vhat vill it take for us to have a real talk?"

"Uh," Sita managed to utter. "I don't know what's going on here, but...why the hell do I feel like I'm living through some déjà vu thingy here?"

"Well, that's a good place to start. How would the two of you feel about continuing this discussion at my place? Perhaps over a bottle of tequila?"

"I'm down for that. But what about Dr. Mason? He has Amy looking over our collective shoulder pretty regularly. You'd think the guy didn't have anything else to worry about. And speaking of which... What am I supposed to be working on right now, so I can report back to the general?"

"Let's try to cut the guy some slack. Funds are tight right now, and he's just worried about losing his job. He's basically a good guy when given half a chance.

"But to answer your question, I want to explore Amy's idea about using microdoses of hallucinogens for treatment. As a matter of fact, I came across an old family recipe that I want to try out."

It was at that moment that Amy Taylor poked her head through the lab's doors and stared at the gathered trio. Jax excused himself and walked towards her. "Hey, Amy, do you have a minute? There's something I need to discuss with you."

Jax gestured to his nearby office, and she nodded her agreement. After being seated, Jax took a moment to look at the gifted woman across the desk from him and tried to find the right words.

"Amy, excuse me if I'm not saying this well, but I'm truly sorry for the way I've treated you. You deserved so much more consideration for everything you've accomplished."

Amy looked at him suspiciously, taking a long beat before responding. "And you're saying this to me now...why exactly?"

"Let's just say my getting away from the lab and the Center for a while has allowed me to reflect on my behavior these past weeks—and months."

"How about these past years?"

"Yes, of course. Probably since we met. I could have handled our...friendship much better than I did. In fact, it was unfair of me to even start a relationship with you. You know, with me being your ex-professor and boss and all."

"Why is it that men always think they're the ones who got the girl into bed? That your charms were so irresistible that I just swooned and fell into your arms? I was an adult, and I knew what I was doing. You breaking it off with me—that isn't even the part that hurt.

"It was after that. After I agreed to continue serving as your lab assistant. You never showed me the least bit of respect that I deserved. You didn't listen to my suggestions, and you sure as hell didn't let me conduct my own research. No, I'm in a much better place now that I'm working for the director."

"I get that. And going forward, I hope you might consider working with me—or with us—a bit more. I'm going to move forward with Dr. Mason to bring on a new lab assistant, but your insight would be invaluable."

"I'm not sure where this is going, but why not? And, yes, I accept your apology."

Jax hesitantly stepped off the elevator and stood looking at the plain white door a few feet away. He had visited her office there in the hospital many times over the years—again, only by his recollection. He had no recent memory of being there, but he had to try. He had to find an answer about why—why weren't they together?

Outside her office, his knuckles barely grazed the doorframe. "Come in," called a woman's voice—soft yet commanding. Unmistakably Tessa.

He pushed the door open, letting it swing wide as he stepped across the threshold. The sight of her behind the desk made his chest tighten. Words formed on his lips, then died as sunlight caught the diamond on her left hand. A quiet exhale escaped him.

"Dr. Beck," she greeted him, her words crisp with her British inflection. "What brings you here?"

"I was wondering..." He paused, trying to collect himself. "That is, I'm interested in how one of your therapeutic approaches might complement my neural research."

"Do have a seat." He lowered himself into the cushioned chair beside her desk, aware of how her presence still affected him after all this time. "Please, tell me more about what you have in mind."

"It has to do with EMDR and its application in calming the pain centers of a patient during, or before, experiencing a migraine. I'm hoping to see if we can train the brain in a way similar to how therapy works, by replacing a traumatic memory with a more favorable one. In our case, it would be swapping pain for calm."

"That sounds rather ambitious coming from a hard-science researcher such as yourself. Didn't you once tell your students that psychology was just a pseudoscience?"

"I don't recall those exact words. However, if I ever gave someone that impression, then I truly apologize. I honestly believe there is an opportunity to discover if the two sciences can complement one another."

Tessa jotted something on a notepad and handed it to him. "This is the name and number of our lead therapist in that area, Dr. Terrance Adler. Terry's the best person to speak with about matters like this. He's off just now, but I'm sure he'll get back to you if you leave a message."

Jax reached out to take the note Tessa had written. His hand wavered with an almost irresistible urge to touch her hand and profess his love for her. To tell her all about their life together. What they could mean to one another...

It was at that moment that a deep male voice spoke from the open doorway. "Ah, Tess. Ready for lunch, are we?" Jax rose to his feet and turned. He recognized the man as one of the hospital's surgeons. He turned back to Tessa with a wounded look on his face that he tried but failed miserably to hide.

"Ah, Dr. Jaxon Beck, this is my fiancé, Dr. Harold Ashcroft. I'm sorry, Dr. Beck, was there anything else you required of me?"

"No, nothing. And, thank you for seeing me without an appointment." As he brushed past Dr. Ashcroft, Jax barely suppressed the urge to shoulder-check him.

Slipping into the open elevator, Jax stabbed the button for the ground floor, his fingertip whitening with pressure. The diamond on her finger flashed in his mind again—a mocking sparkle. His jaw clenched until his molars ached, and he fought the urge to slam his fist into the elevator wall. His throat constricted as if caught in a vise.

"Goddamn it. She's my...wife!"

61

ZANE JR.

THE FIRST WEEK OF October brought an unexpected but welcome guest. Mikey Zane stood at the entrance to Jax's lab, his once boyish features now hardened. The shy countenance that had once defined him was replaced by something more deliberate, more calculated.

Jax's last interaction with Mikey was with him and his father, Leo, right before Curtis showed up. That's what led him to a radical change in his personal history. At that time, Mikey stated that he remembered both the original memories before Jax's 2nd Iteration visits, as well as the changes that occurred afterwards.

Jax wordlessly escorted the younger man down the hall to his private office. As the door clicked shut behind them, a weighted silence filled the room while each man took the measure of what time and circumstance had done to the other.

"It's good to see you again, Mikey. Or would you prefer Michael?"

"I'm feeling much older now, Jax, so make it Michael, please. It's good to see you as well. How are you adjusting to life?"

Jax rubbed his temple, a ghost of pain flickering behind his eyes. "Some days are better than others. But tell me more about you. The last time we talked, you mentioned something fascinating. About being the sole witness to the changes around you. Has that phenomenon continued?"

"Yes and no. It's a damned eerie sensation. It's as if I'm in a play and someone moved the sets around between scenes, but no one told me where to stand."

"What exactly changed for you? I mean, I've managed to lose my entire family. But, hey, the Center and the work are still here."

"Yes, I was sorry to learn about all of that. Well, most recently, my father has turned to building spacecraft—totally convinced he was meant to colonize Mars."

"Damn. So, how is this impacting you and the work of VRMX Technologies?"

Michael leaned forward. "I've taken over VRMX completely—my father's out. That's why I'm here, Jax. I need your knowledge—your ability. The VyzR project? It never happened in this timeline. One day, my dad walked into my office with complete schematics of the visor. He claimed a DARPA connection had handed them to us to manufacture.

“Up to that point, neither of us had any interest in working with medical devices. We had been working with the military to improve the response times between RPAs and their pilots. That and our game consoles had a certain overlap with FPS in battle-type games, and—"

“Michael, I’m sorry to interrupt, but I’m not much of a gamer. None of those terms mean anything to me.”

“Sorry. I often get caught up in the jargon. RPA stands for Remotely Piloted Aircraft, which were used most often in Afghanistan and Iraq. FPS means First-Person Shooter, as in you play the game and see everything as if you were experiencing it. Now we have vests, gloves, and visors.

“You need to understand, I didn’t know what was going on when I initially came up here. At first, I thought I had something medically wrong with me—like a tumor or something. Then you started talking about 2nd Iteration visits, and things started to fall into place for me. I was watching the world change.”

“Which brings me to today. Jax, I want us to build a better VyzR. Maybe even pursue the search for others like you...and me!”

“That’s intriguing, Michael...honestly. I admit, I need to build another VyzR-type unit to undo some damage I created. My concern is that if I involve VRMX, the same people overseeing your government contracts will get curious, and we’ll be back where we started. I've lived through that crap once. I don't plan on doing it again."

Michael rose from his chair and shook his head. He ran his fingers through his hair and let out a long breath that seemed to deflate him. "I really thought you'd be more enthusiastic about this, especially after what I just told you."

"Michael, please sit and listen. I get it, and it makes a lot of sense to partner with you. I'm trying to tell you that I think you're right, and building the unit again is necessary—I have to build it. I could certainly use your help with obtaining certain components, maybe some equipment, but most of all your expertise in this area. There are many things I've learned from this experience, but secrecy is essential.

"Look, can we just stop for a minute and talk? You have a unique perspective given your work. So, in your opinion, what do you think we are dealing with? Either with you seeing changes or me creating them. Are these parallel universes? Is reality something malleable that can be manipulated? What is your take on this whole issue?"

"I don't have a nice, packaged answer for you, although I have read articles on this very issue. Stop me if the jargon I use is not comprehensible. When my company creates video games, we build worlds through code. Do you see where I'm going? The commonalities between that type of work and what we've experienced are too stark to be ignored."

Michael held up a hand to stop Jax from responding. "Wait. Before you say anything, let me add that there are still significant differences that don't align. But the way I work is to start with what I know is fact, then introduce new...let's call them features.

In electronics, we use logic gates. These go back to when the world first started getting into coding, but they're still applicable. Simply put, one such component is called the 'And Gate', which receives a signal and, if all conditions are true, then something else happens. An 'Or Gate' will pass the signal if at least one condition is true, and a 'Not Gate' is when—"

"—neither condition is true," finished Jax. "Kinda like a sophisticated decision tree?"

"Yes. Yes, exactly like that. It helps me see if the datum is true, possible, or false. That's just how I perceive things."

"I like it. I don't accept that we're living in an arcade game, but when I read about quantum mechanics, I start to grasp how much I don't know. Here's what I propose. I was able to get a hold of my original schematics for the VyzR, as well as other equipment we can look at later. Let's start building this new unit at your facility, and maybe, just maybe, we'll get some answers to these questions."

"Okay, I'm in. When do we start?"

"We have to be smart about this, Michael. I just hired a new lab assistant and need to get him up to speed. If your company can support it, I'd like to inform the director that VRMX Technologies is sponsoring some of my research. Then I can get a second assistant to take over the day-to-day operations here at the Center.

"That will free me up to work down in the Springs and provide a good cover for why I'm gone. I've just recruited a couple of very capable people who can help us get this project rolling."

"A grant to the Center won't be a problem. Gifting the university will give me a tax break. So, it's a win-win for everyone."

"You need to accept that I have a priority matter that has to get done before we go too far into experimentation. I have to right that wrong and try to straighten out my timeline before I can look at other things."

"Your father. I get it. It's a deal."

62

VYZR-II

THE TABLE OF POLISHED maple gleamed in the afternoon sunlight, which fell in a concentrated shaft from a skylight thirty feet above, throwing a bright trapezoid across the grain of the wood. Jax removed the VyzR from his face and stared at that rectangle of light for a moment, watching dust motes drift through it. There was always a transitional period between his visits and the return to his present time—a kind of pressure behind the eyes, a ringing in the ears, the slow reassembly of the room around him—but he had never mentioned this to anyone.

This time, the transition lasted a beat longer than usual. His eyes stayed unfocused, the dust motes blurring into streaks. He shook his head once, sharply, the way a swimmer clears water from an ear. Then he reached into his breast pocket for the handkerchief he now made a point of carrying and pressed it briefly to his nose, wiping away the blood. He folded the cloth and tucked it away. He knew his 2nd Iteration visits were doing something to his brain—the nosebleeds, the peripheral distortions, the sounds that arrived half a second before their sources—but this wasn't the time to get into it.

Jax reached over to the side of the recliner in which he sat and hung the VyzR on a padded hook. The newer model that he, Leif, and Michael Zane had developed was significantly larger than the original but weighed half as much. The newer unit had state-of-the-art throat mics and acoustic-tube earpieces. As a government contractor, Michael had no problem acquiring these components. The hope was that Jax would be able to communicate more clearly with his team when he was interacting with people during his visits. So far, all of that was merely theoretical.

"How did it go this time?" asked Michael. "I don't notice anything different about you, but I can't tell if something changed elsewhere in your life."

"You were not gone so long, nei," Leif said. "How is it you feel now?"

"I'm fine, but no, it didn't work. Whenever I try to return to that same time in 1995, I can't seem to stay in my younger body. It's like I get pushed back. My Mom mentioned something similar happening with my grandma when she traveled. If I had to guess, this is what I'm experiencing."

Sita walked up to him and handed him a cup of coffee. "Boss, I know that we don't remember that first trip you took, but may I suggest a workaround? What if you didn't target that specific day again, but went a day earlier? Could you convince your mother, or even your grandmother, to call the people in Oklahoma City?"

"I think that would be asking too much. My Mother just lost her father, and my grandmother her husband. I get that they would probably recognize a fellow traveler, but I don't know if they would be in the proper emotional state to handle all this."

"Okay, but what if you went earlier this time, ja?" Leif asked, leaning in. "Could you...say, go back before your last visit? Dis way Mary can call earlier dan she did before?"

"That won't work because of the time Timothy McVeigh set off the bomb—just after 9 AM in Oklahoma, and 10 AM in Massachusetts. I was lucky enough that Mary reached those two people the first time I did this. Any earlier and the snack bar wouldn't be open. That, and the credit union wouldn't have anyone there to answer phones."

"But, Jax," Michael said, brow drawing up. "You wouldn't necessarily need to reach everyone like before, just George Marshall. Didn't he work for the ATF? If he was a government employee, he would probably be at his desk by 8 AM. If you can reach him, then everything else would play out the way you say it's supposed to."

"What about the other one you saved, and the one you tried to save?" Sita asked. "Isn't it kind of heartless to just let them die in the blast?"

"What you don't recall, and what I never told you this time, is that Anna Toller and her daughter, Sally, died in a school shooting ten months after the bombing. Their fate was pretty much sealed either way. Besides her, the other woman, Susan Sear, was an employee at the credit union, so there wouldn't be any way to reach her."

"Well, that's fucked up," Sita said.

"I don't disagree, but of the four individuals Mary and I were originally able to get away from the blast, only George Jr. lived past a few months. It's not just my dad. George also saved two other members of his squad who, in turn, rescued my father. I have come to believe that he had a specific goal that kept him alive until he could fulfill his purpose. I'm not saying it's my motive, but it seems to be something that's set out in the rules of this game—or with God. Whatever authority you want to label it."

"How much time would you need before we go again?" Michael asked.

"Soon. I want to look through my mom's photo album again. Maybe I missed something that can help me stick the landing. Something about that morning."

"What about a picture?" Sita asked. "Your mother or grandmother. You know, someone who can evoke a strong emotion in you that will spark your memories?"

"Damn good idea, Sita. Give me a few minutes. In the meantime, Leif, can you and Michael run a test on the new components to ensure everything is still in top shape? It might be critical for you three to hear what I'm saying, and with a little luck, even talk to me while I'm there."

Jax opened his eyes to find himself being hugged tightly. He recalled the first time he returned to being five years old and how unusual it felt to be this small and frail. His second return visit was a little easier for him to adjust to his size, yet he still found it difficult to get over that same peculiar sensation.

Unlike his earlier tries, this time he knew he was solidly here. At least he had a chance of completing his mission—save George Marshal—save his dad.

He knew he was being hugged by an adult female, but couldn't tell who it was. After a minute, the woman pulled away and held him at arm's length. He was looking into his Grandmother's face. A face he had nearly forgotten, except for the picture of her at this age in his photo album. She was distracted, yet still radiated great love, interwoven with a trace of grief. Her husband, Jax's grandfather, had died just days ago, and today he would be buried.

Nora Murphy stood, wiping a tear from the corner of her eye. At that moment, he was content to hear her kind voice with an accent that perfectly mixed her Irish and New England roots. "Now, you mind me and listen to our Mary Johnson, Jaxon," she said, her voice soft but steady. "She's a good young lass, and she'll be stayin' with you while your folks and I are out. Can you do that for me, dear?"

Jax found himself tearing up, but told himself to steady his mind and focus. "Yes, Grandma. Mary Johnson will watch me."

"That's my fine young lad," she murmured, pride soft in her voice. "We'll be back before dark, so don't you fret. I love you, boy, I surely do."

All Jax could manage was, "I love you too."

The teenage girl came into view holding a smiling baby in her arms. She reached down with a welcoming hand. "Jaxy, do you want to go downstairs and watch cartoons?"

Placing his small hand in hers, he answered. "Yes, so you can put Jenny in the crib."

"That's right. Babies tend to sleep often, but not for very long. Let's go down each of the stairs slowly so we don't trip, okay?"

When they arrived at the lower level, Mary asked Jax to sit while she put the baby in the crib. Jax looked at the clock and murmured, "It's almost 9 AM now, and I arrived last time at 9:10—I've only got ten minutes to make this happen." He hoped his team back in Colorado heard all of that. He was afraid that if he stayed past his first arrival time, he would be bounced out of his younger self and sent back to his present. If that happened, there was no way he could return to this time again.

He sat on the couch and took deep breaths, preparing himself for what was to come. No time to paint any pictures for Mary on this trip. No time for subtlety. Barely enough time to convince her to act.

When Mary had settled the infant, she asked Jax what he wanted to watch. Jax stood and walked over to the girl who would one day become a senator for this nation. He knew she could handle what was coming, but he still thought it wise to broach the subject gently, regardless.

"Is everything okay Jaxy?" The young girl asked. "Do you need to go potty?"

"Mary, would you please sit on the couch so we can talk?"

"Jeez, Jaxy, look how all polite and mature you are. Sure, buddy, what shall we talk about?" She sat on the couch and met his gaze.

"Mary, please forgive me for my bluntness. I have something important to ask of you, and there's no good way for me to ease into it. Just know that you are the only person who can do this. I'm sorry, but I need your help."

"Wha...Jaxon, why are you... Is this a joke?" Mary raised her voice as if someone were listening to their conversation. "Is someone playing a sick joke here? It's time to stop, whoever you are doing this."

"Mary, I'm going to need you to trust me for the next few minutes. I know you are seeing me as just a young boy, but please try to understand that this isn't a joke. In fact, this is deadly serious."

The girl rose and began backing away from Jax. She turned her head and looked at the staircase, as if calculating the steps necessary to make her escape. Jax walked up and grasped her fingers.

"I know this is a difficult thing to comprehend. But Mary, I know that a part of you recognizes this to be true. That the things I'm about to say to you are the truth. I'm counting on you to be brave and listen to what I have to say. Can you manage to do that...please?"

"I don't know what the hell is going on, but I'm not staying here!" You're a demon, like in the movies or... Or something unholy. I'm taking Jenny and leaving!"

A whisper seeped into Jax's consciousness. Sita's voice, somehow breaching the temporal barrier. Information flowed into his mind. The intrusion sent a chill down his spine. No one had ever reached him during a 2nd Iteration before.

With the baby in her arms, Mary rushed past Jax toward the staircase. Time was slipping away. If he failed now, there would be no second chance—this temporal window would close forever. One phone call stood between his father's life and death.

Drawing a deep breath into his five-year-old lungs, Jax projected his voice against the wood-paneled walls with all the force his child's vocal cords could muster. The infant was crying already anyway. What did he have to lose?

"Mary Johnson, daughter of Mamie and Chip Johnson. You are sixteen years old and your birthday is September 9th. You have one older brother who is attending Amherst College. Your mother teaches history at the local high school, and your father... Your father passed away two years ago from prostate cancer."

Mary froze mid-step. The blanket flew up to shield the baby's face as her own turned ashen. "Stop it," she hissed through clenched teeth, voice cracking. "Just stop."

The infant, Jenny, was now howling her opposition to the noise assaulting her tiny ears. Mary took two more steps towards the stairs, avoiding Jaxon's pleading eyes. She was in tears and trembling as she clutched the child to her chest.

Jax's eyes darted to the clock—9:05. "Mary," he said, his child's voice cracking with adult urgency, "I'm begging you for one thing. Make the phone call to Oklahoma City. Right now. A father and his little boy are about to die unless someone warns them. That boy grows up to save my dad's life. I couldn't stop your father's cancer, but you can prevent my father's death!"

Michael looked at the bank of clocks on the opposite wall. The first showed Colorado time—9:03 AM. The second, a simple digital counter, tracked the duration of Jax's 2nd Iteration visit, its red numerals ticking upward with indifferent precision. The third was an analog clock, its hands frozen, then lurching forward at irregular intervals, approximating the morning of April 19th, 1995, in Massachusetts, synchronized to whatever Jax was experiencing behind the visor.

Five minutes here bled into twenty minutes there—time was not a river but a series of pools, each running at its own depth and speed. Michael watched the three clocks the way you might watch three different people deliver the same bad news. He lowered himself onto his stool, folded his hands on the table in front of him, and waited.

Leif stroked Sita's hair as they held each other. They had listened closely when Jax had repeated Mary Johnson's name. She had run a quick search as planned and provided Jax with what little information she could gather—not knowing if her words could be heard or understood.

They stared down at Jax's still body, strangers to his father but invested in his mission. The stakes were clear. Rescue George Marshall and his son. Mark Beck would be saved, and by extension, the lives of the Marines in those Afghan hills.

"Jax will make this happen," Leif said gently. "Have faith in him, ja?"

Jax's foot twitched first. Then his leg. Then his arm rose and pulled the visor from his face. Leif helped him sit up, and he said nothing for a moment, just nodded once. Then he reached into his pocket for his phone and opened his contacts.

"I need to call to be sure, but Mary came through. She warned George Marshall." He turned the phone around. The listing read *Dad.* He smiled and cried at the same time. Mark Beck was back where he belonged.

63

Epilogue

"Excuse me, Dr. Beck. I didn't catch what you just said."

"It's nothing, Malcolm. I just said it was strange to be clean-shaven again. But I interrupted you. Please continue what you were saying."

"It's about Mrs. Hernandez. She's 79 and exhibiting all the symptoms of the virus. She's in isolation ward two, but she has not been responding well to treatment. I guess I was asking what you'd like me to do for her…if there is anything."

"Keep her on high-dose ibuprofen with mechanical ventilation standing by. Look, I need to run over to the admin office for a minute. The next shift is about ready to start. While I'm gone, would you check with the pharmacy to see if we have any Dexamethasone in stock? I've been reading how doctors in the UK have been using this in severe cases. If she doesn't improve, we may try that on Mrs. Hernandez.

"Doctor, we can both get into serious trouble without the necessary approval."

Jax reached into his pocket, pulled out a prescription pad, and wrote on the order. Handing the slip of paper to Malcolm, he said, "You're covered, my friend. Say, before you go, I see you're not wearing an N95. Are we out?"

"A delivery is due today, but surgical masks are all we have at the moment."

"Yeah, I get it, everything's on backorder. Look, I know you're done seeing patients, but at least change that mask once more before your shift ends. Okay?"

"Of course, Dr. Beck. Thanks for your concern. Not many doctors give a damn."

Jax saw the oncoming physician starting her rounds, so he turned and headed down the hallway that connected to the main hospital. As he exited the clinic, he saw a room full of people and a nurse handing out masks to anyone who lacked one. The room was full of crying babies and sneezing adults. All were waiting to be seen by medical staff who were tired and overwhelmed by the sheer number of people.

Passing the bank of elevators, Jax saw a handwritten sign indicating the temporary administration offices across the main hall. Entering, he noted that the large area was nearly empty and that most of the lights were off. He understood that it was close to the morning shift change, and non-essential personnel sometimes left early.

He zigzagged his way through the warren of empty cubicles until he found a single lighted office in the back. He knocked once on the doorframe and smiled at the woman behind the desk. Although his mask mostly hid his face, there was an unmistakable glimmer of happiness in his eyes.

"Doctor," the woman asked, "is everything alright?"

"Dr. Moreland, I presume?"

"That's correct. I'm Dr. Tessa Moreland. Were you needing something?"

"I was just concerned about one of your people, a Terrance Adler. I was told he's showing initial symptoms of the COVID virus. I believe he's a psychologist but has been assigned to help with administrative duties here during the outbreak."

"Haven't we all. The name sounds familiar, but there are dozens of people working out of this office. I'm sorry, but why is a doctor coming to me to report this? We do have an HR department for such internal matters, Dr...?"

"Beck. Jaxon Beck. Jax. I believe that Mr. Adler is unaware of his condition and isn't wearing the necessary PPE when he interacts with patients or other personnel."

"That is a serious allegation. Let me check the posted schedule." She swiveled in her chair to study a posted document on the wall. Jax couldn't look away from her as she traced her finger along the board. "Yes, Terry Adler is due in at seven. But to be honest, we are not given the higher-grade personal protective equipment. He probably isn't wearing the correct gear because we haven't been issued any."

"I'm not denying that's so, Dr. Moreland, but it's more than just him. I believe that everyone here should undergo testing before they're allowed into work. We're just beginning the middle of 2020, and this COVID-19 virus is hitting hard. I believe it's more serious and much more contagious than what's being publicly reported."

"So, you are saying that the hospital should test every employee? Do you have any idea of the time that would require, not to mention the expense?"

"I'm in the clinic dealing with this crap every day. A lot of people are sick, and too many are dying. So, yes, I believe that in the name of caution and the public's welfare, the hospital should do just that. And that means starting immediately."

"That is a good argument, but I'm just here temporarily. The hospital administrator is due in soon and I will pass along your...recommendation. Will that suffice?"

"It's a start, but until then, I'm afraid it might be up to you to stop Adler from interacting with patients or other employees. Do you have an N95?"

"As I stated, supply has not kept up with demand. We're not on the front line, so the surgical mask you see me wearing is all we've been given."

Jax reached into his scrubs, pulled out a sealed packet, and extended it towards her. "Here, you shouldn't expose yourself if you do end up meeting with Adler. This will provide some degree of protection in the interim."

"Doctor, I cannot take this from you. I am not in a high-risk position, but you are!"

"Tessa, just take the damn mask! I'm coming off shift soon, and I just changed into the one I'm wearing a few minutes ago."

"Well...alright then. Thank you, doctor, that is most considerate of you."

Jax started to leave but paused in the doorway, looking back. "Say, Dr. Moreland. If I haven't shown to be a total lunatic, might I persuade you to have coffee with me sometime? Or a drink, if you are so inclined."

Tessa stopped what she was doing and peered over her glasses to look at him. "You are quite forward and ungentlemanly, aren't you?!"

If it had been anyone else, they would have thought she was angry at him. Even though they had just technically met, in his heart, Jax had loved this woman for over five years. He knew her quirks and her expressions and could tell by her lone raised eyebrow that she was intrigued.

Jax nodded in agreement. “So, my... So, my friends keep telling me.”

64

AUTHOR'S NOTE

THE CHARACTERS IN THIS story are fictitious and are not based on any individual living or dead. Likewise, the hospital and the Neurological Center are composites of many such institutions. VRMX Technologies and the VyzR are fictional as of publication.

Conversely, the science related to the brain is real, as is the medical equipment mentioned. Expanded resources are provided in the Reference Material.

Additionally, several U.S. government studies into parapsychology and related phenomena are fact, as evidenced by the declassified list below. Other programs continue to this day but remain Top Secret to the general public.

Project Stargate - the use of remote viewing for intelligence purposes.

Operation Bluebird - mind control and psychological manipulation techniques.

MKUltra - mind control and the effects of drugs on human behavior.

Project Scanate - an offshoot of Stargate, remote viewing for military applications.

65

Reference Material

The references listed below are for informational purposes and are not meant to be an endorsement of any product or service.

Brunton, B.W. (2024, August). Non-invasive Methods in Neuroscience. https://www.youtube.com.

Clark, A. (2025, August 25). Magnetic pulse stops brain—temporarily. The Morning Review. https://morningoverview.com.

Dubljević, V. and Young, J. (2025). TMS and Neuroethics.

Dubois, J., Field, R. (2024). Kernel Flow Reliability of brain metrics derived from a Time-Domain Functional Near-Infrared Spectroscopy System. Scientific Reports.https://www.nature.com/ar ticles.

Khollam, A. (2025, August). World's first sound-powered microscope sees 5x deeper into brain without altering cells. Interesting Engineering. .

PsyPost. (2025, July), Neuroscientists identify key gatekeeper of human consciousness. Psychological Post. .

Shavit, J. (November 6, 2024). Researchers discovered the part of the brain that controls memory and information recall. The Brighter Side. https://www.thebrighterside.news.

Shavit, J. (2025, August). Revolutionary wearable device uses light to safely scan the brain. The Brighter Side. .

Virture. (2025, September 2, 2025). Luma Pro XR Glasses. Proprietary software allows for use with computers and gaming consoles.

www.ingramcontent.com/pod-product-compliance
Lightning Source LLC
LaVergne TN
LVHW090545110826
845146LV00001B/25

* 9 7 9 8 9 9 5 0 3 6 7 0 8 *